SWEET...

Charles Wy... ...in... ...cor-
rigible—Earl of Billington, needs a bride
before his upcoming thirtieth birthday, if
he hopes to earn his inheritance. The
vicar's vivacious, determined daughter,
Miss Eleanor Lyndon, needs a new
home, since her father's insufferable fiancée is making her old one intolerable.
Destiny has brought Charles and Ellie
together—though their match at the out-
set appears to have been made somewhere rather hotter than heaven.

BRIGHTER THAN THE SUN

Their first meeting is less than auspi-
cious—with a somewhat soused Charles
falling from a tree and landing at
Eleanor's feet. While they agree to marry
for their mutual convenience, Charles is
not prepared to let a woman command
his household. And certainly strong-
willed Ellie refuses to let a rogue run her
life. Yet the rakish earl can be quite
charming—and even tender—when he
puts his mind to it. And there's no denying the sensuous allure of his enchant-
ing, innocent, yet utterly stubborn wife.
Even though mad mishaps and very real
dangers threaten their fragile union, they
must follow where passion leads—to the
rapturous warmth and brilliance of love.

JULIA QUINN

BRIGHTER THAN THE SUN

An Avon Romantic Treasure

AVON BOOKS ◆ NEW YORK

AVON BOOKS
A division of
The Hearst Corporation
1350 Avenue of the Americas
New York, NY 10019

Copyright © 1997 by Julie Cotler Pottinger
Published by arrangement with the author
Visit our website at http://www.AvonBooks.com
Library of Congress Catalog Card Number: 97-93749
ISBN: 0-380-78934-5

First Avon Books Printing: December 1997

AVON TRADEMARK REG. U. S. PAT. OFF. AND IN OTHER COUNTRIES, MARCA REGISTRADA, HECHO EN U.S.A.

Printed in the U. S. A.

WCD 10 9 8 7 6 5 4 3

For Auntie Susan—
Thank you.

—Miss Julie

And for Paul, even though he just doesn't
understand why I can't end all of my titles
with exclamation points.

Chapter 1

Kent, England
October 1817

Eleanor Lyndon was minding her own business when Charles Wycombe, Earl of Billington, fell—quite literally—into her life.

She was walking along, whistling a happy tune and keeping her mind busy by trying to estimate the yearly profit of the East & West Sugar Company (of which she owned several shares) when to her great surprise, a man came crashing down from the sky and landed at, or to be more precise—*on* her feet.

Further inspection revealed that the man in question had fallen not from the sky but from a large oak tree. Ellie, whose life had grown decidedly dull in the last year or so, would have almost preferred that he *had* fallen from the sky. It certainly would have been more exciting than from a mere tree.

She pulled her left foot out from underneath the man's shoulder, hiked her skirts above her ankles to save them from the dirt, and crouched down. "Sir?" she inquired. "Are you all right?"

1

All he said was, "Ow."

"Oh, dear," she murmured. "You haven't broken any bones, have you?"

He didn't say anything, just let out a long breath. Ellie lurched back when the fumes hit her. "Sweet heavens," she muttered, "You smell as if you've imbibed a winery."

"Whishkey," he slurred in response. "A gennleman drinks whishkey."

"Not *this* much whiskey," she retorted. "Only a drunk drinks this much of anything."

He sat up—clearly with difficulty, and shook his head as if to clear it. "Exactly it," he said, waving his hand through the air, then wincing when the action made him dizzy. "I'm a bit drunk, I'm afraid."

Ellie decided to refrain from further comment on that topic. "Are you certain you're not injured?"

He scratched his reddish-brown hair and blinked. "My head pounds like the devil."

"I suspect that isn't only from the fall."

He tried to get up, weaved, and sat back down. "You're a sharp-tongued lass."

"Yes, I know," she said with a wry smile. "It's why I'm a long-toothed spinster. Now then, I can't very well see to your injuries if I don't know what they are."

"Efficient, too," he murmured. "An' why are you so certain I've got an injurty, er, injury?"

Ellie looked up into the tree. The nearest branch which would have supported his weight was a good fifteen feet up. "I don't see how you could have fallen so far and *not* been injured."

He waved her comments aside and tried to rise

again. "Yes, well, we Wycombes are a hardy lot. It'd take more than a—Sweet merciful Christ!" He howled.

Ellie tried her best not to sound smug when she said, "An ache? A pain? A sprain, perhaps."

His brown eyes narrowed as he clutched the trunk of the tree for support. "You are a hard, cruel woman, Miss whatever-your-name-is, to take such pleasure in my agony."

Ellie coughed to cover a giggle. "Mr. Whosis, I must protest and point out that I tried to tend to your injuries, but you insisted you didn't have any."

He scowled in a very boyish sort of way and sat back down. "That's Lord Whosis," he muttered.

"Very well, my lord," she said, hoping that she hadn't irritated him overmuch. A peer of the realm held much more power than a vicar's daughter, and he could make her life miserable if he chose. She gave up all hope of keeping her dress clean and sat down in the dirt. "Which ankle pains you, my lord?"

He pointed to his right ankle, and then grimaced when she lifted it in her hands. After a moment's examination, she looked up and said in her most polite voice, "I am going to have to remove your boot, my lord. Would that be permissible?"

"I liked you better when you were spitting fire," he muttered.

Ellie liked herself better that way, too. She smiled. "Have you a knife?"

He snorted. "If you think I'm going to put a weapon in your hands . . ."

"Very well. I suppose I could just pull the boot off." She cocked her head and pretended to ponder the matter. "It might hurt just a bit when it gets stuck on your hideously swollen ankle, but as you pointed out, you come from hardy stock, and a man should be able to take a little pain."

"What the devil are you talking about?"

Ellie started to pull at his boot. Not hard—she could never be that cruel. Tugging just enough to demonstrate that the boot wasn't coming off his foot through ordinary means, she held her breath.

He yelled, and Ellie wished she hadn't tried to teach him a lesson, because she ended up with a face full of whiskey fumes.

"How much did you drink?" she demanded, gasping for air.

"Not nearly enough," he groaned. "They haven't invented a drink strong enough—"

"Oh, come now," Ellie snapped. "I'm not that bad."

To her surprise, he laughed. "Sweetheart," he said in a tone that told her clear as day that his usual occupation was rake, "you're the least bad thing that has happened to me in months."

Ellie felt an odd sort of tingling on the back of her neck at his clumsy compliment. Thankful that her large bonnet hid her blush, she focused her attention back on his ankle. "Have you changed your mind about my cutting your boot?"

His answer was the knife he placed in her palm. "I always knew there was some reason I carried one of these things around. I just never knew what it was until today."

The knife was a bit dull, and soon Ellie was gritting her teeth as she sawed through his boot. She looked up from her task for a moment. "Just let me know if I—"

"Ow!"

"—poke you," she finished. "I'm dreadfully sorry."

"It is astonishing," he said, his voice liberally laced with irony, "how much sorrow I hear in your voice."

Ellie caught another giggle in her throat.

"Oh, for the love of God," he muttered. "Just laugh. Lord knows my life is laughable."

Ellie, whose own life had descended into the miserable ever since her widower father had announced his intention to marry the village of Bellfield's biggest busybody, felt a pang of empathy. She didn't know what could have prompted this remarkably handsome and well-heeled lord to go out and get himself blindingly drunk, but whatever it was, she felt for him. She stopped her work on his boot for a moment, leveled her dark blue eyes at his face, and said, "My name is Miss Eleanor Lyndon."

His eyes warmed. "Thank you for sharing that pertinent piece of information, Miss Lyndon. It isn't every day I allow a strange woman to saw off my boots."

"It isn't every day I nearly get knocked to the ground by men falling from trees. *Strange* men," she added for emphasis.

"Ah yes, I should introduce myself, I s'pose." He cocked his head in a manner that reminded Ellie that he was still more than a touch inebriated. "Charles Wycombe at your service, Miss Lyndon. Earl of Billington." Then he muttered, "Much as that's worth."

Ellie stared at him unblinkingly. Billington? He was one of the county's most eligible bachelors. So eligible that even she'd heard of him, and she wasn't on anybody's list of eligible young ladies. Rumor had it that he was the worst sort of rake. Ellie had heard him whispered about at village gatherings, although as an unmarried lady she'd never been privy to the juiciest gossip. She tended to think that his reputation must be very black if he did things that couldn't even be mentioned in her presence.

Ellie had also heard that he was fantastically wealthy, even more so than her sister Victoria's new husband, who was Earl of Macclesfield. Ellie couldn't personally vouch for that, as she hadn't seen his personal finance ledgers, and she made it a point never to speculate on financial matters without hard evidence. But she did know that the Billington estate was vast and ancient.

And it was a good twenty miles away. "What are you doing here in Bellfield?" she blurted out.

"Just visiting my old childhood haunts."

Ellie motioned toward the branches above them with her head. "Your favorite tree?"

"Used to climb it all the time with Macclesfield."

Ellie finished her work on the boot and put the knife down. "Robert?" she asked.

Charles looked suspicious and a bit protective. "You're on a first-name basis with him? He's recently married."

"Yes. To my sister."

"The world grows smaller by the second," he murmured. "I'm honored to make your acquaintance."

"You might rethink that sentiment in a moment," Ellie remarked. With a gentle touch, she slid his swollen foot from his boot.

Charles looked down at his mangled boot with a pained expression. "I suppose my ankle is more important," he said wistfully, but he didn't sound as if he meant it.

Ellie expertly prodded his ankle. "I don't think you've broken any bones, but you've a nasty sprain."

"You sound experienced at this sort of thing."

"I come to the rescue of any wounded animal," she said, arching her brows. "Dogs, cats, birds—"

"Men," he finished for her.

"No," she said pertly. "You're the first. But I cannot imagine that you'd be *that* much different from a dog."

"Your fangs are showing, Miss Lyndon."

"Are they?" she asked, reaching up to touch her face. "I shall have to remember to retract them."

Charles burst out laughing. "You, Miss Lyndon, are a treasure."

"That's what I keep telling everyone," she said with a shrug and a wicked smile, "but no one seems to believe me. Now then, I fear you will require a cane for several days. Possibly a week. Have you one at your disposal?"

"Right now?"

"I meant at home, but. . . ." Ellie's words trailed off as she looked around her. She spied a long stick several yards away and scrambled to her feet. "This should do," she said, picking it up and handing it to him. "Do you need assistance getting to your feet?"

He grinned wolfishly as he swayed toward her. "Any excuse to be in your arms, my dear Miss Lyndon."

Ellie knew she should be affronted, but he was trying so hard to be charming, and devil take it, he was succeeding. Handily. She supposed that was why he was such a successful rake. She stepped around to his back and put her hands under his arms. "I warn you, I'm not very gentle."

"Now why doesn't that surprise me?"

"On the count of three, then. Are you ready?"

"That depends, I suppose, on—"

"One, two . . . three!" With a grunt and a heave, Ellie pulled the earl to his feet. It wasn't an easy task. He outweighed her by a good four stone and was drunk, to boot. His knees buckled, and Ellie only just managed to keep herself from cursing as she planted her feet and braced them. Then he started to topple over in the other direction, and she had to scoot to his front to keep him from falling.

"Now that feels nice," he murmured as his chest pressed up against hers.

"Lord Billington, I must insist that you use your cane."

"On you?" He sounded intrigued by the notion.

"To walk!" she fairly yelled.

He flinched at the noise, then shook his head. "It's the oddest thing," he murmured, "but I have the most appalling urge to kiss you."

For once, Ellie was speechless.

He chewed thoughtfully on his lower lip. "I think I just might do it."

That was enough to spur her into motion, and she jumped to the side, sending him sprawling to the ground once again.

"Good God, woman!" he yelled. "What did you do that for?"

"You were going to *kiss* me."

He rubbed his head, which had hit the tree trunk. "The prospect was *that* terrifying?"

Ellie blinked. "Not terrifying, exactly."

"Please don't say repulsive," he grumbled. "I really couldn't bear it."

She exhaled and held out a conciliatory hand. "I'm terribly sorry for dropping you, my lord."

"Once again, your face is a picture of sorrow."

Ellie fought the urge to stamp her foot. "I meant it this time. Do you accept my apology?"

"It appears," he said, raising his eyebrows, "that you might do me bodily harm if I do not."

"Ungracious prig," she muttered. "I am trying to apologize."

"And *I*," he said, "am trying to accept."

He reached out and took her gloved hand. She pulled him to his feet again, stepping out of his reach once he had steadied himself on his makeshift cane.

"I will escort you to Bellfield," Ellie said. "It isn't terribly far. Will you be able to get home from there?"

"I left my curricle at the Bee and Thistle," he replied.

She cleared her throat. "I would appreciate it if you would behave with gentility and discretion. I may be a spinster, but I do have a reputation to protect."

He sent a sideways glance in her direction. "I am considered something of a blackguard, I'm afraid."

"I know."

"Your reputation was probably shredded the moment I landed on top of you."

"For heavens' sake, you fell out of a tree!"

"Yes, of course, but you did put your bare hands on my bare ankle."

"It was for the noblest of reasons."

"Frankly, I thought kissing you seemed rather noble, but you appeared to disagree."

Her mouth settled into a grim line. "That is exactly the sort of flippant remark I am talking about. I know that I shouldn't, but I do care what people think of me, and I have to live here for the rest of my life."

"Do you?" he asked. "How sad."

"That isn't funny."

"It wasn't meant to be."

She sighed impatiently. "Contrive to behave yourself when we reach Bellfield. Please?"

He leaned on his stick and swept into a courtly bow. "I try never to disappoint a lady."

"Will you stop!" she said, grabbing him by the elbow and pulling him upright. "You're going to knock yourself over."

"Why, Miss Lyndon, I do believe you are beginning to care for me."

Her answer was a marginally ladylike grunt. With fisted hands, she began to march toward town. Charles hobbled behind her, smiling all the way. She was walking much more quickly than he, however, and the space between them grew until he was forced to call out her name.

Ellie turned around.

Charles offered her what he hoped was an appealing smile. "I cannot keep up with you, I'm afraid." He held out his hands in a gesture of supplication and then promptly lost his balance. Ellie rushed forward to straighten him.

"You are a walking disaster," she muttered, keeping her hand on his elbow.

"A limping disaster," he corrected. "And I cannot—" He lifted his free hand to his mouth to cover an inebriated burp. "I cannot limp quickly."

She sighed. "Here. You can lean on my shoulder. Together we should be able to get you into town."

Charles grinned and slid his arm over her shoulder. She was small, but she was a sturdy little thing, so he decided to test the waters by leaning on her a little more closely. She stiffened, then let out another loud sigh.

Slowly they moved toward town. Charles felt himself leaning on her more and more. Whether his incompetence was due to his sprain or his drunkenness he didn't know. She felt warm and strong and soft all at once next to him, and he didn't much care how he had gotten himself into this fix—he just resolved to enjoy it while it lasted. Each step pressed the side of her breast up against his ribs, and he was finding that to be a most pleasant sensation indeed.

"It's a beautiful day, don't you think?" he inquired, thinking he ought to make conversation.

"Yes," Ellie agreed, stumbling slightly under the weight of him. "But it is growing late. Is there no way you can move a little bit faster?"

"Even I," Charles said with an expansive wave of his hand, "am not such a cad that I would feign lameness merely to enjoy the attentions of a beautiful lady."

"Will you stop waving your arm about! We're losing our balance."

Charles wasn't sure why, and maybe it was just because he was still decidedly unsober, but he liked the sound of the word *we* from her lips. There was something about this Miss Lyndon that made him glad she was on his side. Not that he thought she would make a vicious enemy, just that she seemed loyal, levelheaded, and fair. And she had a wicked sense of humor. Just the sort of person a man would want standing beside him when he needed support.

He turned his face toward hers. "You smell nice," he said.

"What?" she screeched.

And she was fun to torture. Had he remembered to add that to his list of attributes? It was always good to surround oneself with people who could take a bit of teasing. He schooled his face into an innocent mask. "You smell nice," he said again.

"That is not the sort of thing a gentleman says to a lady," she said primly.

"I'm drunk," he said with an unrepentant shrug. "I don't know what I'm saying."

Her eyes narrowed suspiciously. "I have a feeling you know *exactly* what you're saying."

"Why, Miss Lyndon, are you accusing me of trying to seduce you?"

He didn't think it possible, but she turned an even deeper shade of crimson. He wished he could see the color of her hair under that monstrous bonnet. Her eyebrows were blond, and they stood out comically against her blush.

"Stop twisting my words."

"You twist words very nicely yourself, Miss Lyndon." When she didn't say anything, he added, "That was a compliment."

She trudged along the dirt road, pulling him with her. "You baffle me, my lord."

Charles smiled, thinking that it was great fun to baffle Miss Eleanor Lyndon. He fell silent for a few minutes, and then, as they rounded a corner, asked, "Are we almost there yet?"

"A little more than halfway, I should think." Ellie squinted at the horizon, watching the sun sink ever lower. "Oh, dear. It is growing late. Papa will have my head."

"I swear on my father's grave—" Charles was trying to sound serious, but he hiccupped.

Ellie turned toward him so quickly that her nose bumped into his shoulder. "Whatever are you talking about, my lord?"

"I was trying—hic—to swear to you that I am not—hic—deliberately trying to slow you down."

The corners of her lips twitched. "I don't know why I believe you," she said, "but I do."

"It might be because my ankle looks like an overripe pear," he joked.

"No," she said thoughtfully, "I think you're just a nicer person than you'd like people to believe."

He scoffed. "I am far from—hic—nice."

"I'll wager you give your entire staff extra wages at Christmas."

Much to his irritation, he blushed.

"A-ha!" she cried out triumphantly. "You do!"

"It breeds loyalty," he mumbled.

"It gives them money to buy presents for their families," she said softly.

He grunted and turned his head away from her. "Lovely sunset, don't you think, Miss Lyndon?"

"A bit clumsy as changes of subject go," she said with a knowing grin, "but yes, it is quite."

"It's rather amazing," he continued, "how many different colors make up the sunset. I see orange, and pink, and peach. Oh, and a touch of saffron right over there." He pointed off to the southwest. "And the truly remarkable thing of it is that it will all be different tomorrow."

"Are you an artist?" Ellie asked.

"No," he said. "I just like the sunset."

"Bellfield is just around the corner," she said.

"Is it?"

"You sound disappointed."

"Don't really want to go home, I suppose," he replied. He sighed, thinking about what was waiting for him there. A pile of stones that made up Wycombe Abbey. A pile of stones that cost a bloody fortune to keep up. A fortune that would slip through his fingers in less than a month thanks to his meddling father.

One would think that George Wycombe's hold on the pursestrings would have loosened with death, but no, he still found a way to keep his hands firmly around his son's neck from the grave. Charles swore under his breath as he thought about how apt that image was. He certainly felt like he was being strangled.

In precisely fifteen days, he would turn thirty. In precisely fifteen days, every last unentailed scrap of his inheritance would be snatched away from him. Unless—

Miss Lyndon coughed and rubbed a piece of dust from her eye. Charles looked at her with renewed interest.

Unless—he thought slowly, not wanting his still somewhat groggy brain to miss any important details—unless sometime in these next fifteen days, he managed to find himself a wife.

Miss Lyndon steered him onto Bellfield's High Street and pointed south. "The Bee and Thistle is just over there. I don't see your curricle. Is it 'round back?"

She had a nice voice, Charles thought. She had a nice voice, and a nice brain, and a nice wit, and—although he still didn't know what color her hair was—she had a nice set of eyebrows. And she felt *damned* nice with his weight pressed up against her.

He cleared his throat. "Miss Lyndon."

"Don't tell me you misplaced your carriage."

"Miss Lyndon, I have something of great import to discuss with you."

"Has your ankle worsened? I knew that putting weight on it was a bad idea, but I didn't know how else to get you into town. Ice would—"

"Miss Lyndon!" he fairly boomed.

That got her to close her mouth.

"Do you think you might—" Charles coughed, suddenly wishing he were sober, because he had a feeling his vocabulary was larger when he wasn't tipsy.

"Lord Billington?" she asked with a concerned expression.

In the end he just blurted it out. "Do you think you might marry me?"

Chapter 2

E llie dropped him.

He landed in a tangle of arms and legs, yelping with pain as his ankle gave way beneath him.

"That was a terrible thing to say!" she cried out.

Charles scratched his head. "I thought I just asked you to marry me?"

Ellie blinked back traitorous tears. "It is a cruel thing about which to jest."

"I wasn't jesting."

"Of course you were," she returned, just barely managing to resist the urge to kick him in the hip. "I have been very kind to you this afternoon."

"Very kind," he echoed.

"I did not have to stop and help you."

"No," he murmured, "you did not."

"I'll have you know that I could be married if I so wished it. I am on the shelf by choice."

"I wouldn't have dreamed otherwise."

Ellie thought she heard mocking in his voice, and this time she did kick him.

"Curse it, woman!" Charles exclaimed. "What the devil was that for? I am being utterly serious."

16

"You're drunk," she accused.

"Yes," he admitted, "but I've never asked a woman to marry me before."

"Oh, please," she scoffed. "If you are trying to tell me that you fell head over heels blindingly in love with me at first sight, let me tell you that it won't wash."

"I am not trying to tell you anything of the sort," he said. "I would never insult your intelligence in such a fashion."

Ellie blinked, thinking that he might have just insulted some other aspect of her person, but not sure which.

"The fact of the matter is—" He stopped and cleared his throat. "Do you think we might continue this conversation elsewhere? Perhaps somewhere where I might sit in a chair rather than in the dirt."

Ellie frowned at him for a moment before grudgingly holding out her hand. She still wasn't certain that he wasn't making sport of her, but her recent treatment of him had been less than gentle, and her conscience was nagging her. She didn't believe in kicking a man when he was down, especially when she was the one who had put him there.

He took her hand and eased himself back onto his feet. "Thank you," he said dryly. "You are clearly a woman of great strength of character. It is why I am considering taking you to wife."

Ellie's eyes narrowed. "If you do not cease mocking me. . . ."

"I believe I told you I am utterly serious. I never lie."

"Now that is a clanker if ever I heard one," she retorted.

"Well, then, I never lie about anything important."

Her hands found their way to her hips and she let out a loud, "Harumph."

He exhaled in a vaguely annoyed manner. "I assure you I would never lie about something like *this*. And I must say, you have developed an exceedingly poor opinion of me. Why, I wonder?"

"Lord Billington, you are considered the biggest rake in all of Kent! Even my brother-in-law has said so."

"Remind me to throttle Robert the next time I see him," Charles muttered.

"You very well might be the biggest rake in all of England. I wouldn't know, since I haven't left Kent in years, but—"

"They say rakes make the best husbands," he interrupted.

"*Reformed* rakes," she said pointedly. "And I sincerely doubt that you have any plans in that direction. Besides, I'm not going to marry you."

He sighed. "I really wish you would."

Ellie stared at him in disbelief. "You are mad."

"Thoroughly sane, I assure you." He grimaced. "It is my father who was mad."

Ellie suddenly had a vision of crazy, cackling babies and lurched backward. They said insanity was in the blood.

"Oh, for the love of God," Charles muttered. "Not truly mad. He simply left me in a cursed bind."

"I don't see what this has to do with me."

"It has everything to do with you," he said cryptically.

Ellie took another step backward, deciding that Billington was beyond mad—he was ready for Bedlam. "If you'll beg my pardon," she said quickly, "I'd best be getting home. I'm sure you'll be able to manage from here. Your carriage . . . you said it was around back. You should be able to—"

"Miss Lyndon," he said sharply.

She stopped in her tracks.

"I must marry," he said plainly, "and I must do it within the next fifteen days. I have no choice."

"I cannot imagine that you would do anything that did not suit your purposes."

He ignored her. "If I do not marry, I will lose every drop of my inheritance. Every last unentailed farthing." He laughed bitterly. "I will be left with only Wycombe Abbey, and believe me when I tell you that pile of stones will soon fall into disrepair if I lack the funds to keep it up."

"I have never heard of such a situation," Ellie said.

"It is not wholly uncommon."

"It seems uncommonly stupid, if you ask me."

"On that matter, madam, we are in complete agreement."

Ellie twisted some of the fabric of her brown skirt in her hand as she considered his words. "I don't see why you think I should be the one to aid you," she finally said. "I am certain you could find a suitable wife in London. Don't they call it 'The Marriage Mart?' I should think you would be considered quite a catch."

He offered her an ironic smile. "You make me sound like a fish."

Ellie looked up at him and caught her breath. He was devilishly handsome and thoroughly charming, and she knew she was far from immune. "No," she admitted, "not a fish."

He shrugged. "I have been putting off the inevitable. I know that. But here you are, dropped into my life at my most desperate—"

"Excuse me, but I believe *you* dropped into *my* life."

He chuckled. "Did I mention that you're also vastly entertaining? So I was thinking, 'Well, she'll do as well as any,' and—"

"If your aim was to woo me," Ellie said acidly, "you are not succeeding."

"Better than most," he corrected. "Really, you're the first I've come across I think I could bear." Not, Charles thought, that he had any plans to devote himself to a spouse. He didn't really need anything out of a wife save for her name on a marriage certificate. Still, one had to spend *some* time with one's wife, and she might as well be a decent sort. Miss Lyndon seemed to fit the bill nicely.

And, he added silently, he'd have to get himself an heir eventually. Might as well find someone with a bit of a brain in her head. Wouldn't do to have stupid progeny. He eyed her again. She was staring at him suspiciously. Yes, she was a smart one.

There was something damned appealing about her. He had a feeling that the process of getting that heir would be just as pleasant as the result. He gave her a jaunty bow, clutching onto her elbow for support.

"What do you say, Miss Lyndon? Shall we have a go at it?"

" 'Shall we have a go at it?' " Ellie choked out. Really, this was not the proposal of her dreams.

"Hmmm, I'm a bit clumsy at this. The truth is, Miss Lyndon, that if one's got to get oneself a wife, she might as well be someone one *likes*. We'd have to spend a bit of time together, you know."

She stared at him in disbelief. How drunk *was* he? She cleared her throat several times, trying to find words. Finally she just blurted out, "Are you trying to say you like me?"

He smiled seductively. "Very much."

"I shall have to consider this."

He inclined his head. "I wouldn't want to marry anyone who would make such a decision on the spur of the moment."

"I shall probably need a few days."

"Not too many, I hope. I have only fifteen before my odious cousin Phillip gets his paws on my money."

"I must warn you, my answer will almost certainly be no."

He didn't say anything. Ellie had the unpleasant sensation that he was already trying to decide who he would turn to if she refused him.

After a moment, he said, "Shall I see you home?"

"That won't be necessary. I am only a few minutes down the road. You will be able to manage on your own from here?"

He nodded. "Miss Lyndon."

She bobbed the tiniest of curtsies. "Lord Billington." Then she turned and walked away, waiting until she was out of his sight before falling back against the side of a building and mouthing, "Oh my *God!*"

The Reverend Mr. Lyndon did not tolerate his daughters taking the Lord's name in vain, but Ellie was sufficiently stunned by Billington's proposal that she was still muttering, "Oh my God," when she walked through the front door of their cottage.

"Such language is entirely unbecoming in a young woman, even if she is not so young any longer," a woman's voice said.

Ellie groaned. The only person worse than her father when it came to moral standards was his fiancée, the recently widowed Sally Foxglove. Ellie smiled tightly as she tried to make a beeline for her room. "Mrs. Foxglove."

"Your father will be most displeased when he hears of this."

Ellie groaned again. Trapped. She turned around. "Of what, Mrs. Foxglove?"

"Of your cavalier treatment of the name of our Lord." Mrs. Foxglove stood and crossed her plump arms.

Ellie had half a mind to remind the older woman that she was not Ellie's mother and had no authority over her, but she held her tongue. Life was going to be difficult once her father remarried. There was no need to make it downright impossible by deliberately antagonizing Mrs. Foxglove. Taking a deep breath, Ellie placed her hand over her heart and feigned innocence. "Is *that* what you thought I was saying?" she said, making her voice deliberately breathless.

"What *were* you saying, then?"

"I was saying, 'So I thought.' I hope you did not misunderstand me."

Mrs. Foxglove stared at her with patent disbelief.

"I had misjudged a certain, er, problem," Ellie continued. "I still cannot believe I did. Hence I was saying, 'So I thought,' because, you see, I held a certain thought, and if I had not held that thought, I would not have been mistaken in my logic."

Mrs. Foxglove looked so befuddled that Ellie wanted to whoop with delight.

"Well, whatever the case," the older woman said pointedly, "such bizarre behavior will never land you a husband."

"How did we come to be on this topic?" Ellie muttered, thinking that the subject of marriage had come up entirely too often that day.

"You are three and twenty," Mrs. Foxglove continued. "A spinster, to be sure, but we might be able to find a man who would deign to take you."

Ellie ignored her. "Is my father home?"

"He is out performing his calls, and asked me to remain here in the event any parishioners decide to visit."

"He left you in charge?"

"I will be his wife in two months." Mrs. Foxglove preened and smoothed down her puce-colored skirts. "I have a position in society I must uphold."

Ellie muttered some unintelligible phrases under her breath. She was afraid that if she actually allowed herself to form words, she'd do far far worse than taking the Lord's name in vain. She exhaled slowly and tried to smile. "If you'll excuse me, Mrs. Foxglove, I find I am most weary. I believe I will retire to my room."

A pudgy hand landed on her shoulder. "Not so fast, Eleanor."

Ellie turned around. Was Mrs. Foxglove threatening her? "I beg your pardon."

"We have some matters to discuss. I thought that this evening might be a good time. While your father is gone."

"What could we possibly have to discuss that we could not say in front of Papa?"

"This concerns your position in my household."

Ellie's mouth fell open. "*My* position in *your* household?"

"When I marry the good reverend, this will be *my* home, and I will manage it as I see fit."

Ellie suddenly felt ill.

"Do not think that you may live off my bounty," Mrs. Foxglove continued.

Ellie didn't move for fear that she'd strangle her future stepmother.

"If you do not marry and leave, you will have to earn your keep," said Mrs. Foxglove.

"Are you insinuating that I must earn my keep in some other way than I am currently earning it?" Ellie thought about all of the chores she performed for her father and his parish. She cooked him three meals a day. She brought food to the poor. She even polished the pews in his church. No one could say that she did not earn her keep.

But Mrs. Foxglove clearly did not share her opinion on the matter, because she rolled her eyes and said,

"You live off of your father's largesse. He is entirely too indulgent with you."

Ellie's eyes bugged out. One thing the Reverend Mr. Lyndon had never been called was indulgent. He had once tied up her older sister to prevent her from marrying the man she loved. Ellie cleared her throat in yet another attempt to control her temper. "What exactly do you wish me to do, Mrs. Foxglove?"

"I have inspected the house and prepared a list of chores."

Mrs. Foxglove handed Ellie a slip of paper. Ellie looked down, read the lines, and choked on her fury. "You want me to clean out the chimney?!?"

"It is wasteful for us to spend money on a chimney sweep when you can do it."

"Don't you think I am a bit too large for such a task?"

"That is another matter. You eat too much."

"What?" Ellie shrieked.

"Food is dear."

"Half of the parishioners pay their tithe in kind," Ellie said, shaking with anger. "We may be short of many things, but never food."

"If you don't like my rules," Mrs. Foxglove said, "you can always marry and leave the house."

Ellie knew why Mrs. Foxglove was so determined to see her gone. She was probably one of those women who could not tolerate anything less than absolute authority in her household. And Ellie, who had been managing her father's affairs for years, would be in the way.

Ellie wondered what the old biddy would say if she were to tell her that she'd received a proposal of marriage just that afternoon. And from an earl, no less. Ellie planted her hands on her hips, ready to give her father's fiancée the blistering setdown she'd been holding in for what seemed like an unbearable length of time, when Mrs. Foxglove held out another slip of paper.

"What's this?" Ellie snapped.

"I have taken the liberty of making a list of eligible bachelors in the district."

Ellie snorted. This she had to see. She unfolded the paper and looked down. Without lifting her eyes back up, she said, "Richard Parrish is engaged."

"Not according to my sources."

Mrs. Foxglove was the worst gossip in Bellfield, so Ellie was inclined to believe her. Not that it made a difference. Richard Parrish was stout and had bad breath. She read on and choked. "George Millerton is past sixty."

Mrs. Foxglove sniffed disdainfully. "You are not in a position to be choosy about such a trivial matter."

The next three names on the list belonged to equally elderly men, one of whom was downright mean. Rumor had it that Anthony Ponsoby had beaten his first wife. There was no way that Ellie was going to shackle herself to a man who thought that marital communication was best conducted with a stick.

"Good God!" Ellie exclaimed as her eyes traveled down to the second-to-last name on the list. "Robert Beechcombe cannot be a day over fifteen. What were you thinking?"

Mrs. Foxglove was about to respond, but Ellie interrupted her. "Billy Watson!" she shrieked. "He is not right in the head. Everybody knows that. How dare you try to marry me off to someone like him!"

"As I said, a woman in your position cannot—"

"Don't say it," Ellie cut in, her entire body shaking with rage. "Don't say a word."

Mrs. Foxglove smirked. "You cannot speak to me like that in my home."

"It isn't your home yet, you old bag," Ellie bit out.

Mrs. Foxglove lurched backward. "Well, I never!"

"And *I* have never been moved to violence," Ellie fumed, "but I am always willing to try a new experience." She grabbed Mrs. Foxglove's collar and pushed her out the door.

"You will be sorry you did this!" Mrs. Foxglove yelled from the walkway.

"I will never be sorry," Ellie returned. "Never!"

She slammed the door and threw herself on the sofa. There was no doubt about it. She was going to have to find a way to escape her father's household. The Earl of Billington's face danced in her head, but she pushed it aside. She wasn't so desperate that she had to marry a man she'd scarcely met. Surely there had to be some other way.

By the next morning, Ellie had devised a plan. She wasn't as helpless as Mrs. Foxglove would like to believe. She had a bit of money tucked away. It wasn't a vast sum, but it was enough to support a woman of modest taste and frugal nature.

Ellie had put the money in a bank years ago but had been dissatisfied with the paltry rate of interest. So she took to reading the *London Times*, making special note of items relating to the world of business and commerce. When she felt she had a comprehensive knowledge of the 'change, she went to a solicitor to handle her funds. She had to do it under her father's name, of course. No solicitor would handle money on the behalf of a young woman, especially one who was investing without the knowledge of her father. So she traveled several towns away, found Mr. Tibbett, a solicitor who did not know of the Reverend Mr. Lyndon, and told him that her father was a recluse. Mr. Tibbett worked with a broker in London, and Ellie's nest egg grew and grew.

It was time to draw on those funds. She had no other choice. Living with Mrs. Foxglove as her stepmother would be intolerable. The money could support her until her sister Victoria returned from her extended holiday on the continent. Victoria's new husband was a wealthy earl, and Ellie had no doubt that they would be able to help her find a position in society—perhaps as a governess, or a companion.

Ellie rode a public coach to Faversham, made her way to the offices of Tibbett & Hurley, and waited her turn to see Mr. Tibbett. After ten minutes, his secretary ushered her in.

Mr. Tibbett, a portly man with a large mustache, rose when she entered. "Good day, Miss Lyndon," he said. "Have you come with more instructions from your father? I must say, it is a pleasure to do business with a man who pays such close attention to his investments."

Ellie smiled tightly, hating that her father received all of the credit for her business acumen but knowing that there was no other way. "Not precisely, Mr. Tibbett. I have come to withdraw some of my funds. One-half, to be precise." Ellie wasn't certain how much it would cost to lease a small house in a respectable section of London, but she had close to 300 pounds stashed away, and she thought that 150 would do nicely.

"Certainly," Mr. Tibbett agreed. "I will simply need your father to come here in person to release the funds."

Ellie gasped. "I beg your pardon."

"At Tibbett & Hurley, we pride ourselves on our scrupulous business practices. I could not possibly release the funds into anyone's hands but your father's."

"But I have been conducting business with you for years," Ellie protested. "My name is on the account as a codepositor!"

"A codepositor. Your father is the primary holder."

Ellie swallowed convulsively. "My father is a recluse. You know that. He never leaves the house. How can I get him to come here?"

Mr. Tibbett shrugged his shoulders. "I will be happy to come out to visit him."

"No, that will not be possible," Ellie said, aware that her voice was growing shrill. "He gets most nervous around strangers. Most nervous. His heart, you know. I really couldn't risk it."

"Then I will need written instructions with his signature attached."

Ellie sighed in relief. She could forge her father's signature in her sleep.

"And I will need these instructions witnessed by another upstanding citizen." Mr. Tibbett's eyes narrowed suspiciously. "*You* do not qualify as a witness."

"Very well, I will find—"

"I am acquainted with the magistrate in Bellfield. You may obtain his signature as a witness."

Ellie's heart sank. She also knew the magistrate, and she knew that there would be no way to get his signature on that vital piece of paper unless he actually witnessed her father write out the instructions. "Very well, Mr. Tibbett," she said, her voice catching in her throat. "I will—I will see what I can do."

She hurried out of the office, pressing a handkerchief up to her face to hide her frustrated tears. She felt like a cornered animal. There was no way she was going to be able to get her money from Mr. Tibbett. And Victoria wasn't due back from the continent for several months. Ellie supposed she could throw herself on the mercy of Victoria's father-in-law, the Marquess of Castleford, but she wasn't at all certain that he would be any more amiable to her presence than Mrs. Foxglove. The marquess didn't much like Victoria; Ellie could only imagine how he'd feel about her sister.

Ellie wandered aimlessly through Faversham, trying to gather her thoughts. She had always considered herself a practical sort of female, one who could rely on a sharp brain and a quick wit. She had never dreamed that she might someday find herself in a situation she couldn't talk her way out of.

And now she was stuck in Faversham, twenty miles away from a home she didn't even want to go back to. With no options except—

Ellie shook her head. She was *not* going to consider taking the Earl of Billington up on his offer.

The face of Sally Foxglove loomed in her mind.

Then that awful face started talking about chimneys, and spinsters who ought to be and act grateful for anything and everything. The earl started looking better and better.

Not, Ellie had to admit to herself, that he had ever looked bad to begin with, if one was going to take the word "look" in its literal sense. He was sinfully handsome, and she had a feeling he knew it. That, she reasoned, should be a black mark against him. He was most likely conceited. He would probably keep scores of mistresses. She couldn't imagine he'd find it difficult to gain the attentions of all sorts of females, respectable and otherwise.

"Ha!" she said aloud, then looked this way and that to see if anyone had heard her. The blasted man probably had to beat women away with a stick. She certainly didn't want to deal with a husband with those kinds of "problems."

Then again, it wasn't as if she were in love with the fellow. She might be able to get used to the idea of an unfaithful husband. It went against everything she stood for, but the alternative was a life with Sally Foxglove, which was too horrifying to contemplate.

Ellie tapped her toe as she thought. Wycombe Abbey wasn't so very far away. If she remembered correctly, it was situated on the north Kent coast, just a mile or two away. She could easily walk the distance. Not that she was planning to blindly accept the earl's proposal, but maybe they could discuss the matter a bit. Maybe they could reach an agreement with which she could be happy.

Her mind made up, Ellie lifted her chin and began walking north. She tried to keep her mind busy by guessing how many steps it would take to reach a landmark ahead. Fifty paces to the large tree. Seventy-two to the abandoned cottage. Forty to the—

Oh, blast! Was that a raindrop? Ellie wiped the water from her nose and looked up. The clouds were gathering, and if she weren't such a practical woman, she would swear that they were congregating directly over her head.

She let out a sound that one could only call a growl and trudged onward, trying not to curse when another raindrop smacked her on the cheek. And then another pelted her shoulder, and another, and another, and—

Ellie shook her fist at the sky. "Somebody up there is deuced mad at me," she yelled, "and I want to know why!"

The heavens opened in earnest and within seconds she was soaked to the skin.

"Remind me never to question Your purposes again," she muttered ungraciously, not sounding particularly like the God-fearing young lady her father had raised her to be. "Clearly You don't like to be second-guessed."

Lightning streaked through the sky, followed by a booming clap of thunder. Ellie jumped nearly a foot. What was it that her sister's husband had told her so many years ago? The closer the thunder follows the lightning, the closer the lightning is to oneself? Robert had always been of a scientific bent; Ellie was inclined to believe him on this measure.

She took off at a run. Then, after her lungs threatened to explode, she slowed down to a trot. After a minute or two of that, however, she settled into a brisk walk. After all, she wasn't likely to get any wetter than she was already.

Thunder pounded again, causing Ellie to jump and trip over a tree root, landing in the mud. "Damn!" she grunted, probably her first verbal use of the word in her life. If ever there was a time to begin the habit of cursing, however, it was now.

She staggered to her feet and looked up, rain pelting her face. Her bonnet sagged against her eyes, blocking her vision. She yanked it off, looked at the sky, and yelled, "I am not amused!"

More lightning.

"They are all against me," she muttered, starting to feel just a little bit irrational. "All of them." Her father, Sally Foxglove, Mr. Tibbett, whoever it was who controlled the weather—

More thunder.

Ellie gritted her teeth and moved onward. Finally, an old stone behemoth of a building loomed over the horizon. She'd never seen Wycombe Abbey in person, but she'd seen a pen and ink drawing of it for sale in Bellfield. Relief finally settling within her, she made her way to the front door and knocked.

A liveried servant answered her summons and gave her an extremely condescending look.

"I-I'm here t-to see the earl," Ellie said, teeth chattering.

"Servants' interviews are conducted by the housekeeper," the butler replied. "Use the rear entrance."

He started to shut the door but Ellie managed to jam her foot in the opening. "Noooo!" she yelled, somehow sensing that if she let that door shut in her face she would be condemned forever to a life of cold gruel and dirty chimneys.

"Madam, remove your foot."

"Not in this lifetime," Ellie shot back, squeezing her elbow and shoulder inside. "I'll see the earl, and—"

"The earl doesn't associate with your kind."

"My kind?!" Ellie shrieked. Really, this was beyond tolerable. She was cold, wet, unable to get her hands on money that was rightfully hers, and now some puffed-up butler was calling her a *prostitute*? "You let me in this instant! It's raining out here."

"I see that."

"You fiend," she hissed. "When I see the earl, he'll—"

"I say, Rosejack, what the devil is all this commotion?"

Ellie nearly melted with relief at the sound of Billington's voice. In fact, she *would* have melted with relief if she weren't so certain that any sort of softening on her part would prompt the butler to squeeze her out of the doorway.

"There is a creature on the doorstep," Rosejack replied. "It refuses to budge."

"I'm a 'she,' you cretin!" Ellie used the fist she'd managed to wedge inside the house to bat him in the back of the head.

"For the love of God," Charles said, "Just open the door and let her in."

Rosejack whipped open the door and Ellie tumbled in, feeling very much like a wet rat amidst such splendidly opulent surroundings. There were beautiful rugs on the floors, a painting on the wall that she would swear had been done by Rembrandt, and that vase that she'd knocked over as she fell down—well, she had a sick feeling that it had been imported from China.

She looked up, desperately trying to peel the wet locks of hair from her face. Charles looked handsome, amused, and disgustingly dry. "My lord?" she gasped, barely able to find her voice. She sounded decidedly unlike herself, raspy and hoarse from her arguments with God and the butler.

Charles blinked as he regarded her. "I beg your pardon, madam," he said. "Have we met?"

Chapter 3

Ellie had never had much of a temper. Oh, she was, as her father frequently pointed out, a bit mouthy, but on the whole she was a sensible and levelheaded lady, not given to outbursts and tantrums.

This aspect of her personality, however, was not in evidence at Wycombe Abbey.

"What?!?" she screeched, vaulting to her feet.

"How dare you!" she then shrieked, launching herself toward Billington, who was trying to back up, hindered considerably by his injury and cane.

"You fiend!" she finally squawked, pushing him over and tumbling down to the floor with him.

Charles groaned. "If I have been knocked to the ground," he said, "then you must be Miss Lyndon."

"Of course I'm Miss Lyndon," she shouted. "Who the devil else would I be?"

"I might point out that you look remarkably unlike yourself."

That gave Ellie pause. She was certain she bore more than a passing resemblance to a drowned rat, her clothes were liberally streaked with mud, and her bonnet . . . She looked around. Where the devil was her bonnet?

"Lose something?" Charles inquired.

"My bonnet," Ellie replied, suddenly feeling very sheepish.

He smiled. "I like you better without one. I was wondering what color your hair was."

"It's red," she shot back, thinking that this must be the final indignity. She hated her hair, had always hated her hair.

Charles coughed to cover up yet another smile. Ellie was spitting mad, well beyond furious, and he couldn't remember the last time he'd had so much fun. Well, actually he could. Yesterday, to be precise, when he'd fallen out of a tree and had the good fortune to land on her.

Ellie reached up to push a wet and sticky lock of hair from her face, causing her sodden dress to tighten around her bodice. Charles's skin grew suddenly warm.

Oh yes, he thought, *she'd make a very fine wife*.

"My lord?" the butler interjected as he leaned down to help Charles up. "Do we know this person?"

"I'm afraid we do," Charles replied, earning himself a scathing glare from Ellie. "It appears that Miss Lyndon has had a trying day. Perhaps we might offer her some tea. And"—he eyed her dubiously—"a towel."

"That would be very nice," Ellie said primly. "Thank you."

Charles watched her as she stood. "I trust you have been considering my proposal."

Rosejack halted in his tracks and turned around. "Proposal?" he gasped.

Charles grinned. "Yes, Rosejack. I am hoping that

Miss Lyndon will do me the honor of becoming my wife."

Rosejack went utterly white.

Ellie scowled at him. "I was trapped in a rainstorm," she said, thinking that *that* ought to be self-evident. "I am usually a bit more presentable."

"She was trapped in a rainstorm," Charles repeated. "And I can vouch for the fact that she is usually much more presentable. She will make an excellent countess, I assure you."

"I have not yet accepted," Ellie muttered.

Rosejack looked as if he might faint.

"You will," Charles said with a knowing smile.

"How can you possibly—"

"Why else would you have come?" he interjected. He turned to the butler. "Rosejack, the tea, if you please. And don't forget a towel. Or perhaps two." He glanced down to where Ellie was leaving puddles on the parquet floor, then looked back toward Rosejack yet again. "You had better just bring in a stack of them."

"I have *not* come to accept your proposal," Ellie sputtered. "I merely wanted to talk with you about it. I—"

"Of course, my dear," Charles murmured. "Would you like to follow me to the drawing room? I would offer you my arm, but I fear I cannot provide much support these days." He motioned to his cane.

Ellie let out a frustrated breath and followed him into a nearby room. It was decorated in cream and blue, and she didn't dare sit on anything. "I don't think mere towels are going to be sufficient, my lord," she said. She didn't even want to step on the carpet.

Not with the way her skirts were dripping.

Charles surveyed her thoughtfully. "I fear you are correct. Would you like a change of clothing? My sister is married and now lives in Surrey, but she keeps some dresses here. I'd wager she is about your size."

Ellie didn't like the idea of taking someone's clothing without asking permission, but her other option was coming down with a raging case of lung fever. She looked down at her fingers, which were shaking from the cold and damp, and nodded her head.

Charles rang the bellpull, and a maid entered the room within the minute. Charles gave her instructions to show Ellie to his sister's room. Feeling as if she had somehow lost control of her destiny, Ellie followed the maid out.

Charles sat down on a comfortable sofa, let out a long sigh of relief, then sent up a silent thanks to whomever it was who was responsible for her arriving on his doorstep. He had started to fear that he was going to have to go to London and marry one of those awful debutantes his family kept throwing his way.

He whistled to himself as he waited for tea and Miss Lyndon. What had made her come? He'd been still a bit past tipsy when he'd blurted out that bizarre proposal the day before, but he hadn't been so drunk that he had not been able to gauge her feelings.

He'd thought she would refuse. He'd been almost certain of it.

She was a sensible sort. That much was obvious even after such a brief acquaintance. What would make her give her hand in marriage to a man she barely knew?

There were the usual reasons, of course. He had money and a title, and if she married him, she'd have money and a title as well. But Charles didn't think that was it. He had seen the look of desperation in her eyes when she'd—

He frowned, then laughed as he got up to look out the window. Miss Lyndon had attacked him. Right there in the hall. There really wasn't any other word for it.

Tea arrived a few minutes later, and Charles instructed the maid to leave it in the pot to steep. He liked his tea strong.

A few minutes after that, a hesitant knock sounded at the door. He turned around, surprised at the sound since the maid had left the door open.

Ellie was standing in the doorway, her hand raised to knock again. "I thought you didn't hear me," she said.

"The door was open. There was no need to knock."

She shrugged. "I didn't want to intrude."

Charles motioned for her to come in, watching her with an appraising eye as she crossed the room. His sister's dress was a shade too long for her, and she had to hold up the pale green skirts as she walked. That was when he noticed she wasn't wearing any shoes. Funny how the sight of a foot could cause his midsection to tingle this way . . .

Ellie caught him looking at her feet and blushed. "Your sister has tiny feet," she said, "and my own shoes were soaked through."

He blinked, as if he were lost in thought, then shook his head slightly and looked her in the eye. "No matter," he said, then let his gaze fall to her feet again.

Ellie dropped her skirts, wondering what the devil was so interesting about her feet.

"You look quite fetching in mint," he said, hobbling over to her side. "You should wear it more often."

"All my dresses are dark and serviceable," she said, her voice containing equal parts irony and wistfulness.

"Pity. I'll have to buy you new ones once we're married."

"Now, see here!" Ellie protested. "I have not accepted your proposal. I am merely here to—" She broke off when she realized she was yelling and continued in a softer tone. "I am merely here to discuss it with you."

He smiled slowly. "What do you want to know?"

Ellie exhaled, wishing that she'd been able to approach this interview with a bit more composure. Not that that would have helped much, she thought ruefully, after the entrance she'd made. The butler was never going to forgive her. Looking up, she said, "Do you mind if I sit down?"

"Of course not. How rude of me." He motioned to the sofa, and she took a seat. "Would you care for tea?" Charles asked.

"Yes, that would be lovely." Ellie reached for the tray and began to pour. It somehow seemed a sinfully intimate act, pouring tea for this man in his own home. "Milk?"

"Please. No sugar."

She smiled. "I take mine the same way."

Charles took a sip and assessed her over the rim of his cup. She was nervous. He couldn't blame her. It was a most uncommon situation, and he had to admire her for facing it with such fortitude. He watched as she drained her teacup and then said, "By the way, your hair isn't red."

Ellie choked on her tea.

"What is it they call it?" he mused, lifting his hand and rubbing his fingers together in the air as if that would prompt his brain. "Ah yes, strawberry blond. Although that seems rather inadequate to me."

"It's red," Ellie said baldly.

"No, no, it really isn't. It's—"

"Red."

His lips spread into a lazy smile. "Red, then, if you insist."

Ellie found herself oddly disappointed that he'd given in. She'd always wanted her hair to be something more exotic than just plain red. It was an unexpected gift from some long-forgotten Irish ancestor. The only good thing about it had been that it was a constant source of irritation to her father, who had been known to develop nausea at the merest intimation that there might be a Catholic somewhere in his background.

Ellie had always rather liked the idea of a rogue Catholic hiding out in her family tree. She had always liked the idea of anything out of the ordinary, anything to break up the monotony of her humdrum life. She looked up at Billington, who sprawled elegantly in a chair opposite her.

This man, she decided, definitely qualified as extraordinary. As did the situation in which he'd recently placed her. She smiled weakly, thinking that she ought to be made of sterner stuff. His was a remarkably handsome face, and his charm—well, there was no arguing that it wasn't lethal. Still, she needed to conduct this interview like the sensible woman she was.

She cleared her throat. "I believe we were discussing..." She frowned. What the devil *had* they been discussing?

"Your hair, actually," he drawled.

Ellie felt a blush creeping along her cheeks. "Right. Well. Hmmm."

Charles took pity on her and said, "I don't suppose you want to tell me what prompted you to consider my proposal."

She looked up sharply. "What makes you think there was a specific incident?"

"You have the look of desperation in your eyes."

Ellie couldn't even pretend to be affronted by his statement, for she knew it was true. "My father is remarrying next month," she said after taking a long sigh. "His fiancée is a witch."

His lips twitched. "As bad as that?"

Ellie had a feeling he thought she was exaggerating. "I am not jesting. Yesterday she presented me with two lists. The first consisted of chores I must perform in addition to those I already do."

"What, did she have you cleaning out the chimney?" Charles teased.

"Yes!" Ellie burst out. "Yes, and it was not a joke! And then she had the effrontery to tell me I eat too much when I pointed out that I would not fit."

"I think you're just the right size," he murmured. She didn't hear him, though, which was probably for the best. He didn't need to scare her away. Not when he was this close to having her name on that blessed marriage certificate. "What was the other list?" he inquired.

"Marriage prospects," she said in a disgusted voice.

"Was I on it?"

"Most assuredly not. She only listed men whom she thought I might have a chance at catching."

"Oh, dear."

Ellie scowled. "Her opinion of me is quite low."

"I shudder to think who was on the list."

"Several men over sixty, one under sixteen, and one who is simpleminded."

Charles couldn't help it. He laughed.

"This isn't funny!" Ellie exclaimed. "And I didn't even mention the one who beat his first wife."

Charles's humor faded instantly. "You will *not* be married off to someone who will beat you."

Ellie's lips parted in surprise. He sounded almost proprietary. How very odd. "I assure you that I won't. If I marry, it will be a man of my own choosing. And I'm afraid to say, my lord, that out of all my options, you do seem to be the best of the lot."

"I'm flattered," he muttered.

"I didn't think I would *have* to marry you, you see."

Charles frowned, thinking that she didn't need to sound quite so resigned.

"I have some money," she continued. "Enough to support myself for some time. At least until my sister and her husband return from their holiday."

"Which is in . . ."

"Three months," Ellie finished for him. "Or perhaps a bit longer. Their baby has a small respiratory problem, and the doctor feels a warmer climate would do him good."

"I trust it is not serious."

"Not at all," Ellie said, giving him a reassuring nod. "One of those things one outgrows. But I'm afraid I am still left at loose ends."

"I do not understand," Charles said.

"My solicitor will not give me my money." Ellie quickly recounted the day's events, leaving out her undignified argument with the heavens. Really, the man didn't need to know everything about her. Better not say anything that might lead him to think she was a bit unhinged.

Charles sat quietly, tapping his fingertips together as he listened. "What exactly do you want me to do for you?" he asked when she was finished.

"Ideally, I'd like you to march into the solicitor's office on my behalf and demand that he release my funds," she replied. "Then I could live quietly in London and await my sister."

"And not marry me?" he said, a knowing smile on his face.

"That isn't going to happen, is it?"

He shook his head.

"Perhaps I could marry you, you could get my money, and then, once your inheritance is secure, we could obtain an annulment . . ." She tried to sound convincing, but her words trailed off as she watched him shake his head again.

"That scenario presents two problems," he said.

"Two?" she echoed. She might have been able to talk her way around one, but two? Doubtful.

"My father's will specifically addresses the possibility that I might enter into a sham marriage merely for the sake of my inheritance. Were I to obtain an annulment, my assets would be immediately seized and handed over to my cousin."

Ellie's heart sank.

"Secondly," he continued, "an annulment would require that we not consummate our marriage."

She gulped. "I don't see any problem there."

He leaned forward, his eyes burning with something she didn't recognize. "Don't you?" he asked softly.

Ellie didn't like the way her stomach was jumping about. The earl was far too handsome for his own good—far too handsome for *her* own good. "If we marry," she blurted out, suddenly very eager to change the subject, "you will have to get my money for me. Can you do that? Because I won't marry you otherwise."

"I shall be able to provide for you quite handsomely without it," Charles pointed out.

"But it's mine, and I worked hard for it. I'm not about to let it rot in Tibbett's hands."

"Certainly not," Charles murmured, looking as if he were trying very hard not to smile.

"It's the principle of the matter."

"And the principle is what matters to you, isn't it?"

"Absolutely." She paused. "Of course, principles won't put food on the table. If they did, I wouldn't be here."

"Very well. I shall get your money for you. It shouldn't be that difficult."

"For you, perhaps," Ellie muttered ungracefully. "I couldn't even get the blasted man to acknowledge that I possessed a greater intelligence than a sheep."

Charles chuckled. "Have no fear, Miss Lyndon, I shan't make the same mistake."

"And that money will remain mine," Ellie persisted. "I know that when we marry, all of my possessions—meager though they are—become yours, but I would like a separate account in my name."

"Done."

"And you will make certain that the bank knows that I have full control over those funds?"

"If you so desire it."

Ellie looked at him suspiciously. Charles caught the glance and said, "I have more than enough money of my own, provided we marry in haste. I don't need yours."

She let out a relieved breath. "Good. I do like to play the 'change. I shouldn't want to have to get your signature every time I want to make a transaction."

His mouth fell open. "You play the 'change?"

"Yes, and I'm quite good at it, I'll have you know. I made a tidy profit in sugar last year."

Charles smiled in disbelief. They would do quite well together, he was sure of it. Time spent with his new wife would be more than pleasant, and it sounded as if she would be able to keep herself occupied while he was pursuing his own affairs in London. The last thing he needed was to be shackled to a woman who whined every time she was left to her own devices.

He narrowed his eyes. "I say, you're not one of those managing sorts of women, are you?"

"What does that mean?"

"The last thing I need is a woman who wants to take charge of my life. I need a wife, not a keeper."

"You're rather choosy for someone who has only fourteen days before his fortune is forever lost."

"Marriage is for life, Eleanor."

"Believe me, I know."

"Well?"

"No," she said, looking as if she wanted to roll her eyes. "I'm not. That is not to say that I don't want to manage my *own* life, of course."

"Of course," he murmured.

"But I won't interfere with yours. You won't even know I'm here."

"Somehow I doubt that."

She scowled at him. "You know what I mean."

"Very well, then," he said. "I think we are making quite a fair-minded deal. I marry you, and you get your money. You marry me, and I get my money."

Ellie blinked. "I hadn't really thought of it that way, but yes, that's about the sum of it."

"Good. Have we a bargain?"

Ellie swallowed, trying to ignore the sinking feeling that she had just sold her soul to the devil. As the earl had just pointed out, marriage was forever, and she had known this man but two days. She shut her eyes for a moment, then nodded.

"Excellent." Charles beamed as he rose to his feet, holding on to the arm of his chair while he steadied his cane. "We must seal our bargain in a more festive manner."

"Champagne?" Ellie asked, ready to kick herself for sounding so hopeful. She'd always wanted to know what it tasted like.

"A good idea," he murmured, crossing over to the sofa where she sat. "I'm sure I have some on the premises. But I was thinking of something a little different."

"Different?"

"More intimate."

She stopped breathing.

He sat next to her. "A kiss, I think, would be appropriate."

"Oh," Ellie said quickly and loudly. "That's not necessary." And just in case he missed her point, she gave her head a broad shake.

He caught her chin in a light but firm grasp. "*Au contraire*, my wife, I think it is very necessary."

"I'm not your—"

"You will be."

She had no argument for that.

"We should make sure that we suit, don't you think?" He leaned closer.

"I'm certain we will. We don't need—"

He halved the distance between them. "Has anyone ever told you that you talk a lot?"

"Oh, all the time," she said, desperate to do anything, say anything to keep him from kissing her. "In fact—"

"And at the most inopportune times, too." He shook his head in a sweetly scolding manner.

"Well, I don't really have such an ideal sense of timing. Just look at—"

"Hush."

And he said it with such soft authority that she did. Or perhaps it might have been the smoldering look in his eyes. No one had ever smoldered over Eleanor Lyndon before. It was beyond startling.

His lips brushed against hers, and a sharp tingle

shot up and down her spine as his hand moved to her neck. "Oh, my goodness," she whispered.

He chuckled. "You talk when you kiss, too."

"Oh." She looked up anxiously. "I'm not supposed to?"

He started laughing so hard that he had to pull away from her and sit back. "Actually," he said as soon as he was able, "I find it rather endearing. As long as you're being complimentary."

"Oh," she said again.

"Shall we give it another go?" he asked.

Ellie rather thought that she'd used up all of her protests with the previous kiss. Besides, now that she'd tried it once, she was a bit more curious. She gave her head a tiny nod.

His eyes flashed with something very male and possessive, and his mouth touched her lips once again. This kiss was just as gentle as the previous one, but so, so much deeper. His tongue feathered along the line of her lips until she parted them with a sigh. Then he moved in, exploring her mouth with lazy confidence.

Ellie gave herself up to the moment, sinking into his hard frame. He was warm and strong, and there was something thrilling about the way his hands pressed against her back. She felt branded, burned, as if she'd somehow been marked as his.

His passion grew fierce . . . and scary. Ellie had never kissed a man before, but she could tell that he was an expert at this. She had no idea what to do, and he knew too much, and . . . She stiffened, suddenly overwhelmed. This wasn't right. She didn't know him, and—

Charles pulled away, sensing her withdrawal. "Are you all right?" he whispered.

Ellie tried to remind herself how to breathe, and when she finally found her voice again, she said, "You've done this before, haven't you?" Then she closed her eyes for a moment and muttered, "What am I saying? Of course you have."

He nodded, shaking with silent laughter. "Is there a problem with that?"

"I'm not certain. I have this feeling I'm some sort of . . ." Her words trailed off.

"Some sort of what?"

"Prize."

"Well, you certainly are that," Charles said, his tone clearly marking his statement as a compliment.

But Ellie didn't take it as such. She didn't like to think of herself as an object to be won, and she particularly didn't like the fact that Billington made her head spin so fast that when he kissed her she lost all sense of reason. She stepped quickly away from him and sat down in the chair he'd recently occupied. It was still warm from his body, and she could swear she could smell him, and—

She gave her head a little shake. What on earth had that kiss done to her brain? Her thoughts were skipping along with no sensible direction. She wasn't sure that she liked herself this way, all breathless and silly. Steeling herself, she looked up.

Charles raised his brows. "I can see you have something important to tell me."

Ellie frowned. Was she that transparent? "Yes," she said. "About that kiss . . ."

"I would be more than happy to talk about that

kiss," he said, and she wasn't certain if he was laughing or merely smiling or—

She was doing it again. Losing her train of thought. This was dangerous. "It can't happen again," she blurted out.

"Is that so?" he drawled.

"If I'm going to marry you—"

"You already agreed to do so," he said, his voice sounding very dangerous.

"I realize that, and I'm not one to break my word." Ellie swallowed, realizing that that was exactly what she was threatening to do. "But I cannot marry you unless I have your agreement that we . . . that we . . ."

"That we not consummate the marriage?" he finished for her flatly.

"Yes!" she said with a relieved rush of air. "Yes, that's it exactly."

"Out of the question."

"It wouldn't be forever," Ellie said quickly. "Just until I'm used to . . . marriage."

"Marriage? Or me?"

"Both."

He was quiet for a full minute.

"I'm not asking much," Ellie finally said, desperate to break the silence. "I don't want a lavish allowance. I don't need jewels or dresses—"

"You need dresses," he cut in.

"All right," she agreed, thinking that it would be awfully nice to wear something that wasn't brown. "I do need dresses, but really, nothing more."

He leveled a hard stare in her direction. "*I* need more."

She gulped. "And you shall have it. Just not right away."

He tapped his fingertips together. It was a mannerism that had already become uniquely his in her mind. "Very well," he said, "I agree. Provided that you grant me a boon as well."

"Anything. Well, almost anything."

"I assume that you mean to let me know when you are ready to make our marriage a true one."

"Er ... yes," Ellie said. She hadn't really thought about it. It was hard to think about anything when he was sitting across from her, staring at her so intently.

"First of all, I must insist that your participation in the marital act is not unreasonably withheld."

Ellie's eyes narrowed. "I say, you haven't studied the law, have you? This sounds terribly legal."

"A man in my position must beget an heir, Miss Lyndon. It would be foolish of me to enter into such an agreement without your assurance that our abstinence would not be a permanent state of affairs."

"Of course," she said quietly, trying to ignore the unexpectedly sad feeling in her heart. She'd thought that she might have aroused a deeper passion in him. She should have known better. He had other reasons for kissing her. "I—I will not make you wait forever."

"Good. And now for the second part of my stipulation."

Ellie didn't like the look in his eyes.

He leaned forward. "I reserve the right to try to convince you otherwise."

"I don't catch your meaning."

"No? Come here."

She shook her head. "I don't think that is a very good idea."

"Come here, Eleanor."

His use of her given name shocked her. She hadn't given him permission to do so—and yet, she had agreed to marry him, so she supposed she shouldn't quibble.

"Eleanor," he said again, clearly growing impatient with her wool-gathering. When she didn't respond yet again, he reached out, grasped her hand, and yanked her over a mahogany table and back into his lap.

"Lord Billing—"

His hand covered her mouth as his lips found her ear. "When I said I reserved the right to try to convince you otherwise," he whispered, "I meant *this*."

He kissed her again, and Ellie lost all power to think. Abruptly, he cut the kiss off, leaving her shaking. He smiled. "Fair enough?"

"I . . . ah . . ."

He seemed to enjoy her befuddlement. "It's the only way I'm going to agree to your request."

She nodded jerkily. After all, how often was he actually going to want to kiss her? Stumbling, she rose to her feet. "I had best be getting home."

"Indeed." Charles looked out the window. The weather had cleared, but the sun was beginning to set. "As for the rest of the particulars of our bargain, we can work them out as we go along."

Ellie's mouth opened slightly in surprise. "Particulars?"

"I assumed a woman of your sensibilities would want her duties spelled out."

"You will have 'duties' as well, I presume."

Charles's mouth turned up into an ironic half-smile. "But of course."

"Good."

He took her arm and walked her to the door. "I shall have a carriage bring you home and fetch you tomorrow."

"Tomorrow?" she gasped.

"I haven't much time to dawdle."

"Don't we need a license?"

"I have one. I need only to fill in your name."

"Can you do that?" she gasped. "Is that legal?"

"One can do quite a bit if one knows the right people."

"But I will need to prepare. To pack." *To find something to wear*, she added silently. She had nothing suitable for marrying an earl.

"Very well," he said briskly, "the day after tomorrow."

"Too soon." Ellie planted her hands on her hips in an attempt to look firm.

He crossed his arms. "Three days hence, and that is my final offer."

"I believe we have a bargain, my lord," Ellie said with a smile. She had spent the last five years clandestinely wheeling and dealing on the 'change. Words like *final offer* were comfortable and familiar. Much more so than *marriage*.

"Very well, but if I must wait three days I shall demand something in return."

She narrowed her eyes. "It isn't very gentlemanly to agree to a bargain and then attach further terms."

"I believe that is exactly what you did as pertains to the consummation of our marriage."

Her face colored. "Very well. What precisely is this boon you demand?"

"It is most benign, I assure you. Merely an afternoon in your company. After all, we are courting, aren't we?"

"I suppose one could call it—"

"Tomorrow," he interrupted. "I shall pick you up promptly at one o'clock."

Ellie nodded, not trusting herself to speak.

A few minutes later a carriage was brought around, and Charles watched as a footman helped her up. He leaned on his cane, absently flexing his ankle. The bloody injury had better heal quickly; it looked as if he might have to chase his wife around the house.

He stood on the front steps for several minutes after the carriage disappeared from view, watching as the sun hung on the horizon and painted the sky.

Her hair, he suddenly thought. Eleanor's hair was the exact color of the sun at his favorite time of day.

His heart filled with unexpected joy, and he smiled.

Chapter 4

By the time Ellie arrived home that evening, she was a bundle of nerves. It was one thing to agree to this crazy scheme of marriage to Billington. It was quite another to calmly face her stern and domineering father and inform him of her plans.

As her luck would have it, Mrs. Foxglove had returned, presumably to tell the reverend what an evil, ungrateful daughter he had. Ellie waited patiently throughout Mrs. F.'s tirade until she boomed, "Your daughter"—here she stabbed a stubby finger in Ellie's direction—"will have to mend her ways. I don't know how I will be able to live in peace with her in *my* house, but—"

"You won't have to," Ellie interrupted.

Mrs. Foxglove's head swung around, her eyes blinking furiously. "I beg your pardon."

"You won't have to live with me," Ellie repeated. "I'm leaving the day after tomorrow."

"And where do you think you're going?" Mr. Lyndon demanded.

"I'm getting married."

That was certainly a conversation stopper.

Ellie filled the silence with: "In three days. I am getting married in three days."

Mrs. Foxglove recovered her normally extensive powers of speech and said, "Don't be ridiculous. I happen to know you have no suitors."

Ellie allowed herself a small smile. "I fear you are incorrect."

Mr. Lyndon cut in with, "Would you care to tell us the name of this suitor?"

"I'm surprised you didn't notice his carriage when I arrived home this evening. He is the Earl of Billington."

"Billington?" the reverend repeated in disbelief.

"Billington?" Mrs. Foxglove screeched, clearly unable to decide whether she should be delighted by her imminent connection to the aristocracy, or furious with Ellie for having the audacity to perform such a coup on her own.

"Billington," Ellie said firmly. "I believe we will suit very nicely. Now, if you will both excuse me, I have to pack."

She made it halfway to her room before she heard her father call out her name. When she turned around, she saw him brush off Mrs. Foxglove's grasping hand and make his way to her side.

"Eleanor," he said. His face was pale, and the creases around his eyes were deeper than usual.

"Yes, Papa?"

"I—I know I made a terrible muck of things with your sister. I would—" He stopped and cleared his throat. "I would be honored if you would allow me to perform the ceremony on Thursday."

Ellie found herself blinking back tears. Her father

was proud, and such an admission and request could only be wrenched from deep within his heart. "I don't know what the earl has planned, but I would be honored if you would perform the ceremony." She placed her hand on her father's. "It would mean a great deal to me."

The reverend nodded, and Ellie noticed that there were tears in his eyes. On impulse, she stood on her tiptoes and gave him a small peck on the cheek. It had been a long time since she had done that. Too long, she realized, and vowed that she would somehow make her marriage work. When she had a family of her own, her children would not be afraid to tell their parents what they felt. She just hoped that Billington thought the same way.

Charles soon realized that he had forgotten to ask Ellie for her address, but it wasn't difficult to find the residence of Bellfield's vicar. He knocked on the door promptly at one o'clock and was surprised when the door was opened not by Ellie, not by her father, but by a plump, dark-haired woman who immediately squealed, "You must be the *earrrrrrrrrrrl.*"

"I suppose I must."

"I cannot tell you how *hon*ored and de*light*ed we are to have you join our humble little *fam*ily."

Charles looked about, wondering if he was at the wrong cottage. This creature couldn't possibly be related to Ellie. The woman reached for his arm, but he was saved by a sound coming from across the room that could only be described as a barely suppressed groan.

Ellie. Thank God.

"Mrs. Foxglove," she said, her voice laced with irritation. She quickly made her way across the room.

Ah, Mrs. Foxglove. This must be the reverend's dreaded fiancée.

"Here comes my darling daughter now," Mrs. Foxglove said, turning toward Ellie with open arms.

Ellie dodged the older lady with an artful sidestep. "Mrs. Foxglove is my future *step*mother," she said pointedly. "She spends a great deal of time here."

Charles bit back a smile, thinking that Ellie was going to grind her teeth to powder if she kept glowering at Mrs. Foxglove that way.

Mrs. Foxglove turned to Charles and said, "Dear Eleanor's mother passed on many years ago. I am delighted to be as a mother to her."

Charles looked at Ellie. She looked ready to spit.

"My curricle is waiting just outside," he said softly. "I thought we might make a picnic in the meadow. Perhaps we should—"

"I have a miniature of my mother," Ellie said, looking at Mrs. Foxglove even though her words were ostensibly directed at Charles. "In case you'd like to see what she looked like."

"That would be lovely," he replied. "And then perhaps we should be on our way."

"You must wait for the reverend," Mrs. Foxglove said as Ellie crossed the room and took a small painting off of a shelf. "He will be most sore if he misses you."

Charles was actually rather surprised that Mr. Lyndon had not been present. Lord knew if *he* had a daughter planning to marry at the drop of a hat, he'd want to have a look at the potential groom.

Charles allowed himself a small, private smile at the thought of having a daughter. Parenthood seemed such a foreign thing.

"My father will be here when we return," Ellie said. She turned to Charles and added, "He is out visiting parishioners. He is often detained."

Mrs. Foxglove looked as if she wanted to say something, but she was stopped by Ellie, who brushed rudely by her, holding out a miniature painting. "This is my mother," she told Charles.

He took the small piece from her hands and regarded the raven-haired woman in the portrait. "She was beautiful," he said, his voice quiet.

"Yes, she was."

"She was quite dark."

"Yes, my sister Victoria resembles her. This"—Ellie touched a piece of red-gold hair that had escaped her neat chignon—"was quite a surprise, I'm sure."

Charles leaned down to kiss her hand. "A most delightful surprise."

"Yes," Mrs. Foxglove said loudly, clearly not enjoying being ignored, "we have never known what to do with Eleanor's hair."

"I know exactly what to do with it," Charles murmured, so softly that only Ellie could hear him. She immediately colored beet red.

Charles grinned and said, "We'd best be off. Mrs. Foxglove, it was a pleasure."

"But you only just—"

"Eleanor, shall we?" He grasped her hand and pulled her through the doorway. As soon as they were out of Mrs. Foxglove's earshot he let out a light laugh and said, "The closest of escapes. I thought she would never let us go."

Ellie turned to him, hands fiercely on her hips. "Why did you say that?"

"What, that comment about your hair? I do so love to tease you. Were you embarrassed?"

"Of course not. I've grown surprisedly used to your rakish statements in the three days I've known you."

"Then what is the problem?"

"You made me blush," she ground out.

"I thought you were used to my rakish statements, as you so delicately put it."

"I am. But that doesn't mean I won't blush."

Charles blinked and looked to her left, as if he were speaking to an imaginary companion. "I say, is she speaking English? I vow I have completely lost hold of this conversation."

"Did you hear what she said about my hair?" Ellie demanded. " 'We have never known what to do,' she said. As if she has had a place in my life for years. As if I would let her have a place."

"Yes . . . ?" Charles prompted.

"I wanted to skewer her with a stare, flay her with a frown, impale her with a—I say, *what* are you doing?"

Charles would have answered her, but he was laughing so hard he was doubled over.

"The blush quite ruined the effect," she muttered. "How was I to give her the cut direct when my cheeks were the color of poppies? Now she'll never know how furious I am with her."

"Oh, I'd say she knows," Charles gasped, still laughing at Ellie's attempt at righteous indignation.

"I'm not certain I approve of your making light of my deplorable situation."

"You're not *certain*? It seems rather clear to me." He reached out and playfully brushed his index finger against the corner of her mouth. "That's a rather telling frown."

Ellie didn't know what to say, and she *hated* not knowing what to say, so she just crossed her arms and made a sound like, "Hmmmph."

He let out a dramatic sigh. "Are you going to be in a disagreeable mood all afternoon? Because if you are, I happen to have brought along the *Times* for our picnic, and I can certainly read it while you stare at the countryside and meditate upon the fifty different ways you'd like to do your future stepmother in."

Ellie's jaw dropped, but she snapped it back into place in time to retort, "I've at least eighty methods in mind, thank you very much, and I shouldn't mind if you read at all, as long as *I* get the financial pages." She allowed herself a small smile.

Charles chuckled as he offered her his arm. "Actually, I was planning to check some of my investments, but I wouldn't be averse to sharing with you."

Ellie thought about how close they would have to sit in order to read the paper together on the picnic blanket. "I bet you wouldn't," she muttered. Then she felt rather stupid, because such a comment implied that he wanted to seduce her, and she was fairly certain that women were more or less interchangeable in Charles's mind. Oh, he was going to marry her, that was true, but Ellie had a sinking suspicion that she had been chosen because she was convenient. After all, he himself had told her that he had barely a fortnight to find a bride.

He seemed to enjoy kissing her, but he'd probably enjoy kissing any woman, save for Mrs. Foxglove. And he had clearly spelled out to her the main reason why he wanted to consummate the marriage. What was that he'd said? A man in his position must beget an heir.

"You look rather serious," Charles commented, causing her to look up at him and blink several times.

She coughed and touched her head in a reflexive manner. "Oh, dear!" she suddenly burst out. "I've forgotten my bonnet."

"Leave it," Charles instructed.

"I cannot go out without one."

"No one will see you. We are only going to the meadow."

"But—"

"But what?"

She let out an irritated exhale. "I shall freckle."

"That doesn't bother me," he said with a shrug.

"It bothers *me*!"

"Don't worry. They'll be on your own face, so you won't have to see them."

Ellie gaped at him, astounded by his illogic.

"The simple fact is," he continued, "that I like to see your hair."

"But it's—"

"Red," he finished for her. "I know. I wish you'd cease persisting in calling it that common color when it's really so much more than that."

"Really, my lord, it's only hair."

"Is it?" he murmured.

Ellie rolled her eyes, deciding that it must be time for a change of subject. Something, perhaps, that obeyed ordinary rules of logic. "How does your ankle fare? I noticed you are no longer using the cane."

"Very well. I've still a bit of pain, and I do find myself limping, but I don't appear to be any worse for having fallen out of a tree."

She pursed her lips waspishly. "You shouldn't climb trees on a stomach full of whiskey."

"Sounding like a wife already," Charles murmured, helping her up into the curricle.

"One must practice, mustn't one?" she returned, determined not to let him get the last word, even if her own last words were less than inspired.

"I suppose." He looked down his nose and pretended to inspect his ankle, then hopped up into the curricle. "No, the fall doesn't seem to have done any permanent damage. Although," he added wickedly, "the rest of me is quite black and blue from my altercation yesterday."

"Altercation?" Ellie's lips parted in concerned surprise. "What happened? Are you quite all right?"

He shrugged and sighed in mock resignation as he snapped the reins and set the horses in motion. "I was tackled to the carpet by a wet, red-haired virago."

"Oh." She swallowed uncomfortably and looked out the side, watching as the village of Bellfield rolled by. "I beg your pardon. I was not myself."

"Really? I'd say you were precisely yourself."

"I beg your pardon."

He smiled. "Have you noticed that you always say, 'I beg your pardon' when you don't know what to say?"

Ellie stopped herself a split second before she said, "I beg your pardon," again.

"You're not usually at a loss for words, are you?" He didn't give her time to reply before he said, "It's rather fun befuddling you."

"You don't befuddle me."

"No?" he murmured, touching his finger to the corner of her mouth. "Then why are your lips quivering as if you have something you desperately wish to say, only you don't know how to say it?"

"I know exactly what I want to say, you fiendish little snake."

"I stand corrected," he said with an amused laugh. "Evidently you are in complete command of your rather extensive vocabulary."

"Why must everything be such a game to you?"

"Why shouldn't it be?" he countered.

"Because ... because ..." Ellie's words trailed off when she realized that she didn't have a ready answer.

"Because why?" he prodded.

"Because marriage is a serious thing," she said in a rush. "Very serious."

His answer was swift, and his voice was low. "Believe me, no one knows that as well as I do. Were you to back out of this marriage, I'd be left with a pile of stones and no capital to keep it up."

"Wycombe Abbey deserves a more gracious moniker than 'pile of stones,' " Ellie said automatically. She'd always held a deep admiration for good architecture, and the abbey was one of the more beautiful buildings in the district.

He cast a sharp look in her direction. "It will be a

literal pile of stones if I do not have the funds to support it."

Ellie had the distinct impression that he was warning her. He would be most unhappy with her if she backed out of the marriage. She had no doubt he could make her life utter hell if he so chose, and she had a feeling that should she leave him at the altar, spite alone would be motivation enough for him to devote his life to ruining hers.

"You needn't worry," she said crisply. "I have never broken my word, and I do not intend to begin doing so now."

"I am much relieved, my lady."

Ellie frowned. He didn't sound relieved. He sounded more self-satisfied than anything else. She was contemplating why this disturbed her so when he spoke again.

"You should know something about me, Eleanor."

She turned to him with widened eyes.

"I may treat much of life as a game, but I can be deadly serious when I so choose."

"I beg your pardon?" Then she bit her lip for saying it.

"I am not a man to cross."

She drew back. "Are you threatening me?"

"My future wife?" he said blandly. "Of course not."

"I think you *are* threatening me. And I think I don't like it."

"Really?" he drawled. "Is that what you think?"

"I think," she shot back, "that I liked you better when you were drunk."

He laughed at that. "I was easier to manage. You don't like it when you are not firmly in control."

"And you do?"

"We are two of a kind in that regard. I believe we shall suit each other admirably as husband and wife."

She eyed him doubtfully. "Either that or we'll kill each other in the process."

"That's a possibility," he said, giving his chin a thoughtful stroke. "I do hope that we are able to keep the stakes even."

"What the devil are you talking about?"

He smiled slowly. "I'm considered a fair shot. How about you?"

Her mouth fell open. She was so stunned that she couldn't even manage to say, "I beg your pardon."

"That was a joke, Eleanor."

She snapped her mouth back closed. "Of course," she said in a terse voice. "I knew that."

"Of course you did."

Ellie felt a pressure building up within her, a frustration that this man could repeatedly render her speechless. "I am not a terribly good shot myself," she replied, a tight smile decorating her face, "but I am prodigiously talented with knives."

Charles made a choking sound and had to cover his mouth.

"And I am very silent on my feet." She leaned forward, her smile turning mischievous as she regained control of her wit. "You might want to keep your door locked at night."

He leaned forward, his eyes glittering. "But my darling, my aim in life is to make sure your door is unlocked at night. Every night."

Ellie began to feel quite warm. "You promised . . ."

"And you promised"—he moved in closer, this

time until his nose touched hers—"to let me try to seduce you whenever I wished."

"Oh, for the love of Saint Peter," she said with such disdain that Charles drew back in confusion. "If that isn't the most addlebrained collection of words I have ever heard in a single sentence."

Charles blinked. "Are you insulting me?"

"Well, I certainly wasn't complimenting you," she scoffed. " 'Let you try to seduce me.' Oh, please. I promised you could try. I never said I'd 'let' you do anything."

"I have never had this much trouble seducing a woman in my life."

"I believe you."

"Especially one I've agreed to marry."

"I was under the impression I was the only one to hold that dubious honor."

"Now, see here, Eleanor," he said, his voice growing impatient. "You need this marriage just as much as I do. And don't try to tell me you don't. I've met Mrs. Foxglove now. I know what you have waiting for you at home."

Ellie sighed. He knew just how tight a bind she was in. Mrs. Foxglove and her endless carping had seen to that.

"And," he added irritably, "what the hell did you mean 'you believe' that I've never had so much trouble seducing a woman?"

She stared at him as if he were simpleminded. "Exactly that. I believe you. You must know you're a very handsome man."

He appeared not to know how to reply. Ellie was rather pleased to have set *him* at a loss for words for a change. She continued with, "And you're quite charming."

He brightened. "Do you think so?"

"*Too* charming," she added, narrowing her eyes, "which makes it difficult to discern the difference between your compliments and your flattery."

"Just assume they're all compliments," he said with a wave of his hand, "and we'll both be happier."

"*You* will," she retorted.

"You will, too. Trust me."

"Trust you? Ha! That may have worked with your simpleminded London misses who care for naught but the color of their ribbons, but I am made of sterner—and smarter—stuff."

"I know," he replied. "That's why I'm marrying you."

"Are you saying that I have proven my superior intelligence by my ability to withstand your charms?" Ellie began to chuckle. "How marvelous. The only woman smart enough to be your countess is the one who can see through your superficial rakish veneer."

"Something like that," Charles mumbled, not at all liking the way she had twisted his words but unable to figure out how to twist them back to his advantage.

By now Ellie was laughing in earnest, and he was not amused. "Stop that," he commanded. "Stop it right now."

"Oh, I couldn't," she said, gasping for breath. "I couldn't possibly."

"Eleanor, I will tell you one last time . . ."

She turned to reply, her eyes passing over the road on the way to his face. "But—Good God! Watch the road!"

"I *am* watching the—"

Whatever else he'd meant to say was lost as the curricle hit a particularly large rut, bounced to the side, and tossed both its passengers to the ground.

Chapter 5

❧

Charles grunted as he hit the ground, feeling the jolt in every bone, every muscle, every damned *hair* on his body.

Half a second later Ellie landed on top of him, feeling for all the world like an immense sack of potatoes with very good aim.

Charles closed his eyes, wondering if he would ever be able to sire children, wondering if he'd ever again even want to *try*.

"Ow!" she let out, rubbing her shoulder.

He would have liked to respond, preferably with something sarcastic, but he couldn't speak. His ribs hurt so much that he was certain every last one of them would shatter if he so much as tried to use his voice. After what seemed like an eternity, she rolled off of him, her pointy little elbow finding the tender spot below his left kidney.

"I cannot believe you didn't see that rut," Ellie said, managing to look supercilious even as she sat in the dirt.

Charles thought about strangling her. He thought about getting her fitted for a muzzle. He even thought about kissing her just to wipe that annoying expression off of her face, but in the end he just laid there, trying to find his breath.

"Even I could have driven the curricle with greater skill," she continued, rising to her feet and brushing off her skirts. "I hope you haven't damaged the wheel. They're terribly expensive to replace, and Bellfield's wheelwright is drunk more often than not. You could travel to Faversham, of course, but I wouldn't recommend—"

Charles let out an agonized groan, although he wasn't quite sure what was paining him most: his ribs, his head, or her lecture.

Ellie crouched back down, concern growing on her face. "I say, you're not hurt, are you?"

Charles managed to stretch his lips out far enough to show his teeth, but only the most optimistic sort could have called it a smile. "Never felt better," he croaked.

"You *are* hurt," Ellie exclaimed, her tone rather accusatory.

"Not too much," he managed to get out. "Just my ribs, and my back, and my—" He broke off into a fit of coughing.

"Oh, dear," she said. "I'm terribly sorry. Did I knock the breath out of you when I fell?"

"You knocked it clear to Sussex."

Ellie frowned as she touched her hand to his brow. "You don't sound well. Do you feel hot?"

"Christ, Eleanor, I don't have a bloody fever."

She brought her hand back to her side and muttered, "At least you haven't lost your wide and varied vocabulary."

"Why is it," he said, his breath coming out in a long-suffering sigh, "that whenever you are near, I emerge injured?"

"Now see here!" Ellie exclaimed. "This was not my fault. I wasn't driving. And I certainly didn't have anything to do with your falling out of a *tree*."

Charles didn't bother to reply. His only sound was a groan as he tried to sit up.

"At least let me tend to your injuries," Ellie said.

He shot her a sideways look that reeked of sarcasm.

"Fine!" she burst out, standing up and throwing her arms in the air. "Tend to yourself, then. I hope you have a splendid time walking home. What is it—ten, fifteen miles?"

He touched his head, which was beginning to throb.

"It should be a lovely stroll," she continued, "especially on that ankle."

Charles jammed his fingers more tightly against his temple, hoping the pressure would somehow dull the pain. "I'd wager you have a vengeful streak a mile wide," he muttered.

"I am the least vengeful person I know," she said with a sniff. "And if you think otherwise, then perhaps you ought not to marry me."

"You're marrying me," he ground out, "if I have to drag you to the altar bound and gagged."

Ellie smiled waspishly. "You could try," she taunted, "but in your condition you couldn't drag a flea."

"And you say you're not vengeful."

"I seem to be developing a taste for it."

Charles grabbed at the back of his skull, which felt

as if someone were stabbing long, rusty needles into it. He winced and said, "Just don't say anything. Not a word. Not a"—he gasped as he felt another rush of pain—"single damned word."

Ellie, who had no idea that he even had a headache, interpreted that to mean he thought she was inconsequential, stupid, and a general nuisance. Her spine stiffened, her teeth clenched, and her hands curved into involuntary little claws. "I have done nothing to deserve this kind of treatment," she said in a haughty voice. And then, with a loud, "Hmmmph," she turned on her heel and marched toward home.

Charles lifted his head long enough to see her stride off, sighed, and promptly passed out.

"Why that little snake," Ellie muttered to herself. "If he thinks I'm going to marry him now ... He's worse than Mrs. Foxglove!" She scrunched up her brow, decided that it wouldn't do to start lying to herself at the ripe old age of three and twenty, and then added, "Well, almost."

She tramped along the lane a few more steps, then leaned down when something shiny caught her eye. It looked like a metal bolt of some sort. She picked it up, rolled it around in her hand for a moment, then slipped it into her pocket. There was a little boy in her father's parish who loved trinkets like this. Perhaps she could give it to him next time she went to church.

Ellie sighed. She'd have plenty of time to give the bolt to Tommy Beechcombe. It certainly didn't look as if she'd be moving out of her father's house any time soon. She might as well start practicing her chimney sweeping techniques that afternoon.

The Earl of Billington had brought a brief measure of excitement into her life, but it was now clear they wouldn't suit. She did, however, feel a touch guilty about leaving him lying by the side of the road. Not that he didn't deserve it, of course, but Ellie always tried to be charitable, and . . .

She shook her head and rolled her eyes. One look back wouldn't kill her. Just to see if he was all right.

She twisted around but realized that she'd gone over a little hill and couldn't see him any longer. She let out a deep breath and trudged back toward the scene of the accident. "This doesn't mean you care about him," she told herself. "It just means that you are a fine and upstanding woman, one who doesn't abandon people, however rude and vile"—she allowed herself a tiny smile here—"when they are incapable of looking after—Good God!"

Charles was lying where she'd left him, and he looked quite dead.

"Charles!" she screamed, picking up her skirts and sprinting toward him. She stumbled over a rock and landed next to him, her knee jabbing into his side.

He groaned. Ellie let out her breath, which she hadn't realized she'd been holding. She hadn't *really* thought he was dead, but he'd been so terribly still. "Where are smelling salts when one actually needs them?" she muttered. Mrs. Foxglove was always waving around vile-smelling potions at the least provocation.

"No, I don't have a vinaigrette," she said to the unconscious earl. "No one has ever fainted in my vicinity before." She looked around for something to use to revive him when her eyes fell on a small flask that must have fallen from the upturned curricle. She picked it up, unscrewed the cap, and sniffed the contents.

"Oh, my," she said, holding it back and waving the air in front of her face. Pungent whiskey fumes filled the air. Ellie wondered if the alcohol was left over from the day Charles had fallen out of the tree. He certainly hadn't been drinking today—of that, Ellie was certain. She would have smelled it on him—and besides, she didn't think he was the sort to abuse spirits on a regular basis.

She looked down at this man she was actually considering marrying. Even unconscious, there was a certain air of resolute power about him. No, he wouldn't need alcohol to bolster his self-esteem.

"Well," she said out loud, "I suppose we can at least use it to wake you up." She held the flask in front of her and placed it under his nose.

No response.

Ellie frowned and placed her hand over his heart. "My lord, you haven't gone and died since the last time you groaned, have you?"

Not surprisingly, he didn't reply, but Ellie did feel his heart beating steadily beneath her palm, which reassured her greatly. "Charles," she said, trying to sound stern, "I would really appreciate it if you would wake up immediately."

When he again didn't so much as twitch, she placed her fore and middle fingers against the opening of the flask and tipped it over, dousing her skin with the cool whiskey. It evaporated quickly against her flesh, so she repeated the motion, this time keeping the flask overturned a bit longer. When she was satisfied that her fingers were sufficiently wet, she dabbed them under his nose.

"Whaa . . . Aya . . . Heebelah!"

Charles didn't make much sense as he came to. He shot up like a bullet, blinking and startled, looking very much like a man waking up too quickly from a nightmare.

Ellie lurched back to avoid his flailing arms, but she wasn't quick enough, and he knocked the flask from her hands. It sailed through the air, spewing whiskey all the while. She jumped backward, and this time she *was* quick enough. All of the whiskey landed on Charles, who was still spluttering incoherently.

"What the hell did you do to me?" he demanded once he regained his power of speech.

"What did *I* do to *you*?"

He coughed and wrinkled his nose. "I smell like a drunk."

"You smell very much like you did two days ago."

"Two days ago I was—"

"A drunk," Ellie retorted.

His eyes darkened. "I was drunk, not *a* drunk. There is a difference. And you—" He jabbed his finger in her direction, then winced at the sudden movement and grabbed his head.

"Charles?" Ellie asked cautiously, forgetting that she was rather angry with him for somehow placing the blame for this entire farce on her shoulders. All she could see was that he was in pain. A lot of pain, if his facial expression was any indication.

"Lord almighty," he cursed. "Did someone hit me on the head with a log?"

"I was tempted to," Ellie tried to joke, hoping that levity might take his mind off the pain.

"That I do not doubt. You would have made a superb army commander had you been born a man."

"There are a lot of things I could have done had I been born a man," Ellie muttered, "and marrying you is not one of them."

"Lucky me," Charles replied, still wincing. "Lucky you."

"That remains to be seen."

There was an awkward silence, and then Ellie, feeling that she ought to explain to him what had happened while he was unconscious, said, "About the whiskey . . . I suppose I must apologize, but I was just trying to—"

"Flambé me?"

"No, although the suggestion does have merit. I was trying to revive you. An alcoholic vinaigrette, if you will. You knocked the flask over when you sat up."

"How is it that I feel as if I have been strung out on the rack, and you look completely unhurt?"

Ellie's mouth curved into a wry half-smile. "One would think that a chivalrous gentleman such as yourself would be pleased that his lady was uninjured."

"I am ever chivalrous, my lady. I am also damned confused."

"Evidently you're not chivalrous enough to abstain from cursing in my presence. However"—she waved her hand nonchalantly in the air—"it is lucky for you that I have never been overly fussy about such matters."

He closed his eyes, wondering why it took her so many words to get to the point.

"I fell on you when I was thrown from the curricle," she finally explained. "You must have sustained some injuries to your back when you fell, but any pain you are feeling in your ... ah ... front is probably due to ... ah ... me." She blinked a few times, and then fell silent, her cheeks staining a rather fetching pink.

"I see."

Ellie swallowed uncomfortably. "Would you like a hand up?"

"Yes, thank you." He took her hand and hauled himself to a standing position, trying to ignore the myriad aches and pains that flared with every movement. When he reached his feet, he planted his hands on his hips and stretched his neck to the left. The joint made several cracking sounds, and Charles fought the urge to smile when Ellie winced.

"That doesn't sound very promising," she offered.

He didn't reply, just stretched his neck in the opposite direction, finding some sort of perverse satisfaction in the second round of cracking noises. After a moment, his eyes fell upon the overturned curricle, and he swore under his breath. The wheel had come off and was now crushed beneath the body of the vehicle.

Ellie followed his line of vision and said, "Yes, I tried to tell you that the wheel was quite ruined, but I now realize that you were in far too much pain to listen."

As Charles kneeled down to inspect the damage,

she surprised him by adding, "I'm terribly sorry for walking away a few minutes ago. I didn't realize how hurt you were. If I had, I should never have left. I—I shouldn't have left regardless. It was very bad of me."

Charles was touched by her heartfelt speech, and impressed with her sense of honor. "Your apology is unnecessary," he said gruffly, "but appreciated and accepted nonetheless."

Ellie inclined her head. "We did not travel very far from my home. It shouldn't be difficult to walk back and lead the horses. I am certain my father will be able to arrange transportation home for you. Or we can find a messenger to fetch a fresh carriage from Wycombe Abbey."

"That will be fine," he murmured, giving the damaged curricle a closer look.

"Is something amiss, my lord? Other than the fact that we drove through a rut and overturned?"

"Look at this, Eleanor." He reached out and touched the damaged wheel. "It's no longer attached to the carriage."

"I imagine that is from the accident."

Charles tapped his fingers against the side of the curricle as he thought. "No, it should still be attached. Broken, from when we overturned, but attached right here at the centerpoint."

"Do you think that wheel came off of its own volition?"

"Yes," he said thoughtfully. "Yes, I do."

"But I know we hit that deep rut. I saw it. I felt it."

"The rut was most likely the catalyst for the removal of an already loose wheel."

Ellie leaned down and inspected the damage. "I think you're right, my lord. Look at the manner in which it is damaged. The spokes have been crushed by the weight of the curricle, but the body of the wheel is in one piece. I have studied very little physics, but I should think it would have snapped in two when we overturned. And—Oh! Look!" She reached into her pocket and pulled out the metal bolt.

"Where did you find this?"

"On the road. Just over the hill. It must have come loose and fallen off the wheel."

Charles turned to face her, his sudden movement bringing them nose to nose. "I think," he said softly, "you are correct."

Ellie's lips parted in surprise. He was so close that his breath touched her face, so close that she could *feel* his words as well as hear them.

"I might have to kiss you again."

She tried to make a sound that would convey—well, she didn't know what exactly she wanted to convey, but it made no difference anyway, as her vocal cords refused to make a single noise. She just sat there, utterly still, as he slowly tilted his head to the side and rested his lips upon hers.

"Very nice," he murmured, his words entering her mouth.

"My lord . . ."

"Charles," he corrected.

"We really . . . that is to say . . ." She completely lost track of her thoughts at that point. Having the inside of her lower lip caressed by a man's tongue did that to her.

Charles chuckled and lifted his head a mere inch. "You were saying?"

Ellie did nothing but blink.

"Then I may assume you merely wanted to ask me to continue." His smile turned wolfish before he tipped up her chin and traced the line of her jaw with his lips.

"No!" Ellie burst out, suddenly jolted by a mortified sense of urgency. "That isn't what I meant at all."

"It isn't?" he teased.

"I meant to say that we are in the middle of a public road, and—"

"And you fear for your reputation," he finished for her.

"And yours as well, so you needn't make me out to be a prude."

"Oh, I have no intention of doing that, sweetheart."

Ellie lurched backward at his suggestive remark, promptly lost her balance, and ended up sprawled in the dirt. She bit her lip to keep herself from saying something she might regret. "Why don't we head home now?" she said evenly.

"An excellent idea," Charles replied, rising to his feet and offering her his hand. She took it and allowed him to help her up, even though she suspected that the effort hurt him. A man had his pride, after all, and Ellie rather suspected that the Wycombes had more than their fair share.

The walk back to the vicar's cottage took about ten minutes. Ellie kept the conversation strictly on neutral topics, such as literature, French cuisine, and—even though she winced at the banality of it when she brought it up—the weather. Charles looked rather amused throughout the conversation, as if he knew exactly what she was doing. Worse, his ironic smile was just a touch benevolent, as if he were somehow *permitting* her to talk about thunderstorms and the like.

Ellie wasn't much enamored with the smug look on his face, but she had to be impressed that he could maintain the expression while he was limping, rubbing his head, and occasionally clutching his ribs.

When the cottage came into view, Ellie turned to Charles and said, "My father has returned."

He raised his brows. "How can you tell?"

"He's lit a candle in his office. He will be working on his sermon."

"Already? Sunday is days away. I remember my vicar frantically scribbling away every Saturday eve. He would frequently come up to Wycombe Abbey for inspiration."

"Really?" Ellie asked with an amused smile. "He found you that inspiring? I had no idea you were such an angelic child."

"Quite the opposite, I'm afraid. He liked to study me and then choose which of my sins would serve as his next sermon's theme."

"Oh, dear," Ellie replied, smothering a laugh. "How did you bear him?"

"It was worse than you think. He doubled as my Latin tutor and gave me lessons three times per week. He claimed I had been put on this earth to torture him."

"That seems rather irreverent for a vicar."

Charles shrugged. "He was also overfond of drink."

Ellie reached to pull open the front door, but before her hand connected with the knob, Charles laid a restraining hand on her arm. When she looked up at him in question, he said in a quiet voice, "A word with you before I meet your father?"

"Of course," she replied, moving away from the door.

His mouth was tight when he said, "You are still committed to marrying me the day after tomorrow, are you not?"

Ellie suddenly felt dizzy. Charles, who had been so adamant about holding her to her promise, seemed to be offering her an escape clause. She could cry off, say she had cold feet . . .

"Eleanor," he prodded.

She swallowed, thinking of how tedious her life had become. The prospect of marrying a stranger terrified her, but not nearly as much as a lifetime of boredom. No, it would be worse than that. A lifetime of boredom punctuated by bouts with Mrs. Foxglove. Whatever the earl's faults—and Ellie had a feeling they might be many—she knew in her heart that he was not an evil or weak man. Surely she could find happiness with him.

Charles touched her shoulder, and she nodded. Ellie thought she saw his shoulders sag slightly with relief, but within moments the mask of the dashing young earl was back in place on his face. "Are you ready to go in?" she asked.

He nodded, and Ellie pushed open the door and called out, "Papa?" After a moment of silence she said, "I'll just go to his study and fetch him."

Charles waited and in a moment Ellie reentered the room, followed by a rather stern-looking man with thinning gray hair.

"Mrs. Foxglove had to return home," Ellie said, flashing Charles a secret smile. "But may I present my father, the Reverend Mr. Lyndon. Papa, this is Charles Wycombe, Earl of Billington."

The two men shook hands, silently assessing one another. Charles thought the reverend seemed too rigid and forbidding to have fathered such a bright flame as Eleanor. He could tell by the way Mr. Lyndon looked at him that he fell short of the son-in-law ideal, as well.

They exchanged introductory pleasantries, sat down, and then once Ellie had left the room to prepare some tea, the reverend turned to Charles and said, "Most men would approve of a future son-in-law solely because he is an earl. I am not such a man."

"I didn't think so, Mr. Lyndon. Clearly Eleanor has been raised by a man of stern moral character." Charles had intended the words merely to placate the reverend, but as he spoke, he realized he meant them. Eleanor Lyndon had never even once shown symptoms of being dazzled by his title or his wealth. In fact, she seemed far more interested in her three hundred pounds than his vast fortune.

The reverend leaned forward, his eyes narrowing as if he were trying to discern the sincerity behind the earl's words. "I won't try to prevent the marriage," he said quietly. "I did that once, with my older daughter, and the consequences were disastrous. But I will tell you this: If you mistreat Eleanor in any way,

I shall descend upon you with all of the hellfire and torment I can muster."

Charles couldn't stop one corner of his lips from turning upward in a respectful smile. He imagined that the reverend could muster quite a bit of hellfire and torment. "You have my word that Eleanor will be treated like a queen."

"There is one more thing."

"Yes?"

The reverend cleared his throat. "Are you overfond of spirits?"

Charles blinked, a bit startled by the question. "I certainly have a glass when appropriate, but I do not spend my days and nights in drunken stupors, if that is what you are asking."

"Then perhaps you might explain why you reek of whiskey?"

Charles fought back an absurd urge to laugh, and explained to the reverend what had happened that afternoon and how Ellie had accidentally poured whiskey on him.

Mr. Lyndon leaned back, satisfied. He didn't smile, but then, Charles doubted he smiled often. "Good," the reverend said. "Now that we understand each other, allow me to be the first to welcome you to the family."

"I am glad to be a part of it."

The reverend nodded. "I would like to perform the ceremony, if that is acceptable to you."

"Of course."

Ellie chose that moment to return to the room, carrying a tray with a tea service.

"Eleanor," her father said, "I have decided that the earl will suit you nicely."

Ellie let out a breath she didn't know she'd been holding. She had the approval of her father, something that meant more to her than she'd realized until that very moment. Now all she had to do was actually get married.

Married. She gulped. Lord help her.

Chapter 6

⌒⌒⌒⌒⌒⌒⌒

The next day, a package addressed to Ellie arrived by special messenger. Curious, she untied the string, pausing when an envelope fluttered out. She reached down to the floor, picked up the envelope, and opened it.

My dear Eleanor,

Please accept this gift as a token of my esteem and affection. You looked so lovely in green the other day. I thought you might like to be married in it.

Yrs.
Billington

P.S. Please do not cover your hair.

Ellie could barely suppress a gasp when she felt her fingers touch luxurious velvet. She pulled aside the rest of the wrappings to reveal the most beautiful dress she'd ever seen—much less had the opportunity to wear. Fashioned of the deepest emerald velvet, it was simply cut, without flounces or ruffles. Ellie knew it would suit her perfectly.

With any luck, the man who'd given it to her would suit her as well.

The morning of her wedding dawned bright and clear. A carriage arrived to carry Ellie, her father, and Mrs. Foxglove to Wycombe Abbey, and Ellie truly felt like a fairy princess. The dress, the carriage, the impossibly handsome man waiting for her at the end of her journey—they all seemed like props in some glorious magical tale.

The ceremony was to take place in the formal drawing room of Wycombe Abbey. The Reverend Mr. Lyndon took his place at the front, then, much to everyone's amusement, let out a little yelp of dismay and rushed out of the room. "I have to give away the bride," he explained when he reached the door.

Further laughs ensued when he said, out of rote, "Who gives away this woman?" and then added, "Actually, I do."

But those moments of lightness did not ease Ellie's tension, and she felt her entire body clench up when her father prompted her to say, "I will."

Barely able to breathe, she looked over at the man who would be her husband. What was she doing? She hardly knew him.

She looked at her father, who was gazing at her with uncharacteristic nostalgia.

She looked over at Mrs. Foxglove, who had seemingly forgotten her plans to use Ellie as a human chimney brush and had spent the entire carriage ride over going on and on about how she'd always known that "dear Eleanor would make a splendid catch" and "my dear dear stepson-in-law, the *earl*."

"I will," Ellie blurted out. "Oh, I will."

Beside her, she could feel Charles shaking with laughter.

And then he slipped a heavy gold band onto the fourth finger of her left hand, and Ellie realized that in the eyes of God and England, she now belonged to the Earl of Billington. Forever.

For a woman who had always prided herself on her pluck, her knees felt suspiciously watery.

Mr. Lyndon completed the ceremony, and Charles leaned down and placed a fleeting kiss upon Ellie's lips. To an observer it was nothing more than a gentle peck, but Ellie felt his tongue flick along the corner of her mouth. Flustered by this hidden caress, she'd barely had time to regain her composure when Charles took her arm and led her over to a small group of individuals she assumed were his relatives.

"I did not have time to invite my entire family," he said, "but I wanted you to meet my cousins. May I introduce Mrs. George Pallister, Miss Pallister, and Miss Judith Pallister." He turned to the lady and two girls and smiled. "Helen, Claire, Judith, may I present my wife, Eleanor, Countess of Billington."

"How do you do," Ellie said, not sure if she was supposed to curtsy, or if perhaps they were supposed to curtsy, or if none of them needed to at all. So she just smiled in her most friendly manner. Helen, an attractive blond matron of about forty years, smiled back.

"Helen and her daughters live here at Wycombe Abbey," Charles said. "Since the death of Mr. Pallister."

"They do?" Ellie said with surprise. She looked at her new cousins. "You do?"

"Yes," Charles replied, "as does my maiden aunt Cordelia. I don't know where she's gone off to."

"She's a bit eccentric," Helen said helpfully. Claire, who looked to be thirteen or fourteen years old, said nothing, a sullen expression firmly fixed on her face.

"I'm sure we will get on very well," Ellie said. "I have always wanted to live in a large household. Mine has been quite lonely since my sister left."

"Eleanor's sister recently married the Earl of Macclesfield," Charles explained.

"Yes, but she left home many years before that," Ellie said wistfully. "It has been just my father and me for eight years."

"I have a sister, too!" Judith chirped. "Claire!"

Ellie smiled down at the young girl. "So you do. And how old are you, Judith?"

"I am six," she said proudly, flicking back her light brown hair. "And tomorrow I will be twelve."

Helen laughed. " 'Tomorrow' tends to mean any day in the future," she said, leaning down to kiss her daughter on the cheek. "First you must turn seven."

"And then twelve!"

Ellie crouched down. "Not quite, poppet. Then eight, then nine, then—"

"Ten, then eleven," Judith interrupted proudly, "and *then* twelve!"

"Correct," Ellie said.

"I can count to sixty-two."

"Is that so?" Ellie asked, using her best "impressed" voice.

"Mmm-hmm. One. Two. Three. Four—"

"Mother!" Claire said with a beleaguered sigh.

Helen took Judith by the hand. "Come along, little one. We will practice our counting another time."

Judith rolled her eyes at her mother before turning to Charles and saying, "Mama said it's high time you got married."

"Judith!" Helen exclaimed, turning quite pink.

"Well, you did. You said he contorts with too many women, and—"

"Judith!" Helen fairly shouted, grabbing her by the hand. "This is not the time."

"It's all right," Ellie said quickly. "She meant no harm."

Helen looked as if she wanted to sink into the floor and disappear. She tugged on Judith's arm, saying, "I believe our newlyweds would like a moment alone. I shall show everyone to the dining room for the wedding breakfast."

As Helen hurried the guests from the room, Ellie and Charles heard Judith chirp, "Claire, what is a loose woman?"

"Judith, you are a pest," was Claire's reply.

"Does she fall apart? Are her arms and legs not screwed in tight enough?"

Ellie wasn't certain whether she should laugh or cry.

"I'm sorry about that," Charles said quietly once the room was empty.

"It was nothing."

"A bride shouldn't be subjected to stories of her new husband's peccadilloes on her wedding day."

Ellie shrugged. "It's not so dreadful coming from

the mouth of a six-year-old. Although I imagine she meant that you *consort* with women."

"I can assure you I *contort* with no one."

Ellie actually chuckled.

Charles looked down at the woman who was now his wife and felt an inexplicable sense of pride blossoming within him. The events of the morning could not have been anything but overwhelming for her, and yet she held herself with grace and dignity. He had chosen well. "I'm glad you didn't cover your hair," he murmured.

He chuckled as one of her hands flew to her head. "I can't imagine why you asked me not to," she said nervously.

He reached out and touched a lock of hair that had escaped her coiffure and curled along the base of her throat. "Can't you?"

She didn't answer and he applied pressure to her shoulder until she began to sway toward him, her eyes beginning to glaze over with desire. Charles felt a burst of triumph as he realized that seducing his wife wasn't going to be nearly as difficult as he'd anticipated.

His body quickened, and he leaned down to kiss her, to run his hands through that glorious red-gold hair of hers, and then . . .

She pulled away.

Just like that.

Charles swore under his breath.

"This isn't such a good idea, my lord," she said, looking damnably sure of what she was saying.

"Call me Charles," he bit out.

"Not when you look like that."

"Like what?"

"Like—oh, I don't know. Rather imperious." She blinked. "Actually, you look as if you're in pain."

"I *am* in pain," he snapped.

She took a step back. "Oh. I'm terribly sorry. Do you still ache from the curricle accident? Or is it your ankle? I noticed you still have a tiny limp."

He stared at her, wondering if she could possibly be that innocent. "It's not my ankle, Eleanor."

"You should probably call me Ellie," she said, "if I'm to call you Charles."

"You haven't done so yet."

"I suppose not." Ellie cleared her throat, thinking that this conversation must be proof that she did not know this man nearly well enough to be his wife. "Charles."

He smiled. "Ellie. I like that. It suits you."

"Only my father calls me Eleanor." Her brow furrowed in thought. "Oh, and Mrs. Foxglove, too, I suppose."

"Then I shall *never* call you Eleanor," he vowed, a smile tugging at his lips.

"You probably will," she said, "when you're angry with me."

"Why do you say that?"

"Everyone does when they're angry with me."

"Why are you so certain I will become angry with you?"

She scoffed at that. "Really, my lord, we are to be married for a lifetime. I cannot imagine I will make it that long without incurring your ire at least once."

"I suppose I should be glad I married a realist."

"We are the best sorts in the long run," she replied with a loopy smile. "You'll see."

"I have no doubt."

There was a moment of silence, and then Ellie said, "We should go in to breakfast."

"I suppose we should," he murmured, reaching out to stroke the underside of her chin.

Ellie lurched backwards. "Don't try that."

"Don't try what?" He sounded rather amused.

"To kiss me."

"Why not? That was part of our bargain, wasn't it?"

"Yes," Ellie hedged. "But you know very well I can't think straight when you do that." She supposed she probably ought to have kept that fact to herself, but what was the point if he was just as aware of it as she?

Charles's lips spread into a full-fledged grin. "That's the idea, my dear."

"Perhaps for you," she retorted. "But I wanted the chance to get to know you better before we entered that . . . er . . . phase of our relationship."

"Very well, what do you want to know?"

Ellie was silent for a moment, having no idea how to answer that. Finally she said, "Anything, I suppose."

"Anything?"

"Anything that you think might help me to know the Earl of Billington—excuse me, Charles—better."

He thought for a moment, then smiled and said, "I am a compulsive list-maker. How does that rate for an interesting tidbit?"

Ellie wasn't certain what she'd been expecting him to reveal about himself, but that certainly wasn't it. A compulsive list-maker? That told her more about him than any hobby or pastime ever would. "What sorts of things do you make lists about?" she asked.

"This and that. Everything."

"Did you make a list about me?"

"Of course."

Ellie waited for him to elaborate further, then impatiently asked, "What was on it?"

He chuckled at her curiosity. "It was a list of reasons why I thought you should make a good wife. That sort of thing."

"I see." Ellie wanted to ask how long this list of good reasons was, but thought that might sound a touch too ill-bred.

He leaned forward, the devil lurking in his brown eyes. "There were six items on the list."

Ellie leaned back. "I'm sure I didn't ask you the number."

"But you wanted to."

She kept silent.

"Now then," Charles said, "you must tell me something about Miss Eleanor Lyndon."

"I'm not Miss Eleanor Lyndon any longer," she pointed out pertly.

He laughed at his mistake. "The Countess of Billington. What is she like?"

"She is often a bit too mouthy for her own good," she replied.

"I already *knew* that."

Ellie made a face. "Very well." She thought for a moment. "When the weather is nice, I like to take a book and read outside. I often don't return until the sun sets."

Charles reached out and took her arm. "That is a very good thing for a husband to know," he said softly. "I will know where to look, should I ever lose you."

They walked toward the dining room, and he leaned down and said, "The dress seems to fit you well. Is it to your liking?"

"Oh, yes. It is quite the most lovely gown I have ever worn. It required only the smallest of alterations. How were you ever able to obtain it on such short notice?"

He shrugged nonchalantly. "I paid a dressmaker an obscene amount of money."

Before Ellie could respond, they had rounded a corner and were entering the dining room. The small crowd of guests stood up to cheer the new couple.

The wedding breakfast passed uneventfully, with the exception of the introduction of Charles's greataunt Cordelia, who had been mysteriously absent from the ceremony and much of the breakfast. Ellie couldn't help but glance at the empty seat, wondering if her husband's aunt had an objection to the marriage.

Charles caught her staring, and murmured, "Do not worry. She is merely eccentric and likes to act on her own schedule. I am sure she will make an appearance."

Ellie didn't believe him until an older woman, dressed in a gown at least twenty years out of date, came crashing into the room with the declaration, "The kitchens are on fire!"

Ellie and her family were half out of their seats (indeed, Mrs. Foxglove was halfway out the door) by the time they realized that Charles and his family had not moved a muscle.

"But Charles!" Ellie exclaimed. "Didn't you hear what she said? Surely we must do something."

"She is always claiming that something or another is on fire," he replied. "I believe she enjoys a flair for high drama."

Cordelia made her way to Ellie. "You must be the new bride," she said bluntly.

"Er, yes."

"Good. We needed one of those around here." And then she left, leaving Ellie openmouthed in her wake.

Charles patted his wife on the back. "See? She likes you."

Ellie sank back down into her seat, wondering if every aristocratic family had a crazy maiden aunt stashed away in the proverbial attic. "Are there any other relatives of yours you'd like to introduce me to?" she asked weakly.

"Just my cousin Cecil," Charles replied, clearly trying hard not to laugh. "But he doesn't live here. He's quite a toad, actually."

"A toad in the family," Ellie murmured, the barest hint of a smile brushing along her lips. "How peculiar. I had no idea the Wycombes had an amphibian branch."

Charles chuckled. "Yes, we are all very accomplished swimmers."

This time it was Ellie's turn to laugh. "You shall have to teach me someday. I have never managed to learn."

He took her hand and brought it to his lips. "It should be my honor, my lady. We shall journey out to the pond just as soon as the weather turns warm."

And to all the onlookers, they looked very much like a young couple madly in love.

Several hours later, Charles was sitting in his study, his chair tipped back and his feet balanced against the edge of his desk. He had sensed that Ellie might like a few moments alone to unpack her belongings and adjust to her new surroundings. So he had come here, telling himself that he had a number of business concerns that called for his attention. The responsibilities of administering an earldom were quite time-consuming if one wanted to do a decent job of them. He would complete some work here in his study, take care of all the tasks he had let pile up in the past few days. He'd go about his business while Ellie went about *her* business and—

He let out a loud rush of air, trying very hard to ignore the fact that his entire body was tense with desire for his wife.

He wasn't succeeding.

He certainly hadn't expected to want her quite this badly. He had known he was attracted to her; that was one of the reasons he had decided to ask her to marry him. He had always considered himself a sensible man, and there wasn't much sense in marrying a woman for whom one couldn't muster up a bit of excitement.

But there was something about those little half-smiles of hers—as if she had a secret that she would never divulge—that drove him mad. And her hair—he knew she detested the color, but he wanted nothing other than to run his fingers through the length of it, and—

His feet slipped off the desk and his chair crashed down onto the floor with a loud clunk. How long *was* his wife's hair? It seemed like something a husband ought to know.

He pictured it reaching her knees, swaying about her as she walked. *Not likely*, he decided. Her chignon hadn't been that big.

He pictured it reaching her waist, teasing her navel and flaring gently as it settled upon her hip. He shook his head. Somehow that didn't seem right, either. Ellie—how he liked that nickname!—didn't seem the sort to have the patience for hair that long.

Perhaps brushing along the curve of her breasts. He could see it tucked behind one shoulder, one of her breasts covered by a fall of red-gold hair, and the other laid bare—

He smacked the heel of his hand against his forehead, as if that could knock the mental picture out of his head. Hell, he thought irritably, he didn't want to knock that image just out of his head. He wanted to send it clear across the room and out the window. This particular line of thought was *not* doing anything to ease his discomfort.

He needed to take some action. The sooner he seduced Ellie into his bed, the sooner this madness would leave his blood and the sooner he could get back to the normal routine of his life.

He pulled a piece of paper from his desk and scrawled across the top:

TO SEDUCE ELLIE

He used capital letters without thinking, later deciding that this must be an indication of just how urgent this need to possess her had become.

He tapped the tips of his fore- and middle fingers against his temple as he thought, and then finally began to write.

1. *Flowers.* All women like flowers.
2. *A swimming lesson.* This will require her to remove a great deal of clothing. *Drawback:* weather is quite cold and will remain so for months.
3. *Dresses.* She loved the green dress and has remarked that all her clothes are dark and serviceable. As a countess, she will need to be outfitted in the first stave of fashion, anyway, so this does not constitute an additional expense.
4. *Compliment her business acumen.* Typical, flowery compliments will most likely not work on her.
5. *Kiss her.*

Of all the items on the list, Charles was most enamored with the fifth option, but he did worry that this might merely lead to an intensified state of frustration on his part. He wasn't at all certain that he could manage her seduction with just one kiss; it was probably going to require repeated attempts over the course of several days.

And this would mean several days of rather difficult discomfort on his part. Their last kiss had left him dizzy with desire, and he was still feeling the pain of unfulfilled need several hours later.

Still, the other options weren't viable at this time. It was too late in the evening to go hunting through the hothouse for flowers, and it was definitely too cold for a swim. A full wardrobe would require a trip to London, and as for complimenting her business acumen—well, that would be difficult before he had a chance to assess it, and Ellie was too smart not to see through a false compliment.

No, he thought with a grin. It would have to be a kiss.

Chapter 7

Ellie looked around her new bedchamber, wondering how on earth she could turn this imposing space into her own. Everything in the room screamed of wealth. *Old* wealth. She doubted there was a piece of furniture less than two hundred years old. The countess's bedchamber was ornate and pretentious, and Ellie felt about as at home there as she would have in Windsor Castle.

She reached down into her open trunk, looking for knickknacks that she might use to make the room seem more homey and familiar. Her fingers closed around the miniature of her mother. That would certainly be a beginning. She walked across to her dressing table and set the small painting down, turning it so that the light from the nearby window wouldn't cause the paint to fade.

"There you are," she said softly. "You'll do nicely there. Just don't pay any attention to all of these dour old women staring down at you." Ellie looked up at the walls, which were covered with portraits of earlier countesses, none of whom looked very friendly.

"The lot of you are coming down tomorrow," she

104

muttered, not feeling the least bit foolish for talking to the walls. "Tonight if I can manage it."

Ellie crossed back to her trunk to look for another item that might lend the room a bit of warmth. She was browsing through her belongings when she heard a knock at her door.

Billington. It had to be. Her sister had told her that servants never knocked on doors.

She swallowed and called out, "Come in."

The door opened, revealing her husband of less than twenty-four hours. He was casually attired, having long since discarded his jacket and cravat. Ellie found herself quite unable to take her eyes off of the little patch of skin that peeped through the unbuttoned top of his crisp white shirt.

"Good evening," he said.

Ellie forced her eyes up to his face. "Good evening to you." There, that sounded as if it had come from someone completely unaffected by his nearness. Unfortunately, she had a feeling he could see right through her cheerful voice and bright smile.

"Are you settling in?" he asked.

"Yes, very well." She sighed. "Well, not so well, actually."

He raised a brow.

"This room is quite daunting," she explained.

"Mine is just through the connecting door. You're welcome to make yourself at home there."

Her mouth fell open. "Connecting door?"

"You didn't know there was one?"

"No, I thought—Well, I didn't really think about where all these doors went to."

Charles strode across the room and began opening

doors. "Washroom. Dressing room. A storage room for clothing." He made his way to the only door on the east side of the room and pulled it open. "And voilà, the earl's bedroom."

Ellie suppressed the urge to let out a nervous laugh. "I suppose most earls and countesses prefer connecting rooms."

"Actually," he said, "Many don't. My ancestors were a tempestuous lot. Most of the Earls and Countesses of Billington detested each other quite thoroughly."

"Goodness," Ellie said weakly. "How positively encouraging."

"And those that did *not* . . ." Charles paused for effect and grinned wolfishly. "Well, they were so passionately enamored of one another that separate rooms—and separate beds—were unthinkable."

"I don't suppose any of them found a happy medium?"

"Just my parents," he said with a shrug. "My mother had her watercolors, my father his hounds. And they always had a kind word for each other if they happened to cross paths. Which wasn't very often, of course."

"Of course," Ellie echoed.

"Obviously they saw each other at least *once*," he added. "My very existence is proof of that."

"Goodness, but look how faded the damask is," she said in an overloud voice as she reached forward to touch an ottoman.

Charles grinned at her obvious attempt to change the subject.

Ellie moved forward and peered through the open

doorway. Charles's room was decorated with far less fuss and opulence and was much more to her liking. "Your decor is very nice," she said.

"I had it redone several years ago. I believe the last time the chamber had been refurbished was by my great-grandfather. He had abysmal taste."

She looked around her room and grimaced. "As did his wife."

Charles laughed. "You should feel free to redecorate in any manner you choose."

"Really?"

"Of course. Isn't that what wives are meant to do?"

"I wouldn't know. I've never been a wife."

"And I've never had one." He reached out and took her hand, his fingers stroking her sensitive palm. "I'm rather glad I do."

"You're glad you've managed to keep hold of your fortune," she retorted, feeling the need to keep a bit of distance between them.

He dropped her hand. "You're right."

Ellie was a bit surprised he'd admitted to it when he'd been working so hard to seduce her. Materialism and greed were generally not considered seductive topics.

"Of course I'm rather glad to have you, too," he continued, his voice rather jaunty.

Ellie didn't say anything, then finally blurted out, "This is terribly uncomfortable."

Charles froze. "What?" he asked cautiously.

"This. I barely know you. I don't—I just don't know how to act in your presence."

Charles had a very good idea how he'd *like* her to act, but it required that she remove all of her clothing, and somehow he didn't think that concept would appeal to her. "You didn't seem to have any difficulty being your rather blunt and entertaining self when we first met," he said. "I found it quite refreshing."

"Yes, but now we're married, and you want to—"

"Seduce you?" he finished for her.

She blushed. "Must you say it out loud?"

"It is hardly a secret, Ellie."

"I know, but—"

He touched her chin. "What happened to the fire-breathing woman who tended my ankle, bruised my ribs, and never once let me get the last word?"

"*She* wasn't married to you," Ellie retorted. "*She* didn't belong to you in the eyes of God and England."

"And in your eyes?"

"I belong to myself."

"I'd prefer to think that we belong to each other," he mused. "Or *with* each other."

Ellie thought that was rather a nice way of putting it, but she still said, "It doesn't change the fact that legally, you can do anything you want with me."

"But I have promised that I won't. Not without your permission." When she didn't say anything, he added, "I would think that that would give you leave to relax a bit in my presence. To act more like yourself."

Ellie considered this. His words made sense, but they didn't allow for the fact that her heart raced at triple speed every time he reached out to touch her chin or smooth her hair. She could manage to ignore her attraction to him when they were talking—conversations with him were so enjoyable that she felt as if she were chatting with an old friend. But every so often they would fall silent, and then she'd catch him looking at her like a hungry cat, and her insides would quiver, and—

She shook her head. Thinking about all of this was not helping her in the least.

"Is something wrong?" Charles inquired.

"No!" she said, more forcefully than she'd intended. "No," she said again, this time with a bit more grace. "But I do need to unpack, and I'm very tired, and I'm sure you're very tired."

"Your point being?"

She took his arm and nudged him through the connecting door into his own room. "Just that it has been a most tiring day, and I'm certain we both need some rest. Good night."

"Good—" Charles let out a curse under his breath. The minx had shut the door right in his face.

And he hadn't even had a chance to kiss her. Somewhere somebody was laughing about this.

Charles looked down at his hand and curled it into a fist, thinking that he'd feel a lot better if he could find that "somebody" and plant him a facer.

Ellie awoke early the next morning, as was her habit, donned her finest dress—which she had a suspicion was still a touch too shabby for the Countess of Billington—and set off to explore her new home.

Charles had said she might redecorate. Ellie was thrilled at the thought. She loved nothing better than to have projects to plan and tasks to accomplish. She didn't want to redo the entire house; she rather liked the idea that this old building reflected the tastes of generations of Wycombes. Still, it would be nice to have a few rooms that represented the taste of *this* generation of Wycombes.

Eleanor Wycombe. She mouthed her new name a few times and decided that she could get used to it. It was the Countess of Billington part that might take some time.

She reached the bottom floor and made her way to the great hall, then poked into various rooms. She stumbled into the library, letting out a loud sigh of approval. Books lined the walls from floor to ceiling, their leather spines glistening in the early morning light. She could live until she was ninety and not finish reading all of these books.

She peered more closely at some of the titles. The first she came across was called *Christian Hellfire, the Devil, Earth, and Flesh.* Ellie smiled, deciding that her husband must not have been responsible for the purchase of that particular book.

She saw an open door in the west wall of the library, and she moved forward to explore. Poking her head in, she realized that she must have discovered Charles's study. It was neat and tidy, with the exception of his desk, which was covered with just enough clutter to show that he used the room frequently.

Feeling as if she were somehow intruding, Ellie backed out of the room and made her way to the front hall. Eventually, she found the informal dining room. Helen Pallister was there, sipping a cup of tea and munching on a marmalade-coated piece of toast. Ellie couldn't help but notice that the toast was burnt.

"Good morning!" Helen called out, rising to her feet. "You're up and about early. I have never had the pleasure of anyone's company at breakfast before. No one in this household rises as early as I do."

"Not even Judith?"

That gave Helen cause to laugh. "Judith rises early only on days when she doesn't have lessons. On days like today her governess practically has to dump a bucket of water over her head to get her out of bed."

Ellie smiled. "A most intelligent young girl. I myself have tried to sleep past the sunrise, but I never quite manage it."

"I am the same way. Claire calls me barbaric."

"As did my sister."

"Is Charles awake?" Helen asked, reaching for another teacup. "Would you like a spot?"

"Please. Milk, no sugar, thank you." Ellie watched while Helen poured, then said. "Charles is still abed." She wasn't sure whether her new husband had revealed the true nature of their marriage to his cousin, and she certainly wasn't comfortable enough to do so. Nor did she think it was her place.

"Would you care for some toast?" Helen inquired. "We have two different kinds of marmalade and three jams."

Ellie eyed the black crumbs littering Helen's plate. "No, but thank you."

Helen held her toast in the air and regarded it. "Not very appetizing, is it?"

"Couldn't we possibly teach the cook to make a proper piece of toast?"

Helen sighed. "The housekeeper prepares breakfast. Our French chef insists that the morning meal is beneath his notice. And as for Mrs. Stubbs, I'm afraid she is too old and stubborn to change her ways. She insists that she prepares the toast correctly."

"Perhaps it is the fault of the oven," Ellie suggested. "Has anyone taken a look at it?"

"I haven't the faintest idea."

Feeling a rush of determination, Ellie pushed her chair back and rose to her feet. "Let us go and investigate, then."

Helen blinked several times before asking, "You want to inspect the oven? Yourself?"

"I have been cooking all my life for my father," Ellie explained. "I know a thing or two about ovens and stoves."

Helen rose to her feet, but her expression was hesitant. "Are you certain you want to venture into the kitchens? Mrs. Stubbs won't like it—she's always saying it's unnatural for gentlefolk to be belowstairs. And Monsieur Belmont throws fits if he thinks anyone has touched anything in his kitchen."

Ellie eyed her thoughtfully. "Helen, I think we have to remember that this is *our* kitchen, correct?"

"I don't think Monsieur Belmont will see it that way," Helen replied, but she followed Ellie through the doorway back into the great hall. "He's very temperamental. As is Mrs. Stubbs."

Ellie took a few more steps before she realized she had no idea where she was going. She turned to Helen and said, "Perhaps you should show me the way. It is difficult to play the crusading avenger when one doesn't know the way to the holy land."

Helen giggled and said, "Follow me."

The two women wound through a labyrinth of hallways and staircases until Ellie could hear the unmistakable sounds of a kitchen through the door in front of her. She turned to Helen with a smile on her face.

"Do you know, but at *my* house, our kitchen was right next to our dining room. Exceedingly convenient, if you ask me."

"The kitchen is much too loud and hot," Helen explained. "Charles has done what he can to improve ventilation, but it is still quite stifling. It must have been unbearable when Wycombe Abbey was built five hundred years ago. I cannot blame the first earl for not wanting to entertain his guests so close to the kitchens."

"I suppose," Ellie murmured, and then she opened the door and immediately realized that the first earl had been very smart indeed. The Wycombe Abbey kitchens were nothing like the homey little room she'd once shared with her father and sister. Pots and pans hung from the ceiling, large worktables took up space in the center of the room, and Ellie counted no less than four stoves and three ovens, including a beehive oven set into a large hearth with an open fire. There wasn't much activity at such an early hour, and Ellie could only wonder what the scene would be like before a large dinner party. Utter chaos, she imagined, with every pot, pan, and utensil in use.

Three women were preparing food in the far corner. Two appeared to be kitchen maids, and they were washing and dicing meat. The other woman was a bit older and had her head in one of the ovens. Ellie assumed she was Mrs. Stubbs.

Helen cleared her throat, and the two maids turned to look at them. Mrs. Stubbs rose too quickly and banged her head on the lip of the oven. She let out a short howl of pain, muttered something that Ellie was certain her father would have disapproved of, and stood upright.

"Good morning, Mrs. Stubbs," Helen said. "I would like to introduce you to the new countess."

Mrs. Stubbs bobbed a curtsy, as did the two kitchen maids. "My lady," she said.

"You'll be wanting something cold for that bump," Ellie said briskly, in her element now that she had found a task to complete. She stepped toward the kitchen maids. "Would one of you be so kind as to show me where the ice is stored?"

The maids gaped at her for a moment and then one of them said, "I'll fetch some for you, my lady."

Ellie turned to Helen with a slightly sheepish smile. "I'm not used to having people do and fetch things for me."

Helen's lips twitched. "Obviously not."

Ellie crossed the room to Mrs. Stubbs's side. "Let me have a look at that."

"No, really, it's quite all right," the housekeeper said quickly. "I don't need—"

But Ellie's fingers had already found the lump. It wasn't very large, but she was certain it must be painful. "Of course you do," she said. She picked up a thin towel she saw on a worktable, wrapped it around the ice one of the maids was holding tentatively toward her, and pressed it against the lump on the housekeeper's head.

Mrs. Stubbs let out a grumble and muttered, "It's very cold."

"Of course it is," Ellie replied. "It's ice." She turned to Helen with an exasperated look on her face, but her new cousin had her hand clamped over her mouth and looked as if she were trying very hard not to laugh. Ellie widened her eyes and jutted her chin forward in a silent appeal for cooperation.

Helen gave a little nod, took a couple of breaths to stem her giggles, and said, "Mrs. Stubbs, Lady Billington has come to the kitchen to inspect the ovens."

The housekeeper's head turned slowly in Ellie's direction. "I beg your pardon."

"I couldn't help noticing this morning that the toast was a bit black," Ellie said.

"That is how Mrs. Pallister likes it."

Helen cleared her throat and said, "Actually, Mrs. Stubbs, I do prefer my toast on the slightly less charred side."

"Why didn't you say anything?"

"I did. You said it came out that way no matter how long you toasted it."

"I can only conclude," Ellie interjected, "that something is amiss with the oven. As I have a great deal of experiences with stoves and ovens, I thought I might give it a look."

"You?" Mrs. Stubbs asked.

"You?" Kitchen maid #1 (as Ellie had taken to calling her in her mind) asked.

"You?" Kitchen maid #2 (by default, of course) asked.

All three were gaping visibly. Ellie rather thought that the only reason Helen hadn't let her mouth drop open and echo, "*You?*" was because Helen had already done so upstairs in the informal dining room.

Ellie scowled, planted her hands on her hips, and said, "Contrary to popular opinion, a countess may occasionally possess a useful talent or two. Perhaps even a *skill*."

"I have always found embroidery quite useful," Helen said. She eyed a blackened stovetop. "And it's quite a *clean* hobby."

Ellie shot her a dirty look and hissed, "You are not helping."

Helen shrugged, smiled, then said, "I think we should let the countess take a look at the oven."

"Thank you," Ellie said, with what she thought was great dignity and patience. She turned to Mrs. Stubbs and asked, "Which oven do you use for the toast?"

"That one," the housekeeper replied, pointing a long finger at the filthiest of the lot. "Those other ones belong to the Frenchie. I wouldn't touch them if you paid me."

"They were imported from France," Helen explained.

"Oh," Ellie said, feeling as if she were trapped in a very strange dream. "Well, I am certain they can't compare to our good, sturdy English ovens." She walked over to the oven, pulled the door open, then turned back around to suggest, "Do you know, we could avoid all of this if we just used a toasting fork?"

Mrs. Stubbs crossed her arms and said, "I'll never use one of those. Don't trust them."

Ellie couldn't imagine what could possibly be construed as untrustworthy about a toasting fork, but she decided that it wasn't worth pressing the issue, so she lifted her skirts above her ankles, kneeled, and stuck her head in the oven.

* * *

Charles had been hunting for his new bride for several minutes, his quest finally taking him, most improbably, to the kitchens. A footman swore that he had seen Ellie and Helen head that way a quarter of an hour earlier. Charles couldn't credit it, but he decided to investigate, anyway. Ellie wasn't the most conventional of countesses, so he supposed it was possible that she had taken it in her head to introduce herself to the kitchen staff.

He was not prepared for the sight that awaited him. His new wife was on her hands and knees with her entire head—no, rather half her *torso*—jammed into an oven that Charles was fairly certain had resided at Wycombe Abbey since before the time of Cromwell. Charles's initial reaction was one of terror—visions of flames leaping through Ellie's hair raced through his mind. But Helen appeared unperturbed, so he managed to squelch the urge to run into the kitchen and haul Ellie to safety.

He took a step back from the doorway so that he could watch the proceedings unnoticed. Ellie was saying something—it sounded like nothing so much as a grunt, actually—and then he clearly heard her yell, "I have it! I have it—"

Helen, Mrs. Stubbs, and the two kitchen maids all leaned in closer, clearly fascinated with Ellie's maneuvers.

"Blast. I don't have it," Ellie finished, rather grumpily, in Charles's opinion.

"Are you certain you know what you're about?" Helen asked.

"Absolutely. All I need is to move this rack. It's much too high." Ellie began to yank on something that obviously wouldn't budge, for she landed on her behind several times. "When was the last time this oven was cleaned?" she asked.

Mrs. Stubbs huffed. "That oven is every bit as clean as an oven needs to be."

Ellie muttered something Charles couldn't hear, and then she said, "There. I have it." She pulled a charred rack out of the oven and then inserted it back in. "Now all I have to do is move this farther from this flame."

Flame? Charles's blood ran to ice. She was playing with *fire*?

"There!" Ellie pulled herself out of the oven and landed on her behind on the floor. "That ought to fix it."

Charles decided that this was a good moment to announce his presence. "Good morning, wife," he said, strolling in, his stance deceptively casual. What Ellie couldn't see was that his hands were clenched tightly together behind his back. It was the only way he could keep them from wrapping themselves around her shoulders and hauling her back to their room for a blistering lecture on the safety—or lack thereof—of the kitchens.

"Billington!" Ellie exclaimed in surprise. "You're awake."

"Obviously."

She scrambled to her feet. "I must look a fright."

Charles pulled out a snowy handkerchief. "You do have a bit of soot here"—he wiped the cloth against her left cheek—"and here"—he wiped it against her right—"and of course a bit here." This time he applied the handkerchief to her nose.

Ellie grabbed the cloth out of his hand, not liking the drawl in his voice. "That's really not necessary, my lord," she said. "I'm perfectly capable of wiping my face."

"I don't suppose you would like to tell me what you were doing inside the oven. I assure you that we have ample foodstuffs here at Wycombe Abbey without you offering yourself up as the main course."

Ellie stared at him, not at all certain whether he was funning her or not. "I was fixing the oven, my lord."

"We have servants for that."

"Clearly you don't," Ellie replied, bristling at his tone. "Or you wouldn't have been eating burnt toast for the past ten years."

"I like my toast burnt," he bit out.

Helen coughed so hard that Mrs. Stubbs whacked her on the back.

"Well, I don't," Ellie returned, "and neither does Helen, so you are outvoted."

"I like *my* toast burnt."

Every head swiveled to face the doorway, where Claire stood, her arms planted on her hips. Ellie thought the girl looked rather militant for a fourteen-year-old.

"I want the oven the way it was," Claire stated firmly. "I want everything the way it was."

Ellie's heart sank. Her new cousin was clearly not excited about her arrival into the household. "Fine!" she said, throwing her arms up in exasperation. "I'll change it back."

She made it halfway back into the oven by the time Charles's hand closed around the collar of her dress and yanked her back out. "You will *not* be repeating this dangerous stunt," he said. "The oven will remain the way it is."

"I thought you liked your toast burnt?"

"I will adjust."

At that point, Ellie really wanted to laugh, but she wisely kept her mouth shut.

Charles glared belligerently at the rest of the kitchen's occupants. "I would like a few words alone with my wife." When no one moved, he roared, "Now!"

"Then perhaps *we* should leave," Ellie cut in. "After all, Mrs. Stubbs and the kitchen maids work here. We do not."

"You appeared to be doing a rather fine imitation of it," he grumbled, suddenly sounding more petulant than angry.

Ellie gaped at him. "You are quite the most strange and contrary man I have ever met."

"*I* did not have my head in an oven," he shot back.

"Well, *I* do not eat burnt toast!"

"Well, I—" Charles's head snapped up, as if he suddenly realized that he was not only having a most bizarre argument with his wife, but that he was doing it before an audience. He cleared his throat and wrapped his hand around her slender wrist. "I believe I would like to show you the blue room," he said loudly.

Ellie followed. She didn't have much choice, really. He left the room in quite a hurry, and since her wrist was now attached to his hand, she went with him. She wasn't certain where they were going—probably to the first chamber he found with enough privacy for him to rail at her without anyone else hearing.

Blue room, indeed.

Chapter 8

Much to Ellie's surprise, the room Charles eventually pulled her into actually *was* decorated in blue. She looked around her—taking in the blue sofas, blue drapes—and then let her eyes slide to the floor, which was covered with a blue-and-white carpet.

"Have you anything to say for yourself?" Charles demanded.

Ellie said nothing, temporarily mesmerized by the interlocking pattern on the carpet.

"Ellie," he growled.

Her head snapped back up. "I beg your pardon?"

Charles looked as if he wanted to shake her. Hard. "I said," he repeated, "have you anything to say for yourself?"

She blinked and replied, "This room is quite blue."

He just stared at her, clearly at a loss as to how to respond.

"I didn't think you were serious about taking me to the blue room," she explained. "I thought you merely wanted to take me somewhere where you might yell at me."

"I *do* want to yell at you," he ground out.

"Yes," she mused. "That much is clear. Although I must say that I'm not entirely certain *why* . . ."

"Eleanor!" he fairly roared, "You had your head in an oven!"

"Of course I did," she replied. "I was fixing it. You'll be quite pleased once you start receiving proper toast for breakfast."

"I will *not* be pleased, I could not care *less* about the toast, and you will *never* enter the kitchens again."

Ellie's hands found their way to her hips. "You, sir, are an idiot."

"Have you ever seen a person with his hair on fire?" Charles demanded, jabbing his finger into her shoulder. "Have you?"

"Of course not, but—"

"I have, and it was not a pretty sight."

"I don't imagine it was, but—"

"I'm not certain what ultimately caused the poor fellow's death, the burns or the pain."

Ellie swallowed, trying not to visualize the disaster. "I'm terribly sorry for your friend, but—"

"His wife went insane. Said she heard his screams at night."

"Charles!"

"Good God, I had no idea having a wife would be this disruptive. And only one day into marriage."

"You are being needlessly insulting. And I can assure you that—"

He sighed and rolled his eyes heavenward as he interrupted her. "Was it so much to hope that my life could continue as peacefully as before?"

"Will you let me speak!" Ellie finally burst out.

He shrugged in a deceptively casual manner. "Go right ahead."

"You needn't be so pointlessly macabre," she said. "I have been fixing ovens my entire life. I didn't grow up with servants and luxuries and the like. If we were to eat supper, I had to cook it. And if the oven didn't work, I had to fix it."

Charles pondered that, paused, and said, "I apologize if you feel that I have underestimated you in any way. I certainly do not mean to belittle your talents."

Ellie wasn't entirely certain that fixing an oven qualified as a talent, but she kept her mouth shut.

"It is simply"—he reached out, took a lock of her strawberry-blond hair, and twirled it around his forefinger—"that I shouldn't like to see this go up in flames."

She swallowed nervously. "Don't be silly."

He tugged gently on her hair, drawing her closer to him. "It would be such a shame," he murmured. "It's so soft."

"It's just hair," Ellie stated, thinking that one of them had to keep this conversation grounded in reality.

"No." He brought the lock of hair to his mouth and ran it across his lips. "It's much more than that."

Ellie stared at him, unaware that her lips had parted ever so slightly. She would swear she felt that gentle caress on her scalp. No, on her mouth. No, on her neck. No—blast it, she'd felt that bloody sensation all over her body.

She looked up. He was still running her hair across his mouth. She shuddered. She was still feeling it. "Charles," she croaked.

He smiled, clearly aware of his effect on her. "El-lie?" he countered.

"I think you should . . ." She gasped and tried to pull away as he pulled her even closer to him.

"You think I should what?"

"Let go of my hair."

His free arm stole around her waist. "I disagree," he whispered. "I've grown quite attached to it."

Ellie looked at his finger, around which were now wrapped several coils of her hair. "Clearly," she said, wishing she sounded more sarcastic and less breathy.

He held his finger up so that he could regard it against the undraped window. "Pity," he murmured. "The sun is already well above the horizon. I should have liked to compare your hair to the sunrise."

Ellie stared at him, dumbfounded. No one had ever spoken to her in such a poetic fashion before. Unfortunately, she had no idea how to interpret his words. "What are you talking about?" she finally blurted out.

"Your hair," he said with a smile, "is the color of the sun."

"My hair," she said loudly, "is ridiculous."

"Women." He sighed. "They are never satisfied."

"That is not true," Ellie protested, thinking that she ought to defend her gender.

He shrugged. "*You* are not satisfied."

"I beg your pardon. I am completely satisfied with my life."

"As your husband, I cannot tell you how heartened I am to hear it. I must be better at this marriage thing than I thought."

"I am perfectly satisfied," she said, ignoring his ironic tone, "because I now have control over my own destiny. I am no longer under my father's thumb."

"Or Mrs. Foxglove's," Charles pointed out.

"Or Mrs. Foxglove's," she agreed.

His face adopted a thoughtful air. "But *my* thumb, I could do quite a bit with my thumb."

"I am certain I do not know what you are talking about."

He let go of her hair and let his fingers trail down the side of her neck. "I am certain you don't," he murmured. "But you will. And *then* you will be satisfied."

Ellie's eyes narrowed as she jerked out of his grasp. Her new spouse certainly did not have any difficulties relating to his self-esteem. She rather doubted he had ever heard the word, "No," uttered from female lips. She narrowed her eyes and asked, "You have seduced many women, haven't you?"

"I hardly think that is the sort of question one asks one's husband."

"I think it is *exactly* the sort of question one should be asking one's husband." She planted her hands firmly on her hips. "Women are nothing but a game to you."

Charles stared at her for a moment. Her statement was nothing if not astute. "Not a game, precisely," he said, stalling for time.

"Then what?"

"Well, at the very least, *you* are not a game."

"Oh? And what am I?"

"My wife," he bit off, losing patience with this line of conversation.

"You haven't any idea how to treat a wife."

"I know exactly how to treat a wife," he snapped. "*I* am not the problem."

Offended, Ellie lurched backward. "What, precisely, are you attempting to say?"

"You, madam, do not know how to *be* a wife."

"I have only been a wife for one day," she all but growled. "What do you expect?"

All of a sudden Charles felt the complete cad. He had promised her time to accustom herself to marriage, and here he was snapping at her like a dragon. He let out a soft sigh of regret. "I am sorry, Ellie. I don't know what came over me."

She looked startled by his apology, and then her face softened. "Do not trouble yourself over it, my lord. It has been a stressful few days for us all. And . . ."

"And what?" he prompted when she failed to complete her sentence.

She cleared her throat. "Nothing. Merely that I suppose you could not have been expecting to find me this morning with my head in an oven."

"It was something of a shock," he said mildly.

Ellie fell silent. After a few moments, she opened her mouth, then shut it.

One corner of Charles's mouth turned up. "Did you want to say something?"

She shook her head. "No."

"You did."

"It wasn't important."

"Oh, come now, Ellie. You wanted to defend your kitchen skills, or oven skills, or whatever you want to call them, didn't you?"

Her chin jutted out ever so slightly. "I can assure you that I have adjusted oven racks a million times before."

"You've hardly been alive long enough to have performed the task a million times."

She let out an outraged gasp. "Am I not allowed to speak in hyperbole?"

"Only," he said, a bit too smoothly, "if you are talking about me."

Ellie's face slid into a smirk. "Oh, Charles," she exclaimed, "I feel as if we have known each other for a *million* years." Her tone grew more ironic. "I am *that* weary of your company."

He chuckled. "My thoughts were more along the lines of, 'Oh, Charles, you are the kindest—'"

"Ha!"

"'—most dashing man to ever walk the planet. If I lived a thousand years, I—'"

"I hope I do live a thousand years," Ellie retorted. "Then I should be a wizened old crone whose only purpose in life is to annoy you."

"You should make a fetching old crone." He cocked his head and pretended to study her face. "I can see just where your wrinkles will settle. Right here by your eyes, and—"

She batted away his hand, which was tracing the path of her future wrinkles. "You are no gentleman."

He shrugged. "I am when it suits me."

"I cannot imagine when that is. So far I have seen you drunk—"

"I had quite a good reason for that particular bout of alcohol," he said with a wave of his hand. "Besides, my little drunken stupor brought me you, did it not?"

"That is not the point!"

"Pray do not work yourself into a snit," he said in a weary voice.

"I am not in a snit." She drew back and crossed her arms.

"You do a fine imitation of one, then."

Her eyes narrowed and her lips curved into a confident smile. "My snits are far more lethal than this. You would be well advised not to encourage one."

He sighed. "I suppose I will have to kiss you."

"Whaaaaat?"

Charles grabbed her arm and pulled her quickly up against him until the length of her body molded against his. "It seems the only way to shut you up," he drawled.

"You—" But she couldn't finish her sentence, for his lips were on hers, and they were doing the most devilish things . . . They tickled the corner of her mouth, then caressed the line of her jaw, and Ellie felt as if she were melting. *Yes*, she thought wildly, that could be the only explanation, for her legs felt like butter, and she swayed into him, and she must be on fire, because she felt so very very hot, and the word, "Fire," echoed in her brain and—

Charles let go of her so suddenly that she tumbled into a chair. "Did you hear that?" he asked sharply.

Ellie was far too dazed to respond.

"Fire!" came the shouts.

"Good God!" Charles burst out, heading for the door.

"It's your Aunt Cordelia," Ellie managed to say. "Didn't you say she always shouts, 'Fire'?"

But Charles was already sprinting down the hall. Ellie stood and shrugged, not really believing there was any danger—not after her introduction to Cordelia the day before. Still, this was her new home, and if Charles thought there was something to worry about, she ought to investigate. Taking a deep breath, she picked up her skirts and ran down the hall after him.

Ellie skidded around three corners in her chase before she realized that she was following him back to the kitchens. "Oh, *no*," she groaned, feeling suddenly very sick to her stomach. *Not the oven. Please not the oven.*

She felt the smoke even before she saw the door to the kitchen. It was thick and acrid, and it stung her lungs within seconds. With a grim heart she turned that last corner. Servants were handing off buckets of water, and Charles was in the thick of it, shouting out orders and running in and out of the kitchen as he hurled water onto the flames.

Ellie's heart caught in her throat as she watched him dash into the blaze. "No!" she heard herself shout, and without thinking she ran through the throng of servants and into the kitchen. "Charles!" she screamed, tugging at his shirt.

He whirled around, his eyes filling with horror and rage when he saw her next to him. "Get *out!*" he yelled.

"Not unless you come with me." Ellie grabbed a bucket of water from a servant and threw it on a small blaze that had jumped from the floor to a table. She could put out that small section of the fire, at least.

Charles grabbed her arm and began to drag her to the door. "If you value your life, get *out!*"

Ellie ignored him and picked up another bucket. "We almost have it contained!" she yelled, charging forward with her water.

He grabbed the back of her dress, stopping her short and causing the contents of her bucket to fly forward, landing rather neatly on the fire. "I meant that *I* will kill you," he hissed, hauling her toward the door. Before Ellie realized what was happening, she was on her behind in the hall, and Charles was still in the kitchen, fighting the blaze.

She tried to reenter the kitchen, but Charles must have said something to the servants, because they very efficiently blocked her way. After about a minute of trying to worm her way back in, Ellie finally gave up and joined the bucket line, refusing to consign herself to the impotent position Charles seemed determined to assign her.

After a few minutes more, she heard the telltale sizzle of a blaze put out, and the people in the bucket line began to exhale so loudly that Ellie wondered if any of them had remembered to breathe. They all looked exhausted and relieved, and she decided then and there that her first official act as Countess of Billington would be to make sure that all of these people received some kind of token of appreciation for their efforts. Extra pay, perhaps, or maybe an additional half day off.

The crowd thinned out at the entrance to the kitchen, and Ellie wormed her way forward. She had to get a look at the oven and see if she could somehow determine what had caused the blaze. She knew that everyone would believe that the fire was her fault—she only hoped that they would think she had done a shoddy job fixing the oven and not that she had purposefully set the fire. Better to be thought foolish than evil.

When she entered the kitchen, Charles was in the far corner, conferring with a footman. His back, thank goodness, was to her, and she darted over to the oven, which was still letting off a bit of smoke, and stuck her head in.

She gasped at what she saw. The rack had been moved to its highest position—even higher than it had been before Ellie had fixed it. Any food placed in the oven would catch fire. It was inevitable.

Ellie stuck her head in a little further, wanting to get a better look, but then she heard a sharp curse behind her. Before she had time to react, she felt herself being yanked backward, and she had no doubt as to who the yanker was.

She turned around warily. Charles was standing over her, and his eyes were blazing with fury.

"I have to tell you something," she whispered urgently. "The oven. It's—"

"Not one word," he bit out. His voice was hoarse from the smoke, but that did little to diminish his rage. "Not a single, damned word."

"But—"

"That's one too many." He turned on his heel and stalked out of the room.

Ellie felt traitorous tears stinging her eyes, and she had no idea whether they were caused by hurt or anger. She hoped it was anger, because she didn't much like this feeling in the pit of her stomach that he had somehow rejected her. She rose to her feet and walked to the kitchen doorway so that she could hear what Charles was saying to the servants in the hall.

"... thank you for endangering your lives to help me save the kitchen and indeed all of Wycombe Abbey. It was a noble and selfless act you performed today." Charles paused and cleared his throat. "I must ask, however, were any of you present when the flames began?"

"I had gone to the garden to collect herbs," replied a kitchen maid. "When I returned, Miss Claire was screaming about the fire."

"Claire?" Charles's eyes narrowed. "What was Claire doing down here?"

Ellie stepped forward. "I believe she came down earlier when . . ." She faltered for a moment under the weight of his thunderous glare, but then she reminded herself that she had absolutely nothing of which to be ashamed and continued. ". . . when we were all gathered in the kitchen."

Every servant's eyes were on her, and Ellie felt their collective condemnation. After all, she had been the one to adjust the rack.

Charles turned away from her without a word. "Get me Claire," he said to a footman. Then he turned to Ellie. "A word with you," he barked, and stalked back toward the kitchen. Before he reached the doorway, however, he turned around and said to the assembled group, "The rest of you may go about your duties. Those of you who are sooty may feel free to avail yourselves of the bathing facilities in the guest wing." When none of the servants immediately moved, he said sharply, "Good day."

They all ran off.

Ellie followed her husband into the kitchen. "That was very kind of you to allow the servants to use your bathing facilities," she said quietly, wanting to get in the first word before he started to rail at her.

"They're *our* bathing facilities," he snapped, "and don't think you're going to distract me."

"I hadn't meant to. I can't help it if you did a kind deed."

Charles exhaled, trying to give his heart time to resume a normal rhythm. Christ, what a day it had been, and it wasn't even noon yet. He'd woken up, found his wife with her head stuck in an oven, gotten into his first argument with her, kissed her soundly (and ended up wanting much, much more than that) only to be interrupted by a damned fire that *she* appeared to have started.

His throat was raw, his back was killing him, and his head pounded like a gavel. He looked down at his arms, which appeared to be shaking. Marriage, he decided, was not proving to be a healthful endeavor.

He turned his gaze to his wife, who looked as if she didn't know whether to smile or frown. Then he looked back over at the oven, which was still spewing smoke.

He groaned. A year from now he'd be dead. He was sure of it.

"Is something wrong?" Ellie asked quietly.

He turned to her with a disbelieving expression. "Is something *wrong*?" he echoed. "Is something WRONG?" This time it was more of a boom.

She frowned. "Well, obviously something, er, some things, are wrong, but I was speaking in a more general sense, you see. I—"

"Eleanor, my bloody kitchen is burned to a crisp!" he fairly yelled. "I fail to see anything general about it."

Her chin jutted out. "It wasn't my fault."

Silence.

She crossed her arms and stood her ground. "The rack had been moved. It wasn't where I left it. That oven didn't stand a chance of *not* catching fire. I don't know who—"

"I don't give a damn about the rack. One, you shouldn't have tampered with the oven in the first place. Two"—now he was ticking off on his fingers—"you shouldn't have run in here while the fire was raging. Three, you damn well shouldn't have stuck your head back in the bloody oven while it was still hot. Four—"

"That is quite enough," Ellie bit out.

"I'll tell you when it's enough! You—" Charles stopped himself from continuing, but only because he realized he was shaking with rage. And, perhaps, with a little latent fear.

"You're making a list about me," she accused. "You're making a list of all of my shortcomings. And," she added, wagging her finger at him, "you cursed twice in one sentence."

"God help me," he moaned. "God help me."

"Hmmmph," she said, somehow managing to incorporate a world of scathing reprovement in that one semi-syllable. "He certainly won't if you continue cursing like that."

"I believe you once told me you weren't overly fussy about such things," he ground out.

She crossed her arms. "That was before I was a wife. Now I am expected to be fussy about such things."

"God save me from wives," he groaned.

"Then you shouldn't have married one," she snapped.

"Ellie, if you don't shut your mouth now, God help me, I'm going to wring your neck."

Ellie rather thought that she'd made her opinions clear on the possibility that God was going to help him, so she contented herself with muttering, "One curse is understandable, but two . . . Well, two is really too much."

She wasn't certain, but she thought she saw Charles roll his eyes to the ceiling and mutter, "Take me now."

That did it. "Oh for the love of God," Ellie snapped, uncharacteristically taking the Lord's name in vain. After all, she had been raised by a reverend. "I'm not so bad that death is preferable to marriage with me."

He leveled a look in her direction that told her he wasn't so sure.

"This marriage doesn't have to be permanent," she burst out, humiliated fury making her words shrill. "I could march out that door right this second and obtain an annulment."

"What door?" he drawled. "All I see is a charred piece of wood."

"Your sense of humor leaves much to be desired."

"My sense of humor— Where the hell are you going?"

Ellie didn't reply, just continued on her way past the charred piece of wood she preferred to think of as a door.

"Get back here!"

She kept going. Well, she would have kept going if his hand hadn't found the sash of her dress and yanked her back against him. Ellie heard a ripping sound, and for the second time that day, she found herself pressed up against the hard length of her husband's body. She couldn't see him, but she could feel him intimately against her back, and she could smell him—she would swear she could smell him, even through the lingering smoke.

"You will not get an annulment," he ordered, his lips practically touching her ear.

"I'm surprised you care," she retorted, trying to ignore the way her skin was tingling where his breath warmed her.

"Oh, I care," he growled.

"You care about your blasted money!"

"As you care about yours, so we had better make the best of this."

Ellie was saved from having to admit that he was right by a loud "ahem" from the direction of the doorway. She looked up to see Claire, who was standing with her arms crossed. A huge, irritated frown covered the girl's face.

"Oh, good day, Claire," Ellie said with a tight smile, trying for all the world to appear as if she were quite pleased to be standing in this extremely awkward position in the middle of a burned-out kitchen.

"My lady," Claire replied flatly.

"Claire!" Charles said with a fair amount of feeling, releasing Ellie so quickly that she bumped into the wall. He walked toward his cousin, who beamed at him.

Ellie merely rubbed her elbow where she'd hit the wall and muttered all sorts of unflattering things about her husband.

"Claire," Charles said again, "I understand that you were the one who first discovered the fire."

"Indeed. It began not ten minutes after you and your new wife exited the kitchen."

Ellie narrowed her eyes. Was that a slight note of derision she'd heard in Claire's voice as she said the word "wife"? She *knew* that girl didn't like her!

"Do you have any idea what caused it?" Charles asked.

Claire looked surprised that he'd even asked. "Why, I . . . well . . ." She looked meaningfully over at Ellie.

"Just say it, Claire," Ellie ground out. "You think I set the fire."

"I do not think you did it on purpose," Claire replied, placing her hand over her heart.

"We know that Ellie would never do such a thing," Charles said.

"Accidents happen to everyone," Claire murmured, casting a pitying look toward Ellie.

Ellie wanted to strangle her. She didn't particularly like being condescended to by a chit of fourteen years.

"I am certain you *thought* you knew what you were doing," Claire continued.

At that point Ellie realized she had a choice to make. She could leave the room and take a bath, or stay and kill Claire. With great reluctance, she decided to bathe. She turned to Charles, affected her best shrinking violet posture, and said, "If you'll excuse me, I believe I will retire to my chamber. I'm feeling terribly faint."

Charles eyed her suspiciously and said under his breath, "You've never fainted a day in your life."

"How would you know?" Ellie returned in an equally low voice. "You didn't even know I existed until last week."

"It *feels* like forever."

Ellie stuck her nose in the air and whispered sharply, "I concur." Then she straightened her spine and swept from the room, hoping that her grand exit wasn't too terribly marred by the fact that she was covered with soot, limping slightly, and wearing a dress that was now torn in three places.

Chapter 9

Ellie nursed her wounds for the rest of the day, pleading fatigue when a maid came to her room to fetch her for the evening meal. She knew she'd appear the worst sort of coward, but the truth was that she was so blasted angry with Charles and his entire family that she didn't trust herself to sit with them for an entire meal.

Sulking in one's room was rather boring, however, so she sneaked downstairs and grabbed the latest copy of the newspaper to go over the financial pages. She checked her investments, as was her habit, but then she realized that she no longer knew the status of her savings. Had Charles transferred her accounts yet, as he had promised? Probably not, Ellie thought, trying to be patient. They had only been married for one day. She'd have to remind him, though. She'd read a favorable report on a new cotton mill in Derbyshire, and she was eager to invest a portion of her funds.

She read the newspaper three times, rearranged the knickknacks on her vanity table twice, and stared out the window for an hour before she finally flopped onto her bed with a loud groan. She was bored, hungry, and alone, and it was all the fault of her husband and his blasted family. She could happily strangle the lot of them.

Then Judith knocked on her door.

Ellie smiled reluctantly. She supposed she wasn't furious with her husband's entire family. After all, it was rather difficult to be angry with a six-year-old.

"Are you sick?" Judith asked, climbing up on Ellie's bed.

"Not really. Just tired."

Judith frowned. "When I am tired, Miss Dobbin makes me get out of bed, anyway. Sometimes she puts a cold, wet cloth on my neck."

"I bet that works."

The little girl nodded solemnly. "It is difficult to sleep with a wet neck."

"I'm sure it is."

"Mama said she would send a tray up to your room."

"That is very nice of her."

"Are you hungry?"

Before Ellie could respond, her stomach growled.

Judith squealed with laughter. "You *are* hungry!"

"I guess I must be."

"I think I like you."

Ellie smiled, feeling better than she had all day. "Good. I like you, too."

"Claire said you made a fire today."

Ellie counted to three before she said, "There was a fire, but it was an accident. I didn't cause it."

Judith cocked her head to the side as she considered Ellie's words. "I think I'll believe you. Claire is frequently wrong, although she doesn't like to admit it."

"Most people don't."

"*I* am rarely wrong about anything."

Ellie smiled and tousled her hair. A maid appeared in the doorway with a supper tray. Judith jumped down off the bed, saying, "I had best get back to my room. Miss Dobbin will likely hide my pudding if I am late."

"Goodness, that would be dreadful!"

Judith made a face. "She eats it after I go to bed."

Ellie crooked her finger and whispered, "Come back here for a moment."

Intrigued, Judith climbed back onto the bed and put her face near Ellie's.

"Next time Miss Dobbin eats your pudding," Ellie whispered, "you come to me. We'll sneak down to the kitchens together and find you something even tastier."

Judith clapped her hands together, her face a perfect picture of delight. "Oh, my lady, you are going to be the very best of cousins!"

"As are you," Ellie replied, feeling tears welling in her eyes. "And you must call me Ellie. After all, we are family now."

"Tomorrow I shall show you 'round the house," the little girl stated. "I know all the secret passageways."

"That would be lovely. But you had better run along. We don't want Miss Dobbin to eat your pudding tonight."

"But you said—"

"I know, but the kitchens are in a sorry state this evening. It might prove difficult to find a replacement dessert."

"Oh, dear!" Judith exclaimed, paling at the thought. "Bye!"

Ellie watched her dash from the room, then turned to her tray of food and began to eat.

Despite her hunger, Ellie found that she only had the appetite to eat about a quarter of her food. Her empty stomach did little to calm her nerves, and she practically jumped clear to the ceiling when, later that night, she heard the outer door to Charles's bedroom open. She heard him rustling around, presumably getting ready to go to sleep, and cursed at herself for holding her breath every time his footsteps brought him near the connecting door.

This was madness. Utter madness. "You have one day," she muttered. "One day to feel sorry for yourself and then you must go out and make the best of it. So everyone thinks you set fire to the kitchen. That isn't the worst thing that could happen."

Ellie spent the next minute trying to think of something that was worse. It wasn't easy. Finally she waved her hand in the air and said, a touch louder than before, "You could have killed someone. That would have been very bad. Very very bad."

She nodded, trying to reassure herself that, in the grand scheme of life, the fire was actually a small incident. "Very bad," she said again. "Killing someone. Very bad."

A knock sounded at the connecting door. Ellie yanked her bedsheets up to her chin, even though she knew that the door was locked. "Yes?" she called out.

"Were you speaking to me?" Charles asked through the door.

"No."

"Then may I ask to whom you *were* speaking?"

Did he think she was carrying on with a footman? "I was talking to myself!" And then she muttered, "Save for Judith, I'm the best company I'm going to find in this mausoleum, anyway."

"What?"

"Nothing!"

"I couldn't hear you."

"You weren't meant to!" she fairly screamed.

Silence, and then she heard his footsteps carrying him away from the door. She relaxed slightly, snuggling more deeply into her bed. She had just about gotten comfortable when she heard an awful, terrible clicking sound, and she groaned, just *knowing* what she was going to see when she opened her eyes.

An open doorway. With Charles standing in it.

"Did I remember to mention," he drawled, leaning casually against the doorjamb, "how annoying I find connecting doors?"

"I can think of at least three replies," Ellie retorted, "but none of them are particularly ladylike."

He waved her barb away. "I assure you, I've long since stopped expecting you to behave in a ladylike manner."

Ellie's mouth fell open.

"You were talking." He shrugged. "I couldn't hear you."

It took a powerful force of will to unclench her teeth, but somehow she managed it. "I believe I said that you weren't meant to." Then she grinned in what she hoped was a sickly sort of manner. "I'm a bit batty that way."

"Funny you should say that, because I could swear you were carrying on in here about killing someone." Charles took a few steps toward her and crossed his arms. "The question is: just how batty are you?"

Ellie's eyes flew to his face in horror. He didn't really think she would kill someone, did he? If this wasn't proof that she hadn't known this man well enough to marry him, she didn't know what was. Then she saw telltale crinkles of humor form around his eyes, and she exhaled with relief. "If you must know," she finally said, "I was trying to console myself over the awful incident this morning—"

"The fiery incident, you mean?"

"Yes, that one," she said, not appreciating his facetious interruption. "As I was saying, I was trying to console myself by thinking of all the things that could have happened that would have been worse."

One corner of his mouth turned up in a wry smile. "And killing someone qualifies as worse?"

"Well, that depends on *whom*."

Charles let out a bark of laughter. "Ouch, my lady. You do know how to wound."

"Alas, but not lethally," Ellie replied, unable to suppress a grin. She was having far too much fun sparring with him.

There was a comfortable moment of silence, and then he said, "I do the same thing."

"I beg your pardon?"

"Try to make a bleak situation seem better by imagining all the scenarios that could be worse."

"Do you now?" Ellie felt absurdly pleased that they both dealt with adversity in the same fashion. It made her feel they were better suited, somehow.

"Mmm, yes. You should have heard what I thought up last month, when I was convinced that my entire fortune was going to go to my odious cousin Phillip."

"I thought your odious cousin was named Cecil."

"No, Cecil is the toad. Phillip is merely odious."

"Did you make a list?"

"I always make lists," he said flippantly.

"No," she said with a little laugh. "I meant did you make a list of what would be worse than losing your fortune?"

"As a matter of fact, I did," he said with a slow smile. "*And*, as a matter of fact, I have it in the next room. Would you like to hear it?"

"Please."

Charles disappeared through the connecting doorway for a moment and reemerged carrying a slip of paper. Before Ellie realized what he was about, he hopped up onto the bed and stretched out beside her.

"Charles!"

He looked at her sideways and smiled. "I need one of your pillows to prop me up."

"Get out of my bed."

"I'm not in it, I'm on it." He yanked one of the pillows out from under her head. "There now, this is better."

Ellie, whose head was now perched at a bizarre angle, didn't think it was better in the least and she said so.

Charles ignored her and said, "Did you want to hear my list, or no?"

She waved her hand around in assent.

"Very well." He held the paper in front of him. "'Number One'—Oh, by the way, this list is titled,

'Worse Things that Could Happen to Me.' "

"I hope I'm not on it," Ellie muttered.

"Nonsense. You're quite the best thing that has happened to me in recent memory."

She turned rather pink and was annoyed with herself for being so pleased at his statement.

"If it weren't for a few appallingly bad habits, you'd be perfect."

"I beg your pardon!"

He grinned wickedly. "I love when you beg my pardon."

"Charles!"

"Oh, very well, I suppose you did save my fortune, so I'm inclined to overlook some of the smaller bad habits."

"I have no small bad habits!" Ellie retorted.

"Yes, you're right," he murmured. "Only big ones."

"That is not what I meant and you well know it."

He crossed his arms. "Do you want me to read the list?"

"I'm beginning to think you don't *have* a list. I've never met anyone who changes the subject as often as you do."

"And I have never met anyone who *talks* as much as you do."

Ellie smirked. "I suppose you'll just have to accustom yourself to my mouthy ways, then, seeing as how you married me."

Charles turned his head sideways and looked at her assessingly. "Mouthy ways, eh? What sort of mouthy ways do you mean?"

She scooted away from him until she was almost

falling off the bed. "Don't even think of kissing me, Billington."

"My name is Charles, and I wasn't thinking of kissing you. Although now that you mention it, it's not such a dreadful idea."

"Just . . . Read . . . The . . . List."

He shrugged. "If you insist."

Ellie thought she might scream.

"Now then." He held the list in front of his face and snapped the paper to attention. " 'Number One: Cecil could inherit the fortune.' "

"I thought Cecil *would* inherit."

"No, that's Phillip. Cecil would have to murder us both to inherit. If I hadn't married, he would only have had to kill Phillip."

Ellie gaped at him. "You sound as if you think he has considered it."

"I wouldn't put it past him," Charles said with a shrug. "Now then, 'Number Two: England could be annexed by France.' "

"Were you drunk when you made this list?"

"You must admit it would be a very bad thing. Worse than losing my fortune."

"How kind of you to put the welfare of Britain before your own," Ellie said acerbically.

He sighed and said, "I'm just that kind of man, I suppose. Noble and patriotic to a fault. 'Number Three—' "

"May I interject?"

He looked over at her with a beleaguered expression that clearly said, "You already have."

Ellie rolled her eyes. "I was merely wondering if these items are ranked."

"Why do you ask?"

"If they are ranked, that means you think it would be worse for Cecil to inherit your fortune than it would be for France to conquer England."

Charles let out a whoosh of air. "It's a close call. I'm not sure."

"Are you always this flippant?"

"Only about the important things. 'Number Three: the sky could fall to the earth.' "

"*Surely* that is worse than Cecil inheriting your fortune!" Ellie exclaimed.

"Not really. If the sky were to fall to the earth, Cecil would be a bit too dead to enjoy my fortune."

"So would you," Ellie retorted.

"Hmmm. You're right. I might have to revise." He smiled at her again, and his eyes grew warm, although not, Ellie thought, with passion. His gaze seemed to hold something that was more akin to friendship—or at least that was what she hoped. Taking a deep breath, she decided to take advantage of the lovely moment and said, "I didn't set that fire, you know. It wasn't me."

He sighed. "Ellie, I know you would never do something like that purposefully."

"I didn't do it at all," she said sharply. "Someone tampered with the oven after I fixed it."

Charles let out another long breath. He wished he could believe her, but why would anyone tamper with the oven? The only people who knew how to work it were the servants, and they certainly had no reason to try to make Ellie look bad. "Ellie," he said placatingly, "perhaps you don't know quite as much about ovens as you think you do."

Her posture grew suddenly very tense.

"Or perhaps our oven is fashioned differently than yours."

Her jaw unclenched slightly, but she still looked extremely upset with him.

"Or perhaps," he said softly, reaching out and taking her hand in his, "perhaps you do know every bit as much about ovens as you say you do, but you made a small mistake. A new marriage can be very distracting."

She appeared to soften at that statement, and Charles added, "Lord knows I'm distracted."

To change the subject, Ellie pointed to a bit of writing at the bottom of the sheet of paper in his hand. "What is that? Is it another list?"

Charles looked down, quickly folded the paper, and said, "Oh, that is nothing."

"Now I must read it." She snatched the paper away from him, and when he lunged after it, she hopped off the bed. " 'Five Most Important Qualities in a *Wife*'?" she read incredulously.

He shrugged. "It seemed a worthwhile endeavor to decide in advance just what it was I needed."

" 'What?' Now I'm a 'what?' "

"Don't be obtuse, Ellie. You're far too bright to carry it off."

There was a compliment in there somewhere, but Ellie wasn't about to give him credit for it. With a loud snort, she began to read. " 'Number One: Attractive enough to hold my interest.' *That* is your most important requirement?"

Charles had the decency to look slightly embarrassed. "If you're half as disgusted with me as you look, I'm in big trouble," he muttered.

"I'll say." She cleared her throat. " 'Number Two: Intelligence.' " She looked back up at him with a dubious eye. "You have redeemed yourself slightly. But only slightly."

He chuckled and leaned back, letting his head rest against his interlocked hands. "What if I told you this list wasn't ranked?"

"I wouldn't believe you for a second."

"I thought not."

" 'Number Three: Doesn't nag.' I don't nag."

He didn't say anything.

"I *don't* nag."

"You're nagging right now."

Ellie's eyes shot daggers in his direction, and she continued on with the list. " 'Number Four: Ability to move within my social circle with ease.' " She coughed with disbelief as she read this. "Surely you realize that I have no experience with the aristocracy."

"Your brother-in-law is Earl of Macclesfield," Charles pointed out.

"Yes, but he is family. I needn't put on airs with him. I have never been to a London ball or a literary salon, or whatever it is you indolent types do all day during the Season."

"I shall ignore your misplaced insult," he said, sounding suddenly every bit as haughty as Ellie had always expected an earl to. "Now then, you are an intelligent woman, correct? I am certain you will learn whatever you need to. Can you dance?"

"Of course."

"Can you converse?" He waved his hand. "No, don't answer that. I already know the answer. You converse overwell and overmuch. You shall do just fine in London, Eleanor."

"Charles, I am beginning to find you *over*irritating."

Charles merely crossed his arms and waited for her to continue, beginning to find this process extremely tiresome. He'd made out this list well over a month ago, and he'd certainly never intended to go over it with his future wife. Why, he'd even written—

He suddenly remembered number five. All of the blood in his face abruptly dropped down to his feet. He saw Ellie look down at the list as if at half speed, and heard her say, " 'Number Five.' "

Charles didn't even have time to think. He vaulted off the bed, a primitive cry escaping his mouth, and pounced on her, knocking her down. "The list!" he croaked. "Give me the list."

"What the devil?" Ellie pawed at his arms as she tried to wriggle out of his grasp. "Let go of me, you cur."

"Give me the list."

Ellie, who was now supine on the floor, stretched her arm out over her head. "Get off me!"

"The list!" he roared.

Ellie, unable to think of any alternative, kneed him in the stomach and scurried across the room. She stood up and frantically read the paper in her hands while he caught his breath. Her eyes scanned the lines, found number five, and then she shouted, "You *bastard*!"

Charles just groaned, clutching at his midsection.

"I should have planted my knee lower," she hissed.

"Stop overreacting, Ellie."

" 'Number Five,' " she read in a prissy voice. " 'She

must be worldly enough to overlook my affairs, and may not conduct any of her own until she has produced at least two heirs.' "

Put that way, Charles conceded, it did sound a bit cold. "Ellie," he said placatingly, "surely you realize that I wrote this before I met you."

"What difference does that make?"

"A world of difference. It . . . ah . . . it . . ."

"Am I meant to believe that you fell so head over heels in love with me that all of your notions of marriage were suddenly overthrown?"

Her dark blue eyes seemed to flash fire and ice at the same time, and Charles wasn't sure whether he should be feeling apprehension or desire. He thought about saying something asinine like, "You're beautiful when you're angry." It had always worked wonders on his mistresses, but he had a feeling it wouldn't bring much success with his wife.

He glanced somewhat hesitantly in her direction. She was standing across the room, her posture militant, her hands fisted at her sides. The damned list lay crumpled on the floor. When she caught him looking at her, she glared even harder, and Charles rather thought that he could hear thunder.

No doubt about it, he'd botched this one up but good.

Her intellect, he suddenly thought. He was going to have to appeal to her intellect and reason this out with her. She prided herself on her sensibility and levelheadedness, didn't she? "Ellie," he began, "we never did have the opportunity to discuss marriage with each other."

"No," she bit out, her words dripping acid, "we merely *married* each other."

"I allow that our nuptials were somewhat hasty, but we had good reason to act quickly."

"*You* had good reason," she retorted.

"Don't try to act as if I have taken advantage of you," he replied, his voice growing impatient. "You needed this marriage every bit as much as I did."

"I didn't get as much out of it, though."

"You have no idea what you're getting out of it! You are a countess now. You have more wealth than you have ever dreamed of." He stared at her. Hard. "Don't insult me by playing the victim."

"I have a title. And I have wealth. And I also have a husband to whom I must answer. A husband who does not seem to see anything wrong with treating me like chattel."

"Eleanor, you're growing unreasonable. I don't want to argue with you."

"Have you noticed that you only call me Eleanor when you are speaking to me like a child?"

Charles counted to three and then said, "*Ton* marriages are based on the premise that both parties are mature enough to respect each other's choices."

She stared at him, openmouthed. "Do you have any idea what you just said?"

"Ellie . . ."

"I think what you just said is that *I* may also be unfaithful if I so choose."

"Don't be silly."

"After the heir and the spare, of course, as you so eloquently spelled out." She sat down on an ottoman, clearly lost in thought. "Freedom to live my life as I choose, with whom I choose. It's intriguing."

As Charles stood there, watching her contemplate adultery, his previous views on marriage suddenly sounded as appealing as mud. "You can't do anything about it now," he said. "It's considered very bad form to have an affair before you produce an heir."

She started to laugh. "Item number four suddenly takes on new meaning."

He looked at her with a blank expression.

"You wanted someone who could move about your social milieu with ease. Clearly I am going to have to master the intricacies of what is bad form and what is not. Let's see . . ." She began to tap her forefinger against her jawbone, and Charles had the urge to yank her hand away, just to wipe that sarcastic expression from her face. "It is bad form to carry on an affair too soon in the marriage," she continued, "but is it bad form to have more than one lover at once? I shall have to investigate that."

Charles felt his face growing quite hot, and a muscle was pounding furiously in his temple.

"It is probably bad form to have an affair with one of your friends, but is it bad form to have one with a distant cousin?"

He was starting to see everything through a strange red haze.

"I am almost certain it would be bad form to entertain a lover here in our home," she continued, "but I'm not sure where—"

A strangled, hoarse, half-shout-half-grunt erupted from his throat and he launched himself at her. "Stop!" he yelled. "Just stop."

"Charles!" She squirmed frantically beneath him, which only served to make him crazier.

"Not another word," he rasped, his eyes burning hot holes into her skin. "If you utter one more word, so help me God, I will not be responsible for what I do."

"But I—"

At the sound of her voice, his fingers bit into her shoulders. His muscles shook, and his eyes grew wild, as if he no longer knew or cared what he did next.

Ellie stared up at him, suddenly quite wary. "Charles," she whispered, "maybe you shouldn't . . ."

"Maybe I should."

She opened her mouth to protest, but before she could make a sound he devoured her with a fiery kiss. It felt as if his mouth were everywhere—on her cheeks, on her neck, on her lips. His hands roved up and down her body, pausing to squeeze the curve of her hips and the fullness of her breasts.

Ellie could feel the passion rising within him, and she felt it within herself as well. He ground his hips into hers. She could feel his arousal as he pressed her deeper into the ottoman, and it took several seconds for her to realize that she was meeting his thrusts with her own.

He was seducing her in anger, and she was responding. The mere thought of it was enough to douse her passion cold, and she shoved her hands against his shoulders, squirming out from under him. She made it across the room before he was on his feet.

"How dare you," she breathed. "How dare you."

Charles lifted one shoulder in an insolent shrug. "It was either kiss you or kill you. I thought I made the right choice." He strode to the connecting door and put his hand on the knob. "Don't prove me wrong."

Chapter 10

$\sim\!\!\sim\!\!\supset\!\supset\!\subset\!\subset\!\sim\!\!\sim$

C harles awoke the next morning with a thundering headache. His new wife seemed to have the ability to make him feel hideously hungover without his having imbibed a drop.

There was no doubt about it. Marriage was not good for one's health.

After washing and dressing, he decided that he ought to seek Ellie out and see how she was faring. He hadn't the least idea what he should say to her, but it did seem as if he ought to say something.

What he *wanted* to say was, "Your apology is accepted," but that required that she actually apologize for her scandalous talk the night before, and he doubted she was going to do that.

He rapped on the connecting door and waited for an answer. When none came, he opened the door a crack and called out her name. There was still no response, so he pushed the door open a little wider and poked his head in.

"Ellie?" He glanced at her bed and was surprised to see it neatly made. The servants hadn't come to clean yet that morning. He could be certain of this because he had instructed them to leave fresh flowers on his wife's vanity table every morning, and yesterday's violets were still in evidence.

He shook his head, realizing that his wife had made her own bed. He supposed he shouldn't have been surprised. She was quite a capable woman.

Ovens excepted, of course.

Charles wandered downstairs to the breakfast room, but instead of his wife, he found only Helen, Claire, and Judith.

"Charles!" Claire cried out upon seeing him enter through the doorway. She jumped to her feet.

"And how is my favorite fourteen-year-old cousin this bright morning?" he said as he took her hand and gallantly kissed it. Young girls loved that sort of romantic nonsense, and he doted on Claire enough to remember to treat her to such grand gestures.

"I am very well, thank you," Claire replied. "Won't you join us for breakfast?"

"I think I will," Charles murmured as he took a seat.

"We are not," Claire added, "having toast."

This earned her a reproving look from Helen, but Charles couldn't help but chuckle as he speared a slice of ham.

"You may kiss my hand, too," Judith said.

"A pox on me for having forgotten," Charles said, rising to his feet. He took Judith's hand and raised it to his lips. "My dear Princess Judith, a thousand apologies."

Judith giggled as Charles sat back down. "Where is my wife, I wonder?" he said.

"I have not seen her," Claire put in.

Helen cleared her throat. "Eleanor and I are both early risers, and I saw her here at breakfast before Claire and Judith came down."

"Was *she* eating toast?" her older daughter asked.

Charles coughed to cover a laugh. Really, it wouldn't do to laugh at one's wife in front of one's relations. Even if one was *tremendously* displeased with said wife.

"I believe she had a biscuit," Helen said sharply. "And I will ask you not to bring up the matter again, Claire. Your new cousin is very sensitive about the mishap."

"She is my cousin-in-law. And it wasn't a mishap. It was a fire."

"It was yesterday," Charles interjected, "and I have completely forgotten it."

Claire frowned, and Helen continued with, "I believe Ellie said she was planning to inspect the orangery. She mentioned that she is an avid gardener."

"Is the orangery fireproof?" Claire asked.

Charles leveled a stern stare in her direction. "Claire, that is enough."

Claire frowned again but kept quiet.

Then, as the three of them regarded each other in silence, a sharp cry pierced the air.

"Fire!"

"See!" Claire yelled, sounding a bit smug. "See! I told you she would set fire to the orangery."

"Another fire?" Judith asked, looking rather delighted by the prospect. "Oh, Ellie is ever so exciting."

"Judith," her mother said in a weary voice, "fires are not exciting. And Claire, you know very well that is only Aunt Cordelia. I am certain nothing is on fire."

As if just to prove Helen's point, Cordelia ran through the breakfast room, letting out another cry of, "Fire!" She skidded past the table and through the doorway to the formal dining room, off to destinations unknown.

"There," Helen said. "It is just Cordelia. There is no fire."

Charles was inclined to agree with Helen, but after the previous day's blaze, he found himself a touch nervous. He wiped his mouth with his napkin and stood. "Er, I believe I will take a short walk," he improvised. He didn't want his cousins to think he was checking up on his wife.

"But you barely touched your food," Claire protested.

"I'm not very hungry," Charles said quickly, mentally calculating how fast a fire could spread in the orangery. "I'll see you at the midday meal." He turned on his heel and strode out, breaking into a run as soon as he was out of sight of the breakfast room.

Ellie patted the dirt around a flowering bush, marveling at the wondrous orangery. She had heard of such structures before, but had never actually seen one. The climate was kept warm enough to grow plants all year 'round, even orange trees, which she knew preferred a more tropical clime. Her mouth watered as she touched the leaves of the orange tree. It wasn't giving fruit now but come spring and summer—oh, it would be lovely.

She could get used to luxury, she decided, if it meant that she could eat oranges all summer long.

She wandered about the orangery, inspecting the

various plants. Ellie couldn't wait to get her hands on some of the rosebushes. She had loved to putter about in her father's garden. This had to be the best benefit from her hasty marriage—the opportunity to garden all year long.

She was kneeling down, trying to get a sense of the root system of a particular plant, when she heard a fast footfall growing near. As she looked up, she saw Charles dash into the orangery. Or rather, he dashed to the doorway, then deliberately slowed his pace, as if he didn't want her to know he'd been running.

"Oh," she said flatly. "It's you."

"Were you expecting someone else?" He looked around the room, apparently searching for something.

"Of course not. I simply didn't think you would seek me out."

"Why would you think that?" he asked distractedly, still obviously looking for something.

Ellie stared at him. "Have you a deficient memory, my lord?"

He didn't appear to hear her, so she said loudly, "Charles!"

His head snapped around. "Yes?"

"*What* are you looking for?"

"Nothing."

Just then Cordelia dashed into the orangery and yelled, "Fire! There's a fire, I say!"

Ellie watched her new great-aunt run back out, then turned to Charles with an accusing expression. "You thought I set fire to the orangery, didn't you?"

"Of course not," he replied.

"For the love of—" Ellie caught herself before she blasphemed. Really, her father would have a fit if he'd heard how badly her language had deteriorated in the two days since she'd left his household. Marriage was having a bad effect on her temper, that was certain.

Charles looked at the ground, suddenly feeling rather ashamed. His aunt Cordelia had been crying, "Fire!" once a day since he could remember. He should have had a bit more faith in his wife. "Do you like to garden?" he mumbled.

"Yes. I hope you will not mind if I do some work in here."

"Not at all."

They stood silently for a full thirty seconds. Ellie tapped her toe. Charles drummed his fingers against his thigh. Finally Ellie reminded herself that she wasn't naturally a meek person and she blurted out, "You're still angry with me, aren't you?"

He looked up, clearly surprised that she'd voiced the question. "That might be one way of describing it."

"I'm angry with you, too."

"That fact has not escaped my notice."

His dry tone infuriated her. It was as if he were making fun of her distress. "I'll have you know," she stormed, "that I never imagined my marriage as the dry, bloodless contract you seem to anticipate."

He chuckled and crossed his arms. "You probably never imagined being married to *me*."

"If that isn't the most egotistical—"

"And furthermore," he interrupted, "if our marriage is 'bloodless,' as you so delicately put it, it is because you have chosen not to consummate the union."

Ellie gasped at his crudeness. "You, sir, are despicable."

"No, I merely want you. Why, for the life of me I don't know. But I do."

"Does lust always make men so horrid?"

He shrugged. "I wouldn't know. I've never had this much difficulty getting a woman into bed before. And I was never married to any of the other ones."

Ellie gasped again. She certainly didn't know the ins and outs of a typical *ton* marriage, but she was fairly certain husbands weren't supposed to discuss their amorous pursuits in front of their wives. "I do not have to listen to this kind of talk," she said. "I'm leaving."

She made it halfway to the door when she turned around. "No," she said, "I want to garden. *You* leave."

"Ellie, may I point out that this is my house?"

"It is my house now, too. I want to garden. You don't. Therefore, you leave."

"Eleanor . . ."

"I am finding it very difficult to fully appreciate the pleasure of your company," she ground out.

Charles shook his head. "Fine. Sink yourself into the dirt up to your elbows if you wish. I have better things to do than stand here and argue with you."

"As have I."

"Fine."

"Fine!" He stomped out.

Ellie rather thought they sounded like a pair of squabbling children, but at that point she was too enraged to care.

* * *

The newlyweds managed to avoid each other's company for two days, and they probably would have been able to continue in this solitary manner for even longer had not disaster struck.

Ellie was breakfasting when Helen entered the small dining room, her face scrunched up in an expression of distaste.

"Is something amiss, Helen?" Ellie asked, trying not to notice that the kitchen still hadn't resumed service of toast.

"Have you any idea what that dreadful smell in the south wing is? I nearly swooned on my way over."

"I didn't notice any smell. I came down by way of the side stairs, and . . ." Ellie's heart dropped. *The orangery. Oh, please, not the orangery.* It was off the south wing. "Oh, dear," she mumbled, jumping to her feet. She ran through the halls, Helen right behind her. If something had happened in the orangery she didn't know what she would do. It was the only place in this Godforsaken mausoleum she felt at home.

As Ellie neared her destination, a terrible, rotten stench assaulted her. "Oh, my word!" she gasped. "What is that?"

"It's awful, isn't it?" Helen agreed.

Ellie entered the orangery and what she saw made her want to cry. The rosebushes—which she had already fallen in love with—were dead, their leaves looking almost singed. Petals littered the floor, and the bushes gave off the most hideous stench. She covered her nose. "Who would do such a thing?" She turned to Helen and repeated, "Who?"

Helen stared at her a moment and then finally said,

"Ellie, you are the only one who likes to spend time in the orangery."

"Surely you don't think I . . . You think I did this?"

"I don't think you did this on purpose," Helen replied, looking very uncomfortable. "Anyone could see how much you enjoyed gardening. Perhaps you put something in the soil. Or misted something onto it you ought not have."

"I did no such thing!" Ellie insisted. "I—"

"Good *God!*" Charles entered the orangery, one hand holding a handkerchief over his nose and mouth. "What is that smell?"

"My rosebush!" Ellie nearly wailed. "Look what someone has done to it."

Charles planted his hands on his hips as he surveyed the damage, then accidentally breathed through his nose and coughed. "The devil take it, Eleanor, how did you manage to kill off the rosebushes in only two days? It always took my mother at least a year to do such damage."

"I had nothing to do with this!" she yelled. "Nothing!"

Claire chose that moment to enter the scene. "Did something die in the orangery?" she asked.

Ellie's eyes turned to slits. "No, but my husband is about to if he utters one more derogatory word about me."

"Ellie," Charles said in a placating voice. "I don't think you did this on purpose. It's just—"

"Aaaaargh!" she yelled, throwing up her arms. "If I hear that sentence one more time I shall scream."

"You *are* screaming," Claire pointed out.

Ellie wanted to strangle that child.

"Some people simply aren't very good at gardening," Claire continued. "There is nothing wrong with that. I myself am terrible with plants. I wouldn't dream of interfering with anything here. That is why we employ gardeners."

Ellie looked from Charles to Helen to Claire and back. Their expressions were faintly pitying, as if they had stumbled across a creature who, however likable, was completely inept.

"Ellie," Charles said, "perhaps we should discuss this."

After two days of silent treatment, his sudden willingness to discuss her apparent failure in the orangery simply threw her over the edge. "I have nothing to discuss with you," she ground out. "Any of you!" Then she stomped from the room.

Charles let Ellie stew in her room until evening, then decided that he had better go and talk to her. He had never seen her as upset as she'd been that morning in the orangery. Of course, he'd only known her slightly more than a week, but he certainly had never imagined the spirited and brave woman he'd married getting that upset over anything.

He'd had a few days to cool his temper over their last argument. She'd been testing him, he now realized. She wasn't used to the ways of the *ton* and she was lashing out. She would settle down once she grew more accustomed to marriage.

He knocked softly on the connecting door, then a bit louder when he heard no answer. Finally he heard something that might have been, "Come in," and he stuck his head inside.

Ellie was sitting on her bed, bundled up in a spare quilt she must have brought with her from home. It was a simple piece—white with blue stitching—certainly nothing that would have fit the overblown tastes of his ancestors.

"Was there something you wanted?" Ellie asked, her voice quite flat.

Charles looked at her closely. Her eyes were red, and she looked very small and young in the voluminous quilt. She was clutching something in her left hand.

"What is that?" he asked.

Ellie looked down at her hand as if she'd forgotten she was holding anything. "Oh, this. It's the miniature of my mother."

"It's very special to you, isn't it?"

There was a long pause, as if Ellie were deciding whether or not she wanted to share her family memories. Finally she said, "She had two made when she realized she was dying. One for me and one for Victoria. It was always the plan that we would take them with us when we married."

"So you would never forget her?"

Ellie turned her face to his quite suddenly, her blue eyes surprised. "That is exactly what she said. Exactly." She sniffled and wiped her nose inelegantly with her hand. "As if I would ever forget her."

She looked up at the walls of her bedroom. She hadn't gotten around to taking down the dreadful portraits, and the countesses looked even more imposing than usual when compared to her mother's gentle expression.

"I'm sorry about what happened today in the orangery," Charles said softly.

"I'm sorry, too," Ellie said in a bitter voice.

Charles tried to ignore her harsh tone as he sat beside her on the bed. "I know that you truly loved those plants."

"So did everyone else."

"What do you mean?"

"I mean that someone doesn't want to see me happy. Someone is purposefully ruining my efforts to make Wycombe Abbey my home."

"Ellie, you are the Countess of Billington. That very fact means that Wycombe Abbey *is* your home."

"Not yet. I need to put my mark on it. I need to do something to make at least a piece of it mine. I tried to be helpful by fixing the oven."

Charles sighed. "Perhaps we shouldn't mention the oven."

"I did not set the rack incorrectly," she said, her eyes flashing fire. "Someone tampered with my efforts."

He let out a long breath and placed his hand on hers. "Ellie, no one thinks badly of you. It is not your fault that you're a bit inept when it comes to—"

"Inept! Inept?" Her voice rose halfway to a shriek. "I am not—" She got into a bit of trouble here, for in her haste to jump off the bed and plant her hands on her hips in offended fury, she forgot that Charles was sitting on a corner of her blanket, and she tumbled onto the floor, landing rather clumsily on her bottom. She staggered to her feet, tripping twice—once on her skirt and once on the blanket—and finally ground out, "I am *not* inept."

Charles, for all of his efforts to remain sensitive to her distress, could not keep his mouth from quivering into a smile. "Ellie, I didn't mean—"

"I'll have you know I have never been anything but ept."

"Ept?"

"I have always been supremely organized, brilliantly capable—"

"Ept?"

"I don't procrastinate and I don't shirk my duties. I get things done."

"Is that a word?"

"Is *what* a word?" she burst out, looking very annoyed with him.

"Ept."

"Of course not."

"You just said it," Charles said.

"I did no such thing."

"Ellie, I'm afraid that you—"

"If I did," she said, flushing slightly, "then that ought to prove how upset I have become. Using nonsense words. Hmmmph. It is very unlike me."

"Ellie, I know that you are an extremely intelligent woman." He waited for her to say something and when she didn't, he added, "It's why I married you."

"You married me," she bit off, "because you needed to save your fortune and you thought I would overlook your affairs."

He colored slightly. "It is certainly true that my shaky financial situation had a great deal to do with the haste with which we married, but I assure you that having an affair was the last thing on my mind when I decided to wed you."

She let out a ladylike snort. "One has only to look at your list to know that you are lying."

"Ah, yes," Charles said caustically, "the infamous list."

"Speaking of our marriage agreement," Ellie said, "have you settled my financial affairs?"

"Just yesterday, as a matter of fact."

"You did?" She sounded quite surprised.

"Yes, but—"

"But what?" he asked testily, irritated that she hadn't expected him to keep his word.

"Nothing." She paused, and then added, "Thank you."

Charles nodded his reply. After a few moments of silence, he said, "Ellie, we really must discuss our marriage. I don't know where you obtained your poor impression of me, but—"

"Not now," she interrupted. "I'm too tired, and I really can't bear to hear you explain how little I know of aristocratic marriages."

"Any preconceptions I held of marriage were formed before I met you," he explained.

"I have already told you that I don't believe that I am so heartstoppingly appealing that you would throw over your notions of what a marriage ought to be."

Charles looked at her closely, taking in the wild length of red-gold hair that fell across her shoulders, and decided that "appealing" wasn't nearly a strong enough word to describe her. His body ached for her, and his heart—well, he wasn't so experienced with matters of the heart, but he was fairly sure that his was feeling *something*. "Then teach me," he said simply. "Teach me what a marriage ought to be."

She stared at him in shock. "How would I know? I'm as new to this as you are."

"Then perhaps you ought not to be so quick to scold me."

A vein very nearly popped clear out of her temple before she said, "I *do* know that husbands and wives ought to regard each other highly enough so that they do not laugh and turn the other cheek when their spouse is committing adultery."

"See? I knew you had some firm ideas about marriage." He smiled and leaned back into her bed pillows. "And I cannot tell you how pleased I am to hear that you are not interested in cuckolding me."

"I would be pleased to hear the same thing from you," she shot back.

His smile stretched into a full-fledged grin. "Jealousy never fell upon more appreciative ears."

"Charles . . ." Her voice was laced with warning.

He chuckled and said, "Ellie, I assure you that the thought of adultery has not crossed my mind once since I met you."

"That is reassuring," she said sarcastically. "You have managed to keep your mind on the straight and narrow for an entire *week*."

Charles thought about pointing out that it had actually been eight days but decided that seemed childish. Instead he said, "It seems to me, then, that your role as wife is quite clear."

"I beg your pardon."

"After all, I don't *want* to stray."

"I don't like the sound of this," she muttered.

"I would like nothing more than to spend a lifetime in your arms."

She snorted. "I don't even want to think about how many times you've said that before, my lord."

Charles slid off the bed and onto his feet with the grace of a cat. He took advantage of her disconcertment by picking up one of her hands and raising it to his lips.

"If you're trying to seduce me," she said plainly, "it won't work."

He grinned, the very devil in his smile. "I'm not trying to seduce you, dearest Eleanor. I would never attempt such a gargantuan task. After all, you are noble; you are upright; you are made of stern stuff."

Put that way, Ellie rather thought she sounded like a tree trunk. "Your point being?" she ground out.

"Why, it is simple, Ellie. I think *you* should seduce *me*."

Chapter 11

S he smacked his chest with the heels of her hands, knocking him back onto the bed. "Are you insane?" she screeched.

Charles only smiled. "I assure you that you did not need to resort to force to get me into your bed, dear wife."

"This is nothing but a game to you!"

"No, Ellie. This is marriage."

"You don't know what marriage is."

"By your own admission, you don't know, either." He reached out for her hand. "I suggest we learn together."

Ellie snatched hers away. "Don't touch me. I can't think when you touch me."

"A most encouraging fact," he murmured.

She shot him a scathing look. "I am not going to try to seduce you."

"It wouldn't be that difficult. And it is always rewarding to succeed at one's endeavors."

"It would be exceedingly difficult," she spat back at him. "I shouldn't be able to summon enough desire to make a good go of it."

"Ouch. A well-placed blow, my lady, but clearly false."

Ellie wanted to hiss a stinging retort, but she couldn't think of anything clever to say. Trouble was, she knew her words were false, too. The man had only to look at her and her knees grew weak. When he actually reached out and touched her, she could barely stand.

"Ellie," he said softly, "come to bed."

"I'm going to have to ask you to leave," she said primly.

"Don't you even want to give my plan a try? It doesn't seem fair for you to dismiss my ideas out of hand."

"Fair? Fair! Are you insane?"

"Sometimes I wonder," he muttered.

"See? You know as well as I that this is madness."

Charles swore under his breath and grumbled something about her having better ears than a rabbit. Ellie took advantage of his relative silence to stay on the offensive and say, "What could I possibly have to gain by seducing you?"

"I would tell you," he drawled, "but I'm not certain your tender ears are ready for it."

Ellie turned redder than her hair and tried to say, "You know that wasn't what I meant." But her teeth were so tightly clenched that it came out more like a hiss.

"Ah, my serpentine wife," Charles sighed.

"I am losing my temper, my lord."

"Really? I hadn't noticed."

Ellie had never had the urge to slap someone in her entire life, but she was starting to think that this might be a fine time to start. His mocking, overly confident attitude was too much for her to bear. "Charles—"

"Before you go on," he interrupted, "allow me to explain to you why you ought to seriously consider seducing me."

"Have you made a list?" she drawled.

He waved his hand nonchalantly in the air. "Nothing so formal, I assure you. But I tend to think in lists—it's a habit we compulsive listmakers share— and so naturally I have some key reasons organized in my head."

"Naturally."

He smiled at her attempt at sarcasm. "They are not ranked, of course." When she didn't say anything he added, "Just so there are no misunderstandings about the good of England and the possibility of the sky falling in and all that."

More than anything, Ellie wanted to throw him out of her room. Very much against her better judgment, she said, "Go on."

"Very well, let me see." Charles brought his hands together in a vaguely praying motion as he stalled for time. It hadn't even occurred to him to make a list until Ellie had mentioned it. He looked over at his wife, who was tapping her foot impatiently. "All right, here we are, first we must title the list."

She looked at him dubiously, and he knew she suspected he was making this up as he went along. Not a problem, he decided. This shouldn't be that difficult.

"The title?" Ellie prodded.

"Ah, yes. 'Reasons Why Ellie Should Seduce Charles.' I would have called it 'Reasons Why Ellie Should *Try* to Seduce Charles,' " he added as an aside, "but the outcome seems most certain to me."

She offered him nothing more than a stony stare, so he continued, "I meant that there is little reason to fear that you might make a muck of it."

"I *know* what you meant."

He smiled slyly. "Ah yes, of course you did. Shall we move on to number one?"

"Please."

"I shall begin with the most elementary. Number One: You shall enjoy it."

Ellie very much wanted to contradict this, but she had a sinking suspicion that would be a lie.

"Number Two: I shall enjoy it." He looked up at her and grinned. "Of that I am certain."

Ellie leaned back against the wall, feeling a bit weak.

Charles cleared his throat. "Which leads rather neatly into Number Three: Since I shall enjoy it, I will have no reason to look elsewhere for comfort."

"The fact that you are married to me ought to be reason enough!"

"Yes, it should," he agreed. "But I am the first to admit that I am not the most noble and God-fearing of men. I will need to be taught how blissful and satisfying marriage can be."

Ellie let out a derisive snort.

"Once I do that," he continued, "I am certain that I shall be a model husband."

"You just wrote in your other list that you wanted a sophisticated, worldly marriage, one in which you would be free to stray."

"That was before I met you," he said jovially.

She planted her hands on her hips. "I have already told you that argument won't wash."

"But it's true. To be frank, it had never occurred to me that I might find a wife to whom I wanted to be faithful. I won't tell you that I'm in love with you—"

Ellie's heart surprised her and sank.

"—but I think I might learn to love you, given time and proper encouragement."

She crossed her arms. "You will say anything to seduce a woman, won't you?"

Charles winced. His words had sounded a lot worse than he'd intended. "This isn't coming out right," he muttered.

She raised a brow, gifting him with an expression that was eerily reminiscent of his late nanny's—when she had been really annoyed with him. Charles suddenly felt rather like a scolded child—a most unpleasant sensation for a man of his stature.

"Hell, Ellie," he burst out, jumping off the bed and onto his feet, "I want to make love to my wife. Is that such a crime?"

"It is when you don't care about her."

"I *do* care about you!" He raked his hand through his hair, and his expression grew decidedly exasperated. "I like you better than any female I've ever met. Why the hell do you think I married you?"

"Because without me, your entire fortune would have gone to your odious cousin Cecil."

"Phillip," he corrected automatically, "and I could have married anybody to save my fortune. Believe me, I had my pick of the litter in London."

"Pick of the litter?" she gasped. "What a horrendous thing to say. Have you no respect for women?"

"When was the last time you went to London and took a whirl on the social scene?"

"You know I've never—"

"Exactly my point. Trust me, if you had a chance to meet most of the debutantes, you would know of what I speak. I found only one last year with more than half a brain in her head, and she was already in love with someone else."

"Clearly a testament to the fact that she possessed more than half a brain."

Charles allowed her her little dig. "Ellie," he said in a soft, encouraging tone, "what reason could there possibly be for us not to make ours a true marriage?"

Ellie opened her mouth, but she couldn't figure out what to say. Everything she could think of sounded rather weak and lame. How was she to explain to him that she didn't think she was ready to be intimate because it was a feeling she had? She had no rational arguments, no sound and well thought out reasons, just a *feeling*.

And even if she could somehow convey this feeling, she suspected that she wouldn't be terribly convincing. Not when his constant sensual onslaught was wearing her down, making her want him.

"Ellie," he said. "Someday you're going to have to face the fact that you want me."

She looked up in surprise. Had he somehow read her mind?

"Shall I prove my point?" he murmured. Charles rose to his feet and advanced upon her. "What do you feel when I do"—he reached out and brushed his fingertips lightly across her cheek—"this?"

"Nothing," she whispered, suddenly quite rooted to the spot.

"Really?" His smile was slow and lazy. "I feel a great deal."

"Charles . . ."

"Shhhh. What do you feel when I do"—he leaned forward and captured her earlobe between his teeth—"this?"

Ellie swallowed, trying to ignore the way his hot breath caressed her skin.

He let one of his arms snake behind her, pulling her closer to the raw heat of his body. "What about"—he cupped her backside and squeezed—"this?"

"Charles," she gasped.

"Charles, yes," he murmured, "or Charles, no?"

She didn't say anything, couldn't have made a sound if her life depended upon it.

He chuckled. "I'll take that as a yes."

His lips claimed hers in a hungry movement, and Ellie found herself clinging to him for support. She hated the way he could do this to her, hated herself for loving these feelings so. He was the worst sort of womanizer and had all but admitted that he planned to carry on affairs throughout their marriage, but he only had to touch her and she melted faster than butter.

It was, she supposed, why he had been so successful at womanizing. He had told her that he wanted to be faithful, but how could she believe him? Women must fall into his bed like dominoes—she herself was a perfect example. How could he resist them all?

"You taste like honey," he said hoarsely, nipping

at the corner of her mouth. "You taste like nothing else, like no other."

Ellie felt herself tumbling to the bed, then felt his hard body upon hers. He was more than aroused; he was wild for her, and her feminine heart soared with the knowledge and power of it. Tentatively, she reached out and laid her hand against the strong cords of his neck. His muscles leaped under her fingers and she moved away.

"No," he gasped, pulling her hand back to him. "More."

She touched him again, marveling at the heat of his skin. "Charles," she whispered, "I shouldn't be . . ."

"You *should*," he said fervently. "You definitely should."

"But—"

He silenced her with another kiss, and Ellie let him. If she couldn't speak, she couldn't protest, and dimly she realized that she didn't want to protest. She arched her back, instinctively moving toward his warmth, and gasped when she felt her breasts flatten against him.

He spoke her name, murmuring it over and over. She was losing herself, losing her ability to think. There was nothing but this man, and the things he was making her feel, and . . .

Ellie's ears pricked up.

. . . and a sound at the door.

"Charles," she whispered. "I think—"

"Don't think."

The knocking grew louder.

"Someone is at the door."

"No one would be that cruel," he murmured, his

words disappearing into her neck. "Or that stupid."

"Ellie!" they both heard, and it was immediately apparent that the voice belonged to Judith.

"Damn," Charles swore, rolling off of Ellie. For no one else would he have been able to hold his desire in check. But little Judith's voice was enough to convince him that he couldn't put his own needs first just then. He sat up and buttoned his shirt. When he looked over at Ellie, he saw that she was hurrying to the door, righting her appearance as she moved. He had to smile at her attempts to smooth her hair. He'd certainly done a rather nice job mussing it up.

Ellie pulled open the door to reveal Judith, whose lower lip was trembling. She immediately crouched down. "Judith, whatever is the matter?" she asked. "Why are you so sad?"

"I'm not sad. I'm *mad*!"

Both Ellie and Charles had to smile at that.

"Won't you come in?" Ellie said, keeping her voice appropriately grave.

Judith nodded like a queen and entered. "Oh, good evening, Charles."

"Good evening to you, too, Judith. It's fine to see you. I should have thought you'd be getting ready for bed."

"I would have been, but Miss Dobbin stole my pudding."

Charles looked at Ellie in complete confusion. His wife was trying to suppress an amused smile. Clearly she knew what this was about.

"Did she give you an excuse?" Ellie asked.

Judith's mouth twisted into a most annoyed expression. "She said I had misbehaved when we were practicing my letters."

"And did you?"

"Maybe just a little bit. But certainly not enough for her to take my pudding!"

Ellie turned to Charles. "What was the pudding tonight?"

"Strawberry tarts with custard and cinnamon," he replied. "It was quite nice, actually."

"My favorite," Judith muttered. "And Miss Dobbin's favorite, too."

"Mine as well," Ellie added, placing her hand on her stomach when it let out a loud growl.

"Perhaps you shouldn't have skipped the evening meal," Charles said helpfully.

She shot him a waspish look before turning back to Judith. "I did promise to help you should this occasion arise, didn't I?"

"Indeed you did. That is why I am here. I deserve my pudding! And I can prove it."

Out of the corner of her eye, Ellie could see Charles shaking with laughter. Trying to ignore him, she focused her gaze back on Judith and said, "Is that so?"

"Mmm-hmm." The little girl's head bobbed up and down. "I brought a copy of my lessons. You can see that I got all of my letters perfect. Even Z, which is frightfully hard."

Ellie took the piece of paper Judith had pulled from the pocket of her frock. It was a bit crumpled, but Ellie could see that Judith had written out all of her letters in both lower and upper case. "Very nice," she murmured. "Although you show an extra bump in the 'M.' "

"What?" Judith screeched, clearly horrified.

"I'm only teasing," Ellie replied. Then she turned to Charles and said, "I'm afraid that you will have to excuse us. Judith and I have important business to attend to."

"As master of this house," Charles put in with a mock-concerned expression, "I think that I should be apprised of any devious and underhanded plots that might be stewing."

"Very well," Ellie said. "We are going to sneak to the kitchen to secure another portion of dessert for Judith." She paused as her stomach rumbled. "And for me, too, I should think."

"I shall have to put a stop to this," Charles said.

"Oh, Charles, you wouldn't!" Judith cried out.

"Unless I may be a coconspirator." He turned to Ellie. "Besides, I should have thought you wouldn't want to go down to the kitchens on your own."

She scowled at him. "Judith and I would do quite well by ourselves."

"Of course, but it will be much more fun with me along."

Judith took Ellie's hand and tugged on it. "He's right. Charles can be great fun when he chooses."

He tousled her hair. "Only when I choose?"

"Sometimes you are a bit too stern."

"I keep telling him the same thing," Ellie said with a commiserating shrug.

"Now, now, Eleanor," Charles chided, "You usually tell me the opposite. Perhaps if I were more stern with you . . . Hmmm . . . I might meet with more success."

"I think it is time we were off," Ellie said quickly, ushering Judith toward the door.

"Coward," Charles whispered as he passed her.

"You may call it cowardice," she whispered back, "but I prefer to call it good judgment. Judith is only six years old."

"I am nearly seven," the little girl announced.

"And she hears everything," Ellie added.

"Children do," Charles said with a shrug.

"All the more reason to be more circumspect with your words."

"Are we going to the kitchen now or not?" Judith said with a little stamp of her foot.

"Indeed we are, poppet," Charles said, sweeping forward and taking her hand. "Now then, we must be quiet. Very quiet."

"This quiet?" Judith whispered.

"Even quieter. And you—" He turned to Ellie. "Pipe down."

"I didn't say anything," she protested.

"I can hear you thinking," Charles replied with a wiggle of his eyebrows.

Judith giggled.

Ellie, God help her, giggled too. Just when she was determined to dismiss her husband as a complete ne'er-do-well, he had to go and charm her by turning their trip to the kitchen into a romantic adventure for young Judith.

"Can you hear *me* thinking?" Judith asked.

"Certainly. You are thinking about strawberry tarts."

Judith gasped and turned to Ellie. "He's right!"

Charles looked Ellie straight in the eye, his expression frankly sensual. "Can *you* hear *me* thinking?"

She shook her head quickly.

"Probably not," he agreed. "Else you'd have far more of a blush on your face."

"Look!" Judith squealed. "She *is* blushing. She *does* know what you're thinking!"

"I do now," Ellie retorted.

"What is he thinking?" Judith demanded.

"Goodness!" Ellie said quickly. "Are we nearly to the kitchens? You had best button your lips, Judith. Charles did say we need to be quiet."

The trio tiptoed into the kitchen, which Ellie noted had been cleaned quite thoroughly since her last visit. It looked as if the burnt oven had been put back into use. She was dying to look inside and inspect the rack. Perhaps when Charles's back was turned . . .

"Where do you suppose Monsieur Belmont has hidden those tarts?" Charles asked Judith.

"Maybe in the cupboard?" she suggested.

"An excellent idea. Let us have a look."

While the two of them rummaged through the cupboards, Ellie made a mad—but by necessity quiet—dash to the oven. She shot a glance over at her husband to make sure that he and Judith were still busy, and then quickly stuck her head inside.

She pulled back out just as quickly, but she'd had enough time to see that the oven rack had been reset in exactly the same position she'd put it in. "This is extremely strange," she muttered under her breath.

"Did you say something?" Charles called out without turning around.

"No," she lied. "Did you find the tarts?"

"No. I have a feeling the kitchen staff must have

polished them off this evening. But we did locate a rather tasty-looking cake with butter-cream frosting."

"Butter-cream, eh?" Ellie asked, growing quite interested.

"Mmm-hmm. I'm sure of it."

Ellie believed him as he had one of his fingers in his mouth.

"It's ever so good, Ellie," Judith chirped, plunking her finger down and scooping up a chunk of frosting.

"Aren't either of you going to eat the cake?" Ellie asked.

"No."

"Not I."

"That butter-cream frosting will make you both ill."

"Sadly so," Charles said, giving his finger another lick, "but oh, so very happy."

"Try some, Ellie," Judith said.

"Oh, all right. But only with a piece of cake."

"But that will ruin the effect," Charles said. "Judith and I were planning to strip the cake quite bare and leave a mystery for Monsieur Belmont in the morning."

"He will not be amused, I am sure," Ellie said.

"He is never amused."

"Charles is right," Judith added. "He is forever grumpy and likes to shout at me in French."

Charles held out a frosting-covered finger toward her. "Try it, Ellie. You know you want some."

Ellie turned beet red. His words sounded uncomfortably like those he'd uttered in her bedroom—when he'd been so handily seducing her. He moved his finger toward her lips, but she backed up before he could touch her mouth.

"Pity," he said. "I thought you were going to do it."

"Do what?" Judith asked.

"Nothing," Ellie ground out, and then just to show Charles that she wasn't a complete coward, she reached her finger out to his, scooped up some frosting, and ate it. "Oh, my," she uttered "That's delicious."

"I told you so," Judith said.

Ellie gave up any attempt at trying to be the dignified lady of the house. It took the three of them only two minutes to denude the entire cake.

Chapter 12

~~~❦~~~

Ellie woke up the following morning feeling a bit more amicably disposed toward her husband. It was difficult to maintain a sense of disgust with a man who so obviously adored children.

So he didn't take marriage as seriously as she would have liked. That didn't necessarily make him a bad person. Irreverent, perhaps, but not bad, and after all those years with her father, Ellie was starting to think that irreverent might be kind of nice. Clearly Charles had a way to go before he would be a husband she could trust with her full heart and soul, but the previous evening's escapade with Judith at least gave her some hope that they might be able to make a decent go at their marriage.

Not that she had any plans to fall into his little trap and try to seduce him. Ellie had no doubt as to who would be in control in such a situation. A fat lot *she* knew about seduction. She could picture it easily. She'd lean in to give him a kiss—which was the extent of what she knew how to do, really, and within seconds the seducer would become the seduced.

But to be fair, Charles had held up his end of the

marriage bargain. He had arranged Ellie's financial accounts to her satisfaction, and she was more than eager to get to work. Sometime during the night Charles had slipped a piece of paper under the connecting door with all of the information Ellie would need to take control of her finances. It was remarkably thoughtful of him to have remembered to do this, and Ellie resolved to think of this kindness every time she felt like strangling her new husband—an impulse whose frequency she hoped would decrease.

Ellie left to visit her new solicitor after eating a quick bite of breakfast. No toast, of course; Mrs. Stubbs steadfastly refused to make it, which Ellie thought was just a bit uppity for a housekeeper. But then again, if all she could expect was another brittle, charred square that looked as if it *might* once have originated from a loaf of bread, she wasn't certain it was worth the effort to argue about it.

Then Ellie remembered what she'd seen the night before. Someone had readjusted the stove to her specifications. If she knew what she was doing—and she was still confident she did—then the entire Wycombe household ought to be enjoying lovely toast slathered with lovely jam for the rest of their lives.

Ellie made a mental note to look into it when she returned.

Ellie's new solicitor was a middle-aged man named William Barnes, and it was apparent that Charles had made it very clear that his wife was in charge of her own finances. Mr. Barnes was politeness personified, and he even expressed a large measure of respect for Ellie's financial knowledge and acumen. When she instructed him to put half of her money into a conservative account and half into the risky cotton venture, he clucked approvingly at her appreciation of the value of diversification.

It was the first time Ellie had been able to claim credit for her financial expertise, and she found it a heady feeling, indeed. She liked being able to speak for herself and not having to begin each sentence with, "My father would like . . ." or "It is my father's opinion that . . ."

Her father had never had an opinion on money other than that it was the root of a great deal of evil, and it pleased Ellie to no end to be able to say, "*I* would like to invest my funds in the following way." She supposed that most would consider her eccentric; women did not ordinarily handle their own money. But she didn't care. In fact, she positively reveled in her newfound independence.

By the time she returned to Wycombe Abbey, her spirits were high, and she resolved to improve her efforts to make the grand estate well and truly her home. Her efforts at the Abbey proper had thus far met with nothing but failure, so she decided to spend the rest of the day outside, introducing herself to the tenants. Such an outing would be a worthwhile venture; Ellie knew that landowner-tenant relations often made the difference between prosperous lands and poverty. If there was one thing she'd learned as the daughter of a vicar, it was how to listen to the worries of villagers and help them devise solutions to their problems. As the lady of a great estate, her power and position would be much increased, but Ellie felt confident that the process would be much the same.

This was something she definitely knew how to do.

Of course, she'd also known how to fix stoves and grow roses, and look where that had gotten her.

It was a bit past noon when Ellie returned, and Rosejack informed her that the earl had gone out for a ride. That was just as well; meeting the tenants was something she'd rather do without the imposing presence of the earl behind her. Helen would be a much better choice of companion, and Ellie hoped that she'd be agreeable to such an outing.

As it happened, she was. When Ellie found her in the drawing room, Helen replied, "Oh, but I'd love to. The task of visiting the tenants has rested solely on my shoulders for several years now, and, if truth be told, I'm not terribly good at it."

"Nonsense," Ellie said with a reassuring smile.

"No, it's true. I can be rather shy, and I never know what to say to them."

"Well, then, it's settled. I am more than happy to assume this responsibility, but I will need your assistance this morning to show me about."

The air was crisp when Ellie and Helen got on their way, but the sun was high and bright with the promise of a warm afternoon. It took them about twenty minutes to walk to the first patch of tenants' cottages. Ellie could have probably shaved five minutes off their travel time, but she had long ago learned to adjust her normally brisk and no-nonsense walk to the pace of others.

"This first house belongs to Thom and Bessie Stillwell," Helen said. "They lease a small plot of land where they grow oats and barley. Mrs. Stillwell also takes in mending for a few extra coins."

"Stillwell," Ellie said to herself as she jotted the

name down in a small notebook. "Oats. Barley. Mending." She looked up. "Any children?"

"Two, I think. Oh, wait, it's three now. They had a little girl a few months ago."

Ellie knocked on the door, and they were greeted by a woman of perhaps two and a half decades. "Oh, Mrs. Pallister, how do you do?" she said to Helen, looking rather apologetic. "I wasn't expecting you. May I offer you some tea? I'm afraid I haven't any biscuits."

"No worry, Mrs. Stillwell," Helen replied. "We didn't tell you we were coming, so we certainly cannot expect you to entertain us."

"No, no, of course not," Bessie replied, looking unconvinced. Her gaze shifted to Ellie, and she began to look even more nervous. Clearly she had heard that the earl had married, and was correctly guessing that Ellie was the new countess. Ellie decided that she must immediately put the woman at ease.

"How do you do, Mrs. Stillwell," she said. "I am the new Countess of Billington, and I am very pleased to make your acquaintance."

Bessie dropped a quick curtsy and mumbled her greetings. Ellie wondered what sorts of experiences the tenants had had with the aristocracy for them to be so nervous around her. She smiled her warmest smile and said, "You are the first tenant I have visited. I shall have to rely on you for advice. I am certain you will know the best route for me to take today if I am to meet everyone."

Bessie warmed to the suggestion that she actually could advise a countess, and the rest of the interview proceeded just as nicely as Ellie could have hoped.

She learned that the Stillwell children were called Thom Junior, Billy, and Katey, that they were thinking of buying a new pig, and that there was a small leak in their roof, which Ellie promised to have fixed as soon as possible.

"Oh, but Thom can see to it. He's quite handy," Bessie said. Then she looked down. "We just haven't had the supplies."

Ellie sensed that times had been hard for the Stillwell family this past year. She knew that in Bellfield crops hadn't been as plentiful as usual, and she imagined that farmers had felt the same poor harvest here near Wycombe Abbey. "Then I shall make certain we send the proper supplies over," she said. "It is the very least we can do. No one should have to live with a leaky roof."

Bessie thanked her profusely, and by the end of the day Ellie had had such success with the rest of the tenants that Helen was saying, rather frequently, "I don't know how you do it. You have just met the tenants today, and already I think they would all lay down in front of a speeding carriage for you."

"It is simply a matter of making sure they realize that you are comfortable with them. Once they realize that, they will be comfortable with you."

Helen smiled. "I suppose Mrs. Smith could have little doubt that you were comfortable with her after you climbed up a ladder and inspected the bird's nest in her roof."

"I couldn't very well *not* look at it. If the birds had been pecking into her thatching, they could create serious damage. As it is, I think the nest should be moved to a nearby tree. I am not certain how to do it, though, without disrupting the chicks. I have heard that the mother bird will not tend to her young if a human has touched them."

Helen shook her head. "Where do you learn such things?"

"From my brother-in-law, actually," Ellie said with a wave of her hand. "He has always been quite scientific. Ah, here we are. The last cottage of the day."

"This is the home of Sally Evans," Helen said. "She has been widowed for nearly a year now."

"How sad," Ellie murmured. "How did her husband die?"

"A fever. It swept through the village last year, but his was the only death."

"Is Mrs. Evans able to support herself? Does she have children?"

"No children," Helen replied. "She had been married less than a year. And I am not certain how she makes ends meet. I think she will be looking for a new husband soon. She has a small vegetable garden and a few animals, but when her pigs are gone, I don't know what she'll do. Her husband was a blacksmith, and so she has no land on which to try to grow crops. I doubt she could manage it on her own even if she attempted it."

"Yes," Ellie agreed, lifting her hand to knock on the door, "farming is truly backbreaking work. Surely too much for one woman to do by herself. Or one man, for that matter."

Sally Evans was younger than Ellie had expected, and Ellie could instantly see the lines of grief etched on her pale face. Clearly the woman was still very much in mourning for her husband.

While Helen made the introductions, Ellie looked around the small cottage. It was neat and tidy, but there was a distracted air to it, as if Sally could manage the small tasks of life but couldn't quite tackle the larger ones yet. Everything was in its proper place, but there was a pile of mending as tall as Ellie's hip, and pieces of a broken chair stacked neatly in the corner, waiting to be fixed. The cottage was so cold that Ellie wondered if Sally had lit a fire in days.

During their interview it became apparent that Sally was just going through the motions of life. She and her husband had not been blessed with children, and now she was all alone in her grief.

While Ellie was pondering this, Helen suddenly shivered, and it was a toss up as to who was more embarrassed—Sally for the temperature of her cottage, or Helen for drawing attention to it.

"I am so sorry, Mrs. Pallister," Sally said.

"No, do not worry, it is me, really. I think I am coming down with a touch of a cold, and—"

"You needn't make excuses," Sally interrupted, her face rather melancholy. "It is colder than death in here and we all know it. It is just that there is something wrong with the fireplace, and I haven't gotten around to having it fixed, and—"

"Why don't I have a look at it?" Ellie said, getting to her feet.

Helen looked suddenly and extremely panicked.

"I'm not going to try to fix it," Ellie said with an annoyed expression. "I never try to fix anything I don't know how to fix."

Helen grimaced in such a way that Ellie knew she was dying to bring up the toast incident.

"But I do know how to recognize what is wrong," Ellie continued. "Here, why doesn't one of you help me move this log?"

Sally got up immediately to help her, and a few seconds later Ellie was standing in the fireplace, looking up and seeing nothing. "It's dark as night in here. I say, what happens when you try to light a fire?"

"It spews black smoke everywhere," Sally replied, handing her a lantern.

As her eyes adjusted to the darkness, Ellie looked up and saw right away that the chimney was beyond filthy. "All it needs is a thorough cleaning, in my opinion. We shall send someone over immediately to sweep it out. I am sure the earl would agree with me that—"

"I would agree with you that what?" came an amused voice from the doorway.

Ellie froze. He was not going to be pleased to find her with her head up a chimney.

"Charles!" Helen exclaimed. "What a surprise! Come over here and see—"

"I am certain I heard my lovely wife's voice," he interrupted.

Sally replied, "She has been ever so helpful. My fireplace . . ."

"What?!"

Ellie winced and seriously considered crawling up.

"Eleanor," he said sharply, "remove yourself from the fireplace this instant."

She could see a foothold in the masonry. Just a step or two and she'd be out of sight.

"Eleanor!" Charles, not sounding amused.

"Charles, she was only—" Helen, sounding conciliatory.

"All right, I am coming after you." Charles again, sounding even less amused, although Ellie hadn't really thought that was possible.

"Your lordship! There really isn't room." Sally, sounding quite panicked.

"Eleanor, I will give you to the count of three." Charles again, sounding—well, Ellie didn't really see any point in contemplating how unamused he sounded.

She meant to get out and face the music, she really did. She wasn't naturally a coward, but when he said, "One," she froze, when he said, "Two," she stopped breathing, and if he ever said, "Three," she certainly didn't hear it over the blood rushing in her ears.

Then she felt him squirming into the fireplace beside her, and she suddenly located her brain again, and yelled, "Charles! What the devil are you doing?"

"Trying to pound some sense in that contrary little mind of yours."

"Trying to squeeze it is more like it," Ellie muttered. "Ow!"

"What?" he snapped.

"Your elbow."

"Yes, well, your knee . . ."

"Are you all right?" came Helen's concerned voice.

"Leave us!" Charles roared.

"Well, really, my lord," Ellie said sarcastically, "I think we're quite alone here in—"

"You should really learn when to stop talking, wife."

"Yes, well . . ." Ellie's voice trailed off as she heard

the door slam. She was suddenly very much aware that she was squeezed into a very tight space with her husband, and his body was pressed against hers in ways that ought not be legal.

"Ellie?"

"Charles?"

"Would you care to tell me why you are standing in a fireplace?"

"Oh, I don't know," she drawled, feeling rather proud of herself for her *savoir-faire*, "would you like to tell me why *you* are standing in a fireplace?"

"Ellie, don't test my patience."

Ellie was of the opinion that they had already gone way beyond the testing phase, but she wisely kept that thought to herself. Instead she said, "There wasn't any danger, of course."

"Of course," he replied, and Ellie was impressed despite herself at the amount of sarcasm he managed to pack into those two words. It was a talent, that.

"It would only have been dangerous if there were a fire in the grate, which clearly there wasn't."

"One of these days I'm going to have to strangle you before you kill yourself."

"I wouldn't recommend that course of action," she said weakly, starting to slide downward. If she could just wiggle out before he did, she might be able to buy enough time to make it to the woods. He'd never catch her amidst those trees.

"Eleanor, I—What in God's name are you doing?"

"Umm, just trying to get out," she said, into his belly. That was about as far down as she'd gotten.

Charles groaned. Really groaned. He could feel every inch of his wife's body, and her mouth—her mouth!—was dangerously, deliciously close to his groin, and—

"Charles, are you ill?"

"No," he croaked, trying to ignore the fact that he could feel her mouth move when she spoke, and then trying even harder to ignore the fact that it was moving against his navel.

"Are you certain? You don't sound well."

"Ellie?"

"Yes?"

"Stand back up. Now."

She did, but she had to wiggle an awful lot to get back upright, and after Charles felt her breast against his thigh, then his hip, and then his arm—well, he had to concentrate very hard to keep certain parts of his body from getting any more excited than they already were.

He wasn't successful.

"Ellie?" he said.

"Yes?" She was back to standing, which put her mouth somewhere at the lower part of his neck.

"Tilt your head up. Just a touch."

"Are you certain? Because we might get jammed, and—"

"We're already jammed."

"No, I could wriggle back down and—"

"*Don't* wriggle back down."

"Oh."

Charles took a deep breath. Then she moved. Nothing big, just a slight twist of her hips. But it was enough. And so he kissed her. He couldn't have helped it if France were conquering England, if the sky were falling in, even if his bloody cousin Cecil were inheriting his every last farthing.

He kissed her, and he kissed her, and then he kissed her some more. And then he finally lifted his head for a second—just a second, mind you—to take a breath, and the confounded woman actually managed to get a word in.

"Is that why you wanted me to tilt my head?" she asked.

"Yes, now stop talking."

He kissed her again, and he would have done more, except that they were wedged in so tight that he couldn't have wrapped his arms around her if he tried.

"Charles?" she said, when he took another breath.

"You have a talent for this, you know."

"For kissing?" she asked, sounding more delighted than she'd probably meant to let on.

"No, for rattling on every time I stop to breathe."

"Oh."

"You're rather good at the kissing bit, too, though. A little bit more practice and you'll be superb."

She elbowed him in the ribs, quite a feat considering he couldn't move his own arms an inch. "I'm not going to fall for that old trick," she said. "What I meant to say before you led me into a digression is that Helen and Sally Evans must be terribly worried about us."

"Curious, I imagine, but not worried."

"Yes, well, I think we should try to get out. I'll be terribly embarrassed to see them. I'm sure they know what we're doing, and—"

"Then the harm is already done." He kissed her again.

"Charles!" This time she didn't wait until he took a breath.

"What is it now? I'm trying to kiss you, woman."

"And I'm trying to get out of this bloody chimney." To prove her point, she began to slide back downward, subjecting him to the same erotic torture he'd suffered just a few minutes earlier. Soon she landed on the fireplace floor with a soft thump.

"That ought to do it," she said, crawling out into the cottage and giving him a nice view of her sooty backside. Charles took a few breaths, trying to get a firm rein on his racing body.

"Are you planning to come out?" Ellie asked. She sounded disgustingly chipper.

"Just a moment." He crouched down—moving was much easier now that she'd left the chimney—and crawled out.

"Oh my!" Ellie laughed. "Look at you!"

He glanced down as he sat next to her on the floor. He was covered with soot. "You're rather filthy yourself," he said.

They both laughed, unable to deny the silliness of their appearances, and then Ellie said, "Oh, I forgot to tell you. I visited Mr. Barnes today."

"And was everything arranged to your satisfaction?"

"Oh yes, it was perfect. It was really quite heady, actually, being able to take charge of my finances without subterfuge. And it will be a boon for you, as well."

"How is that?"

"You wanted a wife who won't interfere with your life, correct?"

He frowned. "Er, yes, I suppose I did say that."

"Well, then, it stands to reason that if I have something to keep me busy, I'll stay out of your hair."

He frowned again but didn't say anything.

Ellie exhaled. "You're still angry with me, aren't you?"

"No," he said with a sigh. "But you must stop taking on potentially dangerous tasks."

"It wasn't—"

He held up a hand. "Don't say it, Ellie. Just remember this. You're married now. Your well-being is no longer just your own concern. What hurts you hurts me. So no more unnecessary chances."

Ellie thought that was just about the sweetest thing she'd ever heard, and if they'd been at home, she probably would have thrown herself into his arms on the spot. After a moment, she said, "How did you find us?"

"It wasn't difficult. I simply followed the trail of tenants singing your praises."

She beamed. "I did rather well today, I think."

"Yes, you did," he said softly. "You'll make a fine countess. I always knew you would."

"I'll fix up the muddle I've made at the Abbey, I promise. I checked the oven and—"

"Don't tell me you fiddled with the oven again," he said, looking very much like the most beleaguered man in Britain. "Whatever you do, don't tell me that."

"But—"

"I just don't want to hear it. Tomorrow, maybe. But

not today. I simply don't have the energy to give you the thrashing you deserve."

"Thrashing!" she repeated, her back stiffening in righteous indignation. Before she could go on, however, Helen opened the door to the cottage and poked her head in.

"Oh, good, you're out," she said. "We were beginning to worry about you. Sally was certain you'd be stuck in there all evening."

"Please offer her our apologies," Ellie said. "We have both behaved abominably." When her husband didn't so much as murmur even the barest hint of agreement, she kicked him in the foot. He grunted something, but if it was in English, it wasn't a word Ellie had ever heard before.

She stood, smoothed her skirts—an action that did nothing but get her gloves utterly filthy—and said to the room at large, "I think we ought to be returning to Wycombe Abbey, don't you?"

Helen nodded quickly. Charles didn't say anything, but he did rise to his feet, which Ellie decided to interpret as a "yes." They bid their farewells to Sally and were on their way. Charles had brought a small carriage, which both Ellie and Helen appreciated after a long day on their feet.

Ellie was silent during the ride home, using the time to review the events of the day in her mind. Her visit with Mr. Barnes had been just as splendid as she could have hoped. She had made marvelous headway with the tenants, who now seemed to well and truly accept her as their new countess. And she seemed to have turned some sort of corner with her husband, who, even if he didn't love her, clearly felt something for her that went beyond mere lust and appreciation for the fact that she had saved his fortune.

All in all, Ellie felt remarkably pleased with life.

Chapter 13

Two days later she thought she might like to strangle the entire household. Helen, Claire, the servants, her husband—especially her husband. In fact, the only person she didn't want to strangle was Judith, and that was probably just because the poor girl was only six.

Her success with the tenants had proven to be a short-lived victory. Since then, everything had gone wrong. Everything. All of Wycombe Abbey looked upon her as if she were inept. Good-natured and sweet, but still clumsy and inept. It drove Ellie crazy.

Every day, something new died in her little indoor garden. It had gotten to be a sick little game in her mind—guessing which rosebush had gone to plant heaven each day as she entered the orangery.

Then there was the beef stew she'd made for her husband just to be contrary when he said countesses couldn't cook. It had so much salt that Charles couldn't have hidden the pinched expression on his face even if he'd tried. Which he hadn't. Which irritated her all the more.

Ellie had had to dump the entire pot outside. Even the pigs wouldn't touch it.

"I am sure you *meant* to season it properly," Charles had said while everyone was gagging.

"I did," Ellie hissed, thinking it a wonder that she hadn't ground her teeth down to powder.

"Perhaps you mistook salt for another spice."

"I *know* what salt is," she fairly yelled.

"Ellie," Claire said, just a touch too sweetly. "Clearly the stew is a bit oversalted. You must see that."

"You," Ellie burst out, jabbing her index finger in the fourteen-year-old's direction. "Stop speaking to me as if I were a child. I have had enough of it."

"Surely you misunderstand."

"There is only one thing to understand, and only one person who has some understanding to do." By now Ellie was practically breathing fire, and everyone at the table was agog.

"I married your cousin," Ellie continued. "It doesn't matter if you like it, it doesn't matter if he likes it, it doesn't even matter if *I* like it. I married him, and that is that."

Claire looked as if she were going to protest this tirade, so Ellie cut her off with, "Last time I consulted the laws of Britain and the Church of England, marriage was permanent. So you had better get used to my presence here at Wycombe Abbey, because I'm not going anywhere."

Charles had started to applaud, but Ellie was still so furious with him over the salt comment that she could only glower at him in return. And then, because she was certain she'd do someone bodily harm if she remained in the dining room one moment longer, she stomped off.

But her husband had been hot on her heels. "Eleanor, wait!" he called out.

Against her better judgment, she turned around, but not until she had reached the hall outside the dining room, where the rest of the family would not be able to see her humiliation. He'd called her Eleanor—never a good sign. "What?" she bit off.

"What you said in the dining room," he began.

"I know I ought to be sorry I yelled at a young girl, but I am not," Ellie said defiantly. "Claire has been doing everything in her power to make me feel unwelcome here, and I wouldn't be surprised if—" She cut herself off, realizing that she'd been about to say she wouldn't have been surprised if Claire had been the one to dump so much salt in the stew.

"You wouldn't have been surprised if what?"

"Nothing." He wouldn't make her say it. Ellie refused to make childish and petty accusations.

He waited for a moment for her to continue, and when it became apparent that she would not, he said, "What you said in the dining room ... about marriage being permanent. I wanted you to know that I agree with you."

Ellie only stared at him, not sure what he meant.

"I am sorry if I have bruised your feelings," he said quietly.

Her mouth fell open. He was *apologizing*?

"But I do want you to know that despite these very minor, er, setbacks—"

Ellie's mouth settled into a grim and angry line.

He must not have noticed because he kept talking. "—I think you are becoming a superb countess. Your behavior with the tenants the other day was magnificent."

"Are you telling me I am more suited to life outside Wycombe Abbey than inside?" she asked.

"No, of course not." He exhaled and raked his hand through his thick, brown hair. "I am simply trying to say . . . Hell," he muttered. "What am I trying to say?"

Ellie resisted the urge to make some sort of sarcastic remark and just waited, arms crossed. Finally he thrust a piece of paper in her direction and said, "Here."

"What is this?" she asked, taking it into her hand.

"A list."

"Of course," she murmured. "A list. Just what I wanted. I have been so lucky with lists thus far."

"It is a different sort of list," he said, clearly trying to be patient with her.

Ellie unfolded the sheet and looked down.

ACTIVITIES TO PURSUE WITH WIFE

1. A ride and picnic in the countryside.
2. Revisit the tenants as a unified couple.
3. A trip into London. Ellie needs new dresses.
4. Teach her to write her own lists. They can be devilishly entertaining.

She looked up. "Devilishly entertaining, eh?"

"Mmm, yes. I thought you might like to try something like 'Seven Ways to Silence Mrs. Foxglove.' "

"The suggestion has merit," she murmured, before looking back down at the list.

5. Take her to the seashore.
6. Kiss her until she's senseless.
7. Kiss her until I'm senseless.

Charles could tell the moment when she reached the final two items, for her cheeks turned delightfully pink. "What does this mean?" she finally asked.

"It means, my dear wife, that I have also realized that marriage is permanent."

"I don't understand."

"It is high time we had a normal marriage."

She colored even further at the word "normal."

"However," he continued, "in what must have been a fit of madness, I agreed to your stipulation that you be allowed to get to know me better before we are intimate."

By now she was beyond beet red.

"Therefore, I have decided to give you every opportunity to get to know me better, every last damned chance to grow comfortable in my presence."

"I beg your pardon?"

"Pick something on the list. We'll do it tomorrow."

Ellie's lips parted in delighted surprise. Her husband was actually courting her. She was going to be a wooed woman. She'd never dreamed he'd do something so perfectly romantic. Not that he would ever admit to a romantic bone in his body. Seductive, perhaps. Even rakish, devilish, or amorous. But not romantic.

But she knew better. And that was all that mattered. She smiled and looked back down at the list.

"I suggest number six or seven," he said.

She looked back up. He was grinning in that urbane, devil-may-care fashion of his that must have broken hearts from here to London and back. "I'm not sure I understand the difference," she said, "between kissing me until I'm senseless and kissing me until you're senseless."

His voice dropped to a husky murmur. "I could show you."

"I have no doubt you could," she returned, trying very hard to sound pert even though her heart was racing and her legs felt as steady as marmalade. "But I choose items one and two. It will be very easy for us to picnic and visit the tenants on the same day."

"Items one and two it is, then," he said with a smart bow. "But don't be surprised if I sneak up on you with number six."

"Really, Charles."

He leveled a long, hot stare in her direction. "And seven."

Their outing was scheduled for the very next day. Ellie wasn't particularly surprised by Charles's haste; he had seemed quite determined to do whatever it took to get her into bed. And she was particularly surprised at her own lack of resistance to his plan; she was well aware that she was softening toward him.

"I thought we might ride," Charles said when he met her at noon. "The weather is splendid, and it seems a shame to confine ourselves in a carriage."

"An excellent idea, my lord," Ellie replied. "Or it would be, if I knew how to ride."

"You don't ride?"

"Vicars rarely earn enough to afford mounts," she said with an amused smile.

"Then I shall have to teach you."

"Not today, I hope," she laughed. "I need time to mentally prepare myself for all of the aches and pains I am sure to acquire."

"My curricle is still not repaired from our earlier mishap. Are you up for a constitutional walk?"

"Only if you promise to walk fast," Ellie said with a mischievous grin. "I have never been terribly good at sedate strolls."

"Now why does that not surprise me?"

She looked at him through her lashes. It was a flirtatious expression that was new to her, yet it felt entirely natural in her husband's company. "You're not surprised?" she asked in mock astonishment.

"Let us just say that I have difficulty imagining you attacking life with anything less than complete enthusiasm."

Ellie giggled as she ran ahead of him. "Come along, then. I have yet to attack the day."

Charles followed behind her, matching her run with a gait that was half stride and half lope. "Hold up!" he finally yelled. "Don't forget that I am handicapped by the picnic basket."

Ellie stopped short. "Oh yes, of course. I hope Monsieur Belmont packed something tasty."

"Whatever it is, it smells delicious."

"Some of that roast turkey from yesterday?" she asked hopefully, trying to peer inside the basket.

He held it above his head as he continued down the path. "Now you can't run too far ahead. For I control the food."

"So you plan to starve me into submission?"

"If that is my only chance of success." He leaned

forward. "I am not a proud man. I shall win you by fair means or foul."

"Does starvation count as fair or foul?"

"That, I think, depends upon how long it takes."

As if on cue, Ellie's stomach let out a loud rumble.

"This," Charles said with a slow grin, "is going to be very, very easy."

Ellie scoffed before she continued down the path. "Oh, look!" she exclaimed, stopping before a large oak tree. "Someone hung a swing from this tree."

"My father did it for me when I was eight," Charles recalled. "I swung here for hours."

"Is it still sturdy enough to use?"

"Judith comes here nearly every day."

She looked at him waspishly. "I'm a bit heavier than Judith."

"Not much. Here, why don't you give it a try?"

Ellie smiled girlishly as she sat down on the wooden board that Charles's father had used for a seat. "Will you push?"

Charles swept his body into a courtly bow. "I am your ever faithful servant, my lady." He gave her a starting push, and she began to fly through the air.

"Oh, this is lovely!" she shrieked. "I haven't been on a swing in years."

"Higher?"

"Higher!"

Charles pushed her until she thought her toes might touch the sky.

"Oh, that's quite high enough," she called out. "My stomach is starting to flip about." After she settled down to a more sedate swing, she asked, "Speaking of my poor, beleaguered stomach, do you really plan to starve me into submission?"

He grinned. "I have it planned to the last devious detail. One kiss for a piece of roast turkey, two for a scone."

"There are scones?" Ellie thought she might drool. Mrs. Stubbs might have problems with toast, but the housekeeper made the best scones this side of Hadrian's wall.

"Mmm-hmm. And blackberry jam. Mrs. Stubbs said she slaved over a hot stove for a day to get it just right."

"Jam is not so very difficult," Ellie said with a shrug. "I've made it a thousand times. In fact . . ."

"In fact . . . ?"

"That's a wonderful idea!" she said to herself.

"I don't know why I'm dreading this," he muttered. "Well, in fact I do know. It could have something to do with the fire in my kitchen. Or the odd smells emanating from my orangery. Or perhaps the stew—"

"None of that was my fault," she snapped, stamping her feet on the ground and bringing the swing to a halt. "And if you thought about it for more than half a second, you'd realize that I speak the truth."

Charles decided he'd made a tactical error by bringing up her recent domestic disasters during what was supposed to be an afternoon of seduction. "Ellie," he said in his most conciliatory voice.

She jumped down from the swing and planted her hands on her hips. "Someone is sabotaging me, and I plan to find out why. And whom," she added, almost as an afterthought.

"Perhaps you're right," he murmured, not really meaning it. He just wanted to placate her. But as the words slipped from his mouth, they suddenly rang true. It didn't make sense that Ellie, who seemed so supremely capable in every way, would have set a kitchen on fire, singlehandedly killed every plant in the orangery, and mistaken salt for God only knew what else when she was preparing the beef stew. Even the sorriest dullard couldn't have accomplished quite so much in only a fortnight.

But he didn't want to think of sabotage, nor of fiendish plots nor dead plants. Not today, when he needed to concentrate all of his energies on seducing his wife. "Can we discuss this another day?" he inquired, picking up the picnic basket. "I promise I will look into your allegations, but this is too fine a day to worry over such matters."

Ellie made no reaction for a moment and then nodded. "I don't want to spoil our lovely picnic." Then her eyes crinkled mischievously, and she added, "Monsieur Belmont didn't sneak in any of the leftover beef stew, did he?"

Charles recognized her peace offering and took it. "No, I think you dumped every last bit of it out this morning."

"Ah yes," she murmured. "As I recall, even the pigs wouldn't touch it."

His heart warmed as he watched her. So few people had the ability to laugh at their own foibles. With every passing day, he was developing a deeper appreciation for his wife. He had chosen quickly, but he had chosen well.

Now, he thought with a sigh, if he could only manage to develop an even *deeper* appreciation for her before he exploded.

"Is something wrong?" she asked.

"No. Why?"

"You sighed."

"Did I?"

"Yes, you did."

He sighed again.

"There it is again," she exclaimed.

"I know. It's simply that . . ."

She blinked, a waiting expression on her face, and then finally she prodded him with, "Yes?"

"It's going to have to be number six," he growled, dropping the picnic basket and engulfing her with his arms. "I can't wait another second."

Before Ellie even had a chance to remember what number six entailed, his lips were on hers, kissing her with a fierce possessiveness that was achingly tender. His mouth grew more and more passionate, and his skin turned hot. Without realizing it, he backed her up against a tree, using its sturdy frame to press his body intimately against hers.

He could feel her every curve, from the lush swell of her breasts to the gentle flare of her hips. The wool of her dress was thick, but it didn't hide the way she peaked under his touch. And nothing could have hidden the soft sounds escaping her mouth.

She wanted him. She might not understand it, but she wanted him every bit as much as he wanted her.

He lowered her to the ground, hastily spreading the picnic blanket beneath them. He had long since disposed of her bonnet, and he now loosened her chignon, letting the long strands of hair float between his fingers. "Softer than silk," he whispered. "Softer than the sunrise."

She moaned again, a sound that vaguely resembled his name. Charles grinned, thrilled by the fact that he had inflamed her desire to the point that she couldn't even speak. "I've kissed you senseless," he murmured, his grin sliding into a lazy, masculine smile. "I told you I'd sneak in number six."

"What about seven?" she managed to get out.

"Oh, we're already well past that," he said in a husky voice. He lifted her hand and placed it to his chest. "Feel this."

His heart pounded furiously beneath her small palm, and she looked up at him in wonder. "Me? I did this?"

"You. Only you." His lips found her neck, distracting her while his nimble fingers worked on the buttons of her dress. He had to see her, had to touch her. He'd go insane if he didn't. He was sure of it. He thought about how he'd tortured himself by trying to imagine how long her hair was. Lately he'd been subjecting himself to an even more acute agony, spending his time imagining her breasts. The shape of the them. The size of them. The color of her nipples. The mental exercise always left him in a most uncomfortable state, but he couldn't seem to make himself stop.

The only solution was to get her naked—totally, thoroughly, blessedly naked, and then his imagination could take a break while the rest of him enjoyed reality.

Finally his fingers reached a button near the bottom of her ribs, and he slowly spread open the folds of her dress. She wasn't wearing a corset, just a thin cotton camisole. It was white, almost virginal. It excited him more than the most provocative piece of French lingerie ever could, because *she* was wearing it. And he had never, not once in his life, wanted anyone the way he wanted his wife.

His large hands found the bottom of her camisole and slid beneath, touching the silky warmth of her skin. Her muscles leaped beneath his touch, her stomach instinctively sucking in. He shuddered with need as his hands moved higher, molding themselves over her ribs, then inching even higher until they found the soft, womanly curve of her breast.

"Oh, Charles," she sighed, just as his hands closed around her and gently squeezed.

"Oh, my God," he replied, thinking he might explode then and there. He couldn't see her, but she *felt* perfect. Just the right size for his hands. Hot and sweet and soft, and damn it, if he didn't taste her right then and there, he was going to completely lose control.

Of course there was a very good chance that tasting her would also cause him to lose control, but he forgot that as he pushed her camisole out of the way.

He sucked in his breath when he finally saw her. "My God," he breathed.

Ellie immediately moved to cover herself. "I'm sorry, I—"

"*Don't* say you're sorry," he ordered hoarsely. He'd been a fool when he'd thought that finally seeing her would end the erotic wanderings of his imagination. Reality was so much more exquisite; he doubted that he'd ever be able to resume his daily routine without picturing her in his mind. All the time. Just the way she was right now.

He leaned down and placed the softest of kisses on the underside of her breast. "You're beautiful," he whispered.

Ellie, who had never been called ugly but had certainly not spent her life receiving odes to her beauty, remained silent.

He kissed the underside of her other breast. "Perfect."

"Charles, I know I'm not—"

"Don't say anything unless you're going to agree with me," he said sternly.

She smiled. She couldn't help it.

And then, just when she was about to say something to tease him, his mouth found her nipple and closed around it, and she was lost. Sensation flooded her body, and she couldn't have uttered a word or formulated a thought if she tried.

Which she wasn't. All she was doing was arching her back toward him, pressing herself against his mouth.

"You're better than I dreamed," he murmured against her skin. "More than I imagined." He lifted his head just long enough to gift her with a wicked grin. "And I have a very good imagination."

Once again, she couldn't hold back a tender smile, so touched was she that he was doing so much to keep this first truly intimate experience from overwhelming her. Well, that was not exactly true. He was definitely trying to overwhelm her, working his magic on every last nerve ending in her body, but he was also doing his best to make sure that she had a smile on her face the whole time.

He was a nicer man than he wanted people to think. Ellie felt something warm and sweet moving within her heart, and she wondered if it might be the first stirrings of love.

Moved by a new sense of emotion, she lifted her hands, which had been lying at her sides, and sank them into his thick reddish-brown hair. It was crisp and soft, and she turned his head just so that she could feel his hair against her cheek.

He held her still for a moment, then lifted his body a few inches so that he could gaze down upon her. "My God, Ellie," he said, his words oddly shaky, "how I want you. You'll never know how much . . ."

Ellie's eyes filled with tears at the heartfelt emotion in his voice. "Charles," she began, and then paused to shiver as a chilly wind passed across her bare skin.

"You're cold," he said.

"No," she lied, unwilling to let anything, even the weather, break this beautiful moment.

"Yes, you are." He rolled off of her and began to button her dress. "I'm an animal," he muttered, "seducing you here for the first time outside. Tumbling you on the grass."

"A very nice animal," she tried to joke.

He lifted his face to hers, and his brown eyes burned with emotion she had never seen before. It was hot, and it was fierce, and it was wildly, wonderfully possessive. "When I make you my wife, it will be done properly—in our marriage bed. And then"—he leaned down and dropped a passionate kiss on her mouth—"I'm not going to let you out for a week. Maybe two."

Ellie could only stare at him in amazement, still unable to believe that she could have aroused such passion in this man. He had consorted with the most beautiful women in the world, and yet she, a simple country miss, could set his heart pounding. Then he yanked on her arm, and as she felt herself being dragged back to Wycombe Abbey, she yelped, "Wait! Where are we going?"

"Home. Right now."

"We can't."

He turned around very slowly. "The hell we can't."

"Charles, your language."

He ignored her scolding. "Eleanor, every damned inch of my body is burning for you, and you couldn't possibly deny that you feel the same way. So would you like to give me one good reason why I shouldn't haul you back to the Abbey this minute and make love to you until we both pass out from it?"

She colored at his frank speech. "The tenants. We were to visit them this afternoon."

"Hang the tenants. They can wait."

"But I already sent word to Sally Evans that we would be by in the early afternoon to inspect the work on her chimney."

Charles didn't pause for a moment as he pulled her toward home. "She won't miss us."

"Yes, she will," Ellie persisted. "She has probably cleaned her whole house and prepared tea. It would be the height of rudeness not to show up. Especially after the debacle in her cottage earlier this week."

He thought about the scene in the fireplace, but that

did little to improve his mood. The last thing he needed were memories of being trapped in a very tight space with his wife.

"Charles," Ellie said one last time, "we have to go see her. We don't have any other choice."

"You're not just putting me off, are you?"

"No!" she said, loudly and with great feeling.

He blasphemed out loud and then swore under his breath. "Very well," he muttered. "We visit Sally Evans, but that is all. Fifteen minutes in her cottage and then it's back to the Abbey."

Ellie nodded.

Charles swore again, trying not to dwell on the fact that his body had not yet resumed its normal relaxed state. It was going to be a most uncomfortable afternoon.

Chapter 14

❦

Ellie thought Charles was taking this setback rather well, all in all. He was certainly grumpy, but he was obviously trying to be good-natured about it, even if he wasn't always succeeding.

His impatience showed in a thousand ways. Ellie knew that she would never be able to forget the look on Sally Evans's face as she watched Charles down his entire cup of tea in one extremely fast gulp, clank the cup back onto the saucer, proclaim it the finest beverage of which he'd ever partaken, and grab Ellie's hand and nearly yank her out the front door.

All in ten seconds.

Ellie wanted to be angry with him. She really really did. But she couldn't quite manage it, knowing that his impatience was entirely due to her, to the way he wanted her. And that was too thrilling a feeling for her to ignore.

But it was very important to her that she make a good impression on the villagers, and so when Sally asked if they'd like to inspect the progress on her chimney, Ellie exerted firm pressure on her husband's hand, smiled, and said that they would be delighted.

"It turns out it was a bit more complicated than a regular cleaning," Sally said as they exited the front door. "There was something stuck . . . I'm not really certain what."

"All that matters is that we get it fixed," Ellie replied as she walked outside. "It has been cold of late and it is only going to get colder." She spied a ladder leaning against the side of the cottage. "Here, why don't I go up and take a quick look."

She was only on the second rung when she felt Charles's hands at her waist. In less than a second, she'd been deposited firmly on the ground. "Why don't you stay here," he countered.

"But I want to see—"

"I'll look, if it's so imperative that one of us do so," he grumbled.

There was a small crowd of onlookers gathered around the cottage, all visibly impressed by the earl's hands-on approach to land management. Ellie waited in their midst while Charles scaled the ladder, nearly bursting with pride when she heard such comments as, "He's a right one, the earl," and "Not too hoity-toity to do a spot of work, he is."

Charles moved across the roof and peered into the chimney. "It looks good," he called down.

Ellie wondered if he actually had any prior experience with chimneys upon which to base that opinion, but then decided that that didn't really matter. Charles sounded as if he knew what he was talking about, which was all that really mattered to the tenants, and besides, the man who had done the actual work on the chimney was at her side, and he was assuring her that it was as good as new.

"And so Sally won't have any trouble keeping warm this winter?" she asked him.

John Bailstock, the mason and chimney sweep, replied, "None at all. In fact, she—"

His words were cut off by a sudden cry of, "God almighty! The earl!"

Ellie looked up in horror to see her husband tottering near the top of the ladder. She was momentarily frozen to the spot, feeling as if time were passing before her at half its usual speed. The ladder was making an awful splintering noise, and before she could react, Charles was falling through the air, through the ladder, actually, which was practically crumbling before her eyes.

She screamed and ran forward, but by the time she reached him he had already hit the ground, and he looked terribly still.

"Charles?" she choked out, falling to her knees beside him. "Are you all right? Please tell me that you're all right."

He opened his eyes, thank God. "Why is it," he said wearily, "that I always manage to injure myself when you're near?"

"But I didn't have anything to do with this!" she returned, utterly horrified by his implication. "I know you think I botched the stove, and the orangery, and—"

"I know," he interrupted. His voice was barely audible but he did manage a tiny smile. "I was teasing."

Ellie breathed a sigh of relief. If he could tease her, then he couldn't be that hurt, could he? She willed herself to calm down, sternly telling her heart to stop racing—never could she remember feeling such a paralyzing fright. She needed to be strong just then; she needed to be her usual self—efficient, calm, and capable.

And so she took a deep breath and said, "Where are you hurt?"

"Would you believe me if I said everywhere?"

She cleared her throat. "Actually, I would. That was quite a tumble."

"I don't think I've broken anything."

"All the same, I'd feel better if I checked myself." She started feeling his limbs and inspecting his body. "How does this feel?" she asked as she prodded a rib.

"It hurts," he said plainly. "Although that might be residual pain from our carriage accident before we married."

"Oh, goodness. I'd forgotten all about that. You must think I'm some sort of bad luck charm."

He only closed his eyes, which wasn't quite the, "Of course not!" Ellie had been hoping for. She moved on to his arm, but before she could ascertain whether he'd broken or sprained it, her fingers met with something hot and sticky.

"Good heavens!" she burst out, staring at her red-stained fingers in shock. "You're bleeding? You're bleeding!"

"Am I?" He turned his head and looked at his arm. "I am."

"What happened?" she asked frantically, inspecting his arm even more carefully than before. She'd heard of injuries in which broken bones protruded through the skin. Lord help them if that was the case with Charles; Ellie had no idea how to treat such an injury, and more to the point, she was fairly certain she'd faint before she had a chance to try.

A villager stepped forward and said, "My lady, I think he sliced his skin on a piece of the ladder as he fell."

"Oh yes, of course." Ellie looked over at the ladder, which was laying on the ground in several pieces. Several men were gathered around it, inspecting the remains. "There's a bit of blood on the wood," one of them told her.

She shook her head and turned back to her husband. "You're going to be full of splinters," she said.

"Lovely. I suppose you're going to want to remove them?"

"It's the sort of thing wives do," she said patiently. "And I *am* your wife, after all."

"As I was just beginning to appreciate fully," he muttered. "Very well, do your worst."

Once Ellie got started on a task, there was no stopping her. She had three villagers help her move Charles back into Sally Evans's house and sent two more to Wycombe Abbey to fetch a well-sprung carriage to bring them home. Sally was asked to make bandages out of an old petticoat—which Ellie assured her would be replaced posthaste.

"And boil some water," Ellie requested.

Sally turned around, holding a ceramic pitcher. "Boil it? Wouldn't you rather get started cleaning his wound with what I have here?"

"I would certainly prefer water at room-temperature," Charles interjected. "I have no desire to add burns to my current list of injuries and ailments."

Ellie planted her hands on her hips. "Boil it. At least get it hot. I know that I feel cleaner when I wash with hot water. Therefore it stands to reason that it would do a better job cleaning your wound. And I know that we're not supposed to leave behind any bits of wood."

"I'll boil it, then," Sally said. "Good thing the chimney is fixed."

Ellie went back to work tending to her husband. None of his bones were broken, but he had sustained a number of bruises. She used a pair of tweezers borrowed from Sally to pluck out all of the splinters in his upper arm.

She tweezed. Charles winced.

She tweezed again. He winced again.

"You can yell if it hurts you," she said softly. "I won't think less of you."

"I don't need to—Ow!"

"Oh, I'm sorry," she said sincerely. "I was distracted."

He grumbled something she didn't quite understand, and she had a feeling she wasn't meant to. She forced herself to stop looking at his face—which she'd realized she quite enjoyed looking at—and concentrated on his wounded arm. After several minutes she was satisfied that she'd removed all of the wood.

"Please say you're done," Charles said when she'd announced that she'd gotten the last of it.

"I'm not certain," she replied, her face scrunching as she examined his injury yet again. "I've removed all of the splinters, but I'm not sure what to do about the primary gash. It might need stitching."

He blanched, and she wasn't sure if it was at the

thought of his requiring stitches or her performing them.

Ellie pursed her lips in thought and then called out, "Sally, what do you think? Stitches?"

Sally came over, carrying a kettle of hot water. "Oh, yes. He definitely needs stitches."

"Couldn't I obtain a professional opinion?" Charles asked.

"Is there a doctor nearby?" Ellie asked Sally.

Sally shook her head.

Ellie turned back to Charles. "No, you can't. I'm going to have to stitch you up."

He closed his eyes. "Have you done this before?"

"Of course," she lied. "It's just like stitching a quilt. Sally, have you any thread?"

Sally had already removed a spool from her sewing box and placed it on the table next to Charles. Ellie dabbed a piece of cloth into the hot water and wiped off his wound. "So it will be clean before I close it up," she explained.

When she finished that task, she broke off a piece of thread, and then dunked it in the hot water for good measure. "Might as well do the same for the needle," she said to herself, and then dunked that as well. "Here we go," she said with forced cheerfulness. His skin looked so pink and healthy and well... alive. Rather unlike the last hemline she'd sewn.

"Are you sure you've done this before?"

She smiled tightly. "Would I lie to you?"

"You don't want me to answer that."

"Charles!"

"Just get on with it."

She took a deep breath and plunged in. The first

stitch was the worst, and Ellie soon found out that her little lie actually had some truth to it—it *was* a bit like stitching a quilt. She attacked her task with the same devotion and singleminded concentration she used with all of life's work, and soon Charles had a row of neat, tight stitches in his arm.

He had also consumed what was left of Sally Evans's only bottle of brandy.

"We'll replace that, too," Ellie said with an apologetic smile.

"Buy you a whole new coddage," Charles slurred.

"Oh, that's not necessary," Sally said quickly. "This one's as good as new, what with the chimney working now."

"Ah, yes," he said expansively. "Nice chimney. I saw it. Did you know I saw it?"

"We all know you saw it," Ellie said in her most patient tone. "We watched you on the roof."

" 'Course you did." He smiled, then hiccupped.

Ellie turned to Sally and said, "He tends to get a little silly when he's drunk."

"And who could blame him?" Sally replied. "I would have needed two bottles of brandy if I were receiving those stitches."

"And I would have needed three," Ellie said, patting Charles's arm. She didn't want him worrying that they thought any less of him for drinking spirits to dull the pain.

But Charles was still stuck on the comment about his being drunk. "I'm not drunk!" he said indignantly. "A gennleman never gets drunk."

"Is that so?" Ellie said with a patient smile.

"A gennleman gets *foxed*," he said with a resolute nod. "I'm *foxed*."

Ellie noticed that Sally was covering her mouth to hide a grin. "I wouldn't mind taking you up on a second cup of tea while we wait for the carriage," she said to her hostess.

"You won't have time," Sally replied. "I see it coming around the bend."

"Thank heavens," Ellie said. "I'd really like to put him to bed."

"You joining me?" Charles said as he staggered to his feet.

"My lord!"

"I wouldn't mind taking up where we left off." He paused to hiccup three times in rapid succession. "If you know what I mean."

"My lord," Ellie said sternly, "the brandy has made your tongue deplorably loose."

"Has it? I wonder what it's done to *your* tongue." He swayed toward her, and Ellie darted out of the way just seconds before his lips would have connected with hers. Unfortunately, this caused him to lose his balance, and he tumbled to the floor.

"Heavens above!" Ellie burst out. "If you've torn open your stitches, God help me, I will flay you alive."

He blinked and planted his hands on his hips. This didn't lend him much dignity, however, as he was still sitting on the floor. "That seems rather counter-productive, don't you think?"

Ellie let out a long-suffering sigh. "Sally, will you help me in setting the earl on his feet?"

Sally immediately moved to help her, and in a few

moments they had Charles on his feet and out the door. Thankfully, three grooms had come with the carriage. Ellie didn't think that the two women would have been able to get him into it on their own.

The ride home was uneventful, as Charles fell asleep. Ellie was grateful for that—it was a most welcome respite. She had to wake him up again when they arrived home, however, and by the time she and the grooms got him up to his room, she thought she might scream. He had tried to kiss her fourteen times on the stairs, which wouldn't have bothered her so much if he weren't drunk, completely heedless of the presence of the servants, and in danger of bleeding to death if he fell and broke open his stitches.

Well, she privately allowed, he probably wasn't going to bleed to death, but it certainly made for an effective threat when she finally lost her temper and yelled, "Charles, if you don't stop this this instant, I am going to let you fall and you can bleed to death for all I care!"

He blinked. "Stop what?"

"Trying to kiss me," she ground out, quite unhappy that she'd been forced to say the words in front of the servants.

"Why not?" He leaned forward again, his lips puckered.

"Because we are on the stairs."

He cocked his head and regarded her with a puzzled expression. "Funny how you can talk without opening your mouth."

Ellie tried to unclench her teeth this time before speaking, but she wasn't successful. "Just keep going up the stairs and to your room, if you please."

"And then I can kiss you?"

"Yes! Fine!"

He sighed happily. "Oh, good."

Ellie groaned and tried to ignore the way the footmen were trying to hide their grins.

A minute or so later they nearly had him into his room, but Charles suddenly stopped short and blurted out. "Do you know what your problem is, Ellie, m'dear?"

She kept trying to push him down the hall. "What?"

"You're too damned good at everything."

Ellie wondered why that didn't sound like a compliment.

"I mean—" He waved his good arm expansively, causing him to lurch forward, which required Ellie and both of the footmen to grab him before he tumbled to the ground.

"Charles, I don't think this is the time," she said.

"Y'see," he said, ignoring her, "I thought I wanted a wife I could ignore."

"I know." Ellie looked desperately at the footmen as they pushed Charles onto his bed. "I believe I can handle him from here."

"Are you certain, my lady?"

"Yes," she muttered. "With any luck he'll pass out soon."

The footmen looked dubious, but they filed out nonetheless.

"Close the door behind you!" Charles hollered.

Ellie spun around and crossed her arms. "You do *not* make an attractive drunk, my lord."

"Really? You once told me you liked me best drunk."

"I have reconsidered."

He sighed. "Women."

"The world would be a far less civilized place without us," she said with a sniff.

"I agree wholeheartedly." He burped. "Now, where was I? Oh yes, I wanted a wife so I could ignore her."

"A fine specimen of English good cheer and chivalry, you are," she said under her breath.

"What was that? Didn't hear you. Ah well, doesn't matter. Anyway, here is what happened."

Ellie looked at him with an expression of sarcastic eagerness.

"I ended up with a wife who can ignore *me*." He jabbed himself in the chest and yelped, "Me!"

She blinked. "I beg your pardon."

"You can do anything. Stitch up my arm, make a fortune. Well, aside from blowing up my kitchen . . ."

"Now, see here!"

"Hmm, and you did mess up the orangery something awful, but I did receive a note from Barnes calling you quite the most intelligent female he'd ever met. And the tenants like you better than they ever liked me."

She crossed her arms. "Do you have a point?"

"No." He shrugged. "Well, I probably do, but I'm having a bit of trouble getting to it."

"I would never have noticed."

"Thing is, you don't need me for a damned thing."

"Well, that is not entirely true . . ."

"Isn't it?" He suddenly looked a touch more sober

than he had the moment before. "You've got your money. You've got your new friends. What the hell do you need a husband for? I'm clearly ignorable."

"I'm not sure I'd say *that* . . ."

"I could make you need me, I s'pose."

"Why would you want to? You don't love me."

He pondered that for a moment, and then said. "Don't know. But I do."

"You love me?" she asked disbelievingly.

"No, but I want you to need me."

Ellie tried to ignore the way her heart sank a little when he replied in the negative. "Why?" she asked again.

He shrugged. "I don't know. I just want you to. Now get into bed."

"I certainly will not!"

"D'you think I don't remember what we were doing out in the meadow?"

Her cheeks turned pink, but Ellie honestly wasn't sure if it was from embarrassment or fury.

Charles sat up and leered at her. "I'm eager to finish what we started, wife."

"Not when you're three sheets to the wind!" she retorted, stepping back so that she wouldn't be within arm's reach. "You're liable to forget what you're about."

He gasped, clearly gravely insulted. "I would *neber*—that is to say, *never* forget what I am about. I am an excellent lover, my lady. Superb."

"Is that what all your mistresses have told you?" she could not resist asking.

"Yes. No!" He muttered, "This isn't the sort of thing one wants to talk about with one's wife."

"Exactly. Which is why I'm going to take my leave."

"Oh, no you're not!" With speed that no one who'd imbibed a bottle of brandy should have possessed, he hopped off the bed, dashed across the room, and grabbed her around the waist. By the time Ellie caught her breath she was lying on the bed, and Charles was lying on top of her.

"Hello, wife," he said, looking very much like a wolf.

"A tipsy wolf," she muttered, trying not to cough on the fumes.

He cocked an eyebrow. "You did say I could kiss you."

"When?" she asked suspiciously.

"On the stairs. I pestered and pestered and pestered and you finally said, 'Yes! Fine!' "

Ellie let out an irritated breath. It figured that his memory would still be in perfect working order.

He grinned triumphantly. "The nice thing about you, Ellie, is that you are fundamentally incapable of going back on your word."

She wasn't about to tell him to go ahead and kiss her, nor could she refute his statement—which was, after all, something of a compliment—so she didn't say anything.

That plan backfired, however, for his next words were, "Terribly sporting of you not to start blabbering on, dear wife. Makes it hard to find your mouth."

Then he was kissing her, and Ellie discovered that brandy tasted an awful lot better than it smelled. So much better, in fact, that when he moved to kiss her neck, she surprised herself and grabbed his head to drag his mouth back to hers.

This gave him cause to chuckle, and he kissed her again, this time more deeply. After what seemed like an eternity of this sensual torture, he lifted his head a couple of inches, rested his nose against hers, and said her name.

It was a moment before she was able to say, "Yes?"

"I'm not nearly as foxed as you think I am."

"You're not?"

Slowly, he shook his head.

"But—but you were stumbling. Hiccupping. Burping!"

He smiled at her in amazement. "But I'm not any longer."

"Oh." Ellie's lips parted as she tried to digest this news and decide what it meant. She *thought* it might mean that they were going to consummate their marriage that evening—that hour, in all probability. But she was feeling strangely befuddled, and to be honest rather *hot*, and her brain simply wasn't running at optimum speed.

He stared at her for several moments more, then lowered himself back down to kiss her again. His lips touched everything but her mouth—traveling to her cheeks, her eyes, her ears. His hands were in her hair, streaming it out over the pillows. And then they were running down the length of her body, smoothing over the curve of her hips, caressing the length of her legs, leaving trails of fire wherever they touched.

Ellie felt as if there were two women inhabiting her body. Part of her wanted to lay there and let him work his magic on her, to accept his lovemaking like a rare gift. But part of her yearned to be an active participant, and she wondered what he would do if she touched him back, if she lifted her head and rained soft kisses on *his* neck.

In the end, she couldn't keep her feelings inside. She had always been a doer, and it wasn't in her nature to be passive, even if the activity in question was her own seduction. Her arms wrapped around him and squeezed him tight, and her fingers became passionate claws, and—

"Aaaaargh!" Charles's bloodcurdling scream ripped through the air and quite effectively dampened her ardor.

Ellie let out a surprised yelp and squirmed beneath him, trying to bring her hands down to her sides, and—

"Aaaaaaaaaaaaaaaaaaaargh!" As screams went, this one was worse.

"What on earth?" she finally demanded, wiggling to the side as he rolled off of her, his face a pinched mask of pain.

"You're going to kill me," he said in a dull monotone. "I will be dead before the year is out."

"What the devil are you talking about?"

He sat up and looked at his arm, which had begun to bleed again.

"Did I do that?"

He nodded. "That was the second scream."

"And the first?"

"A bruise on my back."

"I didn't know your back was bruised."

"Neither did I," he said dryly.

Ellie felt extremely inappropriate laughter welling

up within her, and she bit her lip. "I'm terribly sorry."

He only shook his head. "Someday I'm going to consummate this damned marriage."

"You could always try to look on the bright side," she suggested.

"There is a bright side?"

"Er, yes. There must be." But she couldn't think of one.

He sighed and held out his arm. "Stitch me up?"

"Are you going to want more brandy?"

"It'll probably put an end to any amorous intentions I have for the evening, but yes, I would." He sighed. "Do you know, Ellie, but I think this is why people get themselves wives."

"I beg your pardon?"

"I hurt everywhere. Everywhere. It's nice to have someone I can say that to."

"Didn't you before?"

He shook his head.

She touched his hand. "I'm glad you can talk to me." Then she found a spool of thread and a bottle of brandy and got to work.

Chapter 15

As was her habit, Ellie awakened bright and early the next morning. What was out of the ordinary, however, was the fact she was lying on Charles's bed, snuggled up quite close to him, with his arm thrown over her shoulder.

He had fallen asleep very quickly the previous night after she had stitched up his arm for the second time. He'd had a tiring and painful day, and the additional bottle of brandy hadn't helped. Ellie had wanted to leave him to his rest, but every time she tried to ease herself from the bed and creep into her own room, he grew agitated. She had finally dozed off on top of his blankets.

She slipped quietly out of the room, not wanting to awaken him. He still slept quite soundly, and she suspected that he needed his rest.

Ellie, however, was physically incapable of sleeping late; after changing out of her crumpled gown, she wandered downstairs for breakfast. Not surprisingly, Helen was already at the table, perusing the newspaper that arrived in the mail each day from London.

"Good morning, Ellie," Helen said.

"Good morning to you."

Ellie sat down, and it was only a moment before Helen asked, "What was the commotion last evening? I heard that Charles was quite beyond foxed."

Ellie recounted the details of the previous day as she smoothed orange marmalade on one of Mrs. Stubbs's freshly baked scones. "That reminds me . . ." she said when she'd finished telling Helen of Charles's second bout with stitches.

"Reminds you of what?"

"I was trying to think of something special we could do for the tenants as winter and the holidays approach, and I thought I might make them homemade jam."

Helen's hand froze in midair as she reached for another scone. "I don't suppose this will involve your entering the kitchen again."

"It will be a special surprise, as they would never expect a countess to actually cook."

"There might be a reason for that. Although in your case, I believe people have given up trying to figure out *what* to expect."

Ellie scowled at her. "I assure you that I have made jam hundreds of times."

"Oh, I believe you. I just don't think anyone else will. Especially Mrs. Stubbs, who is still complaining that she keeps finding soot in the kitchen corners."

"Mrs. Stubbs merely likes to complain."

"That is, of course, true, but I'm still not sure—"

"*I'm* sure," Ellie said emphatically, "and that is all that counts."

By the time breakfast was finished, Ellie had convinced Helen to help her prepare the jam, and two kitchen maids were sent to town to buy berries. An hour later they returned from town with large quantities of assorted berries and Ellie was ready to get to work. As expected, Mrs. Stubbs was not pleased to see Ellie in her kitchen.

"No no no!" she yelled. "The oven was bad enough!"

"Mrs. Stubbs," Ellie said in her sternest voice, "may I remind you that I am the mistress of this house, and if I want to smear lemon curd up and down the walls, it is my right."

Mrs. Stubbs paled and looked to Helen in terror.

"She is exaggerating," Helen quickly explained. "But perhaps it would be best if you worked outside the kitchen."

"An excellent idea," Ellie agreed, and she practically pushed the housekeeper out the door.

"Somehow I don't think Charles will be happy to hear about this," Helen said.

"Nonsense. He knows that the fire wasn't my fault."

"Does he?" Helen asked dubiously.

"Well, if he doesn't, he should. Now then, let us begin our work." Ellie instructed a scullery maid to pull out Wycombe Abbey's largest pot, and then she dumped the berries into it. "I suppose we could make several different types of jam," she said to Helen, "but I think a mixed berry jam will be delicious."

"And," Helen said, "we can do it all in one pot."

"You're catching on quickly." Ellie smiled and then proceeded to add sugar and water. "We shall probably have to make another batch, though. I doubt this will be enough for all of the tenants."

Helen leaned forward and peered in. "Probably not. But if it's truly this easy, I don't see why that should be a worry. We can simply make another potful tomorrow."

"This is really all there is to it," Ellie said. "Now we just need to cover it up and let the mixture cook." She moved the pot to the perimeter of the stovetop, away from the firebox which burned at its hottest directly underneath the center of the cooking surface. She didn't need any more accidents in the kitchen.

"How long will it take?" Helen asked.

"Oh, most of the day. I could try to cook it faster, but then I would have to monitor the jam more closely, and stir it more frequently. With all that sugar it's likely to stick to the bottom. As it is, I will have to have one of the maids stir it while I'm gone. I shall come back every hour or so to check on its progress."

"I see."

"My brother-in-law once suggested I put rocks on the lid. He said it would cook even faster."

"I see," Helen said automatically, and then she added, "No, actually I don't see."

"It keeps the steam inside, which increases the pressure. That, in turn, allows the jam to cook at a hotter temperature."

"Your brother-in-law must be quite scientific."

"Yes, he is quite." Ellie set the lid on the pot and added, "It is of no matter, anyway. I'm in no rush. I only have to make sure the maids stir it frequently."

"That sounds easy enough," Helen said.

"Oh, it is. Completely foolproof." Ellie held her hand a few inches above the stovetop one last time to check that the heat was not too high, and then they left the kitchen.

Ellie pinned a watch onto her sleeve so that she would remember to check on the jam at appropriate intervals. It cooked slowly but evenly and, in Ellie's opinion, tasted delicious. The pot was thick and didn't get too hot over the low heat, so Ellie was able to grip the handles as she stirred, which was an added convenience.

Since her preparations did not require her undivided attention, she decided to turn some of her energies over to the smelly mess in the orangery. It irked her to no end that she hadn't yet been able to deduce how the saboteur was killing off all of her favorite plants. All that she had been able to figure out was that the smell was not coming from the plants themselves.

The plants were quite dead, that much was irrefutable. But the smell was coming from discreetly placed piles of kitchen garbage that Ellie suspected had been intercepted on their way to a pigpen. Mixed in with the garbage was a suspicious brown substance that could only have been obtained from the ground of the stables.

Whoever wanted to cause her trouble must be very devoted to the cause. Ellie couldn't imagine hating anyone enough to gather horse droppings and rotten food on a daily basis. However, she did love her little indoor garden enough to don a pair of working gloves and haul the smelly mess outside. She located a few sacks and a shovel, resolved not to breathe through her nose for the next hour or so, and dug in.

After five minutes, however, it became apparent that her skirts were getting in her way, so she found some twine and sat down on a stone bench to tie them up.

"A charming sight."

Ellie looked up to see her husband entering the orangery. "Good morning, Charles."

"I have often wished you would lift your skirts for me," he said with a lopsided grin. "Who is the lucky recipient of so charming a gesture?"

She forgot her dignity and stuck out her tongue at him. " 'What' would be a more appropriate word."

Charles followed her gaze to the stinking pile tucked away behind an orange tree. He stepped forward, sniffed the air, and recoiled. "God in heaven, Ellie," he said with a gag and a cough. "What have you done to the plants?"

"It wasn't me," she ground out. "Do you really think I'm stupid enough to think that a rotting sheep's head would help an orange tree to thrive?"

"A *what*?" He walked back over to the tree to get a closer look.

"I've already cleared it away," she said, pointing to her sack.

"Good God, Ellie, you shouldn't have to do this."

"No," she agreed, "I shouldn't. Someone here at Wycombe Abbey clearly does not appreciate my presence. But if you will pardon my pun, I am going to get to the bottom of this mess if it kills me. I won't tolerate this situation any longer."

Charles let out a deep breath and watched as she plunged her shovel into the mess.

"Here," she said, "you can hold the bag open. Although you might want to use some work gloves."

He blinked, unable to believe that she was cleaning this up on her own. "Ellie, I can ask the servants to do this."

"No, you can't," she said, quickly and with more emotion than he would have expected. "They shouldn't have to do this. I'm not going to ask them to."

"Ellie, that is precisely why we *have* servants. I pay them very generous wages to keep Wycombe Abbey clean. This is simply a . . . *smellier* mess than usual."

She looked up at him with suspiciously bright eyes. "They are going to think I did this. I don't want that."

Charles realized that her pride was at stake. Since he knew a thing or two about pride himself, he didn't press her. Instead he said, "Very well. I must insist, however, that you let me wield the shovel. What kind of husband would I be if I sat here and watched while you do all of the hard labor?"

"Absolutely not. You've an injured arm."

"It's not that bad."

She let out a snort. "Perhaps you forget that I am the one who stitched you up last night. I know precisely how bad it is."

"Eleanor, give me the shovel."

"Never."

He crossed his arms and regarded her with a level gaze. God, she was stubborn. "Ellie," he said, "the shovel, if you please."

"No."

He shrugged. "All right. You win. I won't shovel."

"I knew you would see it my—yikes!"

"My arm," Charles said as he yanked her against him, "is working quite well, actually."

The shovel fell to the ground as Ellie twisted her neck to look at him. "Charles?" she asked hesitantly.

He smiled wolfishly. "I thought I might kiss you."

"Here?" she croaked.

"Mmm-hmm."

"But it smells."

"I can ignore it if you can."

"But why?"

"Kiss you?"

She nodded.

"I thought it might get you to stop talking about that ridiculous shovel." Before she could say anything more, he swooped his head down and settled his mouth firmly on hers. She didn't relax right away; he didn't expect her to. But it was so damned fun to hold that overly-determined, wiggling little woman in his arms. She was like a tiny lion, fierce and protective, and Charles found that he wanted all of that emotion directed toward him. Somehow her insistence that he rest while she did the hard labor didn't make him feel like less of a man. It just made him feel loved.

Loved? Was that what he wanted? He'd thought he wanted a marriage like his parents'. He would lead his own life, his wife would lead hers, and they would both be content. Except that he was drawn to his new bride in a way he'd never anticipated, never even dreamed possible. And he *wasn't* content. He wanted her, wanted her desperately, and she was always just out of his reach.

Charles lifted his head an inch and looked down at her. Her eyes were unfocused, her lips were soft and parted, and he didn't know why he had never noticed this before, but she had to be the most beautiful woman in the entire world, and she was right there in his arms, and . . .

. . . and he had to kiss her again. Now. His mouth devoured hers with a new and startling urgency, and he drank in her essence. She tasted like warm berries, sweet and tangy and pure Ellie. His hands bunched the fabric of her skirts, pulling it up until he could reach underneath and grasp the firm skin of her thigh.

She gasped and clutched his shoulders, which only served to make him even hotter, and he slid his hand up until he reached the spot where her stockings ended. He stroked his finger along her bare skin, glorying in the way she shivered at his touch.

"Oh, Charles," she moaned, and that was enough to set him on fire. Just the sound of his name on her lips.

"Ellie," he said, his voice so hoarse he barely recognized it, "we have to go upstairs. Now."

She didn't react for a moment, just sagged against him, and then she blinked and said, "I can't."

"Don't say that," he said, dragging her toward the door. "Say anything but that."

"No, I have to stir the jam."

That stopped him in his tracks. "What the devil are you talking about?"

"I have to . . ." She paused and wet her lips. "Don't look at me like that."

"Like what?" he drawled, his good humor slowly returning.

She planted her hands on her hips and leveled a

stern look in his direction. "Like you want to gobble me up."

"But I do."

"Charles!"

He shrugged. "My mother told me never to lie."

She looked as if she were about to stamp her foot. "I really must leave."

"Wonderful. I'll accompany you upstairs."

"I have to go to the kitchen," she said pointedly.

He sighed. "Not the kitchen."

Her mouth clamped itself into a straight, angry line before she ground out, "I'm making jam to give to the tenants as a holiday gift. I told you about it yesterday."

"Very well, then. The kitchen. And then the bedroom."

"But I . . ." Ellie let her words trail off as she realized that she didn't want to fight him any longer. She wanted his hands on her, she wanted to listen to his soft words of seduction. She wanted to feel like she was the most desirable woman in the world, which was exactly how she felt every time he looked at her with that smoldering, heavy-lidded gaze of his.

Her mind made up, she smiled shyly and said, "All right."

Charles obviously hadn't expected her agreement, because he blurted out, "You will?"

She nodded, not quite meeting his eyes.

"Brilliant!" He looked like an excited young boy, which seemed a little strange to Ellie, considering that she was about to let herself be seduced by him.

"But I have to go to the kitchen first," she reminded him.

"The kitchen. Right. The kitchen." He shot her a sideways glance as he pulled her into the hall. "It takes a bit of the spontaneity away, don't you think?"

"Charles," she said in a warning tone.

"Very well." He switched direction and started dragging her toward the kitchen, moving even faster than he had when he'd been dragging her toward the bedroom.

"Trying to make up for lost time in advance?" she joked.

He pulled her around a corner, pinned her against a wall, and joined his mouth to hers for a brief, proprietary kiss. "You have three minutes in the kitchen," he said. "Three. That is all."

Ellie giggled and nodded, willing to allow him this dictatorial streak because it made her feel all warm inside. He released her again, and they made their way downstairs, Ellie practically having to run to keep up with him.

The kitchen was beginning to bustle with activity as Monsieur Belmont and his staff began their preparations for the day's meals. Mrs. Stubbs was off in a corner, trying to ignore the Frenchman as she supervised the three maids who were cleaning up after breakfast.

"That's my jam on the stove right over there," Ellie said to Charles, pointing to the large pot. "Mixed berry. Helen and I prepared it together, and—"

"Three minutes, Eleanor."

"Right. I just need to stir it, and then—"

"Just stir it," he said.

She walked halfway to the stove and then said, "Oh! I really should wash my hands first. I was wearing work gloves in the orangery, of course, but the mess was so foul."

Charles sighed impatiently. Really, the chit could have been done and gone by now. "Wash your hands, stir, and be done with it. There's a bucket right over on that table."

She smiled, dunked her hands into the water, and then let out a little shriek.

"What now?"

"It's freezing. Monsieur Belmont must have had ice brought up. Perhaps we will have an iced fruit for dessert this evening."

"Ellie, the jam . . ."

She reached out for the pot, scowling as the servants edged away from her. Clearly, they still didn't trust her in the kitchen. "Here, I'm just going to move it to this table over here, where it can cool and—"

Charles would never be quite certain what happened next. He had been watching Monsieur Belmont expertly chop an aubergine when he heard Ellie let out a cry of pain. When he looked up, the large pot of jam was falling to the ground. As he watched in helpless horror, the pot hit the ground and the lid bounced off. Purple jam flew through the air, splattering the stove, splattering the floor, and splattering Ellie.

She howled like an injured animal and collapsed upon herself, sobbing in agony. Charles felt his heart stop and he ran to her side, his boots sliding through the hot, sugary jam as he raced across the kitchen.

"Get it off me," she whimpered. "Get it off me."

Charles looked at her and saw that the boiling jam was stuck to her skin. Good God, her skin was still being burned as he stood there watching. It appeared to be exclusively on her hands and wrists. Without taking time to think, he grabbed the bucket of cold water she'd used earlier and plunged her hands into it.

She jerked against him and tried to yank her hands out. "No," she cried out. "It's too cold."

"Darling, I know it's cold," he said softly, hoping she couldn't hear the way his voice was shaking. "I have my hands in the water, too."

"It hurts. Oh, it hurts."

Charles swallowed and looked around the kitchen. Surely someone would know what to do, how to make her pain go away. It killed him to hear her whimpers, to feel the way her body shuddered. "Shhh, Ellie," he said in his most soothing voice. "Look, the jam is washing away. See?"

She looked down at her hands in the water, and Charles immediately wished he hadn't asked her to. Her skin was a bright and angry red where the jam had washed off.

"Get me more ice," he barked at no one in particular. "The water is growing too warm."

Mrs. Stubbs stepped forward even as three maids scurried to the icehouse. "My lord, I'm not certain that you have chosen the best course of action."

"The jam was still boiling hot. I had to cool it down."

"But she's shaking."

He turned to Ellie. "Does it hurt as much?"

She shook her head. "I can hardly feel anything."

Charles bit his lower lip. He wasn't at all certain as

to the best way to treat a burn. "Very well. Perhaps we should get you bandaged."

He allowed her to lift her hands from the bucket, but it was only ten seconds before she was whimpering in pain again. He plunged her hands back into the water just as the maids returned with ice. "Something about the cold water eases her pain," he told Mrs. Stubbs.

"She can't stay there forever."

"I know. Just another minute. I want to be sure."

"Would you like me to prepare a special burn pomatum for her?"

Charles nodded and returned his attention to Ellie. He held her tightly and placed his lips on her ear, whispering, "Stay close to me, darling. Let me pull the pain out of you."

She nodded.

"Take a deep breath," he instructed. As she did so, he looked back up to Mrs. Stubbs and said, "Get someone to clean this up. I don't want to see it. Throw it all away."

"No!" Ellie burst out. "Not my jam!"

"Ellie, it's just jam."

She turned her face to his, her eyes clearer than they'd been since she'd been burned. "I've been working all day on it."

Charles breathed an internal sigh of relief. If she could focus on the damned jam, maybe she could pull her mind away from the pain.

"*What* is going on here?" came an awful screech.

He looked up to see his aunt Cordelia. Good God, this was all they needed. "Someone get her out of here," he muttered.

"Has she been burned? Has someone been burned? For years, I have been warning all of you about the fire."

"Will someone remove her from the kitchen?" he said more loudly.

"The fire will consume us all." Cordelia began waving her arms wildly in the air. "All of us!"

"Now!" Charles roared, and this time two footmen appeared to escort his aunt from the room. "Good God," he muttered. "The woman is completely unhinged."

"She's harmless," Ellie said shakily. "You told me so yourself."

"You stay quiet and conserve your energy," he said, his voice rough with fear.

Mrs. Stubbs stepped forward with a small bowl in her hands. "Here is the pomatum, my lord. We need to apply it to the burns and then wrap her hands in a bandage."

Charles looked at the sticky mixture dubiously. "What is in that?"

"One beaten egg and two spoonfuls of sweet oil, my lord."

"And you're certain this will work?"

"It is what my mother always used, my lord."

"Very well." Charles sat back and watched as the housekeeper gently applied the mixture to Ellie's splotchy skin, then wrapped her hands in strips of thin linen. Ellie held her neck and shoulders stiffly, and he could tell she was trying not to cry out from the pain.

God, it broke his heart to watch her like this.

A small commotion arose in the doorway, and he

turned to see Judith, closely followed by Claire and Helen. "We heard noise," Helen said, breathy from having run through the house. "Aunt Cordelia was screaming."

"Aunt Cordelia is always screaming," Judith said. Then her eyes fell on Ellie and she asked, "What happened?"

"She burned her hands," Charles replied.

"How?" Claire asked, her voice oddly scratchy.

"The jam," he answered. "She—" He turned to Ellie, hoping that she might forget about some of the pain if he included her in the conversation. "How the hell *did* this happen?"

"The pot," she gasped. "It was so silly of me. I should have noticed it wasn't where I left it."

Helen stepped forward, knelt down, and placed a comforting arm around Ellie's shoulders. "What do you mean?"

Ellie turned to her new cousin. "When we set the jam to cook . . . we wanted it at low heat. Remember?"

Helen nodded.

"It must have been moved closer to the firebox. I didn't notice." She stopped and swallowed down a cry of pain as Mrs. Stubbs pressed one of the bandages into place and began work on the other hand.

"Then what happened?" Helen asked.

"The handles were hot. It surprised me and I dropped the pot. When it hit the floor . . ." Ellie squeezed her eyes tightly, trying not to remember that awful moment when the purple liquid was everywhere, and then it was on her skin, and the burning sensation was awful, so awful.

"That's enough," Charles ordered, clearly sensing

her distress. "Helen, remove Claire and Judith from the kitchen. They don't need to witness this. And see to it that a bottle of laudanum is brought to Ellie's room."

Helen nodded, took her daughters' hands, and left the room.

"I don't want laudanum," Ellie protested.

"You don't have any choice. I refuse to stand by and do nothing to ease your pain."

"But I don't want to sleep. I don't want to . . ." She swallowed and looked up at him, feeling more vulnerable than she had in her entire life. "I don't want to be alone," she finally whispered.

Charles leaned down and dropped a feathery kiss on her temple. "Don't worry," he murmured. "I won't leave your side. I promise."

And when they finally gave her the laudanum and put her into bed, he settled down into a chair at her bedside. He watched her face as she fell into slumber, and then he sat in silence until sleep claimed him as well.

Chapter 16

When Charles awoke several hours later, Ellie was thankfully still asleep. The laudanum he had given her would surely wear off soon, however, so he poured another dose for when she woke up. He wasn't certain how long the burns would remain painful, but he was damned if he was going to let her suffer needlessly. He didn't think he could bear another minute of listening to her trying to suppress her whimpers of pain.

Quite simply, it tore his heart in two.

Charles covered his mouth to silence a yawn as his eyes adjusted to the dim light of the bedroom. He hated late autumn, when the days were short and the sun set early. He longed for the warmth of summer, or even the crisp air of spring, and wondered what Ellie looked like in the summer when the sun stayed high in the sky well into night. Would the light hit her hair differently? Would it look redder? Or perhaps blonder? Or would she look exactly the same, only warmer to the touch?

At that thought, he leaned down and smoothed a lock of hair off her forehead, careful to avoid accidentally brushing against her bandaged hands. He was about to repeat the motion when a soft knock sounded at the door. Charles rose and crossed the room, wincing at the clicking noise his boots made when he stepped off of the carpet and onto the floor. He glanced over at Ellie and breathed a small sigh of relief when he saw she was still sleeping soundly.

He opened the door to reveal Claire, who was standing in the hallway, biting her lip and wringing her hands. Her eyes were puffy and so red that he could see their irritation even in the dim candlelight of the windowless corridor.

"Charles," she blurted out, her voice sounding overly loud. "I have to—"

He raised his finger to his lips and stepped into the hallway, shutting the door carefully behind him. Then, much to Claire's obvious befuddlement, he sat down.

"What are you doing?"

"Removing my boots. I haven't the patience to locate my valet for assistance."

"Oh." She looked down at him, clearly confused as to how to proceed. Charles may have been Claire's cousin, but he was also a belted earl, and one didn't often look *down* upon an earl.

"You wished to speak with me?" he said, grasping the heel of his left boot.

"Er, yes. I did. Well, actually, it is Ellie with whom I need to speak." Claire swallowed convulsively. The reflex seemed to shake her entire body. "Is she awake?"

"No, thank God, and I plan to give her another dose of laudanum the minute she awakens."

"I see. She must be in terrible pain."

"Yes, she is. Her skin has blistered, and she will most likely bear scars for the rest of her life."

Claire flinched. "I-I burned myself once. Just with a candle, but it hurt terribly. Ellie never even cried out. At least not that I heard. She must be very strong."

Charles paused in his efforts to remove his right boot. "Yes," he said softly, "she is. More so than I ever imagined."

Claire was silent for a long moment, and then she said, "May I speak with her when she wakes up? I know you want to give her more laudanum, but it will take a few minutes for it to take effect, and—"

"Claire," he interrupted, "can it not wait until morning?"

She swallowed again. "No. It truly cannot."

His eyes locked onto her face and stayed there even as he rose to his feet. "Is there something you feel you should tell me?" he asked in a low voice.

She shook her head. "Ellie. I need to speak with Ellie."

"Very well. I will see if she is up to a visit. But if she is not, you will have to wait until morning. No arguments."

Claire blinked and nodded as Charles put his hand on the doorknob and turned.

Ellie opened her eyes and then shut them again, hoping that would stem the dizzy sensation that overtook her the instant she blinked herself awake. It didn't help, however, so she opened her eyes again and looked for her husband.

"Charles?"

No answer.

Ellie felt an unfamiliar disappointment settle in her throat. He had said he wouldn't leave her side. It was the only thing that had kept her calm as she'd fallen asleep. Then she heard the door creak, and she looked up to see him silhouetted in the doorway.

"Charles." She had meant to whisper, but her words came out more like a croak.

He rushed to her side. "You're awake."

She nodded. "I'm thirsty."

"Of course." He turned and said over his shoulder, "Claire, ring for tea."

Ellie craned her neck as best as she was able to look behind him. She hadn't realized Claire was also in the room. It was surprising, that. Claire had never shown any interest in her well-being before.

When Ellie looked back to Charles, he was holding a porcelain cup to her lips. "In the meantime," he said, "if you want to moisten your throat, I have a bit of tepid tea here. I've already drunk from it, but it is better than nothing."

Ellie nodded and took a sip, wondering why, after so many kisses, it seemed so intimate to drink from his teacup.

"How are your hands?" he asked.

"They are quite painful," she said honestly, "but not as terribly as before."

"That is the laudanum. It can have very powerful effects."

"I have never used it before."

He leaned forward and kissed her gently. "And I pray you never will again."

Ellie sipped at her tea, trying, unsuccessfully, not to relive the jam accident in her mind. She kept seeing the pot as it dropped to the ground and remembering that one horrific moment when she knew with absolute certainty that she was going to be burned and realized that there was nothing she could do to prevent it. And then, when her hands were in the bucket of icy water, and she could feel everyone's eyes upon her—oh, it was horrible, just horrible. She hated making a spectacle of herself, hated doing anything foolish. It didn't much matter that the accident had been just that—an accident—and it wasn't her fault. She couldn't bear the pity in everyone's eyes. Even Judith had—

"Oh, God," she blurted out, practically choking on her tea. "Judith. Is she all right?"

Charles looked confused. "She wasn't in the kitchen when you dropped the pot, Ellie."

"I know, I know. But she saw me when I—Oh, you must know what I mean. She saw me when I was crying and whimpering and in so much pain, and it must have confused her terribly. I hate to think how she must feel."

Charles placed a gentle finger on her lips. "Shhh. You're going to exhaust yourself if you keep talking at such speeds."

"But Judith—"

This time he actually grasped her lips and held them together. "Judith is fine. Helen has already explained to her what happened. She was very upset but is taking it in her usual, six-year-old stride."

"I should like to speak with her."

"You can do that tomorrow. I believe she is having

supper with her nanny just now and plans to spend the rest of the evening working on her watercolors. She said she wanted to paint you a special picture to inspire you through your recovery."

For a moment Ellie felt so content she didn't even feel the pain in her hands. "That is the sweetest thing," she murmured.

"In the meantime," Charles said, "Claire has asked to speak with you. I told her she may do so only if you feel up to it."

"Of course," Ellie murmured. It was very odd that Claire, who had never bothered to hide her resentment of Ellie, should want to comfort her while she recuperated. But Ellie was still hopeful that they might have a more friendly and familial relationship, so she moved her head a little to the side, made eye contact with her, and said, "Good evening, Claire."

Claire dropped into a bob of a curtsy and said, "I do hope you're feeling improved."

"I am beginning to," Ellie replied. "I expect it will take some time. It is lovely to have people to keep me company, however. It keeps my mind off of my hands."

Ellie wasn't positive, but she rather thought Claire paled when she mentioned her hands. There was a long and awkward silence, and then finally Claire gulped loudly, turned to Charles, and said, "Could I have a private moment with Ellie?"

"I really don't think—"

"*Please.*"

Ellie was startled to hear a touch of desperation in Claire's voice, and she turned to Charles and said, "It will be all right. I'm not sleepy."

"But I had planned to give you more laudanum."

"The laudanum can wait five minutes."

"I won't have you suffering any more pain than is necessary—"

"I will be fine, Charles. I would like a few more moments of lucidity in any case. Perhaps you could go out to the staircase and await the tea."

"Very well." He left the room, but he didn't look happy about it.

Ellie turned back to Claire with a weary smile. "He can be very stubborn, can't he?"

"Yes." Claire chewed on her lower lip and looked away. "And so can I, I'm afraid."

Ellie watched the younger girl closely. Claire was clearly agitated and upset. Ellie desperately wanted to comfort her, but she wasn't certain that her overtures would be welcomed. After all, Claire had made her antagonism clear over the past few weeks. Finally Ellie simply patted the empty side of the bed and said, "Would you like to sit here beside me? I should enjoy the company."

Claire hesitated, then took a few steps and sat down. She didn't say anything for at least a minute, just sat there plucking at the blankets. Ellie finally broke the silence by saying, "Claire?"

The girl was jolted out of her thoughts, looked up, and said, "I haven't been very kind to you since you arrived."

Ellie wasn't certain how best to respond to that so she remained silent.

Claire cleared her throat, as if summoning the courage to continue. When she finally began speaking, the words fell from her lips a mile a minute. "The fire in the kitchen was my fault," she burst out. "I moved the rack. I didn't intend for there to be a fire. I just wanted to burn the toast so you wouldn't appear so bloody smart, and I ruined your stew as well, and I've been poisoning your garden, and . . . and—" Her voice broke, and she looked away.

"And what, Claire?" Ellie prodded softly, knowing what was coming, yet needing to hear it from Claire's lips. More to the point, she rather thought Claire needed to speak the words herself.

"I moved the pot of jam to the hot spot on the cooking surface," she whispered. "I never thought anyone would be hurt. Please believe that. I only wanted to burn the jam. That's all. Just the jam."

Ellie swallowed uncomfortably. Claire looked so miserable, so unhappy, and so damned sorry that Ellie wanted to comfort her, even though she'd been the cause of so much pain. Ellie coughed and said, "I'm still a bit thirsty. Could you . . ."

She didn't have to finish the sentence, for Claire was already picking up the cup of tepid tea and holding it to Ellie's lips. Ellie took a grateful sip, and then another. The laudanum had made her throat terribly dry. Finally she looked back up at Claire, and asked simply, "Why?"

"I can't say. Please just know I'm sorry." Claire's mouth was quivering, and her eyes were filling with tears at an alarming rate. "I know that I've behaved terribly, and I'll never do anything like this again. I promise."

"Claire," Ellie said, keeping her voice gentle but firm. "I am willing to accept your apology, because I do believe that it is sincere, but you cannot expect me to do so without a reason."

Claire squeezed her eyes shut. "I didn't want people to like you. I didn't want you to like it here. I just wanted you to go away."

"But why?"

"I can't say," she sobbed. "I just can't."

"Claire, you must tell me."

"I can't. It's too embarrassing."

"Nothing is ever as awful as one thinks," Ellie said gently.

The younger girl covered her face with her hands and mumbled, "Will you promise not to tell Charles?"

"Claire, he is my husband. We have vowed to—"

"You must promise!"

The girl looked on the verge of hysteria. Ellie rather doubted that whatever secret she was keeping was as terrible as she thought, but she remembered what it felt like to be fourteen, so she said, "Very well, Claire. I give you my vow."

Claire looked away before she said, "I wanted him to wait for me."

Ellie closed her eyes. She'd never dreamed that Claire had been harboring a secret *tendre* for Charles.

"I've always wanted to marry him," Claire whispered. "He's my hero. He saved us six years ago, you know. Poor Mama was pregnant with Judith, and the creditors had taken everything away. Charles barely even knew us, but he paid my father's debts and took us in. And he never made us feel like poor relations."

"Oh, Claire."

"He wouldn't have had to wait much longer."

"But what was the use of trying to scare me away? We were already married."

"I heard you arguing. I know you haven't..." Claire turned beet red. "I can't say it, but I know that the marriage could be annulled."

"Oh, Claire," Ellie sighed, too concerned about the present situation to feel embarrassed that Claire knew that her marriage had never been consummated. "He couldn't have waited for you in any case. You must know about his father's will."

"Yes, but he could have annulled the marriage and—"

"No," Ellie interrupted, "he can't. *We* can't. If he does, he loses the money forever. Charles had to marry before his thirtieth birthday, and the marriage could not be dissolved."

"I didn't know," Claire said quietly.

Ellie sighed. What a muck. Then she realized what she'd just said and opened her eyes very wide. "Oh dear," she said, "Charles's birthday. Did I miss it?" He had said he had *how* many days before his birthday when they met? Fifteen? Seventeen? Ellie pinpointed the day he'd proposed in her mental calendar and began to count forward.

"His birthday is in two days' time," Claire said.

As if on cue, a firm knock sounded at the door. "That will be Charles," both women said in unison.

Then Claire added, "No one else knocks nearly as loud."

"Come in," Ellie called out. Then she turned to Claire and urgently whispered, "You're going to have to tell him. You don't have to tell him why, but you're going to have to tell him you did it."

Claire looked glum but resigned. "I know."

Charles swept into the room carrying a silver tray with a tea service and biscuits. He shooed Claire off the bed and set it down in her place. "Would you care to pour, cousin?" he asked. "It ought to be well-steeped. I waited with it for several minutes on the stairs to give you two more time together."

"That was very kind of you," Ellie replied. "We had a great deal to talk about."

"Did you?" Charles murmured. "Anything you'd care to share with me?"

Ellie sent a pointed look in Claire's direction. Claire answered her with a panicked expression, so Ellie said, "It will be all right, Claire."

Claire merely handed a cup and saucer out to Charles and said, "This is for Ellie."

Charles took them and sat down beside his wife. "Here you are," he said, holding it to her lips. "Be careful. It's hot."

She took a gulp and sighed happily. "Heaven. It's heaven right there in a hot cup of tea."

Charles smiled and dropped a kiss onto the top of her head. "Now then," he said, looking up at Claire. "What did you need to talk with Ellie about?"

Claire held out another cup and saucer in his direction before saying, "I needed to apologize to her."

He took the cup and set it down on Ellie's bedside table. "Why was that?" he asked quietly, giving Ellie another sip of tea.

Claire looked as if she might bolt from the room at any second.

"Just tell him," Ellie said quietly.

"It was my fault that Ellie was hurt today," Claire

finally admitted, her voice barely audible. "I moved the pot so the jam would burn. It did not occur to me that the handles would heat up so much as well."

Ellie gasped as she watched Charles's face harden into an implacable mask. She'd known he'd be angry, had thought he might yell and rage a bit, but this silent fury was unnerving.

"Charles?" Claire choked out. "Please say something."

Charles set Ellie's cup back down in its saucer with the slow, rigid movements of one whose control is about to snap. "I am trying to think of one good reason why I shouldn't pack you off and send you to a work house this minute. In fact," he added, his voice rising by the second, "I am trying to think of one good reason why I shouldn't bloody well kill you!"

"Charles!" Ellie exclaimed.

But by now he was on his feet and advancing in Claire's direction. "What the hell were you thinking?" he demanded. "What the bloody hell were you thinking?"

"Charles," Ellie repeated.

"You stay out of this," he snapped.

"I most certainly will not."

Charles ignored her as he jabbed a finger in Claire's direction. "I suppose you're responsible for the kitchen fire as well."

She nodded miserably, tears streaming down her face. "And the stew," she gasped. "That was my fault, too. And the orangery."

"Why, Claire? Why?"

She clutched at her midsection as she sobbed, "I can't say."

He grabbed her shoulder and spun her to face him. "You will explain yourself to me, and you will do it this instant."

"I can't!"

"Do you understand what you've done?" Charles shook her roughly and turned her to face Ellie's bed. "Look at her! Look at her hands! You did this."

Claire was sobbing so hard that Ellie thought she would crumple to the ground if Charles weren't shaking her by the shoulders. "Charles, stop!" Ellie cried out, unable to watch this any longer. "Can't you see she's upset?"

"As well she should be," he snarled.

"Charles, that is enough! She has told me she is sorry, and I accept her apology."

"Well, I don't."

If Ellie's hands weren't bandaged and throbbing with pain, she would have smacked him. "It isn't your apology to accept," she ground out.

"Don't you want an explanation?"

"She has already given me one."

Charles was so surprised he actually dropped Claire.

"I have given her my vow that I would not tell you about it."

"Why?"

"That is between Claire and me."

"Ellie . . ." His voice held a clear note of warning.

"I will not break my word," she said firmly. "And I believe you value honesty enough not to ask me to do so."

Charles let out an irritated breath and raked his hand through his hair. Ellie had him backed neatly into a corner. "She must be punished," he finally said. "I insist upon it."

Ellie nodded. "Of course. Claire has behaved very badly and must answer to the consequences. But I will decide upon the punishment, not you."

He rolled his eyes. Ellie was so softhearted, she'd probably send the girl to her room for a night and be done with it.

His wife, however, surprised him when she turned to Claire, who was sitting on the floor where Charles had dropped her. "Claire," Ellie said, "how do *you* think you should be punished?"

Claire was also obviously surprised, because she didn't say anything, just sat there with her mouth opening and closing like a fish.

"Claire?" Ellie said gently.

"I could clean up the mess in the orangery."

"That is an excellent idea," Ellie said. "I started clearing it out this morning with Charles, but we didn't accomplish very much. You will need to do a great deal of replanting as well. Many plants have died this past fortnight."

Claire nodded. "I could also clean the jam from the kitchen."

"That has already been done," Charles said, his tone clipped.

New tears formed in Claire's eyes, and she turned to Ellie for moral support.

"What I would like above all else," Ellie said softly, "would be for you to inform every member of this household that the mishaps of the past week were not my fault. I have been trying to find my place here at

Wycombe Abbey, and I have not appreciated being made to look foolish and inept."

Claire closed her eyes and nodded.

"It won't be easy for you," Ellie conceded, "but coming here and apologizing to me wasn't easy, either. You're a strong girl, Claire. Stronger than you think."

For the first time that evening, Claire actually smiled, and Ellie knew that everything was going to be all right.

Charles cleared his throat and said, "I think Ellie has had enough excitement for one day, Claire."

Ellie shook her head and crooked her finger toward Claire. "Come here a moment," she said. When Claire reached her bedside, Ellie whispered in her ear, "And do you know what else I think?"

Claire shook her head.

"I think that someday you will be very glad that Charles wasn't able to wait for you."

Claire turned to Ellie with questioning eyes.

"Love will find you when you least expect it," Ellie said softly. Then she added, "*And* when you're old enough."

Claire giggled, prompting Charles to grumble, "What the devil are you two whispering about?"

"Nothing," Ellie replied. "Now then, let Claire run along. She has quite a bit of work to do."

Charles stepped aside to allow Claire to dash from the room. Once the door had shut behind her, he turned to Ellie and said, "You were too lenient with her."

"It was my decision, not yours," Ellie said, her voice suddenly weary. It had taken a great deal of her already sapped energy to deal with a furious husband and sobbing cousin.

His eyes narrowed. "Are you in pain?"

She nodded. "Could I have that second dose of laudanum now?"

Charles moved quickly to her side and held the glass to her lips, smoothing her hair while she gulped the contents down. Ellie yawned and settled back down against her pillows, resting her bandaged hands carefully atop the bedcovers. "I know you believe I wasn't stern enough with Claire," she said, "but I think she's learned her lesson."

"I shall have to take your word for that, won't I, since you refuse to tell me what she said in her defense?"

"She didn't try to defend herself at all. She knows what she did was wrong."

Charles stretched his legs out on the bed and leaned back against the headboard. "You're a remarkable woman, Eleanor Wycombe."

She gave him a sleepy yawn. "I certainly don't mind hearing you say it."

"Most people would not have been as forgiving."

"Don't let that fool you. I can be quite vindictive when it's called for."

"Is that so?" he asked, amusement lacing his voice.

Ellie yawned again and settled against him. "Will you stay here tonight? At least until I fall asleep?"

He nodded and kissed her temple.

"Good. It's warmer with you here."

Charles blew out the candle and laid back down on top of the covers. Then, once he was sure she was asleep, he touched his heart and whispered, "It's warmer in here, too."

Chapter 17

Ellie spent the next morning recuperating in bed. Charles rarely left her side, and when he did, he was immediately replaced by a member of the Pallister family—most often Helen or Judith, since Claire was busy cleaning up the mess she'd made in the orangery.

By early afternoon, however, she was beginning to lose her patience with Charles and his everpresent bottle of laudanum.

"It is very sweet of you to be so concerned about my burns," Ellie said, trying to placate him, "but truly the pain is not as dreadful as yesterday, and beside that, I can't seem to last through a conversation without falling asleep."

"No one minds," he assured her.

"*I* mind."

"I've already allowed you to reduce your dose by half."

"And it still leaves me half out of my mind. I can bear a little pain, Charles. I'm no weakling."

"Ellie, you don't have to be a martyr."

"I don't want to be a martyr. I just want to be myself."

He looked doubtful, but he put the bottle back on

272

the bedside table. "If your hands start to hurt . . ."

"I know, I know. I—" Ellie breathed a sigh of relief as someone knocked at the door, effectively ending the conversation. Charles still looked as if he might change his mind and pour the laudanum down her throat at the slightest provocation. "Come in!" she called out.

Judith bounded in, her dark blond hair pulled away from her face. "Good day, Ellie," she chirped.

"Good day, Judith. It's fine to see you."

The young girl nodded regally and climbed up on the bed.

"Don't I rate a greeting?" Charles asked.

"Yes, yes, of course," Judith replied. "Good day to you, Charles, but you will have to leave."

Ellie choked down a laugh.

"And why is that?" he demanded.

"I have extremely important matters to discuss with Ellie. *Private* matters."

"Is that so?"

Judith raised her brows in a supercilious expression that somehow fit her little six-year-old face perfectly. "Indeed. Although I suppose you may remain while I give Ellie her present."

"How very generous of you," Charles said.

"A present! How thoughtful!" Ellie said at the exact same time.

"I painted you a picture." Judith held up a small watercolor.

"It's beautiful, Judith," Ellie exclaimed, regarding the blue, green, and red slashes. "It's lovely. It's . . . it's . . ."

"It's the meadow," Judith said.

Ellie breathed a huge sigh of relief that she didn't have to hazard a guess.

"See?" the little girl continued. "This is the grass, and this is the sky. And these are the apples on the apple tree."

"Where is the tree trunk?" Charles inquired.

Judith scowled at him. "I ran out of brown."

"Would you like me to order you some more?"

"I would like that above all else."

Charles smiled. "I wish all women were as easy to please."

"We're not so unreasonable," Ellie felt compelled to say as a general defense of her gender.

Judith planted her hands on her hips, clearly irritated that she didn't understand what the adults were talking about. "You shall have to leave now, Charles. As I said, I need to speak with Ellie. It's very important."

"Is it?" he asked. "Too important for me? The earl? The one who is supposedly in charge of this pile of stones?"

"The key word there would be 'supposedly,'" Ellie said with a smile. "I suspect it is Judith who really runs the household."

"You are no doubt correct," he said wryly.

"We shall need at least half an hour, I should think," said Judith. "Perhaps longer. Either way, you should be sure to knock before you reenter. I shouldn't want you to interrupt us."

Charles stood and headed for the door. "I can see that I have been summarily dismissed."

"A half an hour!" Judith yelled at his retreating form.

He poked his head back in the doorway. "You, poppet, are a tyrant."

"Charles," Ellie said in her best mock-irritated voice, "Judith has requested a private audience."

"Precocious brat," he muttered.

"I heard that," Judith said with a smile, "and it only means that you love me."

"No fooling this one," Ellie said, reaching out to tousle her hair, and then remembering that she couldn't.

"Watch out for your hands!" Charles ordered.

"Run along," Ellie returned, unable to suppress a little chuckle at ordering him about.

They heard his grumbling all the way down the hall. Judith giggled into her hand the entire time.

"Very well, then," Ellie said, "what did you need to talk with me about?"

"Charles's birthday celebration. Claire told Mama and me that you wanted to plan a party."

"Oh yes, of course. I'm so glad you remembered. I'm afraid I won't be able to do much of the work, but I am quite excellent at ordering people about."

Judith giggled. "No, I will be in charge."

"May I be second in command, then?"

"Of course."

"Then I suppose we have a deal," Ellie said. "And since I cannot shake your hand, we will have to seal it with a kiss."

"Done!" Judith crawled across the bed and gave Ellie a loud kiss on the cheek.

"Good. Now I just need to kiss you back, and then we can begin making our plans."

Judith waited while Ellie kissed the top of her head and then said, "I think we should have Monsieur Belmont bake a big cake. Enormous! With butter-cream frosting."

"Enormous, or merely huge?" Ellie asked with a smile.

"Enormous!" Judith yelled, waving her arms in the air to demonstrate. "And we can—"

"Ow!" Ellie yelped in pain as one of the little girl's hands connected with her own.

Judith immediately jumped off of the bed. "I'm sorry. I'm so sorry. It was an accident. I swear it."

"I know," Ellie said, gritting her teeth against the pain. "It's not a problem, poppet. Just get that bottle on the table and pour a little into the cup."

"How much? This much?" Judith pointed with her finger to the middle of the cup, about a half a dose.

"No, half that," Ellie replied. A quarter dose seemed the perfect compromise—enough to take the edge off the pain but hopefully not enough to make her drowsy and disoriented. "But don't tell Charles."

"Why not?"

"Just don't." And then she muttered, "I hate it when he's right."

"I beg your pardon?"

Ellie drank from the cup Judith held to her mouth and said, "It's nothing. Now then, we have plans to make, don't we?"

They spent the next fifteen minutes on the grave topic of butter-cream frosting, arguing the merits of chocolate versus vanilla.

* * *

Later that day, Charles emerged through the connecting door between their rooms carrying a sheet of paper. "How are you feeling?" he inquired.

"Much better, thank you, although it's rather difficult to flip the pages of my book."

One corner of his mouth turned up in amusement. "Have you been trying to read?"

" 'Trying' would be the operative word," she said wryly.

He walked to her side and flipped a page, looking down at her book as he did so. "And how is our dear Miss Dashwood faring this afternoon?" he asked.

Ellie looked at him with a confused expression until she realized he'd been peeking at the copy of *Sense and Sensibility* she'd been attempting to read. "Very well," she replied. "I think Mr. Ferrars is going to propose at any minute."

"How utterly thrilling," he replied, and she had to admire him for keeping such a perfectly straight face.

"Here, turn the book over," she said. "I've had enough reading for the afternoon."

"Do you perhaps need another quarter dose of laudanum?"

"How did you know about that?"

He raised a brow. "I know all, sweetling."

"I imagine what you *know* is how to bribe Judith."

"That is a valuable thing to know, indeed."

She rolled her eyes. "A quarter dose would be much appreciated, thank you."

He poured the liquid and gave it to her, rubbing at his arm as he did so.

"Oh dear," Ellie said. "I'd forgotten all about your arm. How is it feeling?"

"Not half as bad as your hands. You needn't worry about it."

"But I won't be able to remove the stitches."

"I'm sure someone else can do it. Helen, probably. She's forever working at her embroidery and needlework."

"I suppose. I do hope you're not being a stoic, refusing to tell me how much it hurts. If I find out that you have—"

"For the love of God, Ellie, you have been seriously injured. Stop worrying about me."

"It's much easier to worry about you than to sit here and think about my hands."

He smiled understandingly. "It's difficult for you to remain inactive, isn't it?"

"Extremely so."

"Very well, why don't we have one of those conversations I'm told husbands and wives have?"

"I beg your pardon?"

"You say to me something like, 'Darling, darling husband—'"

"Oh, please."

He ignored her. "'—my dearest, darlingest husband, how have you fared this fine day?'"

Ellie let out a big sigh. "Oh, all right. I can play at this game, I suppose."

"Very sporting of you," he said approvingly.

She shot him a peevish look and asked, "How have you been keeping yourself busy, fair husband? I heard you moving about in the next room."

"I was pacing."

"Pacing? That sounds serious."

He grinned slowly. "I've been making up a new list."

"A new list? I am breathless with anticipation. What is it titled?"

" 'Seven Ways to Entertain Eleanor.' "

"Only seven? I had no idea I was that easily amused."

"I can assure you I have put a great deal of thought into this."

"I'm certain you have. The treadmarks on the carpet in your chamber can attest to that."

"Do not poke fun at my poor, beleaguered carpet. Pacing is the least of my woes. If the rest of our marriage is anything like this past fortnight, my head shall be completely gray by the time I turn thirty."

Ellie knew that that momentous occasion was due to happen the very next day, but she didn't want to spoil the surprise party she had planned with the Pallisters, so she feigned ignorance and merely said, "I am certain that our lives will continue on a much more peaceful note now that I have made my peace with Claire."

"I should certainly hope so," he said, sounding rather like a disgruntled young boy. "Now then, do you want to hear my new list? I've been working all afternoon on it."

"But of course. Should I read it or will you recite it aloud?"

"Oh, I think a recitation is in order." He leaned forward and raised an eyebrow in a wolfish expression. "So that I might make certain each word gets its proper emphasis."

Ellie couldn't contain her laughter. "Very well, then. Do begin."

He cleared his throat. " 'Number One: Read to her so that she does not have to flip her own pages.' "

"Let me see that! You're making this up as you go along. You couldn't have known I was reading. And you certainly couldn't have known the trouble I was having with the pages."

"I am merely doing a bit of editing," he said loftily. "It's allowed, you know."

"I'm certain it is, considering that you make up the rules as you please."

"It is one of the few truly beneficial parts of being an earl," he conceded. "But if you must know, number one was indeed that I read to you. I merely amended it to include the bit about flipping pages. Now then, shall I continue?" At her nod, he read, " 'Number Two: Rub her feet.' "

"*My feet*?!"

"Mmm, yes. Have you never had a proper foot massage?" He considered her sheltered background, then considered where he had always received foot massages and from whom, and then decided that she most probably had not. "I can assure you they are most delightful. Would you like a description? Or perhaps a demonstration?"

She cleared her throat several times. "What is the next item on the list?"

"Coward," he accused with a smile. He stretched his arm out along the top of her bedcovers and followed the length of her leg until he found her foot. He tweaked her toe. " 'Number Three: Bring Judith by at least twice a day for a chat.' "

"That is certainly a considerably more innocent suggestion than the last."

"I know you enjoy her company."

"I am certainly growing intrigued by the remarkable variety of this list."

He shrugged. "I didn't put them in any particular order. I jotted them down as they came to me. Well, except for the last, of course. I thought of that one first, but I didn't want to shock you."

"I'm almost afraid to ask what number seven is."

"You should be." He grinned. "It's my favorite."

Ellie's cheeks burned.

Charles cleared his throat, trying not to grin at her innocent distress. "Shall I continue with the next item?"

"Please."

" 'Number Four: Keep her informed of Claire's progress in the orangery.' "

"That is meant to be entertaining?"

"Perhaps not precisely entertaining, but I thought you'd like an update."

"How *is* she doing?"

"Very well, actually. She's been quite industrious. It's bloody cold down there, though. She's opened the outside doors to air the place out. I expect the smell will be gone by the time you're well enough to resume your gardening."

Ellie smiled. "What is the next item on the list?"

He looked down. "Let me see. Ah, here we are. 'Number Five: Bring the dressmaker by with fabric samples and patterns.' " He glanced back up at her. "I can hardly believe we haven't done this already. You're not well enough for a proper fitting, but at least we ought to be able to select a few styles and colors. I'm growing most weary of seeing you in nothing but brown."

"My father was given several bolts of brown cloth as a tithe two years ago. I haven't acquired a colored dress since."

"A most grievous state of affairs."

"Are you such an arbiter of fashion, then?"

"Certainly more so than the good reverend, your father."

"On that point, my lord, we are in agreement."

He leaned in until his nose rested on hers. "Am I really your lord, Eleanor?"

Her lips twisted into a wry smile. "Social protocol does seem to dictate that I refer to you as such."

He sighed and clutched his chest in mock despair. "If you dance as nimbly as you converse, I predict that you shall be the toast of the town."

"Certainly not if I don't purchase a new gown or two. It wouldn't do to attend every function in brown."

"Ah yes, the ever-so-subtle reminder to me to return to the subject at hand." He held up the paper in his hands, flicked his wrists to give it a little snap, and read, " 'Number Six: Discuss with her the terms of her new bank account.' "

Ellie's entire face lit up. "You're interested?"

"Of course."

"Yes, but compared to your finances, my three hundred pounds is a paltry sum. It can't be very important to you."

He cocked his head and looked at her as if she was missing some very obvious point. "But it is to *you*."

Right then and there Ellie decided that she loved him. As much as one could *decide* these things, of course. The realization was shocking, and somewhere in her befuddled mind it occurred to her that this feeling had been building up in her ever since he'd proposed. There was something so very . . . *special* about him.

It was there in the way he could laugh at himself.

It was there in the way he could make her laugh at herself.

It was there in the way he made certain to give Judith a goodnight kiss every night.

But most of all, it was there in the way he respected her talents and anticipated her needs—and in the way his eyes had filled with pain when she'd been hurt, as if he'd felt each and every one of her burns on his own skin.

He was a better man than she'd realized when she'd said, "I will."

He poked her shoulder. "Ellie? Ellie?"

"What? Oh, I'm sorry." Her face colored, even though she knew he couldn't possibly read her thoughts. "Just woolgathering."

"Darling, you were practically hugging a sheep."

She swallowed and tried to come up with a reasonable excuse. "I was merely thinking about my investment strategy. What do you think of coffee?"

"I like mine with milk."

"As an investment," she practically snapped.

"My goodness, we've suddenly grown testy."

He'd be testy, too, she thought, if he'd just realized that he was on a one-way path to a broken heart. She was in love with a man who saw nothing wrong with infidelity. He had made his views on marriage painfully clear.

Oh, Ellie knew he'd remain faithful for the time being. He was far too intrigued by her and by the newness of their marriage to seek out other women. But eventually he'd grow bored, and when he did, she'd be left at home with a broken heart.

Damn the man. If he had to have a fatal flaw, why couldn't he have chewed his fingernails, or gambled, or even been short, fat, and hideously ugly? Why did he have to be perfect in every way except for his appalling lack of respect for the sanctity of marriage?

Ellie thought she might cry.

And the worst part of it was that she knew she'd never be able to pay him back in kind. Ellie couldn't be unfaithful if she tried. Perhaps it was due to her strict upbringing by a man of God, but there was no way she could ever break a vow as solemn as that of marriage. It just wasn't in her.

"You look terribly somber all of a sudden," Charles said, touching her face. "My God! You've tears in your eyes. Ellie, what is wrong? Is it your hands?"

Ellie nodded. It seemed the easiest thing to do under the circumstances.

"Let me pour you more laudanum. And I'll brook no arguments that you just had some. Another quarter dose isn't going to render you unconscious."

She drank the liquid, thinking she wouldn't mind being rendered unconscious just then. "Thank you," she said, once he'd wiped her mouth for her. He was looking at her with such concern, and it made her heart positively *ache*, and . . .

And that was when it came to her. They said reformed rakes made the best husbands, didn't they? Why the devil couldn't she reform him? She'd never backed down from a challenge before. Feeling suddenly inspired and perhaps a little bit dizzy from having doubled her current dose of laudanum, she turned to him and asked, "And when do I learn the mysterious number seven?"

He looked at her with concern in his eyes. "I'm not sure you're up to it."

"Nonsense." She waggled her head from side to side and gave him a jaunty smile. "I'm up for anything."

Now he was puzzled. He blinked a few times, picked up the bottle of laudanum, and regarded it curiously. "I thought this was supposed to make one sleepy."

"I don't know about sleepy," she countered, "but I certainly feel better."

He looked at her, looked back at the bottle, and sniffed it cautiously. "Perhaps I ought to have a nip."

"I could nip *you*." She giggled.

"Now I *know* you've had too much laudanum."

"I want to hear number seven."

Charles crossed his arms and watched her yawn. She was beginning to worry him. She'd seemed to be doing so well, and then she'd practically been in tears, and now . . . Well, if he didn't know better, he'd think she was out to seduce him.

Which worked rather well with what he'd written down for number seven, actually, although he suddenly wasn't too keen on revealing his amorous intentions while she was in such a strange state.

"Number seven, if you please," she persisted.

"Perhaps tomorrow . . ."

She pouted. "You did say you wanted to entertain me. I assure you I shan't be entertained unless I know the last item on your list."

Charles never would have believed it of himself, but he just couldn't read the words aloud. Not when she was acting so strangely. He simply couldn't take advantage of her in this condition. "Here," he said, appalled by the embarrassment he heard in his voice and growing a touch angry with her for making him feel like such a . . . such a . . . Good God, what was happening to him? He was positively domesticated. He scowled. "You can read it yourself."

He placed the paper in front of her and watched while her eyes scanned his words. "Oh, my," she squeaked. "Is that possible?"

"I assure you it is."

"Even in my condition?" She held up her hands. "Oh. I suppose that's why you specifically mention . . ."

He did feel a teeny bit smug when she colored beet red. "Can't say it, darling?"

"I didn't know one could do such things with one's mouth," she mumbled.

Charles's lips spread into a slow grin as the rake within woke up. It felt good. More like himself. "Actually, there's a lot more—"

"You can tell me about it later," she said quickly.

His gaze grew heavy-lidded. "Or perhaps I'll show you."

If he didn't know better, he could have sworn she steeled her shoulders when she said—or rather, gulped—"All right."

Or maybe it was more of a squeak than a gulp. Either way, she was plainly terrified.

And then she yawned, and he realized that it didn't much matter if she was terrified or not. The extra dose of laudanum was taking effect, and she was about to . . .

Let out a loud snore.

He sighed and pulled back, wondering how long it was going to be before he could actually make love to his wife. Then he wondered if he could possibly live that long.

A funny noise erupted from the back of Ellie's throat—a noise through which no normal human being could sleep.

That was when he realized that he had bigger things to worry about and started wondering if she was going to snore every night.

Chapter 18

Ellie awoke the next morning feeling remarkably refreshed. It was amazing what a little grit and determination could do for one's spirits. It was a strange thing, romantic love. She'd never felt it before, and even if it did make her stomach a little flippy, she wanted to hold onto it with both hands and never let go.

Or rather, she wanted to hold onto Charles and never let go, but that was a little tricky with the bandages. She supposed that this was lust. It was as unfamiliar to her as romantic love.

She wasn't completely certain that she could turn him around to her views on love, marriage, and fidelity, but she knew she could never live with herself if she didn't give it a try. If she wasn't successful, she'd probably be miserable, but at least she wouldn't have to call herself a coward.

And so it was with great excitement that she waited in the informal dining room with Helen and Judith while Claire was off fetching Charles. Claire was visiting him in his study under the pretext of asking him to inspect the work she'd done in the orangery. The small dining room was on the way from Charles's study to the orangery, so Ellie, Judith, and Helen were all set to jump out and yell, "Surprise!"

"This cake looks lovely," Helen said, surveying the pale frosting. She looked a little more closely. "Except, perhaps for this little smudge right here just about the width of a six-year-old finger."

Judith crawled under the table immediately, claiming that she'd seen a bug.

Ellie smiled indulgently. "A cake wouldn't be a cake if someone hadn't sneaked a little frosting. At least it wouldn't be a family cake. And those are the best kinds."

Helen looked down to make sure that Judith was occupied with something other than listening to their conversation and said, "To tell the truth, Ellie, I'm tempted myself."

"Then go ahead. I won't tell. I would join you, but . . ." Ellie held up her bandaged hands.

Helen's face immediately grew concerned. "Are you certain you're feeling up to a party? Your hands—"

"—really don't hurt terribly much anymore, I swear."

"Charles said you still need laudanum for the pain."

"I'm taking very little. Quarter doses. And I expect to be through with that by tomorrow. The burns are healing quite nicely. The blisters are nearly gone."

"Good. I'm glad, I . . ." Helen swallowed, closed her eyes for a moment, and then drew Ellie across the room so that Judith could not hear what she was saying. "I can't thank you enough for the understanding you have shown to Claire. I—"

Ellie held up a hand. "It was nothing, Helen. You needn't say anything more on the subject."

"But I must. Most women in your place would have thrown the three of us out on our ears."

"But Helen, this is your home."

"No," Helen said quietly, "Wycombe Abbey is your home. We are your guests."

"This is your home." Ellie's tone was firm, but she smiled as she spoke. "And if I ever again hear you say otherwise, I shall have to strangle you."

Helen looked as if she were about to say something, then she closed her mouth. A moment later, however, she said, "Claire hasn't told me why she behaved as such, although I have a good idea."

"I suspect you do," Ellie said quietly.

"Thank you for not embarrassing her before Charles."

"She didn't need her heart broken twice."

Helen was saved from further reply by Judith, who crawled out from under the table. "I squashed the bug!" she chirped. "He was huge. And very fierce."

"There was no bug, poppet, and you know it," Ellie said.

"Did you know that bugs like butter-cream frosting?"

"So do little girls, I understand."

Judith pursed her lips, clearly not happy with the direction of the conversation.

"I think I hear them!" Helen whispered furiously. "Be quiet, everyone."

The threesome stood to the side of the doorway,

watching and listening with anticipation. Within moments Claire's voice became clear.

"You will see that I have made great progress in the orangery," she was saying.

"Yes," came Charles's voice, growing louder, "but wouldn't it be faster to have gone through the east hall?"

"There was a maid waxing the floor," Claire replied, very quickly. "I'm sure it's slippery."

"Bright girl," Ellie whispered to Helen.

"We can just cut through the informal dining room," Claire continued. "It's almost as fast, and . . ."

The door began to open.

"Surprise!" yelled the four female residents of Wycombe Abbey.

Charles did indeed look surprised—for about one moment. Then he looked rather vexed as he turned to Ellie and demanded, "What the devil are you doing out of bed?"

"And a happy birthday to you, too," she said acerbically.

"Your hands—"

"—do not seem to be hindering my ability to walk in the least." She smiled wryly. "Rather remarkable, that."

"But—"

Helen, in an uncharacteristically impatient gesture, swatted Charles lightly on the back of his head. "Hush up, cousin, and enjoy your party."

Charles looked at the gaggle of females looking at him with expectant faces and realized that he'd been the worst kind of boor. "Thank you, all of you," he said. "I am honored that you have gone to such lengths to celebrate my birthday."

"We couldn't let it pass without at least a cake," Ellie said. "Judith and I chose the frosting. Buttercream."

"Did you?" he said approvingly. "Smart girls."

"I painted you a picture!" Judith exclaimed. "With my watercolors."

"Did you, poppet?" He kneeled down by her side. "It's lovely. Why, it looks just like . . . just like . . ." He looked to Helen, Claire, and Ellie for help, but they all just shrugged.

"Like the stables!" Judith said excitedly.

"Exactly!"

"I spent an entire hour staring at it while I painted."

"An entire hour? How very industrious. I will have to find a position of honor for it in my study."

"You must frame it," she instructed him. "In gold."

Ellie bit back a laugh and whispered to Helen, "I predict a great future for this girl. Perhaps as queen of the universe."

Helen sighed. "My daughter certainly does not suffer from an inability to know what she wants."

"But that is a good thing," Ellie said. "It is good to know what one wants. I have only figured that out for myself very recently."

Charles cut the cake—under the direction of Judith, of course, who had very firm ideas as to how it should be done—and soon he was busy unwrapping his gifts.

There was the watercolor from Judith, an embroidered pillow from Claire, and a small clock from Helen. "For your desk," she explained. "I noticed that it's difficult to see the face of the grandfather clock across the room at night."

Ellie elbowed her husband gently in the side to get his attention. "I haven't a present for you just yet," she said quietly, "but I do have something planned."

"Really?"

"I shall tell you all about it next week."

"I must wait an entire week?"

"I'm going to need full use of my hands," she said, giving him a flirtatious look.

His grin grew positively wolfish. "I can hardly wait."

True to his word, Charles had a dressmaker come to Wycombe Abbey to go over fabric samples and patterns. Ellie would have to get the bulk of her new wardrobe in London, but Smithson's of Canterbury was a quality dressmaker, and Mrs. Smithson would be able to make a few frocks to last until Ellie could travel to town.

Ellie was quite excited to meet the dressmaker; she'd always had to sew her own dresses, and a private consultation was a luxury, indeed.

Well, not quite private.

"Charles," Ellie said for the fifth time, "I am perfectly able to choose my dresses."

"Of course, darling, but you haven't been to London and—" He caught sight of the patterns in Mrs. Smithson's hand. "Oh, no not that one. The neckline is much too low."

"But these aren't for London. These are for the country. And I've been to the country," she added, her voice growing a touch sarcastic. "As a matter of fact, I'm in the country right now."

If Charles heard her, he made no indication. "Green," he said, apparently to Mrs. Smithson. "She's lovely in green."

Ellie would have liked to have been flattered by his compliment, but she had more urgent business. "Charles," she said. "I really would like a moment alone with Mrs. Smithson."

He looked shocked. "Whatever for?"

"Wouldn't it be nice if you didn't know what all of my gowns looked like?" She smiled sweetly. "Wouldn't you like to be surprised?"

He shrugged. "Hadn't really thought about it."

"Well, think about it," she ground out. "Preferably in your study."

"You really don't want me here?"

He looked hurt, and Ellie was immediately sorry she'd snapped at him. "It's just that choosing dresses is a feminine sort of pastime."

"Is it? I was looking forward to it. I've never chosen a dress for a female before."

"Not even your—" Ellie bit her lip. She'd been about to say, "mistresses," but she refused to utter the word. She was thinking positively these days, and didn't even want to remind him that he'd once dallied with the demimonde. "Charles," she continued in a softer voice, "I'd like to choose something that will surprise you."

He grumbled, but he left the room.

"The earl is a very involved husband, is he not?" Mrs. Smithson said as he shut the door behind him.

Ellie blushed and murmured something nonsensical. Then she realized that she needed to act quickly if she wanted to get anything done while Charles was gone. Knowing him, he'd change his mind and come barging in at any moment.

"Mrs. Smithson," she said, "there is no hurry for the dresses. But what I do need . . ."

Mrs. Smithson smiled knowingly. "A trousseau?"

"Yes, some lingerie."

"That can be arranged without a fitting."

Ellie sighed with relief.

"May I recommend pale green? Your husband was most vocal in his praise for that color."

Ellie nodded.

"And the style?"

"Oh, anything. Er, anything you deem appropriate for a young newly married couple." Ellie tried not to put too much emphasis on "newly married," but then again, she wanted to make it clear that she would not be choosing a nightgown on the basis of warmth.

But then Mrs. Smithson nodded in that secretive way of hers, and Ellie knew that she'd send over something special. Maybe something a little racy. Definitely something Ellie would never have chosen for herself.

Considering her lack of experience in the art of seduction, Ellie thought that might be for the best.

A week later, Ellie's hands were nearly healed. Her skin was still tender, but they no longer pained her with every movement. It was time to give Charles his birthday gift.

She was terrified.

She was, of course, rather excited as well, but seeing

as how she was a complete innocent, the terror seemed to be the more gripping of the two emotions.

For Ellie had decided that her gift to Charles on his thirtieth birthday would be herself. She wanted their marriage to be a true union, one of mind, soul, and—she gulped as she thought this—body.

Mrs. Smithson had certainly lived up to her promises. Ellie could hardly believe her reflection in the glass. The dressmaker had chosen a gown of the sheerest pale green silk. The neckline was demure, but the rest of the gown was racier than Ellie could have dreamed. It consisted of two panels of silk, sewn only at the shoulders. There were two ties, on either side of her waist, but they did not hide the length of her leg, or the curve of her hip.

Ellie felt positively naked, and she gratefully donned the matching peignoir. She shivered—partly because there was a chill in the night air, and partly because she could hear Charles moving about in his room. He usually came in to bid her goodnight, but Ellie thought she might develop a case of mad nerves if she sat around and waited for him. She'd never been very patient.

Taking a deep, fortifying breath, she lifted her hand and knocked on the connecting door.

Charles froze in the act of removing his cravat. Ellie never knocked on the connecting door. He always visited her in her room, and besides that, were her hands healed enough to be knocking on wood? He didn't think she'd suffered any burns on her knuckles, but still . . .

He pulled the cravat the rest of the way off, tossed

it onto an ottoman, and strode across the room to the door. He didn't want her turning the knob, so instead of calling out, "Come in," he simply pulled the door open.

And nearly fainted.

"Ellie?" he said, or rather, choked.

She only smiled.

"What are you wearing?"

"I . . . ah . . . it's part of my trousseau."

"You don't have a trousseau."

"I thought I might be able to use one."

Charles pondered the ramifications of this statement and felt his skin grow quite warm.

"May I come in?"

"Oh, yes, of course." He stepped aside and allowed her to enter, his mouth dropping open as she passed by. Whatever she was wearing was cinched at the waist, and the silk clung to every curve.

She turned around. "I suppose you're wondering why I'm here."

He reminded himself to close his mouth.

"I'm wondering myself," she said, laughing nervously.

"Ellie, I—"

She shrugged off the peignoir.

"Oh, God," he croaked. His eyes rolled heavenward. "I'm being tested. That's it, isn't it? I'm being tested."

"Charles?"

"Put that back on," he said frantically, grabbing the peignoir off the floor. It was still warm from her skin. He dropped it and reached for a woolen blanket. "No, better yet, put this on."

"Charles, stop!" She raised her arms to push away the blanket, and he saw that her eyes were filling with tears.

"Don't cry," he blurted out. "Why are you crying?"

"Don't you . . . ? Don't you . . . ?"

"Don't I what?"

"Don't you want me?" she whispered. "Even a little bit? You did last week, but I wasn't dressed like this, and—"

"Are you mad?" he fairly shouted. "I want you so much I'm liable to perish on the spot. So cover yourself up, because otherwise you're going to kill me."

Ellie planted her hands on her hips, growing just a little irritated with the direction of the conversation.

"Watch out for your hands!" he yelled.

"My hands are fine," she snapped.

"They are?"

"As long as I don't run ungloved through a rosebush."

"Are you sure?"

She nodded.

For a split second he didn't move. Then he came at her with a force that knocked the breath clear out of her. One minute Ellie was standing, and the next she was on her back, on the bed, with Charles on *top* of her.

But the most amazing thing was that he was kissing her. Really kissing her, in that deep, dark way he hadn't since before the accident. Oh, he'd written racy things in his lists, but he'd been treating her like a delicate flower. Now he was kissing her with his entire body—with his hands, which had already discovered the side slit of her lingerie and were wrapped around the warm curve of her thigh—with his hips, which pressed intimately against hers—and with his heart, which pounded a seductive beat against her breast.

"Don't stop," Ellie moaned. "Don't ever stop."

"I couldn't if I wanted to," he replied, touching her ear most thoroughly—with his mouth. "And I don't. Want to."

"Oh, good." Her head lolled back, and he immediately moved from her ear to her throat.

"This dress," he groaned, apparently unable to speak in complete sentences. "Don't ever lose it."

She smiled. "You like it?"

He answered by pulling open the bows at her hips. "It should be illegal."

"I can get one in every color," she teased.

His hands grasped her ribcage, his large fingers pressing into the underside of her breasts. "Do it. Send me the bill. Or better yet, I'll pay in advance."

"I paid for this one," Ellie said softly.

Charles held still and lifted his head, sensing something different in her voice. "Why? You know you can use my money to buy whatever you want."

"I know. But this is my birthday gift to you."

"The dress?"

She smiled and touched his cheek. Men could be so obtuse. "The dress. Me." She took his hand and moved it to her heart. "This. I want ours to be a real marriage."

He didn't say anything, just took her face in his hands and gazed rapturously at her for a long moment. Then, with agonizing slowness, he lowered his lips to hers for a kiss more tender than anything she could have ever dreamed. "Ah, Ellie," he sighed against her mouth. "You make me so happy."

It wasn't quite a declaration of love, but it still made her heart sing. "I'm happy, too," she whispered.

"Mmmm." He moved to her neck, nuzzling the length of her throat with his face. His hands slid underneath the silk of her gown, trailing fire along her already hot skin. She felt his touch on her hips, her stomach, her breasts—he seemed to be everywhere, and still she wanted more.

She fumbled with the buttons of his shirt, wanting desperately to feel the heat of his skin. But she was shaking with desire, and her hands were still not as nimble as normal.

"Shhhh, let me," he whispered, lifting himself off her to remove his shirt. He worked the buttons slowly, and Ellie wasn't sure whether she wanted him to go even more slowly, to prolong this tantalizing dance, or whether she wanted him just to rip the damned thing off and move back to her side.

Finally he shrugged off the garment and lowered himself partway back down toward her, leaning on his straightened arms. "Touch me," he ordered, then softened it with an impassioned, "Please."

Ellie reached up hesitantly. She'd never touched a man's chest, never even seen one before. She was a little surprised by the sprinkling of reddish brown hair that played across his skin. It was soft and springy, but it didn't hide the way his skin burned or his muscles leapt beneath her hesitant caress.

She grew more daring, excited and emboldened by the way he sucked in his breath when she reached for him. She didn't even have to touch his skin for him to shudder with desire. She suddenly felt as if she must be the most beautiful woman on earth. At least in his eyes, at least for this moment, and that was all that mattered.

She felt his hands on her, lifting her up, and then the lingerie slid over her head and landed in a pool of silk on the floor. Ellie no longer just felt naked, she *was* naked. Somehow it seemed the most natural thing in the world.

He moved off her and removed his breeches. This time he disrobed quickly, almost frantically. Ellie's eyes widened when she saw his aroused manhood. Charles noticed her apprehension, swallowed, and said, "Are you afraid?"

She shook her head. "Well, maybe a little. But I know you will make everything beautiful."

"Oh, God, Ellie," he groaned, sinking back onto the bed. "I'll try. I promise, I'll try. I've never been with an innocent before."

That made her laugh. "And I've never done this before, so we are even."

He touched her cheek. "You're so brave."

"Not brave, just trusting."

"But to laugh, when I'm about to—"

"That's exactly why I *am* laughing. I'm so happy I can't think of anything but laughter."

He kissed her again, his mouth hot on hers. And while he distracted her in this way, his hand stole down the soft skin of her stomach to the patch of curls that shielded her womanhood. She stiffened for just a moment, then relaxed under his gentle caress. At first, he made no move to touch her more deeply, just tickled her as he moved his mouth along the planes of her face.

"Do you like that?" he whispered.

She nodded.

His other hand moved to her breast, squeezing its fullness before grazing the aroused nipple with his palm. "Do you like that?" he whispered, his voice growing husky.

She nodded again, this time with her eyes squeezed shut.

"Do you want me to do it again?"

And while she nodded for the third time, he moved one finger into the hot folds of her womanhood and began to stroke.

Ellie gasped, then forgot how to breathe. Then when she finally remembered where her lungs were, she let out a loud, "Oh!" that caused Charles to chuckle and slide his finger in deeper, touching her in the most intimate of ways.

"Oh, Lord, Ellie," he groaned. "You want me."

She clutched desperately at his shoulders. "You only just noticed?"

His chuckle came from deep in his throat. His fingers continued their sensual torture, moving and stroking within her, and then he found her most sensitive nub of flesh, and Ellie nearly burst from the bed.

"Don't fight it," he said, pressing his arousal against her belly. "It only gets better."

"Are you sure?"

He nodded. "Positive."

Her legs went slack again, and this time Charles nudged them further open, settling into the space between her thighs. He moved his hand, and then his manhood touched her, softly probing at her entry.

"That's right," he whispered. "Open for me. Relax." He pushed forward, then stopped for a moment. "How is that?" he asked, but his voice was strained, and Ellie could tell that he was exerting extraordinary control to keep himself from making love to her completely.

"It's very strange," she admitted. "But good. It's—Oh!" She yelped as he moved even closer to her center. "You tricked me."

"That's what it's all about, sweetling."

"Charles, I—"

His face grew serious. "This might hurt you a little."

"It won't," she assured him. "Not with you."

"Ellie, I . . . Oh, God, I can't wait any longer." He plunged forward, sheathing himself completely within her. "You feel so . . . I can't . . . Oh, Ellie, Ellie."

Charles's body began to move in its primitive rhythm, each thrust accompanied by sounds that were half-groan, half-breath. She was so perfect, so responsive. He'd never before felt desire with this total, complete urgency. He wanted to cherish her and devour her at the same time. He wanted to kiss her, love her, surround her. He wanted everything from her, and he wanted to give her every last piece of himself.

Somewhere in the back of his mind he realized this was love, that elusive emotion he'd managed to escape for so many years. But his ideas and feelings were overwhelmed by the raging need of his body, and he lost all power of thought.

He could hear her moans grow higher in pitch, and

he knew that she felt the same desperation and need. "Reach for it, Ellie," he said. "Reach for it."

And then she shattered beneath him, muscles tightening like a velvet glove around him, and Charles let out a loud shout as he plunged forward one last time, releasing himself into her womb.

He shuddered a few times with the aftershocks of climax, then collapsed on top of her, dimly realizing that he was probably too heavy for her, but unable to move. Finally, when he felt as if he might have a little bit of control over his body again, he started to roll off of her.

"Don't," she said. "I like feeling you."

"I'll crush you."

"No, you won't. I want to—"

He rolled to his side, pulling her along with him. "See? Isn't this nice?"

She nodded and closed her eyes, looking weary but well-loved.

Charles played absently with her hair, wondering how this had happened, that he had fallen in love with his wife—a woman he'd chosen so impulsively and so desperately. "Did you know I dream about your hair?" he asked.

She opened her eyes in delighted surprise. "Really?"

"Mmm, yes. I always used to think it was the exact color of the sun at sunset, but now I realize that I'm wrong." He pinched a lock and brought it to his lips. "It's brighter. Brighter than the sun. And so are you."

He gathered her into his arms, and then they slept.

Chapter 19

The next week was pure bliss. Ellie and Charles spent more time in bed than out, and when they did venture downstairs, it seemed as if life was conspiring to send only the good things their way. Ellie had her first dress fitting, Claire finished cleaning the orangery and told Ellie she'd very much like to help in the planting, and Judith painted four more watercolors, one of which actually resembled a horse.

Ellie found out later that the painting was in fact meant to be a tree, but Judith's feelings didn't seem to be hurt.

In fact, the only thing that could have possibly made Ellie's life any more perfect would be if Charles were to fall prostrate at her feet, kiss each and every one of her toes, and declare his undying love for her. But Ellie was trying not to dwell on the fact that he hadn't told her he loved her.

Fair was fair, after all, and she hadn't summoned up the courage to tell him, either.

She was optimistic, though. She could tell that Charles enjoyed her company immensely, and there was no denying that they were extremely compatible in bed. She had only to win his heart, and she spent a lot of time reminding herself that she'd never failed at anything she *really* put her mind to.

And she was really putting her mind to this. She'd even started composing lists of her own, the most active of which was called "How to Make Charles Realize He Loves Me."

When Ellie wasn't dwelling on the fact that her husband hadn't yet told her that he loved her or working hard to ensure that he would, she spent her time poring over the financial pages of the newspaper. For the first time in her life, she had real control over her savings, and she didn't want to make a muck of things.

Charles seemed to be spending most of *his* time plotting ways to drag Ellie back into bed. She never put up more than token resistance, and she only did that because he kept writing up lists to coerce her, and they were always terribly amusing.

He presented her with what she would later declare her favorite one night as she mulled over investments in the study.

FIVE WAYS ELLIE CAN MOVE HERSELF
FROM THE STUDY TO THE BEDROOM

1. Walk quickly
2. Walk very quickly
3. Run
4. Smile sweetly and ask Charles to carry her
5. Hop on one foot

Ellie raised her brows over the last one.
Charles shrugged. "I ran out of ideas."

"You realize, of course, that now I will have to hop all the way upstairs."

"I would be happy to carry you."

"No, no, you have clearly thrown down the gauntlet. I have no choice. I must hop or forever lose my honor."

"Mmmm, yes," he said, rubbing his chin thoughtfully. "I can see how you might feel that way."

"Of course if you see me wobble, you may feel free to steady me on my feet."

"Or on your *foot*, as the case may be."

Ellie tried to nod regally, but the impish smile on her face quite ruined the effect. She stood, hopped to the door, then turned back to her husband and asked, "Is switching feet allowed?"

He shook his head. "It wouldn't be a proper hop."

"Of course," she murmured. "Hmmm. I may need to lean on you from time to time."

He crossed the room and opened the door for her. "I would be delighted to assist you in any way."

"I may need to lean *heavily* from time to time."

His smile hovered halfway between a grin and a leer. "That would be even more delightful."

Ellie hopped down the hall, switched feet when she thought he wasn't looking, then lost her balance when she moved from the runner carpet to the bare floor. She waved her arms wildly in the air, shrieking with laughter as she tried to stay upright. Charles immediately moved to her side and draped her arm over his shoulder. "Is this better?" he asked, his face remarkably straight.

"Oh, much." She hopped forward.

"That's what you get for switching feet."

"I would never do that," she lied.

"Hmph." He shot her a *you-can't-fool-me* expression. "Now be careful turning the corner."

"I would never dream of—Oh!" she yelped as she stumbled into the wall.

"Tsk tsk, that's going to cost you."

"Really?" she asked interestedly. "How much?"

"A kiss. Perhaps two."

"I will only agree if I may give you three."

He sighed. "You drive a hard bargain, my lady."

She stood on one tiptoe and kissed his nose. "There is one."

"I think that only counts for one half."

She kissed his lips, her tongue darting out mischievously to tease the corner of his mouth. "There is two."

"And the third?"

"You wouldn't get a third if I hadn't bargained you up so skillfully," she pointed out.

"Yes, but now I've come to expect it, so it had better be good."

Ellie's mouth spread into a slow smile at that challenge. "Lucky for me," she murmured, "that I've learned so much about kissing in the past week."

"Lucky for *me*," he returned, grinning as she dragged his mouth down to hers. Her kiss was hot and passionate, and he felt it in every nerve of his body. Mostly he felt it in his midsection, which was tightening into such a knot of desire that he had to tear himself away and gasp, "You had better hop fast."

Ellie laughed, and they one quarter-hopped, one quarter-skipped, one quarter-stumbled, and one quarter-ran down the hall. By the time they reached the staircase, they were laughing so hard that Ellie tripped and landed on the bottom step smack on her backside. "Ouch!" she yelped.

"Is everything all right?"

They both turned sheepish faces to Helen, who was standing with Aunt Cordelia in the great hall, looking at them questioningly. "It looked as if you were limping, Ellie," she said. "Then it looked like . . . Well, frankly, I don't know what it looked like."

Ellie turned beet red. "He . . . ah . . . I . . . ah . . ."

Charles didn't even bother trying to explain.

Helen smiled. "I see your point exactly. Come along, Cordelia. I believe our newlyweds desire some privacy."

"Newlyweds, hmph!" Cordelia barked. "They're acting like a couple of deranged birds, if you ask me."

Ellie watched as the old lady marched out of the hall, Helen right on her heels. "Well, at least she isn't yelling 'fire' at every opportunity anymore."

Charles blinked. "You're right. I think our myriad accidents in the kitchen may have scared the fire right out of her."

"Thank goodness."

"Unfortunately, or perhaps fortunately, depending on your viewpoint, it has not done the same for me."

"I'm afraid I don't see your point."

"What I mean," he fairly growled, "is that I am on fire."

Ellie's eyes and her mouth made three perfect O's.

"So get that little body of yours upstairs and into the bedroom before I ravish you here on the stairs."

She smiled slyly. "You'd do that?"

He leaned forward, suddenly looking every inch the rake he was reputed to be. "I wouldn't issue any dares, my lady, unless you're prepared to face the consequences."

Ellie scrambled to her feet and started to run. Charles followed, grateful that she'd decided to travel on both of her feet.

Several hours later, Ellie and Charles lounged in bed, propped up against their pillows as they ate the gourmet dinner they'd had delivered to their room. Neither had been in any state to make an appearance downstairs.

"Quail?" Charles asked, holding up a piece.

Ellie ate it right from his fingers. "Mmmm. Delicious."

"Asparagus?"

"I'm going to get dreadfully fat."

"You'd still be delightful." He popped the asparagus tip between her lips.

Ellie chewed and sighed with contentment. "Monsieur Belmont is a genius."

"That's why I hired him. Here, try a bit of this roast duck. I promise you'll adore it."

"No, no, stop. I couldn't possibly eat another bite."

"Ah, ye weak of heart," Charles teased, holding up a dish and a spoon. "You can't possibly stop now. I'm trying to make a complete wanton of you. Besides, Monsieur Belmont will throw a tantrum if you do not eat the custard. It's his masterwork."

"I didn't realize chefs had masterworks."

He smiled seductively. "Trust me on this."

"Very well, I concede. I'll try a small bite." Ellie

opened her mouth and let Charles spoon in some custard. "Good heaven!" she cried. "That is divine."

"I gather you would like some more."

"If you don't give me another bite of that custard I shall have to kill you."

"Said with a straight face," he said with admiration.

She shot him a sideways glance. "I'm not joking."

"Here, have the entire pot. I hate to come between a woman and her food."

Ellie paused in her quest to devour every last speck of custard to say, "Normally I would take offense at that remark, but I'm in far too sublime a state to do so at this moment."

"I'm loathe to speculate whether this sublime state is due to my masculine prowess and stamina or merely to a pot of custard."

"I won't answer that. I would hate to hurt your feelings."

He rolled his eyes. "You're very kind."

"Please say Monsieur Belmont makes this on a regular basis."

"All the time. It's my favorite."

Ellie paused, spoon frozen in her mouth. "Oh," she said, looking rather guilty. "I suppose I ought to share."

"Pay it no mind. I can eat this strawberry tart." He took a bite. "I say, Monsieur Belmont must be angling for a raise in pay."

"Why do you think?"

"Aren't strawberry tarts your favorite? It's uncharacteristically thoughtful of him to prepare both our favorites."

Ellie's face sank into a serious expression.

"Why suddenly so somber?" Charles asked, licking a bit of strawberry off of his lips.

"I am facing a very serious moral dilemma."

Charles glanced around the room. "I don't see one."

"You had better eat the rest of this custard," Ellie said, handing him the pot, which was about two-thirds empty. "I shall feel guilty for weeks if I don't share."

He grinned. "I knew that marrying the daughter of a vicar would have its benefits."

"I know," she sighed. "I have never been able to ignore anyone in need."

Charles spooned a bite of the custard into his mouth with considerable enthusiasm. "I don't know if this counts as 'need,' but I'm willing to pretend it does for your sake."

"The sacrifices one makes for one's wife," she muttered.

"Here, have the rest of the strawberry tart."

"No, I couldn't," she said, holding up a hand. "It seems somehow sacrilegious after the custard."

He shrugged. "Have it your own way."

"Besides, I feel suddenly rather strange."

Charles put the custard down and assessed her. She was blinking quite rapidly, and her skin held a strange pasty quality. "You do look rather odd."

"Oh, dear Lord," Ellie moaned, clutching at her stomach as she curled into a fetal position.

He quickly removed the rest of the dinner plates from the bed. "Ellie? Darling?"

She didn't answer, just whimpered as she tried to pull herself into a tight little ball. Sweat was breaking out on her brow, and her breath was coming in shallow pants.

Charles felt prickly with panic. Ellie, who had been laughing and teasing just moments earlier, now looked as if she were ... as if ... Dear God, she looked like she were dying.

His heart slammed into his throat, and he raced across the room and yanked hard on the bellpull. Then he ran to the door, threw it open, and bellowed, "Cordelia!" His aunt was more than a trifle batty, but she did know a thing or two about sickness and healing, and Charles didn't know what else to do.

"Ellie," he said urgently, running back to her side. "What is wrong? Please talk to me."

"It's like burning swords," she gasped, her eyes shut tight against the pain. "Burning swords in my belly. Oh, God, Oh God. Make it go away. Please."

Charles swallowed in fear, then put a hand on his own stomach, which was also throbbing. He ascribed it to terror; clearly he was not feeling the same agony his wife was experiencing.

"Ooooooohhhhhh!" she yelled, starting to convulse.

Charles sprang to his feet and ran back to the open door. "Someone get here now!" he shouted, just as Helen and Cordelia came running around the corner.

"What happened?" Helen asked breathlessly.

"It's Ellie. She's sick. I don't know what happened. One minute she was fine, and the next ..."

They raced to her bedside. Cordelia took one look at Ellie's pathetic form and announced, "She's been poisoned."

"What?" Helen asked in horror.

"That's ludicrous," Charles said at the same time.

"I've seen this before," Cordelia said. "She's been poisoned. I'm sure of it."

"What can we do?" Helen asked.

"She'll have to be purged. Charles, bring her to the washbasin."

Charles regarded his aunt dubiously. Was he right to trust his wife's welfare to an old woman who was admittedly a touch senile? But then again, he didn't know what else to do, and even if Ellie hadn't been poisoned, Cordelia's suggestion made sense. Clearly they needed to remove whatever was in her stomach.

He picked her up, trying not to let her agonized groans affect him. She twitched violently in his arms, her spasms shaking him to the core.

He looked to Cordelia. "I think she's getting worse."

"Hurry up!"

He hurried to the washbasin and pulled Ellie's hair from her face. "Shhh, darling, it will be all right," he whispered.

Cordelia held up a quill. "Open her mouth."

"What the hell are you going to do with that?"

"Just do what I say."

Charles held Ellie's mouth open and watched in horror as Cordelia thrust the feathered end of the quill down her throat. Ellie gagged several times before she finally vomited.

Charles looked away for a moment. He couldn't help it. "Are we done?"

Cordelia ignored him. "One more time, Eleanor," she said. "You're a strong girl. You can do it. Helen, get something to rinse out her mouth when she's done."

She jammed the feather down her throat again, and Ellie released the rest of the contents of her stomach.

"That's it," Cordelia said. She took a glass of water from Helen and poured some into Ellie's mouth. "Spit that out, girl."

Ellie half spit and half let gravity pull the water from her mouth. "Don't make me do that again," she pleaded.

"At least she's talking," Cordelia said. "That's a good sign."

Charles hoped she was right, because he'd never seen a person look as green as Ellie did right then. He let Helen wipe her mouth with a damp cloth and then carried her back to the bed.

Helen picked up the dirty washbasin with shaking hands, and said, "I'll have someone take care of this," and ran from the room.

Charles picked up Ellie's hand, then turned to Cordelia and asked, "You don't really think she was poisoned?"

His aunt nodded emphatically. "What did she eat? Anything that you didn't?"

"No, except for . . ."

"Except for what?"

"The custard, but I had a bite, too."

"Hmph. And how do you feel?"

Charles stared at her for a long moment, his hand moving to his stomach. "Not very well, actually."

"You see?"

"But it's nothing like what Ellie's been through. Just

a little stabbing pain, as if I'd eaten something that had gone off. That's all."

"And you ate only one bite?"

Charles nodded, and then the blood drained from his face. "She ate nearly the entire pot," he whispered. "At least two-thirds."

"She'd probably be dead if she'd finished it," Cordelia stated. "Good thing she shared it with you."

Charles could scarcely believe the lack of emotion in her voice. "It must be food poisoning. That's the only explanation."

Cordelia shrugged. "My money is on the real thing."

He stared at her in disbelief. "That's impossible. Who would want to do something like this to her?"

"It's that young girl Claire, if you ask me," Cordelia replied. "Everyone knows what she did to the countess's hands."

"But that was an accident," Charles said, not wanting to believe his aunt's words. Claire could be mischievous, but she would never do something like this. "And Claire has made her peace with Ellie."

Cordelia shrugged. "Has she?"

As if on cue, Helen reappeared, dragging Claire, who was crying.

Charles turned his eyes to his cousin, trying very hard to keep any sense of accusation from his gaze.

"I didn't do this," Claire wailed. "I would never, ever. You know I wouldn't. I love Ellie now. I would never hurt her."

Charles wanted to believe her. He truly did, but Claire had been the cause of so much mischief. "Perhaps this is something you set in motion last week, before you and Ellie worked out your differences," he said gently. "Perhaps you forgot—"

"No!" Claire cried. "No, I didn't do this. I swear."

Helen put her arm around her daughter's shoulder. "I believe her, Charles."

Charles looked into Claire's red-rimmed eyes and realized that Helen was right. She was telling the truth and he felt like a heel for ever, even for a moment, considering otherwise. Claire might not be perfect, but she wouldn't poison anyone. He sighed. "It was probably just an accident. Perhaps Monsieur Belmont used bad milk in the custard."

"Bad milk?" Cordelia echoed. "It would have had to be well past rancid to do what it did to her."

Charles knew she had a valid point. Ellie had been violently, deathly ill. Could the convulsions that had shaken her small frame been caused by something as benign as bad milk? But what else could it be? Who would want to poison Ellie?

Helen stepped forward and placed a comforting hand on Charles's arm. "Would you like me to stay with her?"

He didn't answer her for a moment, still lost in his own thoughts. "I'm sorry, what? No. No, I'll stay with her."

Helen inclined her head. "Of course. If you would like any assistance, however . . ."

Charles finally refocused his eyes and gave his cousin his full attention. "I appreciate your offer, Helen. I may very well take you up on it."

"Do not hesitate to wake me up," she said. Then she took her daughter's hand and drew her toward the door. "Come along, Claire. Ellie will never be able to rest with so many people milling about."

Cordelia also strode toward the door. "I'll be back in an hour to check on her," she said. "But she looks to be over the worst of it."

Charles looked down at his now sleeping wife. She certainly looked better than she had just ten minutes ago. But that wasn't saying much; the only way she could have looked worse was if she'd started spitting up blood. Her skin was still translucent and greenish, but her breathing was even, and she didn't appear to be in any pain.

He picked up her hand and brought it to his lips, saying a soft prayer as he did so. It was going to be a long night.

Chapter 20

B y noon the next day, Ellie's color was nearly back to normal, and it was clear to Charles that her bout with food poisoning would not leave her with any lingering illness. Cordelia agreed with his assessment, but she instructed Charles to feed her chunks of bread to sop up whatever poison might be lingering in her stomach.

He took Cordelia's advice to heart, and by suppertime Ellie was alert and begging him not to force her to eat any more bread.

"Not another piece," Ellie pleaded. "It turns my stomach."

"Everything will turn your stomach," he said in a matter-of-fact voice. He'd long since learned that she responded best to plain speaking.

She moaned. "Then don't make me eat."

"I must. It helps to absorb the poison."

"But it was only bad milk. Surely it doesn't linger in my stomach."

"Bad milk, bad eggs ... There is no way to know what really caused the attack." He stared at her with an odd look in his eyes. "All I know is that last night you looked like you were going to die."

Ellie fell silent. Last night she had *felt* like she was going to die. "Very well," she said quietly. "Give me another piece of bread."

Charles handed her a slice. "I think Cordelia has the right idea of this. You do seem less sluggish since you started eating the bread."

"Cordelia does seem considerably more lucid since my unfortunate bout with poison."

He regarded her thoughtfully. "I rather think Cordelia just needed someone to listen to her from time to time."

"Speaking of people who want to be listened to from time to time . . ." Ellie said, nodding toward the open door to her room.

"Good evening, Ellie!" Judith said brightly. "You've slept the whole day away."

"I know. Terribly lazy of me, don't you think?"

Judith just shrugged. "I painted you a picture."

"Oh, it's lovely!" Ellie exclaimed. "It's such a beautiful . . . a beautiful . . ." She looked to Charles who was no help at all. "Rabbit?"

"Exactly."

Ellie let out a relieved breath.

"I saw one in the garden. I thought you'd like his ears."

"I do. I love his ears. They are very pointy."

Judith's face turned serious. "Mama told me you drank some bad milk."

"Yes, it's given me a horrid stomachache, I'm afraid."

"You must always smell milk before you drink it," Judith instructed. "Always."

"I certainly will from now on." Ellie patted the little girl's hand. "I appreciate your advice."

Judith nodded. "I always give good advice."

Ellie smothered a laugh. "Come here, poppet, and give me a hug. That will be the nicest medicine I've had all day."

Judith climbed onto the bed and snuggled into Ellie's embrace. "Would you like a kiss?"

"Oh, indeed."

"It will make you better," the little girl said as she planted a loud smack on Ellie's cheek. "Maybe not right away, but it will."

Ellie stroked her hair. "I'm sure it will, poppet. I'm beginning to feel better already."

As Charles stood in the corner, silently regarding his wife and cousin, his heart swelled to overflowing. Ellie was still recovering from the worst attack of food poisoning he'd ever witnessed, and here she was, cuddling his young cousin.

She was amazing. There was no other way to describe her, and if that weren't enough, she was clearly going to make the best damned mother England had ever seen. Hell, she already made the best wife he could ever have imagined.

He felt his eyes grow suspiciously moist, and he suddenly realized that he had to tell her he loved her. And he had to do it now, this very instant. Otherwise he was certain his heart would burst. Or his blood would boil. Or maybe all his hair would fall out. All he knew was that the words "I love you" were welling up within him and he had to say them aloud. It just wasn't something he could contain within the boundaries of his heart any longer.

He wasn't sure if she returned the sentiment, although he suspected that if she didn't, she felt something at least close to love, and that would be good enough for him right now. He had plenty of time to make her love him. A lifetime, in fact.

Charles was coming to greatly appreciate the permanence of the marriage bond.

"Judith," he said abruptly. "I need to speak with Ellie right now."

Judith turned her head toward him without relinquishing her spot in Ellie's arms. "Go ahead."

"I need to speak with her *privately*."

Judith snorted in a vaguely insulted manner. She climbed off the bed, turned her nose up at Charles, and said to Ellie, "I shall be in the nursery if you need me."

"I shall remember that," Ellie replied gravely.

Judith marched to the door, then turned around, ran back to Charles, and kissed him quickly on the back of his hand. "Because you're such a sourpuss," she said, "and you ought to be a sweetpuss."

He tousled her hair. "Thank you, poppet. I shall try to behave accordingly."

Judith smiled and ran from the room, carelessly letting the door slam behind her.

Ellie switched her gaze to Charles. "You look very serious."

"I am," he blurted out, his voice sounding funny to his ears. Damn, but he felt like a green boy. He didn't know why he should feel so nervous. It was clear she held him in a certain measure of affection. It was just that he'd never said, "I love you," before.

Hell, he'd never expected to lose his heart to a wife,

of all people. He took a deep breath. "Ellie," he began.

"Has someone else taken ill?" she asked, her face growing concerned. "The custard—"

"No! No, it's not that. It is simply that there is something I must tell you, and"—his face grew impossibly sheepish—"and I don't quite know how to go about doing it."

Ellie chewed on her lower lip, feeling suddenly quite heartsick. She'd thought their marriage was progressing so well, and now he looked as if he were about to ask for a divorce! Which was ludicrous, of course—a man in his position would never ask for a divorce, but Ellie had a bad feeling about this all the same.

"When we wed," he began, "I held certain notions about what I wanted out of marriage."

"I know," Ellie interrupted, panic rising within her. He'd made those notions clear, and her heart skipped a beat just thinking about it. "But if you think about it, you'll realize that—"

Charles held up a hand. "Please let me finish. This is very difficult for me."

It was difficult for her, too, Ellie thought glumly, even more so since he wasn't letting her state her case.

"What I'm trying to say is ... Bugger." He raked his hand through his hair. "This is more difficult than I'd anticipated."

Good, she thought. If he was going to break her heart, she didn't want it to be easy for him.

"What I'm trying to say is that I had it all wrong. I don't want a wife who ..."

"You don't want a wife?" she choked.

"No!" he practically yelled. Then he continued in a

more normal tone, "I don't want a wife who will look the other way if I stray."

"You want me to *watch*?"

"No, I want you to be furious."

Ellie was by now on the verge of tears. "You deliberately want to make me angry? To hurt me?"

"No. Oh, God, you've got it all wrong. I don't want to be unfaithful. I'm not *going* to be unfaithful. I just want you to love me so much that if I did—which I'm not going to—you would want to have me drawn and quartered."

Ellie just stared at him while she digested his words. "I see."

"Do you? Do you really? Because what I'm saying is that I love you, and although I very much hope you return the feeling, it's perfectly all right if you don't just yet. But I need you to tell me that I can hope, that you're coming to care for me, that—"

A choking sort of sound emerged from Ellie's throat, and she covered her face with her hands. She was shaking so hard he didn't know what to think. "Ellie?" he said urgently. "Ellie, my love, say something. Please talk to me."

"Oh, Charles," she finally managed to get out. "You're such an idiot."

He drew back, his heart and soul aching more than he ever thought possible.

"Of *course* I love you. I might as well have written the words on my forehead."

His mouth fell slightly open. "You do?"

"I do." It was hard to hear her voice, for she was speaking through laughter and tears.

"I thought you *might*, actually," he said, teasing her

by adopting his favorite rakish expression. "I've never really had much trouble with women before and—"

"Oh, stop!" she said, throwing her pillow at him. "Don't ruin this perfectly perfect moment by pretending you orchestrated the entire scenario."

"Oh?" He raised a brow. "Then what should I do? I've been a rake my entire life. I'm at a bit of a loss now that I'm reformed."

"What you should do," Ellie said, feeling a smile begin at the core of her being, "is come over here to this bed and give me a big hug. The biggest you've ever given."

He closed the distance between them and sat by her side.

"And then," she continued, her smile now on her face, in her eyes, even in her hair and toes, "you should kiss me."

He leaned forward and dropped a feather-light peck on her lips. "Like this?"

She shook her head. "That was much too tame, and you forgot to hug me first."

He gathered her into his arms and pulled her onto his lap. "If I could hold you like this forever, I would," he whispered.

"Tighter."

He chuckled. "Your stomach . . . I don't want to—"

"My stomach feels remarkably restored," she sighed. "It must be the power of love."

"Do you really think so?" he asked, chuckling.

She made a face. "That was the most maudlin thing I've ever said, wasn't it?"

"I probably haven't known you long enough to

make that judgment, but given your rather plainspoken nature, I would venture to agree."

"Well, I don't care. I meant it." She threw her arms around him and held tight. "I don't know how it happened, because I never expected to fall in love with you, but I did, and if it makes my stomach feel better, then so be it."

In her arms Charles shook with laughter.

"Is love supposed to be this much fun?" Ellie asked.

"I doubt it, but I don't plan to complain."

"I thought I was supposed to feel tortured and agonized and all that rot."

He took her face between his hands and gazed at her seriously. "Since you became my wife, you've been seriously burned, suffered a massive case of food-poisoning, and I won't even begin to list Claire's many transgressions against you. I should think you've paid your dues in the realm of torture and agony."

"Well, I did feel agonized and tortured for a moment or two," she admitted.

"Really? When was that?"

"When I realized I loved you."

"The notion was that unpalatable?" he teased.

She looked down at her hands. "I remembered that awful list you wrote before we married, about how you wanted a wife who would look the other way when you strayed."

He groaned. "I was insane. No, I wasn't insane. I was merely stupid. And I just didn't know *you*."

"All I could think about was how I could never be the passive, accepting wife you wanted, and how much it would hurt if you were unfaithful." She shook her head. "I could swear I could *hear* my heart breaking."

"That will never happen," he assured her. Then his expression grew suspicious. "Wait just one second. Why did this give you only a moment or two of agony? I should think the prospect of my being unfaithful would be worth at least a full day of heartbreak."

Ellie laughed. "I was only agonized until I remembered who I was. You see, I've always been able to get what I want if I work hard enough for it. So I decided to work hard for you."

Her words were something less than poetry, but Charles's heart sang nonetheless.

"Oh Oh Oh!" she suddenly exclaimed. "I even made a list."

"Trying to beat me at my own game, were you?"

"Trying to *win* you at your own game. It's in the top drawer of my writing desk. Go fetch it so I may read it to you."

Charles bounded off the bed, oddly touched that she had adopted his habit of making lists. "Shall I read it to myself, or do you want to read it aloud?" he asked.

"Oh, I can—" Her expression froze, and she turned quite red. "Actually, you can read it if you like. To yourself."

He found the list and returned to her side. This was going to be interesting if she'd put something on it so racy that she was embarrassed to read it aloud. He looked down at her neat handwriting and carefully numbered sentences and then decided to torture her. He handed her the list and said, "I really think you ought to read it yourself. After all, it's your debut list."

She turned even redder, which he hadn't thought possible but found very entertaining nonetheless. "Very well," she muttered, snatching the paper from his hands. "But you may not laugh at me."

"I don't make promises I cannot keep."

"Fiend."

Charles leaned back against the pillows, resting his head in his hands, his elbows bent out to the side. "Do begin."

Ellie cleared her throat. "Ahem. This list is titled: 'How To Make Charles Realize He Loves Me.' "

"Amazingly enough, the dolt managed to figure it out all on his own."

"Yes," Ellie said, "the dolt did."

He stifled a smile. "I won't interrupt again."

"I thought you said you don't make promises you cannot keep."

"I shall *try* not to interrupt again," he amended.

She shot him a disbelieving look, then read, " 'Number One: Impress him with my financial acumen.' "

"I've been impressed with that all along."

" 'Number Two: Demonstrate how capably I can run the household.' "

He scratched his head. "Much as I appreciate the more practical aspects of your personality, these aren't very romantic suggestions."

"I was still warming to the task," she explained. "It took a bit of time to get into the true spirit of the endeavor. Now then, 'Number Three: Have Mrs. Smithson send over more silk lingerie.' "

"Now that is a suggestion I can endorse without reservation."

She looked at him sideways, barely turning her head away from the list in her hands. "I thought you weren't going to interrupt."

"I said I would try, and that doesn't qualify as an interruption. You were quite finished with your sentence."

"Your verbal dexterity amazes me."

"I'm delighted to hear it."

" 'Number Four: Make certain he realizes how good I am with Judith so that he will think I will make a good mother.' " She turned to him with a concerned expression. "I don't want you to think that is the only reason I spend time with Judith, though. I love her dearly."

He covered her hand with his own. "I know. And I know that you will be a superb mother. It warms me inside just thinking about it."

Ellie smiled, ridiculously pleased by his compliment. "You shall be an excellent father as well. I am certain of it."

"I must confess that I had never given the matter much thought beyond the simple fact that I would need an heir, but now . . ." His eyes grew misty. "Now I realize there is something more. Something quite amazing and beautiful."

She sank into him. "Oh, Charles. I am so happy you fell out of that tree."

He grinned. "And I am happy you were walking underneath me. Clearly, I have excellent aim."

"And such modesty, too."

"Read me the last item on the list, if you will."

Her cheeks pinkened. "Oh, it's nothing. And it doesn't really matter, since I don't need to make you realize that you love me. As you said, you figured it out all on your own."

"Read it, wife, or I will tie you to the bed."

Her jaw dropped, and she made a strange, choking sort of sound.

"Oh, don't look at me like that. I wouldn't do it tightly."

"Charles!"

He rolled his eyes heavenward. "I suppose you wouldn't know about such things."

"No, it's not that. I . . . er . . . Perhaps you should read item five on my list." She shoved the paper in his direction.

Charles looked down and read, "Number five: Tie him to the—" He dissolved into raucous laughter before he could even utter the *b* in the word *bed*.

"It isn't what you think!"

"Darling, if you know what I think, you're far less innocent than I imagined."

"Well, it certainly isn't whatever you meant when you said—Stop laughing, I'll tell you!"

He might have responded, but it was difficult to tell under the force of his laughter.

"All I meant," she grumbled, "was that you seem rather enamored of me when we are . . . *you know* . . . and I thought if I could keep you here . . ."

He held out his wrists, "I am yours to bind, my lady."

"I was speaking metaphorically!"

"I know," he said with a sigh. "More's the pity."

She tried not to smile. "I should disapprove of such talk . . ."

"But I'm so endearing," he said with a rakish grin.

"Charles?"

"Yes?"

"My stomach . . ."

His face grew serious. "Yes?"

"It feels quite normal."

He spoke carefully. "And by that you mean . . . ?"

Her smile was slow and seductive. "Exactly what you think. And this time, I *do* know what you're thinking. I'm *far* less innocent than I was a week ago."

He leaned down and captured her mouth in a long and melting kiss. "Thank God for that."

Ellie wrapped her arms around him, reveling in the heat of his body. "I missed you last night," she murmured.

"You weren't even conscious last night," he returned, pulling out of her embrace. "And you're going to have to miss me for a little bit longer."

"What?"

He wiggled away and stood on the floor. "Do you really think I'm such a cur that I would take advantage of you in this condition?

"Actually, I'd been hoping to take advantage of *you*," she muttered.

"You were afraid I would fail as a husband because I wouldn't be able to control my baser instincts," he explained. "If this isn't an excellent demonstration of control, I don't know what is."

"You don't have to control them with *me*."

"Nonetheless, you shall have to wait a few days."

"You are a beast."

"You are merely frustrated, Ellie. You'll get over it."

Ellie crossed her arms and glared at him. "Send Judith back in. I think I preferred her company."

He chuckled. "I love you."

"I love you, too. Now get out before I throw something at you."

Chapter 21

Charles's temporary vow of abstinence was just that—temporary—and soon he and Ellie were back to their newlywed habits.

They still had their independent pursuits, however, and one day while Ellie was poring over the financial pages, Charles decided to ride the perimeter of his property. The weather was unseasonably warm, and he wanted to take advantage of the sunshine before it turned too cold to take long rides. He would have liked to bring Ellie along with him, but she didn't know how to ride and adamantly refused to begin lessons until spring, when the weather would be warmer and the ground not quite so hard.

"I shall surely be landing on my behind quite frequently," she had explained, "so I might as well do so when the ground is nice and soft."

Charles chuckled at the memory as he mounted his gelding and took off at an easy trot. His wife certainly had a practical streak. It was one of the things he loved best about her.

Thoughts of Ellie seemed to occupy a great deal of his mind these days. It was getting embarrassing how often people snapped their fingers in front of his face because he was staring off into space. He couldn't help it. All he had to do was think of her and he found himself wearing a silly smile and sighing like an idiot.

He wondered if the bliss of true love ever wore off. He hoped not.

By the time Charles reached the end of the drive, he'd remembered three funny comments Ellie had said the night before, pictured the way she looked when she was giving Judith a hug, and fantasized about what he was going to do with her that night in bed.

That particular daydream made him feel quite warm and left his reflexes a bit dulled, which was probably why he didn't immediately notice when his horse started to grow agitated.

"Whoa there, Whistler. Easy now, boy," he said, pulling back on the reins. But the gelding paid him no attention, snorting in obvious fear and pain.

"What the hell?" Charles leaned down and tried to calm Whistler by patting his long neck. This didn't seem to help, and soon Charles was fighting just to keep his seat.

"Whistler! Whistler! Calm down, boy."

No effect. One minute Charles had the reins in his hands and the next he was flying through the air, with barely time to say, "Damn," before he landed, solid on his right ankle—the same one he'd injured the day he met Ellie.

And then he said, "Damn!" many many more times. The expletive didn't do much to ease the pain shooting up his leg, and it didn't do much to ease his temper, but he yelled it all the same.

Whistler let out one last whinny and took off toward Wycombe Abbey at a full gallop, leaving Charles stranded with an ankle he feared would not be able to bear any weight.

Muttering an astonishing variety of curses, he rose to his hands and knees and crawled to a nearby tree stump, where he sat and swore some more. He touched his ankle through his boot and wasn't surprised to find it swelling at a rapid rate. He tried to pull the boot off, but the pain was too much. Damn. They were going to have to cut through the leather. Another perfectly good pair of boots ruined.

Charles groaned, grabbed a nearby stick that could double as a cane, and started to hobble home. His ankle was killing him, but he didn't see what else he could do. He'd told Ellie that he would be gone for several hours, so no one would notice his absence for some time.

His progress was slow and not particularly steady, but eventually he made his way back to the end of the drive, and Wycombe Abbey came into view.

Thankfully, so did Ellie, who was running toward him at breakneck speed as she shouted his name.

"Charles!" she yelled. "Thank goodness! What happened? Whistler came back, and he's bleeding, and ..." As soon as she reached him, she stopped talking to catch her breath.

"Whistler's bleeding?" he asked.

"Yes. The groom isn't sure why, and I didn't know what happened to you, and—What *did* happen to you?"

"Whistler threw me. I sprained my ankle."

"Again?"

He looked down ruefully at his right foot. "Same one. I imagine it was still weak from the previous injury."

"Does it hurt?"

He looked at her as if she were a halfwit. "Like the devil."

"Oh, yes, I suppose it must. Here, lean on me, and we'll walk back to the Abbey together."

Charles draped his arm over her shoulder and used her weight to support him as they limped home. "Why do I feel like I'm reliving a bad dream?" he wondered aloud.

Ellie chuckled. "We *have* done this before, haven't we? But if you recall, we wouldn't have met if you hadn't sprained your ankle last time. At the very least, you wouldn't have asked me to marry you if I hadn't tended to your injury with such tender and loving care."

"Tender and loving care!" he said with a snort. "You were practically breathing fire."

"Yes, well, we couldn't have the patient feeling sorry for himself, could we?"

As they neared the house, Charles said, "I want to go to the stables and see why Whistler was bleeding."

"You can go after I tend to your foot."

"Tend to it in the stables. I'm sure someone there has a knife you can use to cut the boot off."

Ellie ground to a halt. "I insist that you go back to the house where I can do a proper check for broken bones."

"I haven't broken any bones."

"How do you know?"

"I've broken them before. I know what it feels like."

He tugged at her, trying to shift their direction toward the stables, but the woman had positively grown roots. "Ellie," he ground out. "Let's go."

"You'll find I am more stubborn than you think."

"If that is true, I'm in big trouble," he muttered.

"What does that mean?"

"It means I'd say you're as stubborn as a damned mule, woman, except that might insult the mule."

Ellie lurched back, dropping him. "Well, I never!"

"Oh, for the love of God," he grumbled, rubbing his elbow where he banged it when he fell. "Will you help me get to the bloody stables or do I have to limp there myself?"

She answered by turning on her heel and marching back to Wycombe Abbey.

"Damned stubborn mule of a woman," he muttered. Thankfully, he still had his walking stick, and a few minutes later he collapsed onto a bench in the stables.

"Someone get me a knife!" he shouted. If he didn't get this damned boot off, his foot was going to explode.

A groom named James rushed to his side and handed him a knife. "Whistler's bleeding, my lord," James said.

"I heard." Charles winced as he started sawing at the leather of his second-best pair of boots. His best had already been demolished by Ellie. "What happened?"

Thomas Leavey, who ran the stables and was, in Charles's opinion, one of the finest judges of horseflesh in the country, stepped forward and said, "We found this under the saddle."

Charles sucked in his breath. Leavey held in his hand a bent, rusty nail. It wasn't very long, but Charles's weight on the saddle would have been enough to drive it into Whistler's back, causing the horse unspeakable agony.

"Who saddled my horse?" Charles demanded.

"I did," Leavey said.

Charles stared at his trusted stablemaster. He knew that Leavey would never do anything to hurt a horse, much less a human. "Have you any idea how this might have happened?"

"I left Whistler alone in his stall for a minute or two before you came for him. My only guess is that someone sneaked in and put the nail under the saddle."

"Who the hell would do something like this?" Charles demanded.

No one offered an answer.

"It wasn't an accident," Leavey finally said. "That much I know. Something like this doesn't happen by accident."

Charles knew he spoke the truth. Someone had deliberately tried to injure him. His blood ran cold. Someone had probably wanted him dead.

As he was digesting that chilling fact, Ellie stomped into the stables. "I am far too nice a person," she announced to the room at large.

The stablehands just stared at her, clearly not sure how to reply.

She marched over to Charles. "Give me the knife," she said. "I'll take care of your boot."

He handed it to her without a word, still in shock over the recent attempt against his life.

She sat inelegantly at his feet and began to saw

away at his boot. "Next time you compare me to a mule," she hissed, "you had better find the mule wanting."

Charles couldn't even manage a chuckle.

"Why was Whistler bleeding?" she asked.

He exchanged a glance with Leavey and James. He didn't want her to know about the attempt on his life. He would have to have a talk with the two men as soon as she left, for if they uttered one word about this to anyone, Ellie would learn the truth before nightfall. Gossip could be rampant on country estates. "It was just a scratch," he told her. "He must have stuck himself on a branch while running home."

"I don't know very much about horses," she said, not looking up from her work on his boot, "but that sounds strange to me. Whistler would have had to hit that branch very hard to draw blood."

"Er, I suppose he would."

She eased the mutilated boot from his foot. "I can't imagine how he would have hit a branch while running along the main road or the drive. Both are kept very clear."

She had him there. Charles looked over to Leavey for help, but the stablemaster just shrugged.

Ellie touched his ankle gently, checking the swelling. "Furthermore," she said, "it makes more sense that he sustained the injury before he threw you. After all, there must be some explanation for his distress. He's never thrown you before, has he?"

"No," Charles said.

She turned the ankle slightly. "Does that hurt?"

"No."

"Does this?" She turned it in a different direction.

"No."

"Good." She dropped his foot and looked up at him. "I think you're lying to me."

Charles noticed that Leavey and James had conveniently disappeared.

"What really happened to Whistler, Charles?" When he didn't reply fast enough, she leveled a hard stare in his direction and added, "And remember that I'm as stubborn as a mule, so don't think you're going anywhere without telling me the truth."

Charles let out a weary sigh. There were disadvantages to having such an intelligent wife. There was no way Ellie wasn't going to ferret out the entire story on her own. Better she hear it from him. He told her the truth, finishing up by showing her the rusty nail Leavey had left sitting beside him on the bench.

Ellie twisted her gloves in her hands. She'd taken them off before tending to his ankle, and now they were a wrinkled mess. After a long pause, she said, "What did you hope to gain by hiding this from me?"

"I just wanted to protect you."

"From the truth?" Her voice was sharp.

"I didn't want you to worry."

"You didn't want me to worry."

He thought she sounded unnaturally calm.

"You didn't want me to *worry*?"

Now he thought she sounded a little bit shrill.

"You didn't want me to WORRY?"

By now Charles figured that half the staff of Wycombe Abbey could hear her yelling. "Ellie, my love—"

"Don't try to weasel out of this by calling me 'your love,'" she stormed. "How would you feel if I lied to you about something this important? Well? How would you feel?"

He opened his mouth, but before he could say anything, she yelled, "I'll tell you how you would feel. You would be so angry you would want to *strangle* me."

Charles thought she was most probably right, but didn't see the point in admitting it just then.

Ellie took a deep breath and pressed her fingers against her temples. "All right, all right, Ellie," she said to herself, "calm down. Killing him now would be counterproductive." She looked back up. "I am going to control my temper because this is such a dire and serious situation. But don't think I'm not furious with you."

"There is little danger of that."

"Don't be glib," she bit out. "Someone has tried to kill you, and if we don't figure out who and why, you might end up dead."

"I know," he said softly, "and that is why I am going to hire extra protection for you, Helen, and the girls."

"*We* are not the ones in need of extra protection! You are the one whose life is in danger."

"I will be extra careful as well," he assured her.

"Dear God, this is terrible. Why would someone want to kill you?"

"I don't know, Ellie."

She rubbed her temples again. "My head aches."

He took her hand. "Why don't we go back to the house?"

"Not now. I'm thinking," she said, shaking his hand off.

Charles gave up trying to follow the zigzags of her thought process.

She whipped her head around to face him. "I'll bet you were meant to be poisoned."

"I beg your pardon?"

"The custard. It wasn't bad milk. Monsieur Belmont has been in a rage for days because we even suggested it. Someone poisoned the custard, but it was meant for you, not me. Everyone knows it is your favorite dessert. You told me so yourself."

He stared at her, dumbfounded. "You're right."

"Yes, and I wouldn't be surprised if the carriage accident when we were courting was also . . . Charles? Charles?" Ellie swallowed. "You look quite ill."

Charles felt a rage sweep through him unlike anything he had ever known. That someone had tried to kill him was bad enough. That Ellie had gotten caught in the proverbial line of fire made him want to eviscerate someone.

He stared at her, as if somehow trying to imprint her features on his brain. "I won't let anything happen to you, Ellie," he vowed.

"Will you forget about me for a moment! You're the one someone is trying to kill."

Overcome with emotion, he stood and pulled her to him, completely forgetting about his injured ankle. "Ellie, I—Aaargh!"

"Charles?"

"Damned ankle," he swore. "I can't even kiss you properly. I—Don't laugh."

She shook her head. "Don't tell me not to laugh. Someone is trying to kill you. I need all the laughter I can get."

"I suppose if you put it that way . . ."

She held out her hand. "Let's go back to the house. You'll need something cold on your ankle to bring the swelling down."

"How the hell am I supposed to find the killer when I can't even walk?"

Ellie leaned up and kissed his cheek. She knew how awful it was to feel helpless, but all she could do was comfort him. "You can't," she said simply. "You'll have to wait a few days. In the meantime we will concentrate on keeping everyone safe."

"I am not going to stand idly by while—"

"You won't be idle," she assured him. "We must see to our protection in any case. By the time our defenses are in place, your ankle will be well enough healed. And then you can"—she couldn't suppress a shudder—"seek out your enemy. Although I wish you would just wait for him to come to you."

"I beg your pardon?"

She prodded him until he started moving slowly back to the house. "We haven't the faintest idea who he is. Best to stay at Wycombe Abbey where you will be safe until he reveals himself."

"You were at the Abbey when you were poisoned," he reminded her.

"I know. We shall have to increase our security. But it is certainly safer here than anywhere else."

He knew she was right, but it galled him to sit around and do nothing. And sitting was all he would be doing with this damned ankle. He growled something that was meant to convey his agreement and continued hobbling home.

"Why don't we go through the side entrance?" Ellie

suggested. "We'll see if Mrs. Stubbs can give us a nice cut of meat."

"I'm not hungry," he grumbled.

"For your ankle."

He didn't say anything. He hated feeling foolish.

By the middle of the following day, Charles felt a little more in control of his situation. He might not be well enough to hunt down his enemy, but at least he had been able to do a bit of detective work.

An interrogation of the kitchen staff had revealed that the most recently hired maid had mysteriously disappeared the night of Ellie's poisoning. She had been hired only one week earlier. No one could remember if she had been the one to deliver the custard to the master bedroom, but then again, no one else could remember doing it, so Charles felt it was safe to assume that the missing maid had had ample time to tamper with the food.

He had his men search the area, but he wasn't surprised when they found no trace of her. She was probably halfway to Scotland with the gold she'd undoubtedly been given to dispense the poison.

Charles had also instituted new measures to protect his family. Claire and Judith were expressly forbidden to leave the house, and he would have issued the same edict to Ellie and Helen if he'd thought he could get away with it. Thankfully, both women seemed inclined to stay indoors, if only to keep Judith entertained so that she didn't complain about not being able to ride her pony.

No progress had been made in the search for the

person who had placed the nail under Charles's saddle, however. Charles found this particularly frustrating, and decided to inspect the stables himself for clues. He didn't tell Ellie what he was doing; she'd only worry about him. So while she was busy having tea with Helen, Claire, and Judith, he grabbed his coat, hat, and walking stick, and hobbled outside.

The stables were quiet when he arrived. Leavey was out exercising one of the stallions, and Charles suspected that the rest of the stablehands were taking their afternoon meal. The solitude suited him; he was able to give the stables a more thorough inspection without anyone looking over his shoulder.

Much to his frustration, however, his search produced no new leads. Charles wasn't exactly certain what he was looking for, but he certainly knew when he'd found nothing. He was just preparing to head back to Wycombe Abbey when he heard someone enter the outer door to the stables.

It was probably Leavey. Charles ought to let him know he'd been snooping around. Leavey had been instructed to keep an eye out for anything out of the ordinary, and if Charles had disrupted anything during his search, the stablemaster would surely notice and grow worried.

"Leavey!" Charles called out. "It's Billington. I came to—"

There was a noise behind him. Charles turned but saw nothing. "Leavey?"

No answer.

His ankle started to throb, as if to remind him that he was injured and unable to run.

Another noise.

Charles swung around, but this time all he saw was a rifle barrel swinging down toward his head.

And then he saw nothing.

Chapter 22

E llie wasn't sure just what made her start to worry. She'd never considered herself a fanciful person, but she didn't like the way the sky suddenly clouded over. It made her skin prickle with an irrational fear, and she suddenly felt an intense need to see Charles.

But when she went down to his study, he wasn't there. Her heart skipped a beat, and then she saw that Charles's cane was also missing. Surely if he'd been abducted, his captors wouldn't have taken his cane.

He must have gone off investigating, the blasted man.

But when she realized that more than three hours had gone by since the last time she'd seen him, she started getting a terrible feeling in the pit of her stomach.

She began to search the house, but none of the servants had seen him. Neither had Helen or Claire. In fact, the only person who seemed to have any idea of his whereabouts was Judith.

"I saw him out the window," the little girl said.

"You did?" Ellie asked, practically sagging with relief. "Where was he going?"

"To the stables. He was limping."

"Oh, thank you, Judith," Ellie said, giving her a quick hug. She dashed out of the room and down the stairs. Charles had probably just gone to the stables to try to figure out who had tampered with his saddle. She wished he'd left her a note, but she was so relieved to know where he was that she felt no anger at his oversight.

When she reached her destination, however, there was no sign of her husband. Leavey was supervising several stablehands who were mucking out the stalls, but none of them seemed to know the earl's whereabouts.

"Are you certain you haven't seen him?" Ellie asked for the third time. "Miss Judith insisted she saw him enter the stables."

"It must have been when we were exercising the horses," Leavey replied.

"When was that?"

"Several hours ago."

Ellie sighed impatiently. Where was Charles? And then her eye caught upon something strange. Something red.

"What's this?" she whispered, kneeling down. She picked up a small handful of straw.

"What is it, my lady?" Leavey asked.

"It's blood," she said, her voice shaking. "On the straw."

"Are you certain?"

She smelled it and nodded. "Oh, dear Lord." She looked back up at Leavey, her face going white in an instant. "They've taken him. Dear Lord, someone's taken him."

*   *   *

Charles's first thought upon regaining consciousness was that he was never going to drink again. He'd been hungover before, but never had he felt this brand of skull-pounding agony. Then it occurred to him that it was the middle of the day, and he hadn't been drinking and—

He groaned as splinters of memory shot through his mind. Someone had bashed him over the head with a rifle.

He opened his eyes and looked around. He appeared to be in the bedroom of an abandoned cottage. The furnishings were old and dusty, and the air smelled of mildew. His hands and feet were tied, which didn't surprise him.

Frankly, what *did* surprise him was that he wasn't dead. Obviously someone wanted to kill him. What was the point of kidnapping him first? Unless, of course, his enemy had decided he wanted Charles to know his identity before delivering the final blow.

But in doing so, the would-be killer had granted Charles a little more time to plot and plan, and he vowed to escape and bring his enemy to justice. He wasn't sure how he would do it, bound as he was and with a sprained ankle to boot, but he'd be damned if he'd depart this world mere weeks after discovering true love.

The first order of business was clearly to do something about the ropes binding his hands, so he scooted across the floor to a broken chair sitting in the corner. The splintered wood looked sharp, and he started rubbing the rope against the jagged edge. It was clearly going to take a long time to break through the heavy rope, but his heart lifted with each tiny fiber that snapped under the friction.

After about five minutes of rubbing, Charles heard a door slam in the outer room of the cottage, and he quickly brought his hands back to his side. He started to move back to the center of the room, where he'd been dumped unconscious, but then decided to stay put. He could make it look like he had moved across the room simply to lean up against the wall.

Voices drifted through the air, but Charles couldn't make out what his captors were saying. He caught a snatch of a cockney twang, and deduced that he was dealing with hired thugs. It just didn't make sense that his enemy would be from London's underworld.

After a minute or two, it became apparent that his captors had no intention of checking up on him. Charles decided that they must be waiting for whomever was in charge, and he went back to work fraying the rope.

How long he sat there, moving his wrists back and forth across the jagged wood, he didn't know, but he was barely a third of the way through the rope when he heard the outer door slam again, this time followed by a distinctly upper-class voice.

Charles yanked his hands back to his body and pushed the broken chair away from him with his shoulder. If he guessed right, his enemy would want to see him right away, and—

The door opened. Charles held his breath. A silhouette filled the doorway.

"Good day, Charles."

"*Cecil?*"

"The very one."

Cecil? His mealy-mouthed cousin, the one who had always tattled when they were children, the one who had always taken an inordinate amount of pleasure in stepping on bugs?

"You're a hard man to kill," Cecil said. "I finally realized I was going to have to do it myself."

Charles supposed he should have paid more attention to his cousin's fixation with dead bugs. "What the hell do you think you're doing, Cecil?" he demanded.

"Ensuring my place as the next Earl of Billington."

Charles just stared at him. "But you're not even next in line to inherit. If you kill me, the title goes to Phillip."

"Phillip is dead."

Charles felt sick. He'd never liked Phillip, but he'd never wished him ill. "What did you do to him?" he asked hoarsely.

"Me? I did nothing. Our dear cousin's gambling debts did him in. I believe one of his moneylenders finally ran out of patience. He was fished out of the Thames just yesterday."

"And I suppose you had nothing to do with his debts."

Cecil shrugged. "I might have steered Phillip in the direction of a game or two. But always at his request."

Charles swore under his breath. He should have watched out for his cousin, realized that his gambling habit was becoming a dangerous problem. He might have been able to counteract Cecil's influence. "Phillip should have come to me," he said. "I would have helped him."

"Don't scold yourself, cuz," Cecil said with a clucking sound. "There's really very little you could have done for dear Phillip. I have a feeling those money-lenders would have gotten to him no matter how promptly he repaid his debts."

Bile rose in Charles's throat as he realized what Cecil meant. "You killed him," he whispered. "You threw him in the Thames and made it look like the moneylenders did him in."

"Rather clever, don't you think? It's taken over a year to execute; after all, I needed to make certain Phillip's connections with London's underbelly were common knowledge. I laid my plans out very care-fully." His face grew ugly. "But then you ruined it all."

"By being born?" Charles asked, baffled.

"By marrying that stupid vicar's daughter. I wasn't going to kill you, you know. I never cared about the title. It was just the money I was after. I was biding my time until your thirtieth birthday. I have been re-joicing over your father's will since the day it was read. Nobody thought you'd actually obey his terms. You've been acting out just to spite him your entire life."

"And then I married Ellie," Charles said in a dull voice.

"And then I had to kill you. It was as simple as that. I saw it coming when you began to court her, so I tampered with your curricle, but all that gave you were a few bruises. And then I engineered your fall from the ladder—that was difficult to do, I'll tell you. I had to work very quickly. I wouldn't have been able to do it if the ladder hadn't been in a bit of disrepair to begin with."

Charles remembered the searing pain he'd felt when his skin had been sliced open by the splintered ladder, and he shook with rage.

"There was quite a bit of blood," Cecil continued. "I was watching from the forest. I thought I had you that time until I realized you'd only cut your arm. I'd been hoping for a chest wound."

"I'm sorry to have disobliged you," Charles said in a dry voice.

"Ah yes, that famous Billington wit. Such a stiff upper lip you possess."

"Clearly I need it at times like these."

Cecil shook his head slowly. "Your wits won't save you this time, Charles."

Charles stared his cousin hard in the eye. "How do you plan to do it?"

"Quick and clean. I never intended to make you suffer."

"The poison you fed my wife did not precisely sit gently in her stomach."

Cecil let out a long-suffering sigh. "She is ever getting in the way. Although she did cause that nice kitchen fire. If the day had been windier she might have done my job for me. I understood you fought the flames yourself."

"Leave Ellie out of this."

"At any rate, I do apologize for the virulence of that poison. I had been told it would not be painful. Clearly I was misinformed."

Charles's lips parted in disbelief. "I cannot believe you're apologizing to me."

"I am not without manners—just scruples."

"Your plan is going to fail," Charles stated. "You

can kill me, but you won't inherit my fortune."

Cecil tapped his finger against his cheek. "Let me see. You have no sons. If you die, I become the earl." He shrugged and laughed. "It seems simple to me."

"You'll become the earl, but you won't get the money. All you'll get is the entailed property. Wycombe Abbey is worth quite a bit, but as the earl, you will be legally barred from selling it, and it costs a bloody fortune to keep it up. Your pockets will feel even more pinched than they do right now. Why the hell do you think I was so bloody desperate to get married?"

Beads of sweat appeared on Cecil's brow. "What are you talking about?"

"My fortune goes to my wife."

"No one leaves a fortune like that to a woman."

"I did," Charles said with a slow smile.

"You're lying."

He was right, but Charles didn't see any reason to inform him. In all truth, he'd planned to amend his will to leave his fortune to Ellie; he just hadn't gotten around to doing it yet. Charles shrugged and said, "That's a gamble you'll just have to take."

"That's where you're wrong, cuz. I can just kill your wife."

Charles had known he would say that, but it made his blood boil all the same. "Do you really think," he drawled, "that you can kill both the Earl and Countess of Billington, inherit the title and the fortune, and not be a suspect in our murders?"

"I can . . . if you're not murdered."

Charles narrowed his eyes.

"An accident," Cecil mused. "A terrible, tragic accident. One that takes both of you away from your loving relatives. We shall all grieve terribly. I will wear black for a full year."

"Very sporting of you."

"Damn, but now I'm going to have to send one of those idiots"—he flicked his head toward the outer room—"back out after your wife."

Charles began to struggle against his bindings. "If you harm a hair on her head . . ."

"Charles, I just told you I'm going to *kill* her," Cecil said with a chuckle. "I shouldn't worry too much about her hair, were I you."

"You will rot in hell for this."

"Undoubtedly. But I shall have a grand time here on earth beforehand." Cecil scratched his chin. "I don't really trust them to do a good job with your wife. I'm amazed they managed to get you here without mishap."

"I wouldn't call this lump on my head 'without mishap.' "

"I have it! You shall write her a note. Lure her out of the safety of her home. I understand the two of you have been quite amorous of late. Make her think you have arranged a lovers' tryst. She'll come running. Women always do."

Charles started thinking quickly. Cecil didn't realize that he and Ellie had already guessed that someone was out to do them harm. Ellie would never believe that Charles would plan a tryst amidst such danger. She would immediately suspect foul play. Charles was sure of it.

But he didn't want to raise Cecil's suspicions by appearing too eager to write the note, so he twisted his face away and spat out, "I won't do anything to lure Ellie to her death."

Cecil strode forward and yanked Charles to his feet. "She's going to die in any case, so she might as well do it with you."

"You'll have to untie my hands," Charles said, keeping his voice sullen.

"I'm not as stupid as you think."

"And I'm not as dexterous as *you* think," Charles shot back. "Do you want my handwriting to look like chicken scrawl? Ellie isn't stupid. She'll be suspicious if she receives a note that doesn't look to be in my hand."

"Very well. But don't try anything heroic." Cecil pulled out a knife and a pistol. He used the knife to cut through the rope around Charles's wrists and kept the pistol pointed at his head.

"Have you any paper?" Charles asked sarcastically. "A quill? Ink, perhaps?"

"Shut up." Cecil paced across the room, keeping the pistol pointed at Charles, who couldn't have gone far in any case with his feet tied together. "Damn."

Charles started to laugh.

"Shut up!" Cecil screamed. He turned to the doorway and yelled, "Baxter!"

A burly man opened the door. "Wot?"

"Get me some paper. And ink."

"And a quill," Charles said helpfully.

"I don't think there's any of that 'ere," Baxter said.

"Then go buy some!" Cecil screamed, his entire body shaking.

Baxter crossed his arms. "You 'aven't paid me for nabbing the earl yet."

"For the love of God," Cecil hissed. "I'm working with idiots."

Charles watched with interest as Baxter's expression grew dark. Perhaps he could turn him against Cecil.

Cecil threw a coin at Baxter. The large man stooped to pick the coin up, but not before glaring viciously in Cecil's direction. He started to leave, then turned back around when Cecil barked, "Wait!"

"Wot now?" Baxter demanded.

Cecil jerked his head toward Charles. "Tie him back up."

"Why'd you untie 'im in the first place?"

"That's none of your concern."

Charles sighed and held his wrists out toward Baxter. Much as he'd like to fight for his freedom, now wasn't the time. He could never win against both Baxter and Cecil, who was still armed with a knife and gun. Not to mention the fact that his ankles were tied together and one of them was sprained.

Charles sighed as Baxter looped new rope around his wrists. All that work wearing down the other rope for nothing. Still, Baxter tied a looser knot than the previous one, which at least allowed him some measure of circulation.

Baxter left the room, and Cecil followed him to the doorway, waving the gun once in Charles's direction with a harsh, "Don't you move."

"As if I could," Charles muttered, trying to bend his toes inside his boots to get the blood moving in his feet. He listened while Cecil spoke to Baxter's friend, whom he had not yet seen, but he couldn't make out what they were saying. After a minute or two Cecil returned and sat down in a ramshackle chair.

"Now what?" Charles demanded.

"Now we wait."

After a few moments, however, Cecil started to fidget. Charles took some satisfaction in his discomfort. "Bored?" he drawled.

"Impatient."

"Ah, I see. You want me dead and done with it."

"Exactly." Cecil started tapping his hand against his thigh, making clucking sounds with his mouth as he did so.

"You are going to drive me bloody insane," Charles said.

"That is not high on my list of worries."

Charles closed his eyes. Clearly he had already died and gone to hell. What could possibly be worse than being trapped for hours with a tapping, clucking Cecil, who, incidentally, planned to kill him and his wife?

He opened his eyes. Cecil was holding a deck of cards.

"Want to play?" Cecil asked.

"No," Charles said. "You've always been a cheat."

Cecil shrugged. "Won't matter. I can't collect from a dead man. Oh, I beg your pardon, I *can*. In fact, I'll be collecting everything you own."

Charles closed his eyes again. He had been courting the devil when he wondered what could be worse than being trapped with Cecil.

For now he knew. He was going to have to play *cards* with the cur.

There was no justice in the world. None at all.

* * *

Ellie's hands shook as she unfolded the note the butler had just given to her. Her eyes scanned the lines, and she caught her breath.

My dear Eleanor,

I have spent all day preparing a romantic outing for us alone. Meet me at the swing in one hour.

Your devoted husband,

Charles

Ellie looked up at Helen, who had been keeping a vigil with her for the past hour. "It's a trap," she whispered, handing her the note.

Helen read it and looked up. "How can you be sure?"

"He would never call me Eleanor in a personal note such as this. Especially if he were trying to do something romantic. He would call me Ellie. I'm sure of it."

"I don't know," Helen said. "I agree with you that something is amiss, but can you really read all that into whether he uses your proper name or a nickname?"

Ellie waved her question aside. "And besides that, Charles has instituted draconian measures since someone tampered with his saddle. Do you really think he'd send me a note asking me to come out alone to a deserted area?"

"You're right," Helen said firmly. "What will we do?"

"I'll have to go."

"But you can't!"

"How else am I to discover his whereabouts?"

"But Ellie, you will be hurt. Surely whomever has taken Charles means to do you ill as well."

"You will have to summon help. You can wait at the swing and watch what happens. Then you can follow me after I am snatched."

"Ellie, it seems so dangerous."

"There is no other way," Ellie said firmly. "We cannot save Charles if we do not know where he is."

Helen shook her head. "We won't have time to summon help. You're supposed to be at the swing in an hour."

"You're right." Ellie let out a nervous exhale. "We shall have to save him ourselves then."

"Are you mad?"

"Can you shoot a gun?"

"Yes," Helen replied. "My husband taught me how."

"Good. I hope you don't need it. You shall go with Leavey to the swing. There is no other servant Charles trusts more." Then Ellie's face crumpled. "Oh, Helen, what am I thinking? I cannot ask you to do this."

"If you're going, I'm going," Helen said firmly. "Charles saved me when my husband died and I had no place to go. Now it's my turn to return the favor."

Ellie grasped her hands tightly. "Oh, Helen. He's lucky to have you for a cousin."

"No," Helen corrected. "He's lucky to have you for a wife."

Chapter 23

Ellie hadn't counted on getting smacked over the head, but other than that, her scheme was proceeding exactly according to plan. She'd waited out by the swing, acted stupid and called out, "Charles?" in a silly voice when she'd heard footsteps, and struggled—although not too hard—when someone had grabbed her from behind.

But obviously she'd struggled a little bit harder than her attacker had expected, because he'd let out a loud curse and whacked her over the head with something that felt like a cross between a giant boulder and a grandfather clock. The blow didn't knock her out, but it did leave her dizzy and nauseated, which wasn't helped when her captor stuffed her in a burlap bag and threw her over his shoulder.

But he hadn't searched her. And he hadn't found the two small pistols she had strapped to her thighs.

She groaned as she bounced along, trying really hard not to empty the contents of her stomach. After about thirty seconds, she was dumped onto something hard, and it soon became apparent that she was in the back of a wagon or cart of some sort.

It was also apparent that her captor was *aiming* for every bump in the road. If she got out of this alive, she was going to have bruises on every inch of her body.

They traveled for about twenty minutes. Ellie knew that Leavey and Helen were on horseback, so they ought to be able to follow her with ease. She only prayed that they were able to do so without being seen.

Finally the wagon rolled to a halt, and Ellie felt herself being lifted roughly in the air. She was carried for a moment, then she heard a door swing open.

"I got 'er!" her captor yelled.

"Excellent." This new voice was well-bred, very well-bred. "Bring her in."

Ellie heard another door swing open and then the bag was being untied. Someone picked up the bottom of the sack and dumped her out, rolling her onto the floor in a tangle of arms and legs.

She blinked, her eyes needing time to adjust to the light.

"Ellie?" Charles's voice.

"Charles?" She scrambled to her feet, then stopped short at what she saw. "Are you playing *cards*?" If he didn't have a good explanation for this, she was going to kill him herself.

"It's actually quite complicated," he replied, holding up his hands, which were bound together.

"I don't understand," Ellie said. The scene was positively surreal. "What are you doing?"

"I've been flipping his cards for him," the other man said. "We're playing *vingt-et-un*."

"Who are you?" she asked.

"Cecil Wycombe."

Ellie turned to Charles. "Your cousin?"

"The very one," he answered. "Isn't he simply the picture of filial devotion? He cheats at cards, too."

"What can you possibly hope to gain from this?" Ellie demanded of Cecil. She planted her hands on her hips, hoping that he hadn't noticed that he'd forgotten to tie her up. "You're not even next in line to inherit."

"He killed Phillip," Charles replied in a flat voice.

"You. Countess," Cecil barked. "Sit on the bed until we finish our hand."

Ellie's mouth dropped open. He wanted to continue playing cards? More out of surprise than anything else, she moved docilely to the bed and sat down. Cecil dealt out a card to Charles and then flipped one end up so that Charles could see what it was.

"Do you want another?" Cecil asked.

Charles nodded.

Ellie used the time to assess her situation. Cecil obviously didn't see her as much of a threat, because he hadn't bothered to tie her up before ordering her to sit on the bed. Of course, he had a pistol in one of his hands, and she had a feeling he wouldn't hesitate to use it on her if she made a false move. Not to mention the two burly men who were standing in the doorway, their arms crossed as they watched the card game with irritated expressions.

Still and all, men could be such idiots. They always underestimated women.

Ellie caught Charles's eye while Cecil was occupied with his cards, and she flicked her gaze toward the window, trying to let him know that she'd brought reinforcements.

Then she had to ask, "Why are you playing cards?"

"I was bored," Cecil replied. "It took longer to get you here than I anticipated."

"Now we have to keep playing," Charles explained, "because he refuses to quit while I'm ahead."

"I thought you said he cheated."

"He does. He just doesn't do it well."

"I'll let that pass," Cecil said, "since I'm going to kill you later today. It seems only sporting. Do you want another card?"

Charles shook his head. "I'll stand."

Cecil turned over his cards, then flipped over Charles's. "Damn!" he swore.

"I win again," Charles said with a careless smile.

Ellie noticed one of the men in the doorway roll his eyes.

"Let's see," Charles mused. "How much would you owe me now? If, of course, you weren't to kill me?"

"Unfortunately for you, that point is moot," Cecil said with a malicious hiss. "Now be quiet while I deal."

"Can we get on with this?" one of the guards demanded. "You're only paying us for one day."

"Shut up!" Cecil screamed, his whole body shaking from the force of his order. "I'm playing cards."

"He's never beaten me at anything before," Charles told the guard with a shrug. "Games, hunting, cards, women. I guess he wants to do it once before I die."

Ellie chewed on her lower lip, trying to decide how best to exploit the situation to her advantage. She could try to shoot Cecil, but she doubted that she could draw one of her guns before the guards overpowered her. She had never been terribly athletic and had long since learned to rely on her wits rather than her strength or speed.

She glanced back over at the guards, who were now looking very irritated with Cecil. She wondered how much he was paying them. Probably a lot, for them to put up with such nonsense.

But she could pay them more.

"I have to relieve myself!" Ellie shouted loudly.

"Hold it," Cecil ordered, flipping over the cards. "Damn."

"I win again," Charles said.

"Stop saying that!"

"But it's true."

"I said shut your mouth!" Cecil waved his gun wildly in the air. Charles, Ellie, and both the guards ducked, but thankfully no bullets were forthcoming. One of the guards muttered something that sounded unflattering toward Cecil.

"I really need a moment of privacy," Ellie said again, purposefully making her voice strident.

"I told you to hold it, bitch!"

Ellie gasped.

"Don't speak to my wife that way," Charles bit out.

"Sir," Ellie said, hoping she wasn't pushing her luck. "Obviously you do not have a wife, or you would realize that women are a bit more . . . *delicate* . . . than men in some ways, and I am quite simply unable to do as you ask."

"I'd let her go," Charles advised.

"For the love of Christ," Cecil muttered. "Baxter!

Take her outside and let her do her business."

Ellie jumped to her feet and followed Baxter out of the room. As soon as they were out of Cecil's earshot, she hissed, "How much is he paying you?"

Baxter looked at her with a shrewd look in his eye.

"How much?" Ellie persisted. "I'll double it. Triple it."

He glanced back at the doorway and yelled, "Hurry up!" Then he jerked his head toward the front door, signaling her to follow him outside. Ellie scurried after him, whispering, "Cecil is an idiot. I'll bet he cheats you once you've killed us. And has he offered you double for having to kidnap me, too? No? That's not fair."

"You're right," Baxter said. "He should've given me double. He only promised to pay me for the earl."

"I'll give you fifty pounds if you come to my side and help me free the earl."

"And if I don't?"

"Then you'll have to take your chances that Cecil will pay you. But from what I've seen in there at that so-called card table, you're going to end up with empty pockets."

"All right," Baxter agreed, "but I want to see the money first."

"I haven't got it with me."

His face grew menacing.

"I wasn't expecting to be abducted," Ellie said, talking quickly. "Why would I have brought that much coin with me?"

Baxter stared hard at her face.

"You have my word," Ellie said.

"All right. But if you cheat me I'll swear I'll slit your throat as you sleep."

Ellie shivered, having no doubt that he told the truth. She held up a hand in a prearranged signal to Leavey and Helen that all was well. She couldn't see them, but they were supposed to have followed her. She didn't want them charging out and spooking Baxter.

"What are you doing?" Baxter demanded.

"Nothing. Just brushing my hair from my face. It's windy."

"We've got to get back inside."

"Yes, of course. We don't want Cecil to grow suspicious," Ellie said. "But what are we going to do? What is our plan?"

"I can't do anything until I talk to Riley. 'E needs to know we've changed sides." Baxter's eyes narrowed. "You'll be giving him fifty quid, too, right?"

"Of course," Ellie said quickly, assuming that Riley was the other thug guarding the doorway.

"All right. I'll talk to 'im as soon as I can get 'im alone and then we'll make our move."

"Yes, but—" Ellie wanted to say that they needed more of a strategy, more of a plan, but Baxter was already dragging her back inside. He pushed her through the door to the inner room, and she stumbled onto the bed. "I'm feeling much better now," she announced.

Cecil grunted something about not caring, but Charles regarded her thoughtfully. Ellie shot him a quick smile before looking back to Baxter, trying to remind him that he needed to speak with Riley.

But Riley had other ideas. "I gotta go, too," he announced, and he lumbered off. Ellie glared at Baxter, but he didn't follow Riley. Maybe he thought it would look too suspicious for him to go so soon after coming back with Ellie.

After a minute or so, however, they heard a terrible commotion from outside the cottage. Everyone jumped to their feet, except Charles, who was tied up, and Baxter, who was already standing.

"What the hell is going on?" Cecil demanded.

Baxter shrugged.

Ellie's hand flew to her mouth. Oh God, Riley didn't know that he was working for her now, and if he'd found Helen or Leavey outside . . .

"Riley!" Cecil yelled.

All of Ellie's worst fears were realized when Riley thundered back into the room, holding Helen close to his body, a knife pressed against her throat. "Look what I found!" he cackled.

"Helen?" Cecil said, looking amused.

"Cecil?" Helen didn't look amused at all.

"Baxter!" Ellie shouted in a panicked voice. He needed to let Riley know the change in plans *now*. She watched in horror as Cecil sidled up next to Helen and yanked her next to him. His back was to Ellie, however, and she used his inattention to grab one of the pistols strapped to her legs and hide it under the folds of her skirt.

"Helen, you really shouldn't have come," Cecil said, his voice practically a croon.

"Baxter, tell him *now*!" Ellie yelled.

Cecil whirled around to face her. "Tell who what?"

Ellie didn't even stop to think. She whipped up the pistol, cocked it, and pulled the trigger. The explosion jolted her clear up to her shoulder and knocked her back to the bed.

Cecil's face was a picture of surprise as he clutched his chest near his collarbone. Blood seeped through his fingers. "You bitch," he hissed. He raised his gun.

"Nooooo!" Charles yelled, pitching forward from his chair and hurling himself at Cecil. His aim wasn't good, but he managed to hit his cousin in the legs, and Cecil's arm was thrown up in the air before he pulled the trigger.

Ellie felt a burst of pain in her arm as she heard Helen scream her name. "Oh my God," she whispered in shock. "He shot me." Then her shock was replaced by anger. "He shot me!" she exclaimed. She looked up just in time to see Cecil readjusting his aim on Charles. Before Ellie even had time to think, she reached down with her good arm, grabbed her other pistol, and fired it at Cecil.

Silence fell over the room, and this time there was no doubt that he was dead.

Riley was still holding a knife to Helen's throat, but now he looked like he didn't know what to do with her. Finally Baxter said, "Let 'er go, Riley."

"What?"

"I said let her go."

Riley dropped his knife arm and Helen ran to Ellie's side.

"Oh, Ellie," Helen cried out. "Are you badly hurt?"

Ellie ignored her and glared at Baxter. "A fat lot of good you were."

"I told Riley to let 'er go, didn't I?"

She scowled at him. "If you want to earn your pay, at least go and untie my husband."

"Ellie," Helen said, "let me look at your arm."

Ellie looked down at where her hand clutched her wound. "I can't," she whispered. If she let go, then the blood would start pouring out, and . . .

Helen tugged at her fingers. "Please, Ellie. I must see how serious the wound is."

Ellie whimpered and said, "No, I can't. You see, when I see my own blood . . ."

But Helen had already pried Ellie's fingers from her arm. "There now," Helen said. "It's not so bad. Ellie? Ellie?"

Ellie had already fainted.

"Who would have thought," Helen said several hours later, when Ellie was comfortably settled in her own bed, "that Ellie would have turned out to be so squeamish?"

"Certainly not I," Charles replied, lovingly smoothing a lock of hair from his wife's forehead. "After all, she put a row of stitches in my arm that would set any seamstress to shame."

"You don't need to talk as if I'm not here," Ellie said peevishly. "Cecil shot me in the arm, not the ear."

At the mention of Cecil's name, Charles felt a now-familiar rush of rage. It would be some time before he would be able to look back upon the events of this day without shaking in fury.

He had sent someone out to collect Cecil's body, although he hadn't really decided what he was going to do with it. Charles certainly wasn't going to allow him to be buried with the rest of the Wycombe family.

Baxter and Riley had been paid and sent on their

way after Riley showed them where he'd left poor Leavey, who hadn't even had a moment to scream before Riley had clubbed him over the head and grabbed Helen.

His attention was on Ellie, and on making certain her gunshot wound wasn't any more serious than she'd claimed. The bullet didn't seem to have hit any major vessels or bones, although Charles had had the scare of his life when Ellie had passed out.

He patted his wife on her good arm. "All that matters is that you are healthy. Dr. Summers says that with a few days of bed rest you should be as good as new. And he also said that it's quite common to faint at the sight of blood."

"I don't faint at the sight of *any* blood," Ellie muttered. "Just my own."

"How peculiar," Charles teased. "After all, my blood is the same color as yours. It looks quite the same to me."

She scowled at him. "If you can't be nice, then just leave me to Helen."

He could tell by her tone that she was also teasing, so he leaned down and kissed her nose.

Helen abruptly stood up and said, "I'll fetch some tea."

Charles watched his cousin leave the room and shut the door behind her. "She always knows when we want to be left alone, doesn't she?"

"Helen is far more perceptive and tactful than either of us," Ellie agreed.

"Perhaps that is why we are so well matched."

Ellie smiled. "We are, aren't we?"

Charles settled in beside her and draped his arm

over her shoulders. "Do you realize that we can finally have a normal marriage now?"

"Having never been wed before, I was not aware that ours was an abnormal marriage."

"Perhaps not precisely 'abnormal,' but I doubt that most newlyweds must contend with poisonings and gunshot wounds."

"And do not forget carriage accidents and jam explosions," Ellie said, actually laughing.

"Not to mention stitches in my arm, carcasses in the orangery, and fires in the kitchen."

"Goodness, it has been an exciting month."

"I don't know about you, but I could do with a bit less excitement myself."

"Oh, I don't know. I don't mind a bit of excitement, although I'd rather it be of a different sort."

He raised a brow. "What do you mean?"

"Merely that Judith might like another little Wycombe to boss around."

Charles felt his heart drop to his toes, a remarkable feat considering he was horizontal. "Are you . . . ?" he gasped, unable to get the full sentence out. "Are you . . . ?

"Of course not," she said, swatting him on the shoulder. "Well, actually I suppose I could be, but considering we only started . . . *you know* . . . so recently, I haven't even had the opportunity to *know* if I were or not, and—"

"Then what is your point?"

She smiled coyly. "Merely that there is no reason we cannot begin trying to make this particular dream a reality."

"Helen will be back with the tea at any minute."

"She'll knock."

"But your arm . . ."

"I have every faith that you will be careful."

A slow smile crept across Charles's face. "Have I told you lately that I love you?"

Ellie nodded. "Have I told you?"

He nodded back at her. "Why don't we wiggle you out of that dressing gown and see about turning your dreams into reality?"

Epilogue

 ̶ ̶ ̶ ̶ ̶ ̶ ̶ ̶ ̶ ̶ ̶ ̶

Nine months and one day later, Ellie was the happiest woman alive. Not that she hadn't thought herself the happiest woman alive the day before, and the day before that, but this day was special.

Ellie was finally certain that she and Charles were going to have a child.

Their marriage, which had begun almost as an accident, had grown into something truly magical. Her days were filled with laughter, her nights with passion, and her dreams with hope and wonder.

Not to mention her orangery, which was filled with oranges, thanks to her and Claire's diligent gardening.

Ellie looked down at her abdomen with a sense of amazement. How strange that a new life was growing there, that a person who could eventually walk and talk and have her own name and ideas was resting inside of her.

She smiled. She was already thinking of this new baby as a girl. She didn't know why, but she was certain it would be female. She wanted to name her Mary, after her mother. She didn't think Charles would mind.

Ellie strode through the great hall, still looking for her husband. Drat and blast, where was he when she needed him? She had waited months for this moment, to tell him the wonderful news, and now she couldn't find him anywhere. Finally she gave up all pretense of decorum and yelled his name. "Charles? Charles?"

He appeared across the hall, tossing an orange between his hands. "Good afternoon, Ellie. What has you in such a tizzy?"

Her face erupted into a smile. "Charles, we've finally done it."

He blinked. "Done what?"

"A baby, Charles. We're going to have a baby."

"Well, I should think so. I've been trying my damnedest for the last nine months."

Her mouth fell open. "*That* is your reaction?"

"Well, if you think about it, you'd be delivering right now instead of announcing your pregnancy if we'd gotten it right the first time."

"Charles!" She swatted him on the shoulder.

He chuckled and gathered her into his arms. "Hush up, Ellie. You know I'm teasing."

"Then you're happy?"

He kissed her tenderly. "More than I could ever say."

Ellie smiled up into his face. "I never thought I could love another person as much as I do you, but I was wrong." She placed her hands on her flat stomach. "I love this little one already, so very, very much, and she's not even born yet."

"She?"

"It's a girl. I'm sure of it."

"If you're sure of it, then I'm sure you're right."

"Is that so?"

"I've long since learned never to argue with you."

"I had no idea I had you so well trained."

Charles grinned. "I do make a fine husband, don't I?"

"The best. And you'll be an excellent father as well."

His face grew emotional as he touched her midriff. "I love this little one already, too," he whispered.

"Do you?"

He nodded. "Now then, shall we show our daughter her first sunset? I peeked out the window. The sky is almost as bright as your smile."

"I think she'd like that. And I would, as well."

Hand in hand, they walked outside and watched the sky.

Dear Reader,

If you've just finished this Avon romance title and are looking for more of the best in romantic fiction, then be on the watch for these upcoming romance titles—available at your favorite bookstore!

Affaire de Coeur says Genell Dellin is " . . . one of the best writers of ethnic romances starring Native Americans." And her latest, AFTER THE THUNDER, is Native American romance filled with sensuality and emotion. When a young Shaman falls for a scandalous young woman he must decide if he will fulfill the needs of the spirit—or the body.

For lovers of Scotland settings, don't miss the luscious A ROSE IN SCOTLAND by Joan Overfield. When a desperate young woman marries the handsome, brooding Laird of Lochhaven, she expects nothing more than a marriage of convenience. But what begins as duty turns into something much more.

Maureen McKade's A DIME NOVEL HERO is a must-read for those who like their heroes tough and their settings western. This tender romance about a woman who writes dime novels, her adopted son and the man she's turned into an unwilling hero—and who is unknowingly the boy's father—is sure to touch your heart.

Contemporary romance fans are sure to love SIMPLY IRRESISTIBLE by debut author Rachel Gibson. A sassy charm school graduate is on the run—from her own wedding. She's rescued by a sexy guest but never dreams that, nine months later, she'll have a little bundle of joy—proof of their whirlwind romance. And when he barges back into her life, complications ensue—and romance is rekindled.

Remember, look to Avon Books for the very best in romance!

Sincerely,
Lucia Macro
Avon Books

AEL 1197

Avon Romantic Treasures

*Unforgettable, enthralling love stories,
sparkling with passion and adventure
from Romance's bestselling authors*

EVERYTHING AND THE MOON *by Julia Quinn*
78933-7/$5.99 US/$7.99 Can

BEAST *by Judith Ivory*
78644-3/$5.99 US/$7.99 Can

HIS FORBIDDEN TOUCH *by Shelley Thacker*
78120-4/$5.99 US/$7.99 Can

LYON'S GIFT *by Tanya Anne Crosby*
78571-4/$5.99 US/$7.99 Can

FLY WITH THE EAGLE *by Kathleen Harrington*
77836-X/$5.99 US/$7.99 Can

FALLING IN LOVE AGAIN *by Cathy Maxwell*
78718-0/$5.99 US/$7.99 Can

**THE COURTSHIP OF
CADE KOLBY** *by Lori Copeland*
79156-0/$5.99 US/$7.99 Can

TO LOVE A STRANGER *by Connie Mason*
79340-7/$5.99 US/$7.99 Can